PRAISE FOR
THE DARK DAYS CLUB

"Helen's torn between her desire for a proper future and her fascination with her strange abilities, and it's in those moments of doubt when her courage and reason shine through the most. Lucky for us, this fantastic introduction leaves us hungry for more." —*ENTERTAINMENT WEEKLY*

"A masterful, beguiling story from start to finish."
—*NEW YORK DAILY NEWS*

"*The Dark Days Club* captivates with a mix of history and fantasy. [An] immersive, action-packed narrative." —*USA TODAY'S* **HAPPY EVER AFTER**

"It's London 1812 like you've never seen it: with demonic creatures and their slayers. Lady Helen Wrexhall takes the Buffy-esque role in *The Dark Days Club* . . . Helen has to fight between two sides of herself as a proper lady and a kickbutt slayer. Feminists swoon!" —**BUSTLE.COM**

★ "[A] Regency romance/supernatural mash-up . . . Fast-paced, rich in description, with fascinating characters and excitement."
—*SLJ*, **STARRED REVIEW**

★ "A delicious collision of Regency romance and dark fantasy."
—*PUBLISHERS WEEKLY*, **STARRED REVIEW**

"A nail-bitingly exciting story of espionage and gallantry, with a horribly well-imagined demonic element."
—*JANE AUSTEN'S REGENCY WORLD* **MAGAZINE**

"Not your mother's Regency romance . . . Goodman's prose is assured; her impeccable research shines through on every page." —*KIRKUS REVIEWS*

"Try this with fans of genre twisters such as Jane Austen and Seth Grahame-Smith's *Pride and Prejudice and Zombies*." —*BOOKLIST*

"Goodman's research is evident as interesting details are revealed concerning the time period's social, environmental, and political issues . . . The paranormal aspect of Helen's world is well-conceived." —*VOYA*

"Spectacular." —*SHELF AWARENESS*

OTHER BOOKS YOU MAY ENJOY

Bitterblue	Kristin Cashore
The Dark Days Club	Alison Goodman
Eon	Alison Goodman
Eona	Alison Goodman
Fire	Kristin Cashore
Flame in the Mist	Renée Ahdieh
The Half Bad trilogy	Sally Green
The Legend trilogy	Marie Lu
Rebel of the Sands	Alwyn Hamilton
The Rose & the Dagger	Renée Ahdieh
The Wrath & the Dawn	Renée Ahdieh
The Young Elites trilogy	Marie Lu

ALISON GOODMAN

THE
DARK DAYS
PACT

A Lady Helen Novel

speak

SPEAK
An imprint of Penguin Random House LLC
375 Hudson Street
New York, New York 10014

First published in the United States of America by Viking,
an imprint of Penguin Random House LLC, 2017
Published by Speak, an imprint of Penguin Random House LLC, 2018

LIBRARY OF CONGRESS CATALOGING-IN-PUBLICATION DATA IS AVAILABLE.
ISBN 9780670785483 (hardcover)

Speak ISBN 9780142425114

Printed in the United States of America

Set in Carre Noir Std
Book design by Kate Renner

1 3 5 7 9 10 8 6 4 2

To my father, Douglas Goodman,
a gentleman and a hero

German Place, Brighton,
30 June 1812

Delia, my dear friend,

I am now residing in Brighton for the summer season,
and according to my guidebook, your village is but
twenty miles from this town. I urge you to write back
promptly and name a day for me to call upon you and
your parents.

    I have a great deal to tell you, much of which will
explain your Mr. Trent's horrifying demise. I promise it
will also put an end to your fear that you are going mad.
All is not as it seems in this world, Delia—tricksters
walk among us with deadly menace in their hearts—and
I believe your recent encounter with this hidden realm
entitles you to an explanation.

    We must, however, find time to speak of this alone,
for I cannot offer the same explanation to your parents
and restore their trust in you. It is unfair, I know, but
my reasons are sound. My hope is that a formal call
from myself and my chaperone, Lady Margaret
Ridgewell, will soften their belief that you are ruined for

decent society, and put a stop to any talk of confinement and sanatoriums.

I fear you did not receive my earlier letters. Therefore, I have instructed my messenger to place this in your hands, and yours only. He will return in two days for your reply.

Stand strong, my friend: I am nearby.

Helen

One

Friday, 3 July 1812

A t Lord Carlston's bidding, Lady Helen Wrexhall studied the gentleman walking rapidly toward them up the rise of Brighton's Marine Parade. Even at such a distance she could see that he was a thin, bitter-faced man in a sober blue coat rather badly cut across his stooped shoulders, and an unfashionable tricorn hat drawn low over his brow.

"Can you really see him in detail from this far away?" Mr. Hammond asked, squinting at the tiny figure. "He is little more than a blur to me."

"Of course she can: it is part of the gift," his sister said. "Do stop making comments, Michael."

"I can even see his expression, Mr. Hammond," Helen said across Lady Margaret's rebuke. The woman was forever criticizing and correcting. "I can report that the gentleman's countenance is quite sour. Probably a bad kipper for breakfast."

Mr. Hammond laughed. "Bad kipper. Did you hear that, Margaret?"

"Quite," his sister said, her expression as sour as the one under discussion.

Lord Carlston thumped the ebony tip of his cane into the dirt path. "Lady Helen, focus. What do you notice about his gait?"

She smothered a sigh. So it was to be another lesson on manly pedestrianism. His lordship was adamant that she perfect a male disguise; their duties, he said, would take them into taverns and the like, and she must convince as a man. Clearly, however, she had not yet mastered her understanding of the masculine stride.

She studied his lordship from the corner of her eye. Today he looked older than his twenty-six years, weary and distant, the bold angles of his face set into stern command. The forbidding expression was becoming all too familiar. Ever since she had been cast out of her uncle's house four weeks ago, she had watched Lord Carlston retreat from the strange energy that leaped between them when they touched, pushing it behind his new role of instructor. It felt as if a shared pulse was slowly being extinguished. Yet what could she say? Nothing between them had ever been voiced, could *ever* be voiced. He was, by law, still married. She must quash the energy, too, although she did not know how. Whenever he guided her arm through a sword stroke or showed her how to punch, it felt as if her body were aflame.

He had noticed her scrutiny. She saw something flicker in his eyes—that pulse perhaps, not totally quelled—and then a lift of his dark slanted eyebrows called her to the task at hand. She shifted her parasol, taking refuge behind the green silk shield—*Dear God, do not let him see the flush upon my cheeks*—and returned her attention to the fast-approaching figure.

"He moves his arms with vigor," she ventured. "And keeps his eyes to the fore."

"No, forget his eyes and arms. Do you see how each pace is at least this long?" Lord Carlston's cane plunged into the dirt again, measuring a good length from the toe of his right Hessian boot. "And despite those rounded shoulders, there is confidence in his upper body. You must take up more space when you walk and move with greater purpose."

Space and purpose. Helen took an experimental step alongside the flimsy fence that safeguarded the sheer drop to the beach. The hem of her promenade gown brought her up short, the sudden halt causing her touch watch to swing out on the end of its silk neck-cord and slap back against her ribs. Despite its compact size, the watch was no small weight—a product of the hidden crystal lens folded inside—and its impact left a definite sting, even through her layers of muslin and lawn. She gathered up the green enameled case and cupped it in her palm, the diamond arrow at its center pointing to the large emerald set at the eleven o'clock mark. Lord Carlston had given her the watch to replace the miniature portrait of her mother that had contained its own lens, which she had lost to the enemy. A most forgiving gesture on his lordship's part, considering the alchemy built into the miniature, and how dangerous it was to them all.

"Lady Helen?" Lord Carlston's voice sharpened. "Do I have your attention?"

She jerked her head up and let the watch drop back to the end of its cord. "Of course. More space and purpose."

She had no difficulty with the idea of more *purpose.* Surely that was just a matter of taking a longer stride—something that would be far more achievable when she was clad in breeches. Her long, lean measurements had already been given to a London tailor to sew her a pair of buckskins and all the other gentlemanly accoutrements. She was to be a fine young man, at least in the cut of her clothing. Her manner, however, was not so easily stitched into masculinity. According to his lordship, she still needed to deepen her voice, be less careful with the placement of her arms and legs, and now also take up more *space.* No easy task, since she had spent most of her life learning to control any excess gesture or movement. Nevertheless, she gathered up the hem of her gown, squared her shoulders, and rocked forward onto the balls of her feet.

"For goodness' sake, you cannot go striding around with your skirts up," Lady Margaret hissed. "Someone may see."

"It is not as if she is galloping along the seafront in her chemise, my dear," Mr. Hammond said.

"That may be so," his sister replied, her delicate features pinched beneath her straw-chip hat, "but it is past the breakfast hour, and we are in full view of everyone's drawing rooms."

They all looked across at the row of houses that lined the Parade. Most of them were still shuttered, but enough had their windows exposed to the bright July morning to give credence to Lady Margaret's alarm.

"I doubt that one or two steps will bring us undone," his lordship told her, "but your caution is exemplary."

Helen let go of her skirts and turned toward the sea to hide her pique, her eyes fixed upon a three-masted war-sloop no doubt making its way to Plymouth before joining the newly declared war with the United States. Perhaps it could aim its cannons at Lady Margaret and her *exemplary caution* instead, Helen thought, then immediately felt churlish. The woman was irritating, but she and her brother had been valued members of the Dark Days Club for over five years, whereas Helen had only just joined the secret order that protected mankind from the Deceivers. And although Lady Margaret and her brother were not *Reclaimers* like herself and Lord Carlston—rare warriors born to fight the hidden creatures—it could not be denied that they were also placing themselves in great danger. Not to mention the fact they had been kind enough to take her in after she had been expelled from her Uncle Pennworth's house.

"You must weigh and consider every action now," Lady Margaret added, her severe tone drawing Helen around to face her again. "One slip and you will—"

"I am aware of it." Helen smiled through clenched teeth. "But I am obliged to you for the reminder."

Lady Margaret regarded her warily, clearly recognizing the strain in her voice. They had been confined together over the past four weeks in a rented town house in German Place, not without some sharp words from both sides. The unhappy incarceration had been ordered by Lord Carlston, as it was imperative to the Dark Days Club that Helen start her Reclaimer training in earnest. It was a time-consuming project, and his lordship had insisted that they establish a reason why such a well-connected young lady staying in Brighton would be absent from many of the town's social delights. Convalescence was the most believable excuse, and so Helen had stayed indoors alongside Lady Margaret and feigned poor health. She had also braved a visit from the proprietor of Awsiter's Baths with his foul elixir of seawater and milk, and engaged the services of Martha Gunn, a sturdy old woman who dipped young ladies in the sea for their health—both clear indicators to society that she had come to the seaside resort for her constitution and not for the busy Season.

When she had asked his lordship why they had not gone to a quieter town instead—to her mind, a perfectly reasonable question—he had merely given her an endless shark-eyed stare. One of his more maddening traits. At least her *convalescence* story was now established to his satisfaction, and this morning he was permitting them to unobtrusively walk into town to sign the subscription book at Donaldson's Circulating Library: the very hub of fashionable Brighton life and, according to Lord Carlston, its center of illicit information.

Helen felt her gaze drawn to him again. He was back to watching the progress of the man walking up the hill. The clean lines of his profile were set and unyielding, and he reminded her of one of the Roman centurion statues she seen in Bullock's Museum. Forever waiting for the enemy. Yet she could not forget that beyond those noble features she had seen a deep darkness within his soul. At first, she had thought it was the black mark of his wife's murder—a crime that he had never denied—but now she knew it was a slow poisoning from the Deceivers' foul energy. Every time he reclaimed a Deceiver's offspring back to humanity, the blight he ripped from its soul took root within his own. Helen knew that every Reclaimer had to eventually retire from saving souls, else it would send them mad. Yet Mr. Hammond had said his lordship refused to stop.

"I believe we are about to receive a visit from the Home Office," Lord Carlston said dryly, his attention still fixed upon the approaching figure. Helen looked back at the stooped man: his intention was now clearly aimed at the four of them.

Mr. Hammond tilted back the brim of his beaver hat. "By Jove, is that—?"

"Ignatious Pike," Carlston said. "I recognized him when he started up the hill. Hard to mistake that deplorable Whitehall style."

Helen saw a fleeting frown tighten Mr. Hammond's face, and knew he felt as exasperated as she did. If his lordship had known it was the government man all along, why had he not offered the information? He kept his own counsel too much. It was even more maddening than his shark-eyed stare.

"What is he doing here?" Lady Margaret asked.

"I would hazard a guess that the new Home Secretary has finally been informed about the Dark Days Club," Carlston said.

It was near two months since the Prime Minister, Lord Perceval, had been assassinated in the House of Commons. After much mayhem, His Royal Highness the Prince Regent had finally ratified a new government on the eighth of June, and along with it a new Home Secretary, Lord Sidmouth, who would, among other duties, oversee the clandestine Dark Days Club.

"Well, at least we do not have Ryder over us anymore," Mr. Hammond said.

Carlston nodded his agreement. "They could not keep him, not after he covered up Benchley's involvement in the Ratcliffe murders."

Just the mention of Lord Carlston's old Reclaimer mentor sent a crawling sensation across Helen's nape. It was Samuel Benchley who had forced her mother to absorb the Deceiver darkness within him, and it had all but killed Lady Catherine's soul. He had planned to do the same to Helen, but her mother had bequeathed her a *Colligat*—an alchemical way to strip herself of her Reclaimer heritage—hidden in the miniature portrait alongside the Reclaimer lens. Benchley had attacked Helen in her uncle's house, bent on stealing the miniature and its power, but had been killed by the Deceiver posing as a footman in the household.

Even in the bright sunlight and warmth of the Brighton morning, Helen shuddered at the memory of Benchley's bulging eyes and popping veins as he died at the Deceiver's hands. The creature would have attacked her as well, but Lord Carlston had intervened and absorbed all of its lethal whip energy. The Deceiver had then grabbed for the *Colligat*, and Helen had been forced to make a terrible choice: leap for the *Colligat* herself and protect her only way to a normal life; or absorb half of the whip energy raging through Lord Carlston and save his life but lose the *Colligat*.

She had flung herself atop the Earl, and the intensity of that moment still sang in her blood. There had been so much power between them as their bodies locked together in an intimate embrace, which, if she were honest, had not been fueled only by the overwhelming hold of the Deceiver energy. Even now, standing on the road above the beach, the memory of his arms around her brought a wave of heat across her skin. She found the lever on her parasol and pulled down the canopy, trying to distract herself from the disturbing images. Had she not just vowed to reject these wayward emotions?

With the parasol folded and her composure back in place, she turned her attention to the arrival of Ignatious Pike. He was taller than she had expected—the downhill perspective must have skewed her reckoning—and if he had stood straight, he would have been almost Lord Carlston's commanding height. He did not, however, have the Earl's breadth of shoulder nor his air of strength. Still, his breath was unhurried even after his rapid climb, and he moved with some agility. The man was more athletic than his spindly, round-shouldered frame suggested.

He bowed to Carlston. "My lord." A cool glance took in Helen. "My lady, we are not yet acquainted. I am Ignatious Pike, Second Secretary to the Home Office."

Helen stared at him, taken aback. Was he grossly ill-mannered, or did his position allow him to sidestep the conventions of polite introduction? She looked across at his lordship, knowing he would see the question in her eyes. His answer came in the flick of one eyebrow and a wry cast to his mouth: *Acknowledge him.* So it was the latter: the man had some kind of status.

"How do you do, Mr. Pike," she said, and found his gaze had narrowed into shrewd evaluation.

Two could play at that game: she met his close scrutiny with her own. It was difficult to place an age upon him. His face had a wizened quality, but his cold blue stare was bright, and his pasty skin still had the tautness of youth. No more than thirty, Helen guessed, and that was all she could glean from his sharp features.

Usually she could read a person's truth within their face—it was one of the Reclaimer abilities—but this man was even more closed than his lordship.

He allowed a wintry smile of triumph to touch his lips: he had seen her attempt *and* her failure.

"Mr. Pike, I believe you are already acquainted with Lady Margaret and Mr. Hammond," Lord Carlston said.

"Yes." Pike afforded the brother and sister a quick nod, before turning back to his lordship. "No doubt you know why I am here. You are requested to return to London immediately to meet with Lord Sidmouth. He has now been apprised of the Dark Days Club and its activities."

"Hopefully he will not be as corruptible as Mr. Ryder," Mr. Hammond said.

Pike turned a hard look upon him. "Mr. Ryder made the necessary decisions to contain the damage created by Benchley and to protect the Dark Days Club from public knowledge." The hard look traveled to his lordship.

"I think we all know that those *necessary* decisions were more yours than Mr. Ryder's," Carlston said. "You certainly know how to survive, Mr. Pike."

"Your lordship gives me credit that I am not due."

Carlston made a small sound of disbelief. "Has our new prime minister been fully apprised of the Dark Days Club as well? *And* the current situation?"

Pike let the question hang between them for a moment, his icy smile appearing again. "Lord Liverpool has been fully briefed, and I assure you, he gives Lord Sidmouth his full support."

"I would not have thought otherwise."

Although Carlston's tone was pleasant, Helen heard the draw of steel within it. The two men, it seemed, were stepping back into an old battle.

Pike crossed his arms. "Neither of them is convinced by your evidence that a Grand Deceiver has arrived in England."

"Not convinced?" Helen exclaimed. "But the Deceiver who attacked me *said* he served a Grand Deceiver."

"They are Deceivers, Lady Helen," Pike said with a note of condescension in his voice. "They manage to live as humans and fool us all. Deception is their nature."

"And yet we saw a number of them working together at Bellingham's hanging," Carlston said. "You know that is out of the ordinary."

"It is," Pike allowed. "But nothing in the archives even hints that such an occurrence points to the arrival of a Grand Deceiver."

Carlston drew a breath through pinched nostrils. "Then what about Lady Helen herself? She is a direct inheritor: the Reclaimer daughter of a Reclaimer mother. That, at least, is documented."

The wave of a thin hand dismissed his lordship's words. Or, Helen thought, maybe it dismissed such a *female* lineage.

"If I remember correctly, that archive only states that a direct inheritor has powers beyond a normal Reclaimer, to stand against all that may come." Pike looked inquiringly at Helen.

She felt obliged to shake her head: she had not yet exhibited any extra powers. A small mercy, in her opinion; she was having enough difficulty with the ones she already had.

"To stand against all that may come," Pike repeated. "Not a Grand Deceiver in particular; such a creature is never named. We cannot chase phantoms, Lord Carlston, especially with the Luddites rioting through the country and Bonaparte across the channel." He drew himself up. "You are expected at Lord Sidmouth's house to dine this evening, my lord. I suggest you start your journey as soon as possible."

He gave a small bow, his eyes meeting Helen's again for an odd, intense moment, then he turned and walked back the way he had come, looking neither to the left at the sea, nor to the right at the handsome row of houses. Mr. Pike, it seemed, had not the time or inclination for a beautiful view.

Lady Margaret lifted her shoulders as if struck by a sudden chill. "Horrid man."

"Why does he not believe you?" Helen asked Lord Carlston. A jab of pain in her hand drew her attention to the fact that she was holding her parasol like a club, the lever biting into her palm. She eased her grip.

"Because it is I who brought the news," he said acidly. "Ignatious Pike is the bureaucratic heart of the Dark Days Club and its senior officer, yet he just delivered a summons that could easily have been carried by one of his underlings. So why did he make the journey?"

"Good point," Mr. Hammond said. "Perhaps it was to acknowledge you as new leader of the Reclaimers."

"No, he is here on some other business," his lordship said. "But what, I wonder."

Mr. Hammond pulled his fob watch from his breeches pocket. "He is right about one thing. If Sidmouth expects you tonight, that does not give you much time to get back to Mayfair. It is already near eleven thirty."

Helen calculated the journey. It had taken her and Lady Margaret seven hours to travel to Brighton, but that had been in a coach-and-four, using the ill-matched teams that went for hire at the posting inns. His lordship had driven down in his curricle, a far lighter equipage, and he kept his own thoroughbreds stabled at the inns for each change. He could possibly make it back to London within five hours. Still, it would mean he would most probably not start his return to Brighton until the following morning.

The thought brought a small slump of disappointment. She

had begun to look forward to her training. The long hours under his lordship's tutelage were never easy—he gave no quarter—but the challenge was exhilarating, and it took her away from Lady Margaret's *reminders* of her duty.

Now he would be away for a day. Probably two.

Two days without the chance of touching him.

She coughed, shocked by the thought. Could she not even last five minutes without her mind taking a lascivious path?

"I shall make London by evening, and return Sunday afternoon," Carlston said, confirming her estimate. Yet she heard something in his tone that made her observe him more closely. He was uneasy in a way she had not seen before.

He turned to address her, once more the stern instructor. "While I am away, I want you to start reading the Romford book on alchemy—pay particular attention to the binding rituals—and practice your male disguise. The pitch of your voice is coming along well, but your gait needs a lot more work. Mr. Hammond, I trust you will assist Lady Helen and deal with any other issues that arise?"

Mr. Hammond straightened. "Of course, sir."

"I take my leave, then." Carlston bowed, then plainly bethought himself of something else and turned back to Helen, his eyes finding the touch watch around her neck. "When I gave that to you, I am sure I told you not to wear it on your person."

"You said not to wear it on a chain." She hooked the cord around her thumb. "See, it is on silk. And you said the enameling was made of glass and would insulate—"

"I said the enameling *may* insulate the metal underneath from creating a pathway for a Deceiver's whip-energy. But do you really want to take the chance?"

"No."

"I thought not." His tone sharpened. "Carry it in your reticule, and listen more carefully."

Helen pulled the cord over her head, opened the tiny purse, and dropped the dangling watch inside. "You wear yours," she muttered. Even to herself she sounded like a sullen child.

"I wear mine in a specially prepared leather-lined pocket in my breeches. As far as I know, ladies' gowns do not have pockets. Until they do, or you are wearing your own breeches, carry the watch in your reticule. For once, do as you are told."

Helen stiffened at the unfair criticism; she did everything she was told.

He pressed his fingers hard into his forehead. "I beg your pardon, Lady Helen. Forgive my ill humor. I clearly misled you regarding the effectiveness of the enameling." With that, he strode away in the direction of his lodgings.

They watched his progress up the hill, each silent and unmoving as if his departure had somehow suspended them. At the corner of Camelford Street, he paused and looked back at them, then was gone.

"He is far more ill-tempered than usual," Mr. Hammond said.

"It is just weariness," Lady Margaret said quickly. "They place too much upon him. It is a strain."

Helen glanced at her: she was half-right. Lord Carlston *was* weary and strained, but not only from the burden of his responsibilities. It was also the constant battle against the Deceiver darkness that shadowed his soul. She had seen the canker within him, had felt its corruption spreading, sapping the light from him, creeping a little deeper into his heart every time he reclaimed another Deceiver offspring. Yet he would not stop. Was it duty that compelled him to such risk, or something else?

She laid her hand on her chest where the touch watch had hung.

There was only one known way to cleanse a Reclaimer's soul: by pouring the darkness into another Reclaimer and destroying them instead. It had been Benchley's despicable solution, but neither she nor his lordship would ever resort to such a heinous act.

She turned her gaze back to the empty street corner where his lordship had stood only moments before. Yet what would happen if Lord Carlston finally descended into the tormented madness of a poisoned soul?

She closed her eyes. Yes, what then?

Two

MR. HAMMOND WAS first to break the pensive silence. "Even after all this time, Pike holds a grudge," he said, offering his arm to his sister.

"What did you expect?" Lady Margaret replied. "He will always hate Lord Carlston."

Shaking off her sense of dread, Helen put up her parasol again and considered what had just passed between his lordship and Mr. Pike. They seemed to dislike each other in equal measure.

"What has caused such animosity?" she asked as they started down the hill.

The brother and sister looked at each other. Mr. Hammond gave a tiny shrug, as if to say, *What is the harm?* "Have you heard the name Sir Dennis Calloway?" he asked.

"He was another Reclaimer, was he not?"

Mr. Hammond nodded. "And a friend to his lordship. He was killed four years ago by an Unreclaimable."

"Unreclaimable?" Helen had not heard the word before.

"It is as the name suggests," Hammond said. "A Deceiver offspring who is too affected by the vestige within it to be returned to humanity. Some are highly promiscuous, some are prone to fits of violence, and some are just insane. Apparently the Unreclaimable was a small woman, and Sir Dennis underestimated her strength and cunning. Pike was his Terrene at the time."

"Really?"

Helen could not picture the thin, stooped Pike as a Reclaimer's guard and aide. Terrenes were usually chosen for their large size and natural strength, like Lord Carlston's man, Mr. Quinn, or her own maid and Terrene-to-be, Darby. Their build was essential, as it was a Terrene's duty to wrestle their Reclaimer to the ground and force him—or, indeed, her—to release the lethal energy captured from a Deceiver. It was a difficult task at the best of times, made even more dangerous by the seduction of the deadly power. A Reclaimer would kill to keep it.

Helen had only shared the Deceiver's whip-energy with Lord Carlston but could still feel an echo of it in her flesh. Faith, it had been like the sun coursing through her veins, so bright and hot and triumphant. Their bodies entwined within the delight—

"Lady Helen?" Lady Margaret's voice broke through the heady sensation. "Are you quite well?"

Helen felt heat rise to her cheeks. She had been lost again in the memory of that power rushing through her body. She smiled, covering her disorientation. "Pike does not look like a Terrene."

"He used to," Lady Margaret said. "He was almost as big as Mr. Quinn. But when a Reclaimer dies, the alchemical bond he had with his Terrene declines. Within a year after Sir Dennis's death, Pike lost all his enhanced abilities—his speed and strength and that wondrous accelerated healing—and became the man we see today. A shadow of what he once was."

"It must have been a wretched experience," Helen said.

She knew herself the exhilaration of that extraordinary physical power; how devastating to have it drain away.

"The loss has certainly made him bitter, especially toward his lordship," Mr. Hammond said. At Helen's querying glance, he added, "Pike blames him for Sir Dennis's death. He says Lord

Carlston knew Sir Dennis was not up to the task but did not heed Pike's request for assistance."

His sister sniffed. "That was not the case at all."

"And yet his lordship has never denied it, Margaret."

The path narrowed abruptly, forcing Helen to take a step back behind the brother and sister. It seemed Lord Carlston never denied any accusation of wrongdoing: not the murder of his wife, Lady Elise, nor Sir Dennis's death. Did he just not care that he was blamed for such crimes, or was there more to it?

Mr. Hammond looked back over his shoulder. "I suggest we go to Donaldson's first and then walk across to the Castle Tavern. His lordship wants us to subscribe to their balls and card assemblies now that the Season has truly started."

"Are you sure he wants me to subscribe?" Helen asked. "I thought I was supposed to be too unwell to attend balls."

Mr. Hammond shrugged. "That is what he said. No explanation."

He turned back to navigate the path. As Helen followed him and Lady Margaret past the Marine Library—as good as Donaldson's, according to her guidebook, but without its central position—she was struck anew by the similarity in the way the brother and sister moved: a graceful precision that gave him a wiry self-possession, and her a dainty elegance. Just in that trait, their relationship to one another was obvious, but it became even more so when they turned to one another to speak and their features were mirrored: the same well-shaped nose, broad brow, and expressive eyes, with a softer mouth for Lady Margaret, and the firmer lines of masculinity set upon Mr. Hammond's jaw and chin.

Helen had assumed Lady Margaret was the elder by a year or two, but such close similarity suggested they might be twins. It would explain the bond between them. For all their bickering, they had a true affection for one another. A true ease.

She looked out at the expanse of ocean, suddenly overcome

by an ache that seemed to hollow her out. There was no one among her new companions with whom she could share a passing thought or laugh at the absurdity of others, no one she could trust with a silly secret. It was all Dark Days Club and *focus, Lady Helen.* Even Darby was intent upon training, all alight with her new Terrene responsibilities. But back in London, before all this madness, Helen had laughed and talked with Aunt, and her brother, Andrew, and Millicent, the best of all friends. Not now, of course. Nothing would ever compel her to drag them into the darkness of the Deceivers' world.

Yet there was someone close to her who had already stepped halfway into the shadows of that world. Someone who would be better off with the knowledge of the Deceivers than without it. Her friend Delia. Helen wet her lips, tasting the sea's salt on the tip of her tongue. It was just over two months since she had learned of Delia's failed elopement. Aunt Leonore had returned from a trip to Ackermann's Repository of Arts full of the latest gossip that Delia Cransdon had run away with a Mr. Trent, who had then shot himself in front of her under the strangest of circumstances. Well, they had seemed strange at the time, but now it was obvious— to Helen, at least—that Mr. Trent had been a Deceiver, and Delia had witnessed his fiery demise.

Poor Delia. She had been whisked away to her family's country estate, disgraced, disbelieved, and fearing for her own sanity. Helen had written from London to say that she would soon be in Brighton, close enough to call upon her friend, but Delia had never replied, or perhaps had not been allowed to reply. Whatever the case, the ominous silence had prompted Helen to post another letter soon after her arrival in Brighton, and one a week after that too. Still no reply. In desperation, she had sent another missive two days ago, this time by hired messenger. The man was due back that morning, hopefully carrying an invitation from Delia to call upon her and her parents.

And if not . . . ?

Helen quelled the thought. She had to see her friend, with or without an invitation. She was the only one who could tell Delia the whole truth and reassure her she was not mad. It was even possible that she could arrange for Delia to accompany her back to Brighton as her companion, reinstate her in society, and get her away from the threat of the sanatorium. Surely Delia's parents would welcome such a solution, particularly since their spinster daughter's upkeep would be someone else's responsibility.

It was a good plan, except for one rather large, curt problem: Lord Carlston. Helen wiped her mouth with a gloved forefinger, feeling the salt scratch her lips into a burning sting. He would be furious that she had taken it upon herself to tell an innocent about the Deceivers. Yet Delia was not wholly an innocent; and if it was already done, his lordship could not change it, could he? Knowledge, after all, could not be unlearned.

They reached the bottom of the hill, and Helen paused to take in the view of the beachfront: a stretch of pale pebbles that looked rather dangerous to unshod feet. She started to comment upon it to Mr. Hammond, then realized she was standing alone. He and Lady Margaret had already walked ahead and made the turn into South Parade.

Helen quickened her pace to catch up, and so came upon Brighton's famous promenade: the Steine. According to the guide-book, no other place in the kingdom was frequented by more beauty and fashion during the mornings and evenings of the Season.

That may be so, Helen thought as she surveyed the large expanse of fenced grass circled by a gravel path, but the Steine before her now seemed decidedly bare of both. The warmer weather had enticed very few visitors into the town center, and the shops and amenities that clustered around the Steine had an air of disappointed expectation. Then again, Helen conceded, half past eleven was counted as obscenely early for many of the fashionable set.

Mr. Hammond and Lady Margaret were waiting for her to join them. She fell in beside Lady Margaret, ignoring her impatient scowl, and appraised a jeweler's window as they strolled past. A thin gold armlet in the Egyptian style demanded a second look.

As Helen paused, she caught sight of two men in the periphery of her vision, crossing the road near the Castle Tavern: a tall figure with a reddish cast to his hair beneath a shabby gray beaver hat, and a smaller, swarthier man. It was just a glimpse, but her entire body clenched with cold alarm. The way the taller man moved, his breadth of shoulder, the bright glint in his hair—all reminded her of Philip. She spun around, her eyes fixed upon the now empty street corner.

"Lady Helen, is something wrong?" Mr. Hammond asked.

"I thought I saw the Deceiver who posed as my uncle's footman. The one who stole the *Colligat* and killed Benchley."

"Where?" Lady Margaret demanded.

Helen pointed across the Steine. "He walked along there with another man, and crossed into that street." It was quite a distance to be claiming recognition from one glance, even with her Reclaimer eyesight. Maybe she was overreacting. "I cannot be sure it was him."

"Still, if there is any chance of retrieving the *Colligat*, we must investigate," Mr. Hammond said, urging them forward. "What does he look like?"

Helen gave a brief description of Philip as they crossed the road at an unseemly trot and took the pathway that cut through the green expanse of the Steine. Helen clasped her bonnet to her head, murmuring an apology to a startled elderly lady as the three of them hurried past. They reached the corner and peered down the road. A pair of giggling maidservants walked arm in arm, a brewer hauled a barrel from his cart, and a fashionable gentleman stood viewing a window display of books. No sign of a tall young man in a gray beaver, or his shorter dark-haired companion.

"Are you sure you saw him come down here?" Lady Margaret asked.

"I am not sure it was him at all. It was just something about the way he walked that—"

"Lady Helen! Upon my soul, it is you!"

They all turned.

"Good Lord," Mr. Hammond said, raising his quizzing glass to look at the figure waving exuberantly from the main promenade path. "Who is that?"

"Lady Elizabeth Brompton," Helen said. "And that is her mother, Lady Dunwick, coming behind."

It was inevitable that she would meet London acquaintances in Brighton; it was one of the most fashionable sea-bathing towns. But why did it have to be Pug and her mother? They were so cheerfully and relentlessly inquisitive. Moreover, they'd both been at her ball and would, without a doubt, have awkward questions about that fateful night.

"We cannot pretend we have not seen them," Hammond said. He gave one last look down the road. "If that was indeed the Deceiver, he could be anywhere in that maze of lanes."

Helen braced herself as Pug, resplendent in pink and green stripes, dragged her mother across the road and bobbed into a breathless curtsy. Her protuberant blue eyes—the reason for her nickname—popped even wider under the tall, luxuriously feathered crown of her bonnet.

"How are you, Lady Helen? I've not seen you since the night of your ball. Are you recovered now?" She caught Helen's hands, squeezing them sympathetically. "It was such a shock to learn that you had fallen ill straight after dancing before His Royal Highness. Was the dancing too much for you after your fall? Is your darling mare all right? Are you here for your health?"

Helen aimed a curtsy at Lady Dunwick, trying unsuccessfully to extricate herself from Pug's grip. "Yes, here for my health," she echoed, ignoring all the other questions. "Allow me to present my friends. This is Lady Margaret Ridgewell and her brother, Mr. Hammond."

Lady Dunwick, who had clearly passed on her bulbous eyes to her daughter, nodded graciously to the brother and sister. "How do you do." Her gaze turned back to Helen, the bulging expanse of white around each blue iris giving her an expression of perpetual urgency. "Is your aunt here with you, my dear? I had thought she and your uncle were set upon spending the summer at Lansdale Hall?"

"Yes, they will be at Lansdale," Helen said, fixing a smile upon her face. In truth, she did not know what her guardians intended—not since her uncle had expelled her from his house. "Lady Margaret has been so kind as to invite me here for the summer."

"Then you must all come to supper next Friday," Lady Dunwick said, the abundance of orange feathers on her bonnet nodding vigorously as if to second the invitation. "A little announcement of our arrival in Brighton. It will be just those families who are already in town. It is such a shame that all this hoo-ha with the government and the American war is keeping the Prince Regent in London. It leaves us rather light for company. I see you are hesitating, my dear, but I insist. Let me tempt you with dancing. Some of the officers from the Tenth Light Dragoons will be attending." She raised an emphatic finger and shook it. "Elizabeth has told me about your riding accident, so we will make sure you are not overtaxed. Only every second dance, and a rest in between."

"Oh, yes, you must come," Pug urged. "The Prince of Wales's

regiment always has the best dancers. Say you will. Please say you will."

Under such kind pressure, Helen knew she could not demur. "Thank you."

She saw Lady Margaret's jaw tighten before she murmured her own thanks, along with Mr. Hammond.

"Wonderful!" Pug beamed around the small circle. "Where are you heading now?"

"Donaldson's," Helen said.

"To sign the book?" Pug asked. "We are on our way too. Let us go together." She linked arms with Helen. "It is across the Steine and very well-placed for watching the street. Have you seen the bathing boxes with their little ponies—aren't they divine? I'm so keen to bathe, although it is not yet warm enough. Surely you must be considering it, too?"

Helen opened her mouth to reply, but was not quick enough.

"Of course you are, what with your fall and everything. So beneficial to the health. Why, I was just telling Mother . . ."

And so Pug continued for the whole of the short walk to the library. Helen nodded and smiled and caught the appalled eye of Lady Margaret, who was enduring a similar one-sided conversation with Lady Dunwick.

"Well, here we are," Pug announced unnecessarily as they drew up to the clearly signed frontage of the library. "We shall soon find out who else is in town. Everyone subscribes to Donaldson's."

A young footman clad in neat drab stood at the entrance. Seeing their intention to enter, he pulled open the doors and bowed as Pug led the way inside. Helen happened to glance at the young man as she passed, and as their eyes met, she saw something dawn upon his round-cheeked face: recognition.

Before she could react, she'd been herded over the threshold by Lady Dunwick's bulk. She looked back, but the young man had already closed the doors behind them and disappeared from his post. Through the large front windows, Helen searched the pedestrians walking along the Parade until she found him again, standing on the corner of the road opposite Raggett's Club. A rather abrupt departure for a footman. The anomaly hardened into a sudden suspicion: perhaps he was a Deceiver who had sensed her Reclaimer energy and bolted.

Then again, maybe her phantom sighting of Philip had made *all* footmen into Deceivers. Was she overreacting again? Even if she were, it would do no harm to check. Most of the time it was impossible to prove the identity of a Deceiver. However, if this footman had been skimming life force from oblivious passersby, then maybe she would be able to see his feeding tentacle through her Reclaimer lens. It was a hundred-to-one chance, nevertheless she opened her reticule and scooped up the touch watch, finding the tiny clip that held the case shut.

But how could she assemble the lens and raise it to her eye without causing comment? A swift glance about the room gave her the answer: she could not. There were too many people around, and Pug had already noticed the watch cupped in her hand. Lord, how she missed her mother's miniature. Somehow, the *Colligat* alchemy within it had allowed her to see Deceiver energy just by holding the tiny portrait; no need to assemble a lens. But its power was in the hands of the Deceivers now. With one last look at the young man rapidly crossing the road, Helen let the watch drop back into her bag.

"I say, that is a pretty timepiece," Pug said. "It looks just like the one that Lord Carlston carries, except his is blue. Are they from the same maker?"

"I would not know. I have never noticed his lordship's watch," Helen lied, and walked further into the library, leaving Pug in her wake.

Mr. Hammond came to stand at her side. "Grand, is it not? This is only the first of many rooms beyond." He added under his breath, "Is everything all right?"

"It is," she said to both questions, and turned her attention to the library in an effort to throw off her sense of unease.

A remarkably large skylight in the ceiling allowed the day's brightness into the long spacious room. The walls were lined with shelves of books—as was to be expected—most of them bound in the serviceable blue cardboard that was the badge of the modern circulating library. A handsome mahogany counter stood to the right, manned by a portly individual dressed in a black coat and with luxurious whiskers who was showing a periodical to a young lady. Three older gentlemen sat bent over newspapers at a long reading table set beneath the skylight; at one end of the table was spread a neat display of that day's *Times*, *Gazette*, and *Morning Post*, and the local *Brighton Herald*. The smell of fresh newspaper ink and the fustiness of the books mixed with a faint trace of rose perfume. A curiously pleasant scent. Helen breathed it in, finding a measure of calm again.

A number of small tables had been arranged around the floor with enough distance between them for a quiet *tête-à-tête*, and some were already occupied by ladies and gentlemen conversing in soft tones. Nearby, a pair of young ladies strolled arm in arm past a series of glass-topped display cases, pausing now and again to study an array of jewelry and stationery for sale, their coos of delight like distant doves.

"Oh, look!" Pug's voice cut through Helen's newfound serenity. "They carry rings. I do love a ring. And perfume, too!" She leaned closer to Helen's ear, although did not drop her volume. "It's probably smuggled from Paris."

The gentle activity in the room ceased for a moment, and all eyes turned to the new arrivals. The portly librarian, having concluded his business with the young lady, rapidly made his way toward them.

"Lady Dunwick," he said in a rich voice that seemed more suited to the stage than a library. A neat bow showed the shiny freckled top of a balding head. "It is an honor to see you here again. How may I be of service?"

Lady Dunwick waved an expansive hand, collecting Helen, Lady Margaret, and Mr. Hammond into its arc. "We are here to subscribe, Mr. Fountwell."

"You are all most welcome," he said. "Please, come this way and sign the book." He gestured to the counter where a large green bound ledger sat open. "Our terms have not changed since last summer, Lady Dunwick, and I think you and your companions will agree they are most moderate. Five shillings for one month or ten shillings for three months." He turned his attention to Helen and Lady Margaret. "And if you are so inclined, we also sell subscriptions to the concert series."

"I do not know if my health will allow me to attend the concerts," Helen said, stepping up to the counter, "but I will subscribe to the library. For two months."

"I believe one month will be sufficient, my dear," Lady Margaret said.

Helen met her eyes for a fleeting moment—were they only staying a month more, then?—and saw the affirmative.

"Of course, just a month," she amended. Why was she always the last to know these things?

"Excellent," Mr. Fountwell said, casting a rather narrow look at Lady Margaret. He offered Helen a well-trimmed quill. "If you would be so kind as to sign the register."

Helen took the pen, dipped it into the ink, and bent to the ledger, her eye skimming down the names already written across the page.

"Who is here?" Pug leaned in to study the book. "Oh, look, the Comte and Comtesse d'Antraigues. It says here they have a house in Marlborough Row. They must be near us, then. You know she was a famous opera singer in Paris?"

"Yes," Helen said, but her attention had fixed—horribly—on another name in the register. In almost the same moment, Pug's gloved finger jabbed at the bold signature.

"Oh, my goodness, His Grace the Duke of Selburn is here!" She turned her head, the feathers in her bonnet brushing Helen's face. "Did you know he was coming?"

"No," Helen managed.

Just six weeks ago, a few days before her presentation ball, the Duke had asked her to marry him—an honor that she had more or less accepted on the condition that he still wished to do so *after* her ball. Admittedly, it had been a strange caveat, but she had expected to strip herself of her Reclaimer powers that night, and the effect of such alchemy could have destroyed her wit and intelligence forever. She had felt she could not in all conscience accept his proposal as a bright, lively woman, and then expect him to live an entire life with a diminished, idiot version of herself. All that had changed, of course, with Philip's attack upon her in her bedchamber and her choice to be a Reclaimer, not a Duchess. She had written to the Duke and released him from any obligation, but had not seen him since that letter had been delivered.

Pug's thick fingertip traced the ledger line across to the date column. "His Grace arrived the day before yesterday. I rather thought he would have stayed in the city, what with the new government and all."

"Two days ago?" Helen looked at Mr. Hammond and saw a flash of guilt cross his face. He had known; and beside him, Lady Margaret's face told the same story. Without a doubt, their silence was on Lord Carlston's orders. Helen's anger heated her cheeks.

Pug sent her a knowing glance. "You are blushing. Perhaps his arrival is a compliment to you, Lady Helen. The general view in London is that there is an understanding between you."

"You are mistaken. There is no understanding."

Helen bent to the page again and signed her name, the nib almost puncturing the paper. She placed the pen back in its stand and stood aside so that Pug could sign the book.

The inevitability of meeting the Duke sometime soon settled like a cold stone within her stomach. She would not be able to avoid him in a town as small as Brighton. What on earth would she say to him? More to the point, what would he say? The man had every right to be angry—she had abandoned her promise with little explanation and, to her eternal shame, by letter. However, that would pale by comparison if the Duke found her in the company of Lord Carlston. At her ball, the two men had nearly come to blows on the dance floor, and, if her brother was to be believed, the Duke's rancor had only increased since that night.

"Shall we take a turn around the room, Lady Helen?" Pug asked as her mother bent to the subscription book.

Helen had no objection—a walk would at least channel her anxiety into action—and she allowed Pug to take possession of her arm. They strolled across the floor to the neat line of display cases, nodding to the other pair of young ladies who were studying an array of beaded reticules.

"To my mind, a ring should not be too plain," Pug said, rather forcefully steering Helen toward the jewelry case near the door. "Plain rings vex me. I think pearls . . ."

But Helen did not hear the rest of the sentence, for she had looked through the window and seen the library's footman again, departing Raggett's Club. And before him strode a familiar tall blond figure: the Duke of Selburn. The footman had not been a Deceiver; he was an informer.

"Oh my," Pug whispered, her eyes also fixed on the Duke who was now crossing the road. She looked at Helen. "You've gone so pale. There *was* an understanding, wasn't there?"

Helen managed a nod. "But not now. It is most . . . awkward."

"What are you going to do?" Pug asked. "Can I be of service?"

"Don't leave me," Helen whispered. "Please."

She felt Pug squeeze her arm. "Of course. Nailed to your side, dear thing."

Helen fought back the impulse to throw propriety aside and embrace Pug Brompton right there in the middle of the library. She made do with a return squeeze.

"Let us pretend we are engrossed in the display," Pug whispered, leading her to the nearest case. "Look, Lady Helen, what lovely stationery," she said loudly and with patently false enthusiasm.

Helen stared at the sheaves of paper bound with red ribbon, the bundles of uncut quills, and the stacked boxes of sealing wafers. "Lovely," she echoed.

Behind her, she heard the front door open, felt the cooler street air push its way into the room, and, from the corner of her eye, saw the straightening of male spines and flutter of female hands. She tucked her chin down and stared fiercely at the uncut quills.

"Your Grace. May I be of service?" Mr. Fountwell's voice rolled with deference.

"Not at this time. Thank you." He was still near the door.

"His Grace is coming this way," Pug whispered.

Barely time to draw a steadying breath.

"Lady Helen."

His voice held a grave note of inquiry. Yet she could not lift her eyes.

Pug's arm pulled on her own for a moment as she dipped into a curtsy. "Good morning, Your Grace."

"Lady Elizabeth. How pleasant to see you again."

"Indeed," Pug said. "We have not been in Brighton long and—"

"Excuse me." He was moving, and every nerve in Helen's body followed his trajectory around Pug to take the position at her other side. One of his hands—ungloved—curled around the edge of the glass case near her own. "Ah, I see what has your attention, Lady Helen. It is indeed an enthralling display, particularly the pyramid of wafers. Almost on par, I think, with Mr. Turner's epic painting *The Battle of Trafalgar.*"

She bit her lip. He could always make her smile.

"The composition is less convincing, I fear," she said, and finally looked sideways at him. "Good morning, Your Grace."

She met the relief in his warm hazel eyes, then ducked her head in a belated curtsy.

"Good morning," he said. "How opportune to find you here."

That brought her eyes back to his face. She glanced pointedly at the returned doorman. "Opportune perhaps, but not a coincidence."

"No." He smiled, a wry acknowledgment that made her own lips twitch again. "Perhaps not." He turned to Pug. "Lady Elizabeth, would you please leave us for a moment? I have a message of a *private* nature to give to Lady Helen. From her brother."

"Your Grace, I am . . . Well, in fact . . ." Pug looked wildly at Helen.

"It is all right, Lady Elizabeth." Helen braced her feet more firmly into the thick rug. "I will hear the message."

With another curtsy to the Duke, Pug retreated to the next display case. A flat stare from him moved her further back, out of earshot.

Helen could hear Lady Margaret and Mr. Hammond in whispered conference at the subscription counter. Some part of her—not the bravest part—wanted them to cross the floor and save her from the impending *tête-à-tête*, but another part knew she must hear what His Grace had to say.

For a moment, they were both silent. She had once thought his long narrow face rather plain. Not now. At some point in their friendship, his kindness and humor had subtly rearranged his features into something quite appealing.

"I received your letter," he said. "You did not say *why*."

She turned from the pain in his voice. It had been the most difficult letter she had ever had to write and she had known her carefully crafted words had not been equal to the task. There was no satisfactory way to tell a man that his accepted offer of marriage was now to be rejected.

"You said you had a message from Andrew?"

"Helen, please." He was claiming the lover's right to use her first name, and she could not find it within herself to admonish him. "Am I to have no reason, then? No understanding of why you have changed your mind?"

She gave a slight shake of her head—unfair, but necessary—and saw his hand tighten around the edge of the case.

Three heartbeats of awkward silence; she could not take her eyes from his long slim fingers pressed hard against the glass.

"Your brother comes to Brighton as my guest on the thirteenth," he finally said. "He has asked me to inform you that he will call upon you at the first opportunity."

"He is coming here?" The last thing she needed.

"He wishes to ensure that you are happy and safe. He says he cannot be easy when you are with people so closely associated with Lord Carlston."

She looked up. That was not only Andrew's concern speaking. "What makes him think they are closely associated?"

"He is not a fool, Helen. Carlston is known to be here too. Your brother, like yourself, is suspicious of coincidences."

"Most of London society comes to Brighton for the summer, Your Grace. There is nothing extraordinary about my friends and Lord Carlston being in the same town."

Across the room, those friends were now valiantly trying to extricate themselves from Lady Dunwick's loud opinions on literature. Helen caught Lady Margaret's eye, sending a clear plea for help.

"That may be so," His Grace said. "But it has been noted in town that he has visited your address a number of times."

Was he repeating gossip? Or was he having the house watched, like the library?

"There is no mystery to that. Lord Carlston is related to my family. Naturally he would visit."

"Yet, as I understand it from your brother, that connection between Carlston and your family is no longer welcome." His shrewd gaze searched her face. "Particularly after your ball."

What had Andrew told him?

She saw him note the flicker of her eyelids, the catch in her breath. She had to end this interview. Now.

"Then you understand more than I do, Your Grace," she said, her tone as clipped as she could manage. "I am honored by your attentions, but I have released you from your obligation. You have no need to concern yourself with my welfare."

He leaned closer. "You may have released me, Helen, but I have not released you. Not in my heart." His voice held a new implacability. "I am not a man to give up, and I have your family's blessing for our union. Do not think I will sit by and watch that man draw you into his corruption. He has already stolen one future from me. He will not take another."

He made a graceful bow, and strode to the door. She watched him pause outside and draw a deep breath, as if to collect himself, then he crossed the street toward Raggett's Club again.

What did he mean, *stolen one future?*

Of course: he had courted poor Lady Elise and lost her to Lord Carlston.

Helen took her own steadying breath, and glanced around the library. Holy heaven, every eye in the room was fixed upon her, only now sliding away from her affronted stare. This was not quite the unobtrusive visit to town that Lord Carlston had envisioned.

Three

HELEN QUICKENED HER pace up the hill of Marine Parade, her speed fueled as much by agitation as the need to get away from Lady Margaret's accusing tone.

"I do not understand why you allowed private conversation with the Duke, Lady Helen. You should have made your curtsy and moved away."

"He contrived the meeting," Helen snapped over her shoulder, the sea breeze whipping at the end of each word. She glanced at Mr. Hammond, who, as ever, walked at his sister's side. At least his face held understanding and some sympathy. "If I had refused to speak to him on this occasion, he would just have arranged another."

How many times did she need to say it? She caught a moment of Lady Margaret's sucked-lemon mouth then turned back to her march. They underestimated the Duke: he was a man of resolution, and now he had declared he would not give up his pursuit of her under any circumstance. Helen held no delusion that it was her charms that made him so determined; she was not one of those fascinating females who could crook a finger and bring a man to her side. No, it was his hatred of Lord Carlston and their shared history with Lady Elise that had brought the Duke to Brighton. A most worrisome situation. By all reports, the Duke had not come out well from his last physical confrontation with Lord Carlston. Selburn had threatened to flog his lordship and had his own horsewhip turned upon him. Would he be so foolish as to challenge the Earl again? Perhaps Andrew was encouraging him to do so; her brother had made it very clear that he did not want her to associate with Lord Carlston. She stifled a groan. Andrew's imminent presence in Brighton was going to complicate matters a hundredfold.

Mr. Hammond drew up by her side, his breathing labored. "Slow down, Lady Helen. You are moving like a Reclaimer."

It was true; her body had angled forward, ready for the uncanny speed of her calling. She eased back to a more sedate pace.

"Margaret is not blaming you," he said, matching her slower stride. "It was bound to happen sooner or later."

Must he always smooth the edges of his sister's tongue?

Helen rounded on him. "You both knew the Duke was here in town. I saw it in your faces. Why did you not tell me?"

Mr. Hammond shrugged. "His lordship did not want you distracted from your training."

"Does he think me so weak-willed that just the presence of the Duke would pull me from my purpose? Surely even he would not be so insulting." Her vehemence caused her to accelerate again. With gritted teeth, she steadied her pace and forced moderation into her tone. "No, he did not tell me because it is a habit with him to keep his own counsel."

"You do not know his lordship well enough to make such comment upon his character," Lady Margaret said, catching up to them. "Besides, why should you expect him to tell you anything? You have been with us for little more than a month. We have been with him for five years."

"He was in exile for three of those years, Margaret," Mr. Hammond said.

"That may be so, but my point is that he does not tell *us*—his aides—everything, and we have proved our loyalty. Lord Carlston always has good reason for what he does. Everything is planned. He understands the whole canvas, whereas we see only a small corner of it."

"Perhaps we would see more," Helen said, "if he were not always standing in front of the canvas and obscuring whatever part of it he does not wish us to . . . or that we should be . . ." She broke off: the metaphor was in danger of imminent collapse. "All I am saying is that he keeps from me—and undoubtedly you as well—information that is important." She turned to Mr. Hammond. "Do you not agree?"

"Of course not," Lady Margaret said.

"I think Lady Helen has a point," Mr. Hammond said. "His lordship has always had an inclination to secrecy, and since his return from exile it is worse. He has been by himself far too long, and has been reclaiming too many offspring souls."

His sister gave him a long stare. "Is that so, Michael?"

"It is what Quinn says," Mr. Hammond said, returning her stare.

They had reached German Place. In heavy silence, they walked along the narrow pavement to number 20, the town house that Mr. Hammond had rented on his sister's behalf. Although not situated on Marine Parade itself, the five-story dwelling was close enough to that fashionable address to be beyond reproach, and was furnished, according to Lady Margaret, in an entirely adequate style.

The front door opened as they climbed the steps. Garner stood at the threshold, ready to take parasols and hats as they entered. The butler's bony face was, as ever, set in the dour lines of the upper servant, but Helen saw a slight tightening around his watchful eyes.

"Is something wrong, Garner?" she asked, untying her bonnet.

Before he could answer, a bustle from the basement stairwell heralded the arrival of Darby, Helen's maid, and Tulloch, Lady Margaret's maid. It was a narrow hall, and by all rights the more senior Tulloch should have had right of passage, but Darby's quick energy and broad shoulders edged her past the smaller woman. She entered the already crowded vestibule with her fair skin flushed in triumph, and curtsied to Helen before taking the bonnet from her hands. Tulloch stalked up a moment later and retrieved Lady Margaret's reticule.

Garner regarded both maids for a steely moment, then directed his answer to his mistress. "Mr. Pike and another gentleman are in the drawing room, my lady. Mr. Pike insisted upon waiting for Mr. Hammond and Lady Helen to return."

Lady Margaret paused in unclasping her spencer. "Pike? Here?" She turned to her brother, but he was already making his way up the stairs to the drawing room.

"I shall see what this is about," he said.

"Mr. Pike was most insistent upon seeing you and Lady Helen *together*, sir," Garner told Mr. Hammond, then turned back to his mistress. "I am afraid, my lady, that he made it clear you were not to be present."

"I see," Lady Margaret said. "Did you hear that, Michael?"

Mr. Hammond stopped on the first landing and peered up through the balustrade as if he could divine the Second Secretary's purpose through the walls. "Most irregular."

"I shall be in the morning room, then," Lady Margaret said. "You will come to me straight after?"

"Of course," Mr. Hammond said.

Lady Margaret stalked away to the morning room, her maid trailing behind. Mr. Pike had a great deal of presumption to exclude Lady Margaret in her own home, Helen thought. He clearly had more power than she had imagined. She placed her reticule on the hall table and peeled off her gloves, passing them to Darby.

"Did you see them come in?" she asked softly.

Darby nodded. "I think the other man is a Reclaimer," she murmured. "He moves like you."

Helen looked up from unbuttoning her pelisse. That was unexpected. Another of her kind, upstairs.

"He follows Mr. Pike's orders," Darby added, "but I don't think he likes him."

Helen nodded. Her maid had good instincts about people: a useful asset in a Terrene-to-be. She shrugged off her pelisse into Darby's waiting hands, using the close quarters to whisper, "Has the messenger to Miss Cransdon returned?"

"No, my lady."

He was not yet overdue, but Helen could not shake her sense of unease. "Find me when he does. I wish to speak to him."

"Even if he comes while you're . . . ?" Darby glanced upstairs.

Helen recalled Mr. Pike's manner. "No. Wait until I am free."

She passed Darby her reticule—a tap on the beaded silk alerting her maid to its precious contents—then climbed the staircase to join Mr. Hammond on the first landing.

"It would seem Mr. Pike was waiting for his lordship's absence," she said, leading the way up the remaining steps.

"Yes; a rather troubling thought," Mr. Hammond said. "Still, we must remember that Pike is on the same side as us."

"Not the enemy, you mean?"

He gave a wry smile. "I wouldn't go that far."

⌒

THEIR ARRIVAL ON the first floor brought Geoffrey and Bernard, the two footmen standing on either side of the drawing room door, into stiff-backed attention. Helen knew that Geoffrey and the senior servants were members of the Dark Days Club, but now she realized that all of Lady Margaret's staff, down to the lowliest kitchen maid, must be involved with the secret society in some way. How else would the strange goings-on in the house—her training, for instance, or the arrival of the Second Secretary—stay within its walls?

She considered the closed door. What did her training tell her about this situation? It was obvious that Mr. Pike was a dubious ally, and therefore, by association, so was the other Reclaimer. She would count them as possible adversaries and follow his lordship's advice: approach with extreme care, but also calm confidence.

Helen inclined her head, and the two footmen opened the double doors.

"Mr. Pike, I understand that you wish to see us," she said as she entered the drawing room.

The Second Secretary stood at the window looking down at the street. He held a small cloth-wrapped parcel in one hand and two letters—official-looking packets—in the other.

The Reclaimer stood next to him: a blond, curly-headed man of about thirty-five, tall and thin like all of their kind. According to Lord Carlston, such lean dimensions allowed captured Deceiver energy to move through a Reclaimer's body into the earth with greater ease. If that were the case, Helen thought, such energy would fly through the long bones of this man. Underneath the room's ambient fragrance of wax candles, wood polish, and charcoal from the hearth, she smelled his scent: a mix of hay and horse and soap. Not wholly unpleasant. He wore a dark blue jacket of fair quality, with buckskins and boots that looked more a practical choice than one of fashion. A country gentleman, then, of modest means.

He watched her with blatant curiosity, sizing up the oddity of a female Reclaimer and a direct inheritor. Helen was not entirely sure she was passing his inspection. For all of that, she had to admit she rather liked his face. The whole could not be called handsome—his nose was too sharp and his chin too wide—but his hazel eyes held a steady intelligence, and a rather small mouth was made more amenable by a resting expression of humor.

He glanced at Pike, but the Second Secretary continued to study the view from the window. "It would seem I must introduce *myself*, Lady Helen," the Reclaimer said, bowing. His voice held a soft lilt: Cambridgeshire perhaps, or somewhere further northeast. "I am George Stokes, Reclaimer. But I think you already knew that."

She returned his smile, surprised by the sudden sense of camaraderie. "A pleasure to meet you, Mr. Stokes."

No bow from Pike. Not even an acknowledgment of her arrival. She knew this game; her uncle used to ignore people when they entered a room too. A way to assert his authority.

She crossed to the damask armchair set opposite its matching sofa, and noted a portable mahogany writing box on the low marble table, with trimmed pen, inkwell, and sand pot laid out. Mr. Pike had come prepared, but for what?

"Geoffrey," she said over her shoulder to the footman. "Tea, please."

"No," Pike said. "No tea. I do not want any interruptions."

Helen paused in taking her seat. The man was a boor. "As you wish. No tea, Geoffrey. You may go."

The footman bowed and withdrew, closing the door. At the corner of her eye, Helen saw Mr. Hammond take up a position beside her chair—an unmistakable declaration. The lines were drawn.

"Gentlemen, would you care to sit?"

Finally Pike turned. "This is not a social call, Lady Helen."

"I think we have ascertained that, Mr. Pike. Does your business preclude you from sitting?"

The wintry smile appeared. "Not at all."

He walked to the sofa and sat, placing the parcel and letters next to the writing slant on the table between them. Helen glimpsed the wax fastening on one of the packets. A Royal seal. She had seen one before, on the letter from her long-dead mother that the Queen had held and delivered—Helen counted back to the Sunday when Sir Desmond had placed the letter in her hands—forty-seven days ago. Forty-seven days since her world had been torn apart. Yet the pain still felt as sharp as if it had arrived yesterday.

Mr. Stokes remained standing. He had the same *ready* quality as Lord Carlston, although not quite as much presence.

"Lady Helen, I am here to swear you in to the Dark Days Club," Pike announced. "Am I correct in thinking that you have not yet taken your oath?"

"No, not yet. But Lord Carlston—"

"It is well overdue. We will do it now."

"But his lordship is not here," Mr. Hammond said, finishing Helen's protest.

She nodded. It did not seem right to take the oath without him.

"Lord Carlston does not need to be present," Pike said. "All that is needed are three members of the Dark Days Club to stand witness. Myself, Stokes here"—he nodded at the Reclaimer, who politely bowed again—"and you, Mr. Hammond. I presume you will do so?"

"Of course, but—"

"Then let us begin."

Pike held Mr. Hammond's gaze in some kind of challenge or warning—it was not clear to Helen which—but it silenced the younger man. Pike picked up the cloth parcel and unwrapped it, bringing out a Bible with a cross tooled into its worn red leather cover.

"This was Mr. Henry Fielding's. When he founded the Dark

Days Club, he used it to swear in the first Reclaimer, and now it has become somewhat of a tradition to use it for all Reclaimers."

Mr. Stokes nodded, confirming that his own oath had been sanctified upon it.

"I have no objection, however, if you would prefer to use your own Bible," Pike added.

"Mr. Fielding's?" Helen took the holy book Pike held out to her and cradled it in both hands. Perhaps the famous author and magistrate had held it in exactly the same manner; her fingers could be resting where his had lain too. "I will be glad to swear upon it."

Pike fastidiously folded the cloth into three and placed it back on the table. "Before you do so, it is my duty to inquire if you have any questions or are unsure of what you are undertaking. I assume you have been given a copy of the oath and the regulations?"

"Yes, I have."

A week ago, Lord Carlston had supplied the documents to both her and Darby, along with the instruction to think carefully upon them. A solicitor had obviously written the regulations, for they were unnecessarily long and almost impenetrable, but Helen had managed to skim through most of them. The oath, on the other hand, was barely a page long, and she had quickly realized that beneath the elegant language was a solemn pledge to kill. A troubling discovery that had led to an even more troubling question: Did an oath written by men override one of God's own sacred laws, *Thou shalt not kill*?

"By taking this oath, you will be dedicating your life to the Dark Days Club and its mission to ensure the safety of mankind," Pike said. "You will be swearing it to God, King, and country, and breaking it would be treason. Do you understand?" He fixed her with a hard stare, as if he could peel back her skin and expose any weakness or doubt. "Treason carries the death penalty."

He was trying to make her balk; some kind of test. Well, she would not be cowed by an ill-mannered official.

"I am fully aware of the gravity of this oath, Mr. Pike," she said, pasting on a smile as cold as his own. "I remind you that I have stepped away from my family and from the normal expectations of a woman of my rank to take on this duty. My decision has not been without due consideration."

A fine statement, Helen thought, but in all truth, the decision had been made in a split second on the night of her ball. She had chosen her path the moment she had saved Lord Carlston and lost the *Colligat* to Philip. A large part of that choice had come from her sense of duty and her rather shameful allegiance to Lord Carlston, but she had to admit now that another part had been self-preservation. She was a Reclaimer, and as such, a target for those renegade creatures that would choose to break the peace pact between human and Deceiver. She could not afford to be without the training and support of the Dark Days Club.

Pike gave a nod and rose from his seat. "Then place your hand upon the Bible."

With the precious book in hand, Helen stood and pressed her palm against the soft leather. Although she had stated her commitment only seconds before, the magnitude of the moment caught her in her chest. She closed her eyes for a heartbeat and steadied her breath.

Pike motioned the other two men closer. "Mr. Hammond, Mr. Stokes, stand as witness with me."

They both stepped forward. Mr. Hammond met her eyes: appropriately solemn, but with a lingering tension around his mouth. He was still uneasy about the absence of Lord Carlston. She had to agree it did feel wrong.

Pike handed her a piece of parchment. "When you are ready, Lady Helen."

She cleared her throat and read: "I, Helen Catherine Wrexhall, of my own voluntary will, do declare and swear to God Almighty and to my King and my country that from this day onward I am a serving member of the secret order known as the Dark Days Club attached to the Home Office of His Majesty's government. I acknowledge that I am subject to its rule, that I serve at the King's pleasure, and that I will never, by deed or word, place the Dark Days Club in jeopardy. As a Reclaimer, I swear to uphold and police the Compact that stands between mankind and those creatures known as Deceivers, and in the event of that Compact being broken, I will protect mankind with my life and put out of the world any renegade creature. I take upon myself the duty to save the souls of Deceivers' offspring and reclaim them back to humanity when possible, and when it is not, to save them from a life of torment. I swear this in the presence of three witnesses, and under the penalty of death with my name and character forever held in abhorrence." She raised her eyes to say the final vow and found Pike intent upon her face, an unsettling avidity in his expression. "So help me God."

"Amen," all three men said in unison.

Helen eased her grip on the Bible, her thumb pad ridged from the edge of the tooled cross. It was done now, sworn in the presence of God and on her honor. An unbreakable oath.

"Well done, Lady Helen," Mr. Stokes said. "You are truly one of us now."

He said it with such conviction, as if the vow immediately created the Reclaimer, but Helen was not so sure. Could she really *put out of the world* any renegade creature or its offspring? Even just imagining such an act brought disquiet to her soul. Yet surely if such duties were sanctified by God, they could not be wrong?

"The oath, please," Pike said, hand outstretched. "And the Bible."

Helen passed both to him, her unease swamped by irritation

at the man's lack of occasion. He might at least acknowledge the solemnity of the moment.

"We must all sign it," Pike said, smoothing the oath across the writing slant.

He passed the pen to Helen. She dipped the nib in the ink, then scratched her name along the bottom of the paper.

"Allow me," Pike said. He picked up the sand pot and sprinkled the fine dust upon her signature, then shook it off. "Your turn, Mr. Stokes."

One by one the men signed and sanded their names. Pike studied the completed document. All, it seemed, was to his satisfaction, for he said, "I understand that Lord Carlston intends to train you in combat."

"Yes," Helen replied warily.

"And that your maid, Miss Darby, is to be your Terrene?"

Helen nodded. "She is being trained by Mr. Quinn, Lord Carlston's Terrene."

Pike looked up from his task. "I know who Quinn is, Lady Helen. Your maid is not yet bound to your power, is that correct?"

Helen searched his face, but could read nothing in its bland expression. "Lord Carlston said she must be fully trained before the binding ritual."

"Lord Carlston is right. She must be trained, and then she must be tested by myself and another Reclaimer. A Reclaimer other than Lord Carlston."

Helen glanced at Mr. Stokes. Was that the real reason why Pike had brought him to Brighton, to test her and Darby? If so, it was clearly news to Mr. Stokes, too. He shifted his feet and clasped his hands behind his back, but made no comment.

Mr. Hammond was not so circumspect. "That is not how it is done. There is no Terrene test."

"It is how it will be done in this case," Pike said. "There has never been a female Terrene, let alone a female Reclaimer and Terrene partnership trained to fight as well as reclaim. There is doubt that such a pairing could be effective."

"Doubt from whom?" Helen demanded.

"Myself and Lord Sidmouth."

The new Home Secretary did not have any faith in them. Now that was bad news.

"Darby is a most resolute young woman," Helen said firmly. "I assure you that we will be as effective as our male counterparts."

"That seems highly unlikely, Lady Helen. Two weak elements do not make a strong whole. We would prefer that you have a male Terrene. I am sure you are most intelligent, but you are still a woman and therefore reliant upon emotion rather than logic, and subject to your sensibilities as are all your sex. You cannot be expected to have the same strength, strategic mind, or logical competence as a man. A male Terrene would counter that deficit."

"I see," Helen said through her teeth. She had heard that opinion of women over and over from her uncle; there was no use trying to gainsay it. She glanced at Mr. Stokes, but his face was impassive. No help there. She tried another tack. "Lord Carlston has no reservation about Darby's capabilities. Or mine for that matter."

"Nevertheless, she will be tested."

"What if she fails?"

"Then we will pair you with a more suitable Terrene, and Miss Darby's status will be reconsidered."

Reconsidered? Helen frowned: What did that mean? She opened her mouth to ask, but Pike had already turned to address the other Reclaimer.

"Mr. Stokes, I believe you have business elsewhere." It was a blatant dismissal.

Mr. Stokes paused for a beat, eyes narrowing at Pike's manner, then said, "As you wish, Second Secretary." He turned to Helen and made his bow. "It was an honor to witness your oath, Lady Helen. Please, give my regards to Lord Carlston."

He left the room. As soon as the door closed behind him, Mr. Pike rose from his seat and walked back to the window.

Mr. Hammond cleared his throat. "I think the test is unf—"

"Quiet," Pike ordered. His attention was on the street below.

Mr. Hammond regarded him from under a resentful brow, but refrained from speaking.

Pike must be watching for Stokes, Helen realized. She focused her hearing and tracked the Reclaimer as he walked down the stairs, retrieved his hat from Garner, and departed through the front door. He had almost reached the corner of Marine Parade, and the full extent of Helen's hearing, before Pike spoke again.

"Mr. Hammond, dismiss the footmen. I do not want our conversation overheard."

Lud, he had been waiting for Stokes to be out of Reclaimer earshot. What was coming now?

As Mr. Hammond obediently dismissed both footmen and closed the door again, Helen watched Pike carefully wrap the Bible back into its linen, then fold the oath parchment in two and place it in the writing box. Every movement exact and considered. Perhaps it was his cold precision that sent a chill down her back, or maybe it was the way in which Stokes and Hammond jumped to his command. Certainly, he had the weight of the Home Office behind his orders, but it was more than that. He had an air of menace and ruthless intensity that was entirely his own.

He picked up the letters and placed one in her hands and passed the other to Mr. Hammond. "Read these, please. They will be destroyed once you have finished."

Helen sat and turned the packet over, aware of Mr. Hammond doing the same. She heard the sharp draw of his breath as he recognized the Royal seal at the back. So she was right to be apprehensive.

A flick of her thumbnail broke the wax on her own packet. She unfolded the paper, finding the signature at the bottom.

In his Name and on behalf of His Majesty,
George PR

The letter was from the Prince Regent. Helen's eyes flew up to the date. *Carlton House, Wednesday, 1 July 1812.*

Three days ago.

Lady Helen,

I have lately been apprised of your astounding abilities and your selfless decision to join the endeavors of that most noble of societies, the Dark Days Club.

So the Prince Regent, like his mother, Queen Charlotte, knew about the Deceivers.

On behalf of my father, I thank you for your devotion to our interests and to the protection of our realm and the British people.
You see before you Mr. Ignatious Pike. He stands as the emissary of my wishes via Lord Sidmouth, whom I have newly appointed as Home Secretary. The duties that Mr. Pike places upon you have my full endorsement. By following his instruction you may be assured that you are serving your King, his Regent, and your country. I shall, of course, never speak of this to you or any other, but I wish you to understand that you have my full

admiration and the eternal thanks of a grateful nation.
May God go with you.

She was to obey Pike; not an attractive proposition. Yet she had given her solemn word to do her duty, and if that meant following Pike's orders, that was what she must do. One's word was binding. And one's word sworn upon the Bible was unbreakable.

"I wonder," Mr. Hammond said, bringing Helen's eyes up from the flourish of the Prince Regent's mark, "why it has been deemed necessary for me to be reminded of my duty to his Royal Highness?" His voice was as tight as his hold upon his own letter. "Is my loyalty in question?"

"The letter is a reminder that your loyalty is to the Dark Days Club and not to Lord Carlston," Pike said. He held up a forestalling hand. "Do not waste my time denying that your loyalty lies with his lordship. We both know it is the case."

"And what if it is?" Mr. Hammond said. "Since his lordship is loyal to the Dark Days Club, then I am too, by default."

"Ah, now we come to the crux of the matter." Pike paused. "We are not convinced that Lord Carlston is still loyal to his King and country. He has been in exile on the Continent for over three years. Reports have had him in contact with French agents. There is every possibility that he is now working for the enemy."

Mr. Hammond snorted. "That is ridiculous."

"Outrageous," Helen said. "Have you seen what his lordship braves for his country? Besides, the other Reclaimers have made him their leader, and you, the Home Office, have agreed to it. Why would you do so if you do not trust him?"

"As a former Terrene"—Helen caught Pike's almost imperceptible wince of loss—"I am well aware of what he faces, and I am also well aware that none of the other Reclaimers have the ability to lead as Lord Carlston does. Nevertheless, the reports must be investigated. We would be fools to assume that he is still loyal. Three years is a long time to be exiled from one's country. Particularly under such ugly circumstances."

"You want us to spy on him." Mr. Hammond drew himself up into ramrod opposition. "I refuse to do so. Most adamantly I refuse."

Pike sighed, the sound of a weary adult dealing with a truculent child. "You and I both know you will do as I say, Mr. Hammond. You have put yourself in a position where you cannot refuse."

Mr. Hammond stepped back as if he had been physically hit. "Are you threatening . . . ?" He paused, clearly trying to compose himself. "Mr. Ryder said that would never be used against me."

Pike lifted an eloquent shoulder. "I am sure God will forgive Mr. Ryder's broken promise more readily than he will forgive your sick perversions."

Helen's breath caught at the disgust in Pike's voice. Sick perversions? She looked up at Mr. Hammond. His eyes slid from her own.

"Lady Helen," Pike said, "I see that you are wondering—"

"No!" Mr. Hammond lurched forward. "I will do as you ask."

Pike nodded. "I know you will." He plucked the letter from Mr. Hammond's hands. "Nevertheless, Lady Helen should know that you are a sodomite."

The word burst through Helen, sending freezing shock into her very core. *Sodomite.* Could it be true?

Mr. Hammond gave a small breathy moan, like a wounded animal, and backed away. The very shape of his body, curled into anguish, confirmed Pike's words. And, of course, now it made sense. That fierce loyalty to Lord Carlston, and the terrible sadness behind it. Poor man; it seemed not only the sister was in love with his lordship. Yet how could she, a Reclaimer, have missed such clear devotion? Helen shook her head. Because it had not even entered her mind to see it, let alone name it as such. Dear God, if it came into public knowledge, Mr. Hammond would be hanged. No wonder he was at Pike's mercy.

"You must forgive me for being so indelicate, Lady Helen," Pike said, taking the letter from her slackened grasp. He walked to the hearth and tossed both letters into the fire. They ignited, burning in a tall reach of bright orange. "But there is no place for a lady's sensibility now that you are a Reclaimer. I have no doubt you are disgusted by his presence, but you must overcome your revulsion."

Mr. Hammond whirled around, a fist raised. "Stop, or I'll . . ."

Pike stepped up to him. "You'll what?"

"Mr. Hammond!" Helen sprang up from her chair to stand between them.

"He will not hit me; he is a molly," Pike sneered. "Don't make me reconsider, Hammond. Your proclivities have made you useful. Be thankful for that."

Helen saw Mr. Hammond's eyes bulge, his judgment gone in a blaze of fury. His fist tightened. He was going to hit Pike—she could see it in her mind's eye, a possible projection of the next few seconds that could never be taken back.

Gathering all her authority, she thrust her face in front of his and yelled, "Mr. Hammond, sit down!"

He met her eyes for a terrible moment, and she saw the anger and fear and humiliation coursing through him.

"Please," she said more gently, "sit down." She touched his arm, directing him to the sofa.

He lowered his fist and sat, stiff and slow as an old man. "Lady Helen, you should not be burdened with my—"

"I am not as delicate as some would have me, Mr. Hammond. Do not be anxious on my account." She gave him a fleeting smile.

In truth, it was a strain to put aside her shock, but it was worth the effort: the dreadful fear and rage in his face had gone. Shame, however, still lingered in his eyes.

She took her own seat again. "What is it you want us to do?" she asked Pike coldly. "I cannot see why Mr. Hammond's . . ." She paused, searching for a way to spare the man more humiliation. "Why *his nature* has anything to do with spying upon Lord Carlston."

"I do not need you to spy upon his lordship," Pike said. "You two have an entirely different task."

Helen glanced at Mr. Hammond. Whatever surprise Pike was about to deliver, they must stand together. Mr. Hammond gave a small nod.

Pike walked to the fireplace again. "I believe you have both met the man who was Mr. Benchley's Terrene."

"Lowry," Mr. Hammond said grimly. "Bartholomew Lowry."

"Yes, that is the man."

"You saw him at Vauxhall Gardens, Lady Helen," Mr. Hammond said.

Helen nodded. She clearly recalled the man at Samuel Benchley's side: lank hair, oily brow, and barely contained violence. A low man, Mr. Hammond had said at the time. Even Benchley had remarked upon his Terrene's "predilections" with distaste. She glanced at Mr. Hammond. Did he share the same proclivity as Lowry? Was that why Pike had said he would be useful?

"Lowry claims he has Benchley's journal and it contains a register of Deceivers that we do not know about," Pike said. "He is offering to sell it to us. You two will meet with him and strike the deal."

Helen sat back. Why on earth would Pike choose her to deal with someone like Lowry? She opened her mouth to ask, but Mr. Hammond was already on the attack.

"Lowry is trying to gammon you," he told Pike. "Lord Carlston says Benchley did not leave any papers."

"Lowry has proved the journal's existence and the usefulness of the information within it," Pike said flatly.

"In what way?" Helen asked.

"In a way that has satisfied those who need to be satisfied."

He was not going to give her any more than that; it was in the stiff set of his shoulders.

"But surely the man should just hand it over to you," she said. "He is a member of the Dark Days Club."

Pike's wintry smile appeared again. "Mr. Lowry's sense of duty toward the Dark Days Club and, indeed, mankind extends only to offering us the journal first, before he puts it on the open market. Now that Benchley is dead, Lowry's powers will diminish; in less than six months he will be a normal man again. Perhaps even less than he was before." Pike looked down at his own hand, closing his fingers into a fist. "He is taking the opportunity to make his fortune while he still has the alchemical strength to bargain with Reclaimers or Deceivers."

"Still, a Terrene cannot overcome two or more Reclaimers," Mr. Hammond said. "Why not just take it from him? He has betrayed us, after all."

"Why use an ax when a scalpel will do the job?" Pike said. "Lowry has already offered the journal to us. We will buy it. The fact of his betrayal will be dealt with later."

Mr. Hammond crossed his arms. "No, there is something else that is stopping you from forcing him to hand over the journal." He contemplated Pike, the quick turn of his mind mirrored in the tap of his fingers on his arm. "You want to keep this quiet. An old fox like Benchley wouldn't just make notes about the Deceivers, would he? I'll wager that journal has information about the other Reclaimers as well, particularly Lord Carlston—he was Benchley's protégé. You don't want to send any of the other Reclaimers because they will get their hands on the information first. You certainly wouldn't want to lose that advantage."

Pike stared at him.

"Is Mr. Hammond correct?" Helen asked.

Pike turned and walked to the window, the silence making his answer.

"What is it supposed to contain?" Helen demanded, forcing back a flare of pique. Pike clearly did not care that she would see the journal; he must think her a malleable nonentity, no threat to himself or his plans. She clasped her hands in her lap. Perhaps he was right. What would she do with such information?

Pike's eyes were fixed on the street below. "According to Lowry, Benchley knew what really happened to Lord Carlston's wife—the man would hint at it when he was in his cups—and also about his lordship's activities on the Continent. All of this, by Lowry's account, is detailed in the journal, along with information about a number of Deceivers that Benchley had unearthed. He also made a dossier on each of his fellow Reclaimers, including you, Lady Helen." He turned to face them at last, his expression forbidding. "The Home Office does not want that information in anyone's hands other than our own."

Helen shook her head. "I think you just want to incriminate Lord Carlston."

"You seem to think this is entirely about Carlston," Pike said. "I assure you it is not. Lord Sidmouth wants to make sure the Dark Days Club is not compromised. It is just as feasible that the journal exonerates Lord Carlston." He narrowed his eyes. "You do believe in his innocence, don't you, Lady Helen?"

"Of course I do," Helen said stoutly, ignoring the flutter of doubt that always accompanied her thoughts about his lordship's past.

"Then you have every reason to believe that Benchley's journal will be to his benefit. It may be to your benefit too. Lowry claims there is information about your parents' death in it."

Helen felt her body lock. "But my parents drowned. It was an accident. Are you saying it was not?"

"Perhaps. We will not know until we have the journal in hand, will we?"

Hammond made a soft sound of disgust. "Do not believe him, Lady Helen. He has just thrown that in to season the pot."

"No," Pike said. "I am merely reporting what Lowry's letter claimed."

Helen stared unseeingly at the carpet, trying to comprehend the possibility that her parents had been murdered. By whom? Benchley? Perhaps Mr. Hammond was right, and it was just a lie to give her more incentive to retrieve the journal. If it was, it was a cruel invention.

"Lady Helen, you are not listening."

She jerked her head up to meet Pike's rebuke. "I beg your pardon. What did you say?"

"I said Lowry has made it clear that he will deal only with you."

It was a startling caveat. "Why me?"

"No doubt he thinks that your sex and inexperience will give him an advantage."

Helen frowned. "Is that what *you* think?"

He paused. Plainly, he did. "This is a simple agreement of terms and exchange of goods, Lady Helen. A fool could do it. Mr. Hammond will be there to assist you. Since he shares the man's perversions, he will help you navigate the Lewes stews where we believe Lowry is taking refuge."

"God's blood, Pike, I have nothing in common with that man," Mr. Hammond said, his face bright with anger again. "He finds his pleasure in others' pain, especially young women who do not consent to such treatment."

Helen sat back in her chair. "That is monstrous."

"It is," Mr. Hammond said. "And it is nothing to do with me."

Pike shrugged. "Nevertheless, your assignment is to help Lady Helen meet Lowry so that she can secure the journal." He turned to Helen. "We expect him to demand somewhere between five and ten thousand pounds for it."

Helen drew in a surprised breath: a small fortune. Yet it was clear that Lowry was an opportunistic man. "What if he asks for more than that?"

"You have the authority to offer up to fifteen thousand pounds in gold. If he pushes for more, make it clear to him that it is our final offer before the scalpel turns into an ax."

Mr. Hammond sat forward. "Fifteen thousand in gold! There must be something highly incriminating in the journal to warrant such an amount. What are you not telling us?"

Pike's brows lifted. "Obviously the government would prefer not to pay that much, but it may come to it. We must have that journal." He walked to the table and picked up the wrapped Bible and the writing box. "You are both bound by oath to the Dark Days Club. You are also bound by the express written order from His Royal Highness the Prince Regent to obey my instructions. You now have those instructions, and I leave you with one more. This assignment must not be discussed with anyone else. That includes your sister, Mr. Hammond. Am I clear?"

Mr. Hammond nodded, his hands clenched on his thighs.

"Say it," Pike ordered.

"Yes, it is clear," Mr. Hammond said, each word viciously distinct.

"Good, because if either of you decides to inform Lady Margaret or Lord Carlston, or anyone else for that matter, you will be in violation of your oath. High treason." Pike drew back his stooped shoulders. "Allow me to elaborate. Not only treason, but treason in a time of war. They would hang you, Mr. Hammond, and it would be our duty to add the black charge of sodomy to your name." His cold gaze turned to Helen. "And beheading is still the method of execution for a treasonous noble, Lady Helen. It would be rather ironic, don't you think, if you had the end that was going to be your mother's?"

Helen jammed her fingers together, forcing her fear and fury into the tight weave of her flesh. "I have given my oath, Mr. Pike," she said, glad that her voice did not quaver. "I am the daughter of an Earl. My word is my bond. It is a matter of honor and conscience; things you clearly know nothing about. You do not need to threaten me or Mr. Hammond for us to do our duty."

He regarded them both, his thin top lip curled in disgust. "A young noblewoman and a molly—you are the very essence of moral weakness. There could be no one in this world more in need of the impetus of fear."

He gave her a small, ironic bow and walked to the door. "Send a messenger to me when you have struck the deal," he said. "I will arrange your access to the gold."

And then he was gone, the door closing behind him. The sound of his footsteps receded down the staircase. Helen strained her Reclaimer hearing, picking through the sound of Lady Margaret pacing across the morning room floor, a maid singing off-key, and the scrape of pots in the kitchen, to finally find Garner murmuring "Good day" and the front door closing.

"He has left," she said.

Mr. Hammond drew in a long breath. "Whoreson bag of shit!"

Helen flinched.

He glanced at her, his lips pressed together in contrition. "I beg your pardon."

"I understand your sentiment, Mr. Hammond." She smoothed out the skirt of her gown, trying to cover her own rage. How dare Pike call her morally weak. She had never broken her word, and she never would. "Perhaps I should learn such language for my male persona."

He gave a mirthless smile. "It is probably the one thing I can teach you with more authority than his lordship."

Helen returned his smile, but a new problem was taking hold. "What should we say to Lord Carlston and your sister? She will certainly tell him that Pike came to visit."

Mr. Hammond hunched over, his hands pressed to his face.

"Mr. Hammond?" He made no move. "Mr. Hammond!"

Was he sinking into despair? He must not; they had to stand firm together. She touched his shoulder. "Michael!"

He lifted his head, and she saw that it was not despair in his face. It was fear.

"I think we should stay with the truth as much as possible," she said, hoping her quick words would draw him back. "We will say that Pike came here to swear me into the Dark Days Club. No other reason. Will that serve, do you think?"

"I don't know. Possibly."

"Then that is what we will say." She smiled encouragingly, forcing back her own fear. "It will be as Pike says: a straightforward exchange. Then we will be done with it."

"Yes, done with it." He stood, hands clenched. "Lady Helen, I ask you . . . no, I beg you, please do not say anything to his lordship."

"Of course I will not say anything." She rose as well, alarmed by the anguish in his voice. "Pike has my oath on the matter, just as he has yours. Besides, I believe him when he says he would bring us both to ruin."

"No, not about the journal," he said. "About the other . . ."

Helen flushed at her own stupidity. "I will not say a thing; I swear it. But do you truly think his lordship does not know? He is a Reclaimer: he would have seen your devotion in your face."

Mr. Hammond bowed his head. "Of course he knows. How could he not? But there is a chasm between what is known and what is said."

Helen nodded. There surely was, particularly when it came to Lord Carlston and Ignatious Pike.

Four

LADY MARGARET WALKED across the morning room yet again, the tips of her fingers pressed into a ruminative steeple. "No, there must be more to Pike's visit," she said, pacing back to the small tiled hearth. "He would not come all the way to Brighton to swear in a new Reclaimer. He would expect the Reclaimer to go to him in London."

"Not this time," Mr. Hammond said from the armchair.

Helen, seated on the opposite chair, met Lady Margaret's searching gaze with as much nonchalance as she could muster. "He does not have much faith in a female Reclaimer and Terrene partnership. He intends to test Darby before she is bound to my power."

"Test her?" Lady Margaret sent a questioning glance to her brother.

Mr. Hammond nodded. "Some new thing he and Sidmouth have concocted between them. A test to be given by himself and a Reclaimer when Lady Helen and Darby are fully trained. Most irregular. A slap in the face, if you ask me."

"Is that why Stokes is here?" Lady Margaret asked. "It seems odd that he has been pulled from Norwich with all the Luddite riots up there, especially since Lady Helen and Darby are not yet close to being fully trained. It does not make sense. None of it makes sense."

"What kind of man is Stokes?" Helen asked quickly. "Is he Pike's creature?"

"Good heavens, no," Lady Margaret said. "Stokes is his own man, and a fair one by all accounts. He was in the army until quite late. His abilities didn't come to the notice of the Home Office until five or so years ago. I know Lord Carlston considers him both trustworthy and a friend."

"He seems very obedient to Pike," Helen said.

Lady Margaret shook her head. "I doubt it is from any particular devotion. Stokes was a soldier; he follows orders. And Pike has the authority of the Home Secretary to give those orders. He does what Pike says because he must."

At the corner of her eye, Helen saw Mr. Hammond flinch. As they all must.

"You are right," he told his sister. "I don't know if Stokes is here for the test or not, but all in all, I think it is a slap in the face for Lady Helen."

He was repeating himself, his words over-fast—the sure sign of a guilty conscience. Helen aimed a slanted look at him: *End the conversation.*

"Pike has probably created the test to irritate his lordship," he added abruptly, rising from his chair.

Lady Margaret tilted her head as she considered the notion, her fingers twirling a long black ringlet arranged over her shoulder. "Maybe. . . . He is a vindictive man. Still, I am uneasy."

"I am too," Helen said. That, at least, was the truth.

"We are all uneasy," Mr. Hammond said. "That is Pike's raison d'être: he likes nothing better than to create anxiety."

"But why did he exclude me from witnessing the oath?" Lady Margaret asked. "I have taken my own vow, and I was present when you took yours."

"Probably to drive you mad with the wondering of it," her

brother said. "Think no more on it, Margaret. He swore Lady Helen into the Club, and that is that. Pike and God move in mysterious ways." He turned to Helen with a small bow. "His lordship wished me to instruct you further on your male gait. Shall we repair to the salon?"

"Of course." Helen stood, using the upward motion to scrutinize Lady Margaret's expression. She saw musing distance in the navy eyes, and full lips pressed into a tight line. A mix of distrust and mystification. Had she sensed their lie, or was all her suspicion directed at Pike?

"No, I cannot dismiss it," Lady Margaret said, her eyes snapping back to the moment. "I think we should send a message to his lordship. He questioned Pike's presence in Brighton, and now we have an answer for him. Or some kind of answer. I am sure his lordship will make better sense of it than we can. He will want to know that Stokes is here too."

"By the time a message gets to London, his lordship will have started back," Mr. Hammond said. "It will miss him."

"No, you are mistaken. If we send a man now, we should catch him." His sister gathered up the filmy skirt of her white cambric gown and sat at the secretaire beside the front window. She pulled open the two lacquered cabinet doors. "Are we out of paper?"

"No, Margaret, we will not send a message. It is unnecessary." She stopped rifling through the shelves. "I beg your pardon?"

Mr. Hammond drew himself up to the extent of his small stature. "I believe his lordship placed me in charge. For once, Margaret, do as I say."

Helen held her breath; she had not heard that note of command in Mr. Hammond's voice before. The brother and sister stared at one another, their chins lifted at exactly the same angle.

"I see," Lady Margaret finally said. She turned her back and shut the cabinet doors with a snap.

"Good."

Mr. Hammond widened his eyes at Helen, jerking his chin toward the door. Yes, it was definitely time to go. She edged past the armchair, ready to make her own escape.

"Lady Helen, wait." The coldness in Lady Margaret's voice brought her to a standstill. "Do not forget what his lordship said this morning. Space and purpose. It is where your gait fails."

"Space and purpose," Helen repeated, managing to keep the edge from her voice. She nodded a brusque farewell and followed Mr. Hammond from the room.

By silent consensus, Helen and Mr. Hammond did not speak until the door of the grand reception salon was firmly shut behind them and they had walked to the far corner of the bare room. The salon was the reason the terrace house had been rented: it ran the length of the whole dwelling, front to back, with a line of side windows that faced a blank brick wall. With the front shutters closed, privacy was assured, while the high-set windows allowed enough natural light for them to dodge bullwhips and swing ceramic swords well into the summer evenings.

Mr. Hammond rubbed at his forehead. "That did not go so well."

"On the contrary, I think she believed us," Helen said. "Or at least I think she believes that *we* think Pike came to hear my oath and inform me of the test."

"Perhaps. I am not well-practiced at keeping secrets from my sister. In fact, it sometimes feels as if we can read the other's mind. It does not make for successful secret keeping. The curse of a twin, I suppose."

Ah, she had guessed correctly. "Is Lady Margaret the elder?"

He smiled. "By half an hour. It is why she thinks she must look after me."

"Does she know about . . . ?"

"Oh, yes." He gave an odd, light laugh. "Perhaps even before I did." He turned his face away and dug his fingernail into a crack in the wall, picking at the plaster. "We were barely thirteen. She said it was how I was made. She was never disgusted."

Helen heard the query buried within the statement.

"I think . . ." she said, then stopped. In truth, she did not know what she thought, or felt. It was not disgust. All of that sentiment was reserved for Pike and his foul coercion, not for this young man who had only ever acted with honor and courage. No, she did not feel disgust. She felt fear. For his very life. "I think Lady Margaret is right."

He gave a slight nod, his eyes meeting hers in fleeting gratitude. "At present Margaret is angry at me, which will divert her from pursuing the Pike matter. But she will return to it. She is like a terrier."

"It is a good tactic."

"The fact that I need such a tactic makes me . . ." He slammed his palm against the wall, sending a spray of plaster dust into the air. "Let us get this task done, Lady Helen."

"Yes." She nodded fervently. "As quickly as possible."

He dusted off his hands. "I will go to Lewes tomorrow and hunt out Lowry to arrange a meeting. It will be best, I think, if you were to meet him as a young man rather than a woman, especially if he nominates a tavern or inn for the assignation."

Helen wrapped her arms around her body, trying to contain a spidery crawl of doubt along her spine. "Your sister does not think I am ready to go out into the world as a young man."

His mouth twisted in mute apology. "Margaret is too hard upon you; it is her own pique talking. You may not be quite ready yet, but with some hard work you soon will be."

"I was not even asked," Helen said.

"Asked?"

"Whether or not I wanted to masquerade as a man. Or even if I thought I could. It was just expected that I would do so."

"That is Lord Carlston's way," Mr. Hammond said. "I doubt that it even enters his mind that any of us would refuse to do whatever it takes to fulfill our duty. We have, after all, taken our own oaths." He cocked his head. "Does it upset you to masquerade as a man? I am sure it will be only on occasion. It will be just as valuable for you to police the Deceivers as a woman; probably more so, since you are the only Reclaimer who can move in female society."

Helen waved away the question. "No, I am more than willing to take on the male guise. It is just . . ."

"You would have preferred to have had the decision of it." He shrugged, not from indifference but in sympathy. "Like Stokes, we are all soldiers now, and Lord Carlston is our general, leading us against an enemy that outnumbers us five hundred to one. He believes you are a sign that the Grand Deceiver is among us—the creature's opposite, if you will—and he is trying to make you a general too, before it strikes."

"A general? I am barely even a Reclaimer. How am I to lead men?"

"You doubt yourself?"

"Of course I do. Men will not follow a woman."

"They followed Queen Elizabeth," Mr. Hammond said.

True, although the Virgin Queen had forgone marriage and called herself a prince. Perhaps pretending to be a man was the only way for a woman to lead.

"If Lord Carlston thinks you can do it, trust him," Mr. Hammond advised. He gestured to the center of the room with a small bow. "Come, let us work on your gait."

Shaking off her unease, Helen turned her mind to the task. Her breeches had not yet been delivered; somehow she would have to raise her skirts to allow free movement. She lifted the scalloped hem of her pale green gown a few inches and felt heat suffuse her face. Less than a month ago she would never have stood unchaperoned in a room with a man, let alone shown her legs to him.

"I shall have to tie up my skirts, Mr. Hammond, in order to take a proper stride."

He glanced at the show of her ankle, then looked up with an earnest face. "Lady Helen, after today's revelations you must know you are safe with me."

For a moment, Helen was nonplussed. "Oh, lud," she said on a wave of understanding. "Of course."

They looked at one another—an instant of shared absurdity—then burst out laughing, both bent over and gasping.

⌒

TWO HOURS LATER, Helen had walked the length of the salon fifty-two times, training her body to stride purposefully through the space rather than step prettily across it. Over and over Mr. Hammond had patiently corrected every part of her, until she felt she swaggered as well as any young gent. Finally he called a stop, nodding approvingly as Helen followed him with her best manly saunter to the beer jug set on the mantel.

"You have it now," he said, lifting the jug. "The trick, however, is to maintain the disguise even in times of high duress. It must become second nature, and that means practice."

He passed her a glass of beer, then poured his own. "Small beer. You'd best get used to it."

Helen looked at the murky brew and took an experimental mouthful. It was malty, warm, and somewhat sour.

"Bigger mouthfuls," Mr. Hammond urged. "Do not be so delicate."

She obeyed, reveling in the chance to gulp rather than sip. "It tastes a bit like . . ."

"Cat piss?"

She choked. "No. I was thinking more of . . ."

"Donkey piss?"

Ah, a test. A young man in the company of another would not balk at such language.

"Exactly," she said. "Donkey piss."

He grinned his approval. "It is the least alcoholic of the beers." He held his glass to the light and regarded the amber liquid with distaste, then looked past it to meet her eyes, the lightness gone from his face. "As you have seen at many a dinner party, most men drink the heavier wines and spirits, and well into excess. It is even more so when men are alone. While you are in disguise, you will have to pace your liquor intake."

Helen peered into her glass again. "I have never been inebriated."

"Of course not." He waved his hand in dismissal of such a possibility, the elegant gesture drawing Helen's eye. "In the male milieu, however, it does not matter if a man falls over drunk. Sometimes it is even expected. In *our* world, however, it can be fatal."

He raised his glass again. It was empty. Helen frowned. A minute ago it had been full, and she was sure he had not drained it.

He winked. "Remind me to show you some tricks that will help you discard a glass or two without being seen. It can mean all the difference when trying to keep one's wits."

"How did you do that?"

"Practice," he said, reaching for the jug again. "A lot of practice. I have been doing this for a very long time."

Helen eyed him speculatively. "Longer than the Dark Days Club?"

He poured himself another glass, intent upon the action. "So, young fellow. That latest mill was a smoky affair. The first bruiser had bottom, but it was all a bit of the home brew, if you ask me."

Helen blinked at the sudden shift in language. He was speaking cant, the dialect of the lower classes. Many young gentlemen used phrases from the London underworld—it was a fashionable affectation—but Mr. Hammond spoke it with the confidence of a native. It would seem his past held a great deal more color than was usual for a young landed gentleman, and clearly he was not going to share it.

"What did I just say?" he asked, placing the jug back on the mantel.

Another test. For the past two weeks, she had been studying Mr. Grose's recently published *Dictionary of the Vulgar Tongue* alongside her alchemy books, trying to treat the startling revelations of attitude and behavior within it as if she were merely learning another language. It had to be said that learning cant was far more fascinating than the impenetrable codes of the alchemists.

"You said, the latest boxing match was a curious affair. The first fighter had courage, but . . ." She faltered.

"But?"

"No, don't tell me"—she raised a forestalling finger—"it was all a bit amateur and untrained."

"Good work!" A slap on her back forced her forward a step, slopping half her beer onto the floor. "And be prepared for that kind of thing. Men like to hit each other."

"So I have noticed."

A loud knock turned them both toward the door.

"Wait," Helen called. She thrust her glass into Mr. Hammond's hand and, with a wild glance at him, dug her fingers into the knot of her skirt. It came free, the hem dropping back around her feet in a creased swirl of linen. "Yes, enter."

The door opened to admit Geoffrey, the first footman. He walked across the room—a solid, masculine stride, Helen noted—and bowed. "My lady, Miss Darby asks that you join her in the rear yard. She said to tell you it is *most* urgent."

The messenger she had sent to Delia must have returned, and with bad news. But why had Darby sent Geoffrey and not come herself?

"In the rear yard?" Mr. Hammond said. "That's an odd request."

"I am sure it is something to do with her Terrene training," Helen said. How quickly lies came to her lips now; a requisite of this new world. She dipped into a curtsy. "If you will excuse me, Mr. Hammond."

He bowed. "Of course. We are done here anyway."

⸺

THE WAY TO the rear yard was via the busy basement kitchen, and Helen passed through it apace, barely acknowledging the startled curtsies from Cook and her two girls. The warm air held the aroma of cooking pastry and braised meat—game pies for dinner— the rich smell following her as she climbed the three stone steps to the back door.

It was already standing open, the framed view of the yard affording her a glimpse of a large bay horse, a dusty young man, and a corner of Darby's brown calico dress. Good, the messenger had arrived.

"That is true," she heard Darby say, "but it is also true that my lady is not expecting you."

Her tone was far too polite for a messenger, and anyway Helen had been expecting him. To whom was Darby speaking? Helen's innards clenched with terrible intuition as she stepped into the yard. Three people stood beside the horse: the messenger, Darby, and, yes, her friend Delia. Holy heaven, Delia had taken matters into her own hands and come for her explanation.

Helen stopped still. She had just sworn a Royal oath that commanded silence. She could not tell Delia *anything*, let alone the true identity of her dead suitor.

"Helen! My dear! There you are." Delia crossed the stone flags, her hands held out. "I am sorry to arrive without any warning. It is unpardonable, I know, but I could not stay with my parents a minute longer."

Helen received Delia's gloved hands in her own and stared at her friend. Suffering, it seemed, had whittled her back to her bones: her features had sharpened into a somewhat haggard elegance, and a figure that had once been pronounced shapeless by whispering matrons now curved in a very fashionable way under her blue velvet spencer. Beneath her plain straw bonnet, her fair hair clustered in natural ringlets around her face—far more suited to her new angles than the coiffures forced upon her by her mother—and her skin, usually prone to ruddiness, was as pale as Caroline Lamb's.

"Upon my soul, Delia, I hardly recognize you."

She nodded. "I have not eaten or slept in weeks, Helen, and I have endured so many blood-lets. Papa thinks he can have the madness drained from me."

"Delia, you are not mad. Do not even think it." She could at least assure her friend of that, couldn't she?

The messenger cleared his throat. Helen dragged her eyes from her friend's transformation, practicalities overtaking the shock of her appearance. She read the expectant look in the man's dirt-streaked face: he was waiting for his payment.

"Delia, how exactly did you get here?" she asked, a dreadful thought dawning. "You did not ride behind this young man, did you?"

"Of course not," Delia said. "I rode, and your man walked."

No point telling her that the messenger was not a private servant, but a hired man. "You walked?" Helen said to him. "All that way?"

"Yes, my lady." He bobbed his head. "Miss Cransdon insisted

on coming back with me, so I put her up on Polly-girl and walked her back. Didna take more than five hours."

Helen shot a glance at Delia, who nodded.

"That was very gallant of you . . . ?"

"Leonard, my lady." He cast a wary look at Delia. "I couldna do much else. Miss Cransdon was ad-a-mant." He sounded out the word, obviously newly learned.

"I see." Helen smiled inwardly. Delia had always been known for her tenacity. "Thank you, Leonard. Darby, give him an extra crown for his quick thinking and courtesy."

"My lady, thank you," he said breathlessly, bowing.

"It is for your discretion, too, Leonard," Helen said. "And before you go, you may feed your horse and take your dinner with the servants."

Darby drew Helen's purse from her apron pocket and counted out the money. "Mind what her ladyship says," she warned, her eyes fierce as she passed over the coins. "No breath of this around the taverns."

Leonard shook his head. "I'd not get much in the way of work if I blabbed everyone's business, now, would I?" He bobbed another bow to Helen and Delia, then with a click of his tongue led his horse toward the mews.

"You must think me very forward," Delia said. "But when he arrived with your letter and was so secretive in passing it to me, I saw my chance." She gathered Helen's hands again, holding them as if they were the only anchors that held her from a wild sea. "Helen, my father has decided to send me to a sanatorium. I over-heard him telling Mother."

"Oh no. That is awful, Delia."

"You said you would tell me the truth about Mr. Trent's demise. Whatever it is, can you tell my parents, too?" Delia's gray eyes were fixed upon her own, the plea in them sending a jab of guilt through Helen. How could she refuse such desperation? "I know you wrote that you could not, but perhaps if they knew—"

"Delia, this is not the place." She softened the interruption with a squeeze of her friend's hands.

She had to get Delia inside as discreetly as possible; she needed time to think through this complication. The explanation she had promised was now impossible to deliver under the mandate of her oath, yet she could not abandon her friend to self-doubt and incarceration. She saw no clear way through: either she broke her word to her friend or to the Palace. And either way, lives were at stake: Delia's, or Mr. Hammond's and her own. Still, even with such a dilemma on her hands, she could not leave Delia in the yard. Somehow they had to get past the beady attentions of Mrs. Kent, the housekeeper, and Garner and delay the advent of Lady Margaret.

"Come inside," she said. "I hope you do not mind that we pass through the kitchens; it is the quickest way. Did you not bring any luggage?"

"No, I just got on the horse and came."

Helen heard the slur of fatigue in Delia's voice. Whatever difficulties her arrival had caused, her well-being must come first.

"I can see you are exhausted. You need to eat and rest, and then we will talk. Wait here for a moment." With a reassuring pat upon her friend's shoulder, Helen stepped away and motioned Darby to her side. "Is Garner in his pantry?" she asked softly.

"No, my lady. He and the footmen are preparing the dining room for luncheon."

"Even better. Make sure Mrs. Kent does not see us on our way up the back stairs. I want to keep this quiet for as long as possible."

Darby nodded, but her brow furrowed. "It will not be very long—someone will tell her ladyship."

"I know."

Darby gave another nod and hurried to the kitchen door.

With an eye to her maid's progress, Helen asked Delia, "To be clear, am I to understand that your parents do not know where you are? You did not leave a note?"

"No." Delia bit her lip. "I am afraid they will see this as yet more evidence of an unsound mind. What sane young woman would abandon her parents and a safe home?"

Helen gave a sympathetic nod as she concentrated upon her Reclaimer hearing and reached into the house. Under the clang of pots and orders from Cook, she found Darby's voice: ah, she was telling the housekeeper about a cleaning mishap in the vestibule. And they were already moving toward the front of the house. Good girl.

She brought her attention back to Delia. "You know we must send a messenger to your parents to tell them of your whereabouts. They will be greatly disturbed by your disappearance."

"Must we?"

"Yes, but I think we may delay a little longer until we decide what is to be done."

Delia clutched at her hand again. "Thank you."

Darby should have Mrs. Kent in the vestibule by now; it was time to move. Helen steered Delia down the steps into the kitchen, past the cook and her staff intent upon taking the pies from the ovens, and around to the back staircase. It was blessedly deserted.

"Oh my, those pies do smell good," Delia said.

Helen touched her finger to her lips. Delia ducked her head in apology.

"It is just that we need some time before Lady Margaret knows you are here," Helen whispered. "She will insist a message be sent to your parents immediately."

Or more likely, Helen thought, she would pack Delia into a

carriage and send her back to her parents immediately, but her friend need not know that.

Delia nodded, her mouth pressed into obedient silence.

Cautiously they climbed the stairs, Helen leading the way with ears strained for any sounds of approaching servants. On the ground floor, she heard the tutting of Mrs. Kent in the vestibule, the scritch of a nib, and an irritated sigh in the morning room—Lady Margaret answering correspondence—and Garner in the dining room, ordering a footman to replace a butter knife.

They hurried up the next set of steps. Helen found two voices murmuring: maids indulging in an illicit chat as they tidied the drawing room. Otherwise, all was silent. They crept up to the second floor. Near the top of the flight, Helen paused and listened carefully to a new set of footsteps. Was it a maid in her bedchamber? No, the movement was in Lady Margaret's room: no doubt her woman, Tulloch. Grabbing Delia's hand, she pulled her along the corridor and into her own bedchamber, shutting the door firmly behind them.

"These are my rooms," she said, gesturing around the royal-blue-and-gold interior that had been decorated—rather unpatriotically—in the French empire style. The adjoining door that led to her small dressing room stood open. She walked across and closed it. "We shall be private here. Come, sit down and rest."

She pulled out the gilt chair from beneath the matching writing desk and waved Delia over. It was not the most comfortable of seats, but it was the only one in the room apart from the bed. Delia slumped into its delicate curves and plucked fretfully at the ribbons of her straw bonnet.

"You are very good to help me, Helen. I fear I have placed you in a very difficult position with your chaperone." She sighed and lifted the bonnet from her head, a dusty arc of road grime across her forehead. "I have waited so long to know the truth, and now I am here." She smiled wearily. "At last."

"At last." Helen echoed. "Would you not like to wash before we talk? Let me send for my maid."

"No!" Delia half rose from the chair. "I do not want to wash. I just want the truth."

"Of course," Helen said, dropping her hand from the bell-pull.

Delia perched on the edge of the seat. "Forgive me. I have been waiting to hear it for so long." The bonnet's straw brim buckled under her grip.

"I do want to tell you," Helen said, feeling the weight of her oath thundering toward her like a runaway coach. "But things have changed."

"Changed? How?"

Helen hesitated. Whichever way she tried to frame an answer, some kind of explanation about the Dark Days Club was required. Even why she could not offer an explanation. Not many young girls in their first Season were held to silence by the Home Office. No, all avenues of discussion were blocked. Yet here was Delia, sitting before her and rightfully expecting her to keep her word.

She took a deep breath. "I am so sorry, but I cannot say."

There, the words had been spoken. May God forgive her for such a betrayal of her friend's trust.

Delia looked up at her, a knit of bewilderment between her brows. "Are you funning with me? If you are, it is most cruel."

"I am not, I swear."

"Then why can you not say?"

"I am bound to silence by an oath."

"To whom?" Delia rose from her chair, her voice shrill. Her bonnet, crushed beyond repair, dropped to the floor. "Tell me."

"I cannot."

At the edge of her senses, Helen heard the thud of approaching footsteps. A summons from Lady Margaret already?

"Why are you doing this, Helen? Do you want me to be locked away in an asylum?" Delia stopped, something awful overtaking her indignation. "Oh, dear God, I *am* insane." She grabbed Helen's forearm, her fingers digging hard into the tender flesh. "Did you send me letters that promised the truth, or did I imagine them? Did you? Did you send letters?"

"Yes. I sent the letters." Helen pulled herself free from the desperate grip. Delia's eyes were wide, the whites showing like a panicked deer's. She had to tell her friend something to wipe the ghastly horror from her face. "I am bound by an oath to the government, Delia. To His Royal Highness the Prince Regent. On my honor, it is true."

The door burst open, wrenching them both around to face the small rigid figure of Lady Margaret on the threshold.

"Lady Helen!" There was no mistaking her fury; her voice shook with it, and both hands were clenched into fists. "Who is this? What is she doing here?"

"Lady Margaret," Helen said, clutching at the safe haven of civility, "may I present Miss Delia Cransdon."

Delia curtsied. "How do you do. Please forgive me for imposing—"

"Lady Helen, come with me, please," Lady Margaret said abruptly. "Wait here, Miss Cransdon."

Helen hurried past Lady Margaret into the passageway. She caught a glimpse of Delia's pale, set face, then Lady Margaret pulled the door shut, turned on her heel, and without a word led the way down the stairs. Helen could feel the rage pounding against the woman's silence. Her spine was ramrod straight, the artfully arranged black curls swinging with every stiff stride toward the salon. She flung open the door, stood aside as Helen entered, then closed the door with the barest of clicks, the self-control more alarming than if she had slammed it shut.

She turned, hands on hips, navy eyes brilliant. "What have you told her?"

Helen stepped back. "Nothing."

"Liar. I heard you say you had taken the oath." Her disgust was distilled into every word. "Did you tell her about the Dark Days Club?"

"No. I only said I could not tell her anything *because* of the oath."

"Who is she? Why is she here?"

Helen pressed her hands against her forehead. "She is a friend, from my seminary days. Delia Cransdon. She eloped with a man who shot himself in front of her at an inn. Do you remember the scandal?"

For a moment the fury in Lady Margaret's eyes shifted into recollection. "About two months ago?"

"Yes. I believe the man—no, I am *sure* the man was a Deceiver. Delia saw him light up from within when he died and passed into his next body. No one believes her story. Her parents think her mad and are going to send her to an asylum. I thought . . ." Helen paused. How could she explain the creeping suspicion that somehow it was all her fault, that her friendship with Delia had placed her in the path of a Deceiver? "I sent her some letters; I did not want her to think herself mad. I promised to explain why Mr. Trent had killed himself and died in such an odd way." Helen looked away. "I may have hinted that he was not of this world."

"God's blood!" Lady Margaret said. "What were you thinking? You have taken an oath—"

"I sent the letters before I had taken the oath," Helen protested.

Lady Margaret batted away the defense with a vicious hand. "You knew weeks ago that your membership in the Dark Days

Club required secrecy. We cannot have the truth leaking out into the world, yet here you are blithely telling a school friend that you have sworn an oath to the Home Office."

"That is all I was going to say, I swear upon my soul. Even so, she saw one of the creatures, Lady Margaret. She knows they exist—"

Helen stopped. She had heard a sound; no more than a hardening of breath. She lunged for the door and jerked it open. Delia jumped back, her body hunched with guilt.

"Good God, she is eavesdropping like some low servant," Lady Margaret said.

Delia lifted her chin. "I have had enough of people deciding my future behind closed doors."

Helen shook her head. "That is no excuse for—"

"What exactly is a Deceiver, Helen?" Delia looked defiantly at Lady Margaret. "What is the Dark Days Club? I demand answers."

"You do not have the right to demand anything, Miss Cransdon," Lady Margaret said. She rounded on Helen. "This will not be discussed again until his lordship returns from London. Do you understand? Until that time, Miss Cransdon shall be our *guest*." The last word came through gritted teeth.

"Yes. I understand." Helen hesitated, not sure she should add more fuel to Lady Margaret's fire, but there was no getting away from the fact of Delia's family. "I'm afraid her parents do not know she is here."

Lady Margaret made a sound low in her throat, rather like a snarl. "She left their house without telling them?" She shook her head and raised her palms to ward off the answer. "Do not even try. I shall write immediately and inform them of the whereabouts of their daughter and extend an invitation for her to stay with us for a few days. Let us hope that they do not arrive on our doorstep, outraged." On that, she departed the salon, sweeping past Delia without another glance.

Helen drew a steadying breath. "I cannot believe you listened through the door."

Delia flushed. "It was reprehensible, I know, but it is the only way I learn anything at home. I am sorry."

Helen gave her friend a wan smile. "At least you may stay."

"Until his lordship returns. Who does she mean? Her husband?"

"No. She means Lord Carlston."

"The one who murdered his wife? What does he have to do with it?"

"Everything," Helen said heavily. She was not looking forward to facing his lordship's fury. "You heard Lady Margaret. I cannot discuss any of this until he returns."

"Surely you can tell me about Mr. Trent?" Delia pleaded. "I already know some of it. You said he was a Deceiver—what does that mean?"

Helen shook her head. The next two days were going to be very long indeed.

Five

Sunday, 5 July 1812

HELEN JABBED HER needle into the linen of her embroidery and forcibly quelled the desire to spring from her chair and run from the drawing room. Delia's arrival two days ago had stopped any Reclaimer training or Dark Days business, and it felt excruciating to be thrust back into the slow rhythm of a lady's life. The service that morning at the new Chapel Royal had been interminable, and now they were filling the afternoon with needlework and reading. It did not help that the ponderous turn of every minute also held the weight of Lord Carlston's imminent return. Mr. Hammond had gone to meet him at his lodgings and, no doubt, to inform him of the trouble that awaited at German Place.

Helen looked across at Lady Margaret, who was seated at the small table beside the front window, her back straight and pen traveling across paper with fierce purpose. She must have felt Helen's gaze, for she raised her eyes and stared back, her message plain: *This is your own fault.*

The previous evening, Geoffrey had arrived back from the Cransdon estate with a note from Mrs. Cransdon full of thanks and the intelligence that Delia could stay as long as her ladyship graciously allowed. The note was accompanied by two traveling trunks full of clothes; far more than a few days required. Delia's parents, it seemed, were eager to be rid of their daughter, whether it was by dumping her upon another household or incarcerating her in a sanatorium. What must she be feeling, Helen wondered, to be so abandoned?

There was no clue upon Delia's face. She sat on the opposite sofa, eyes on the open book in her hands, but her sight clearly inward. Helen did not blame her retreat. Lady Margaret's cold courtesy and swift check of any remark beyond the banal did not lend itself to vivacity. Lady Margaret was determined to give Helen and Delia no opportunity for private conversation. She had even posted Tulloch outside Delia's bedchamber door at night.

Helen returned her attention to her embroidery. She had not been able to speak to Mr. Hammond, either. He had arrived back from his expedition to Lewes well after everyone had retired for the evening, and emerged late from his room for breakfast. There had been no opportunity for any communication under Lady Margaret's eye other than a brief, meaningful nod from him across the silent breakfast table. He had found Lowry. The knowledge had settled heavily in her stomach, and sat there still: a cold, hard knot of thwarted questions.

The sound of hooves on flags brought Helen's head up again. No, what was she thinking? Camelford Street was but one road away; his lordship and Mr. Hammond would walk, not ride or take a carriage. Surely it would not be long now before they arrived. While she did not look forward to meeting his lordship's anger, the waiting for it was beyond endurance. Even with the arguments she had rehearsed on Delia's behalf, she had little hope of affecting his lordship's decision. Delia would be sent back to her parents and their plans of a sanatorium. The thought of it chilled Helen to her core.

It was another half an hour before Lady Margaret straightened in her chair, her regard on the street below. She patted her lips with a fingertip, her other hand finding the back of her coiffure to smooth the braided knot. Helen knew only one person could prompt such unconscious primping.

"Is that his lordship?" she asked, needing to break the silence as much as warn Delia of the impending arrival.

"It would seem so." Lady Margaret bent her head back to her writing, but the high line of her shoulders betrayed her anticipation.

Delia glanced at Helen, her gray eyes dark with fear. Helen smiled back with as much reassurance as she could muster, and pointedly returned to her embroidery. It was important to remain calm. She drew in a deep breath. Holy heaven, she could barely place the next stitch. So much for calmness.

She listened, following the procession of footsteps up the staircase: Garner first, then his lordship and Mr. Hammond. She threaded her needle through the linen in preparation to put it down.

A knock sounded.

Lady Margaret meticulously placed her pen back into its rest and rose from her chair. "Yes?" she called as Helen and Delia stood and readied themselves.

Garner entered and stepped aside as Lord Carlston and Mr. Hammond strode into the room. The two men bowed.

Helen focused on the impeccable fit of his lordship's dark blue jacket across his shoulders, the strong line of his neck, the beginning of a curl in his clipped dark hair. As he straightened, she tried to fix her eyes upon the wall behind him, but found her gaze relentlessly pulled back to his face. Lud, it was as if he were the north and her eyes a compass. She braced herself against the inevitable effect of him upon her body. There it was: the little skip within her chest. A response to harmonious symmetry and line, she told herself. Even so, she could feel a deeper pulse within herself, an insistent beat that seemed to reach toward him.

From the corner of her eye she saw Lady Margaret curtsy and hurriedly bobbed into her own.

"I hope your journey was not too tiresome, Lord Carlston," Lady Margaret said.

"Not at all." His expression was at its most unreadable. Not a good sign, but there was no use delaying the inevitable.

Helen stepped forward. "Lord Carlston, may I present my friend, Miss Delia Cransdon." She could not keep the defiance from her voice.

His eyebrows lifted at the tone, but he turned his attention to Delia. "Miss Cransdon," he said, bowing again.

"Lord Carlston." Delia executed a graceful curtsy.

"Would you like a glass of wine, Carlston?" Lady Margaret asked.

"I thank you, no." His attention was once again upon Helen.

Lady Margaret waved a dismissal to the butler. "That will be all, Garner."

"Mr. Hammond," Carlston said as the door closed behind the servant, "would you please escort your sister and Miss Cransdon to the morning room. I wish to speak to Lady Helen alone."

Helen felt all the air leave her body.

"Of course," Mr. Hammond said. He look anxiously at Helen. "My lord, I—"

"Thank you, Mr. Hammond," Carlston said pleasantly. "Leave us now."

Silently Delia and Lady Margaret crossed the room. Helen kept her eyes fixed upon the dusky pink carpet as they passed. She had a fair idea what was in their faces, and right then she did not want to meet Delia's fear or Lady Margaret's grim satisfaction. She heard the click of the door opening, the creak of the landing as it took three people, and finally the soft thud of the door as it once again shut. Alone with his lordship.

She took another deep breath and raised her eyes. He had not moved, and his face was still impassive. If he was angry, the emotion was under strict control.

"Lord Carlston, allow me to explain. Miss Cransdon was tricked into eloping with a suitor by the name of Trent, whom I believe was a Deceiver. The creature shot itself before her and she witnessed the illumination as it passed from its body—"

"I am aware of what Miss Cransdon witnessed," he said, cutting her short. "They were pursued by Mr. Hallifax, the Reclaimer who was tracking that creature, and he has provided me with a full report."

"Oh." Helen took a moment to digest the implications of this knowledge. "Did you know that she was my friend at the time?"

"Of course. As soon as I became aware of your abilities, I instructed our Tracers to check the lineage of all the people around you. We had to determine if they could be of a known Deceiver line. Although"—he tilted his head in wry acknowledgment—"we failed to find the Deceiver who infiltrated your house as a footman."

"Philip," Helen said. With a start, she remembered her possible sighting. Should she tell Lord Carlston? Surely Pike's ban did not cover that information. "I thought I saw him on Friday, in the township."

"Here?" His lordship frowned.

"I cannot be certain," she added quickly. "It was but a glimpse, and I could not sight him again, although we made a search. It was probably just someone who looked like him."

"I will make inquiries." He rubbed his forehead. "Philip is definitely one who slipped through our Tracer net. Nevertheless, our people are as thorough as possible with the limited registers that we have in our archives. We checked everyone around you against that information, including Miss Cransdon."

"Everyone?" That little demon of defiance made her add, "Even the Duke of Selburn? I know he is here in Brighton too."

His jaw tightened, but he did not rise to her jibe. "Yes, we checked even the Duke of Selburn."

"And did you find anything?"

"No one is of a Deceiver line that we can detect."

"But what if Delia *had* been a Deceiver?"

"That would make it a great deal simpler. She would be dispatched."

"You mean killed, don't you?" Helen stared at him. "Just like that?"

"Just like that," he repeated. "There could be only two reasons for a Deceiver to work its way into your life: to harm you or to gather information about the Dark Days Club." He walked to the window and looked out to the street, his profile a sharp-edged silhouette against the light. "Mr. Hammond informs me that you wrote a letter to Miss Cransdon that promised the truth about the Deceivers."

"I did." Helen squared her shoulders. "But that was before I took my oath before Mr. Pike."

"Yes, Mr. Pike." His tone was flat. "I believe you met Mr. Stokes as well."

He abandoned the window and crossed to the hearth. She turned to face him again.

"Yes, I did." She waited, but he did not reply. The silence felt accusatory. "I kept my oath, Lord Carlston," she added sharply. "I did not tell Delia anything. I hope Mr. Hammond made that clear."

"He told me that Miss Cransdon has a penchant for listening at doors."

He walked around the sofa. She found herself pivoting again. He was circling her, like some predatory beast.

"It was not well done of Delia, I know, but you must understand that her family is determined to send her to a sanatorium. They tell her nothing about her fate, and she must find out through any means."

"So now she is aware of the existence of the Deceivers and the Dark Days Club."

"Yes." She watched him pace, trying to find some little clue that would help gauge his mood. He was certainly angry—it was in the stiff length of his fingers—but there was something else as well. "I was hoping that you would allow her to join us. I am sure she could be of use."

He stopped by the two large Chinoiserie urns set against the wall and crossed his arms. "It is not my decision."

Helen paused. Of course, he had a hierarchy to consider. "You mean the Home Office must agree?"

He shook his head. "She has been cleared by the Tracers. It is now your decision."

Her decision? Helen frowned. "But I have only just joined. I have barely begun my training."

"Nevertheless, you have created a breach that may threaten the organization. Miss Cransdon must either be brought into the fold or her silence guaranteed. If she is to stay, you must take her as one of your aides."

"Yes," Helen said promptly. "Of course I want her to stay. She cannot go home to—"

He held up his hand, stopping her midsentence. "Do not base your decision upon pity or friendship, Lady Helen. You are a Reclaimer now; you must think strategically. If you take Miss Cransdon as an aide, you will be responsible for her from that moment onward: for her safety, her training, and, because of her circumstances, her upkeep. You will be placing her in mortal peril for the rest of her life, and you will be held accountable by the

Dark Days Club for her actions. Do you understand?" His voice was implacable. "Do you even know if Miss Cransdon would want to take on such a dangerous role? Is she strong enough in both mind and body for such service? Can you be assured that she will be committed and useful to you and the Dark Days Club?"

Helen hesitated. How could she guarantee any of those things? Moreover, could she really ask Delia to shoulder such responsibility and danger?

"What if I decided she was not suitable?"

The severity in his face softened a little. Almost sympathy, Helen thought, but not quite.

"You and I are here to protect mankind from the Deceivers, Lady Helen. That is what you swore to do in the presence of Mr. Pike, Mr. Stokes, and Mr. Hammond. Sometimes we must make hard decisions for the good of mankind rather than the good of just one man, or woman."

"But what would happen to Delia? Surely you would not *dispatch* her. An innocent girl."

He frowned. "Of course not. She would be sent back to her parents. I suspect that their decision to incarcerate her would be expedited by the Home Office. Pike is very good at managing the concealment of the Dark Days Club."

"They would have her labeled a madwoman and locked away? That is despicable."

"So you would rather she was killed?"

She bristled at his sarcasm. "The high-handedness of it is reprehensible. This is a young woman's life."

"It is, and you must take responsibility for your part in Miss Cransdon's unfortunate situation." His face was stern again. "It is your own foolish actions that have caused it."

"My foolish actions?"

"Your womanish need to comfort and pacify."

In four outraged strides she was across the room and standing a step too close to him. Courtesy be hanged! "Womanish need? All I did was write a letter to reassure a friend that she was not mad."

"No, you wrote a letter that acknowledged the existence of the Deceivers." He jabbed the air with his forefinger. "You did it knowing full well that it was a stupid thing to do."

Deep down she knew he was right. But his manner was obnoxious.

"How can I know anything *full well* when you keep so much important information to yourself? I must always be guessing!"

He leaned forward, his face hard. "Perhaps if you used the intelligence that God gave you instead of relying upon sentimental impulses, I would trust you with more information."

She drew in a furious breath. "It was my sentimental impulses that saved your life. By your logic I should have left you to die!"

Their angry eyes locked. The raw connection was no more than a second, but it blazed with pulsing heat. Helen felt herself sway forward. Dear heaven, it was as if a force were driving her toward him.

She saw the shock in his face too. Heard the sharp intake of breath as if he had been struck. He reached for her, his hand so close to cupping her cheek. But no; he turned on his heel and strode to the door.

"Make your decision," he snapped over his shoulder.

Before she could gather breath to answer him, he was gone.

She stared at the closed door, hand pressed to her chest. Now she understood. He had not been circling her at all. He had been keeping his distance.

HE LEFT THE house at once, not even stopping to take his leave from Lady Margaret and Mr. Hammond. Helen, left alone in the drawing room, listened to his progress out of the front door and as far along the street as her Reclaimer hearing could reach. Even then, she stood for a few minutes more, trying to calm the pulse that drummed through her body to the ends of her fingers and toes.

At last composed, she ventured downstairs to find Delia and end her friend's agonizing wait. To Helen's mind, there was no decision to be made. Delia could not be sent back to her parents or exposed to the malignant intentions of the Home Office; such ruthlessness was inconceivable. That left only one path: to tell her about the Deceivers and persuade her to join the Dark Days Club.

It was this last part that caused Helen some anxiety as she made her way to the morning room where her friend, Lady Margaret, and Mr. Hammond had retreated. What if Delia quailed at the idea of such a dangerous life?

She need not have worried. Although shocked, Delia neither flinched at the revelation that her suitor had been an otherworldly creature living in a stolen body, nor did she shrink from the invitation to step into a life that held as much peril as it did purpose.

"You wish me to be your aide?" Delia sat forward in her chair, both hands grasping the edge of the table that held one of Mr. Wedgwood's new fine china tea sets and an untouched fruitcake. "You want *me*?"

Helen stopped pacing and caught sight of herself in the large mirror that graced the gaily painted yellow wall behind her friend. She looked almost as pale as Delia, the shock of her encounter with Lord Carlston still etched into her face. She averted her eyes from her pinched reflection and returned to her seat.

"Yes. Just as Mr. Hammond and Lady Margaret are aides to Lord Carlston."

Across the table, Mr. Hammond put down his delicately gilded teacup. Both he and Lady Margaret were frowning; clearly they had not expected this outcome.

"You must think very carefully upon this, Miss Cransdon," he said. "It is a decision that will affect your entire life."

"I will, sir. I think I—"

"Lady Helen," Lady Margaret interrupted. "Are you certain Lord Carlston approves of this . . . addition?" A sideways glance at Delia punctuated her disapproval.

Helen clenched her teeth over a sharp retort. She had already twice confirmed his lordship's knowledge of the matter. Still, she should not snap at Lady Margaret. The woman was providing her with a home and all earthly comforts until Helen's brother made good on his promise of an allowance. Such largesse at least deserved gratitude and civility.

Gathering all the pleasantness she could muster, Helen said, "His lordship made it very clear it was my decision, Lady Margaret."

"It stands to reason, my dear," Mr. Hammond said to his sister. "Lady Helen is now a sworn Reclaimer. She must have her own aides."

"She has had little more than a month's training. How can she be responsible for an aide when she is barely responsible for herself? She is not ready."

Although it had been her own concern, Helen bristled. "On the contrary, since his lordship has placed this in *my* hands, he must feel I am ready."

"Really?" Lady Margaret picked up the elegantly curved teapot and poured herself another cup, the precise action full of disdain. "More likely he is testing you to see which way you go." She replaced the pot with a sharp click on the polished tabletop. "And you are patently going the wrong way."

"Is that so?" Helen said. Gratitude could only stretch so far.

"Am I to gather that you know his lordship's mind better than he does?"

"Well, I *certainly* know that he—"

"Mr. Hammond, please tell me your duties," Delia said, the force and volume of her interruption swinging all attention to her. "So that I may make a proper decision. Do you and your sister fight the creatures too?"

Her eyes cut to Helen in a moment of solidarity. It seemed her friend was already in the business of peacemaking.

"No," Mr. Hammond said, regarding Delia with new respect. "We help Lord Carlston in other matters, but we do not fight the Deceivers. When that is required, it is the duty of a Reclaimer. Most Deceivers live according to the Compact. It is only those who break the pact that are hunted."

Delia frowned. "The Compact?"

"Perhaps you will answer this for Miss Cransdon, Margaret?" Mr. Hammond smiled coaxingly at his sister.

She crossed her arms. "We should not be sharing information like this with someone who is not yet sworn to keep her silence."

"Delia needs to know what she will be facing," Helen said, abandoning all attempt to keep the sharpness from her tone. "Surely you were told about the Deceivers before you took your oath."

"Naturally we were," Mr. Hammond said, sending a stern glance at his sister. "Margaret, please!"

With a sniff of reluctance, Lady Margaret turned to Delia. "The Compact is our agreement with the Deceivers. It allows the creatures to feed upon human energy by skimming a tiny amount from many people. It is not their preferred way of feeding, of course; they would much rather glut upon the energy of one person at a time. That, however, is forbidden. Glutting, you see, almost always kills the victim, and the influx of their life force allows the creatures to build the energy whips that they use as weapons."

"Oh my," Delia breathed. "Stolen bodies, energy whips, feeding upon human energy. It is all so"—her shoulders twitched—"*Gothic*."

Helen shifted on her seat. "It is not like a novel, Delia. Real people get hurt and killed."

"Of course," Delia said. "I did not mean to sound flippant."

"The creatures are not visible to our eye, so it is hard to believe at first," Mr. Hammond said kindly. "Part of the Compact requires them to maintain their anonymity. There are too many of them to destroy, and so we must live alongside them. We cannot, however, have their existence known to the general populace. The panic would rip apart society. We must maintain stability, especially in a time of war. Our country cannot fight both the French and the Deceivers."

Delia nodded gravely. "How many of them are there?"

Helen glanced at Mr. Hammond. This was the number that had shocked her so thoroughly.

"At least ten thousand in England alone," he said.

Helen watched her friend's face. Delia had always been phlegmatic, but her calm acceptance of the Deceivers so far seemed remarkable. Perhaps she did not truly understand the magnitude of what they faced.

"That is one Deceiver in every one thousand people," Helen added. "And probably as many in every other country."

Delia's mouth formed a soundless O. "That many," she said faintly.

There it was: the horrible realization. Helen still felt it herself.

"Most of them congregate in the towns and cities," she said, "places with the highest concentrations of human energy. Many will follow the *beau monde* here for the summer Season. Some will even be people with whom you converse and dance."

Delia flinched. "Yes, of course, like Mr. Trent," she said, her attention suddenly fixed upon her teacup.

Helen felt a flick of guilt. It was perhaps unkind to drive home the idea that anyone could be a Deceiver, particularly after Delia's experience with her false suitor. Still, it was better that she should know the full extent of the matter.

Mr. Hammond broke the uncomfortable silence. "There are some that have even worked their way into high positions. It seems Deceivers cannot breed with their own kind to create Deceiver offspring. Instead, the creatures breed with humans to produce human offspring. At the time of conception, a spark of the parent Deceiver's own energy, called a vestige, is planted within the human child. When the parent Deceiver's inhabited human body eventually dies—as all human bodies must die—it uses that vestige as a pathway to colonize the body of one of its human children, thus surviving from generation to generation. Some have used those centuries to build large fortunes and strongholds of power in the upper echelons of society."

That brought Delia's eyes up from her cup. "Who do you mean? How high up in society? The Royal family?"

"The Royal family is as human as you and I," Lady Margaret said. She bent a fierce frown toward her brother. "Really, Michael. These are secret matters."

Delia turned to Helen. "What happens to the offspring child already inhabiting the body?"

"The Deceiver destroys the child. Mind and soul."

"Heaven forfend." Delia closed her eyes for a horrified moment. "Where did these creatures come from?"

"No one is certain. Some of the old writings say they are from Hell itself. Others say they are made from the yearnings of humanity, or are the angry spirits of the dearly departed."

"What do you think they are?" Delia asked.

Helen shook her head. "I cannot rightly say. We do know there are at least four *kinds* of Deceiver." She counted each off on a finger. "The Hedons who seek out the energy of creativity, the Pavors who thrive on pain and anguish, the Cruors who follow bloodlust and battle, and the Luxures who seek . . ."

She paused, feeling her skin heat. What was she doing dragging her friend into such a sordid, dangerous world?

"Who seek sexual pleasure," Mr. Hammond finished, his voice carefully flat. "And do not forget the fifth and worst kind: the Grand Deceiver."

Delia sat up straighter. "That sounds rather ominous."

Lady Margaret made a warning noise deep in her throat. "Does she really need to know about the Grand Deceiver at this point?"

"I think she does," Helen said. "It is a rare, special kind of Deceiver, Delia. It has more power, more cunning, and the ability to draw all of the other Deceivers into an army."

At the corner of her eye she saw Lady Margaret's mouth purse.

"If you are going to tell her about it, Lady Helen, you should at least give her some context. Usually Deceivers do not band together, Miss Cransdon; they are territorial. It is why we are able to police them with so few Reclaimers. A Grand Deceiver, however, has the power to bring them together."

"*Is* bringing them together," Mr. Hammond said grimly. "It is possible that Napoleon is one, and now we believe there is one in England, too. It has been proven that some of the Deceivers are working together, and Lord Carlston is convinced it is a sign that a Grand Deceiver is among us." He gestured to Helen. "Another sign is the emergence of a Reclaimer who is a direct inheritor."

"My mother was a Reclaimer too," Helen explained to her friend. "It is not supposed to be an inherited gift, and yet here I am, with Reclaimer powers."

Delia gaped at her. "You have powers?"

"As a direct inheritor she has more powers than a normal Reclaimer," Mr. Hammond said.

"That remains to be seen," Helen said.

She felt a sudden need to downplay her abilities. Everyone was expecting so much from her heritage. What if she could not even control the powers she had?

"Lady Helen has uncanny speed, sharpened senses, and near twice the strength of a normal man," Mr. Hammond supplied. "Not to mention the ability to heal at a great rate—a boon that the Deceivers do not have."

"She will need all that, and more, if we are to find and defeat the Grand Deceiver," Lady Margaret said.

"We will find him," Mr. Hammond said firmly. "And Lord Carlston is convinced Lady Helen will exhibit more powers."

"You aim to defeat this creature, Helen?" Delia shook her head as if trying to clear a way through so much wonder. "I cannot conceive of the kind of power that would do so. Will you show me?"

Helen hesitated. It was all well and good to talk of Reclaimers and Deceivers, but once Delia saw what she could do, she knew her friend would never look at her in the same way. She already felt like one of Sir Joseph Banks's specimens under a magnifying glass. Yet Delia had to see the truth.

She rose from her chair and walked to the side bureau. It was small but made of heavy oak, at least eighty pounds or so in weight. Lifting it would probably suffice as a show of strength. She swung around to scan the rest of the furniture. Perhaps the striped silk armchair near the window would be a better demonstration. Not only heavy, but large as well.

Mr. Hammond rose from his chair. "Why don't you lift *me*?"

Lady Margaret placed her hand on his arm. "Do not be ridiculous, Michael."

"No, I cannot," Helen said, for once finding herself in agreement with her chaperone. "What if I were to harm you?"

"I am sure you will take care. It will be good practice: if you are to fight the creatures, you must get used to such bodily contact. I insist. Come, let us move away from the table to be safe."

He strode to the other end of the room and pushed one of the armchairs to one side.

Helen followed. "Are you sure, sir?"

"I am." He waved her closer. "Come, you cannot lift me from two feet away."

She stepped in front of him, hands hovering, not quite sure exactly where to take hold.

He patted his chest. "Do take care with my cravat; it is one of my best efforts."

She nodded earnestly, then saw the crinkles around his eyes. He was joking. With a smile, she grasped the front of his waistcoat and shirt. The action pulled him closer. As she gathered the layers of blue silk and snowy linen into one fist, he turned his head, his mouth almost against her ear, and murmured, "I found Lowry."

Helen stiffened. So this was why he had wanted to go to the other side of the room: to deliver his message.

His voice dropped even lower, to a register that only a Reclaimer could hear. "We are to meet him two nights hence. In the Bear at Lewes."

Lud, a meeting at night in another town. Nevertheless, she met his eyes and gave the slightest of nods. At least it would all be over by Tuesday.

"Are you ready?" she asked.

"I am."

She braced herself, and with a deep breath hauled him upward. She had expected to lift him a foot or so, but in one easy hoist she had him a good three feet off the floor.

He looked down at her, eyes slightly bulging, his cravat and shirt bunched around his chin. She was shocked as well. Mr. Hammond was at least 150 pounds and, although she was using only one hand, she was not straining at all. Holy star, her strength must have increased in the last few days. Was that normal? She almost laughed at the thought. What was normal about a young woman lifting a man so easily from the ground?

Delia stood and clapped. "Amazing! How wonderful to be so strong, and you did it with such ease." She peered up at Mr. Hammond. "He seems to be rather red in the face."

"Oh!" Helen lowered him abruptly back to his feet. "Forgive me, Mr. Hammond. I was not expecting to lift you so high."

He lurched back, coughing. "Quite all right," he gasped, pulling at his cravat.

Lady Margaret sprang from her chair and passed him a cup. "Here, Michael, take some tea."

"I do apologize," Helen said, hovering behind Lady Margaret.

He shook his head and took a spluttering mouthful.

Lady Margaret turned on Helen. "You have choked him! You are too careless."

"That is not fair, Margaret," Mr. Hammond croaked. "Neither of us was expecting such"—he cleared his throat—"such an increase in strength."

"Would you like some wine?" Helen asked. "I shall call for some."

Lady Margaret waved her away. "You have done enough."

"Helen," Delia said, taking her hands and drawing her back across the room, "let him have some air." She dropped her voice. "And let her do her fussing."

"I did not mean to choke him."

"Of course not," Delia said, squeezing her hands. "You were just trying to help me make my decision. Well, I have made it. I do not want another girl ever to experience what I did with Mr. Trent." She gave a grimace of resignation. "And in the end, I have nowhere else to go."

Helen looked into her friend's face, searching for any kind of doubt. "Are you sure? It is not an easy life."

Delia nodded. "I would be most honored to serve as your aide."

Helen smiled. She was, of course, glad to have Delia by her side. Very glad. Yet within that bright elation ran a darker streak of foreboding. She had just persuaded her friend to enter a world of extreme danger. Delia was now her responsibility, and she already felt the weight of her friend's soul upon her own.

Delia cocked her head to one side. "Perhaps it is you who are not sure?"

"No, I am very sure," Helen said quickly. She leaned forward and kissed Delia on one cheek and then the other, her friend's fragrant white skin soft beneath her lips.

Dear God, she added silently, *please help me keep her safe.*

Six

Monday, 6 July 1812

EARLY NEXT MORNING, Helen woke to hear murmuring in the adjoining dressing room. She rolled onto her back and concentrated on the soft voices. Darby of course, and Geoffrey the footman.

"Lord Carlston is downstairs and waiting," Geoffrey whispered.

"What is he doing here so early? My lady has not even had her morning chocolate yet."

Helen almost heard the footman shrug. "According to Mr. Quinn, his lordship wants to start her training sessions earlier." He dropped his voice lower still. "Says she's not progressing fast enough. Too frightened of her own power."

Helen drew in a sharp breath.

"That's not true," her maid said stalwartly.

Dear faithful Darby. Yet the comment had stung with some kind of truth.

"He's got a cove with him from London, and bid me deliver these bandboxes to you. You'd best wake her."

Helen sat up, her night plait swinging heavily against her back. A man from London? She had no idea who that might be. The bandboxes, however, were not so mysterious: her gentleman's

garb. No doubt Lord Carlston would have given them to her yesterday if they had not quarreled.

Wretchedness prickled across her skin. He had not returned
to the house after that unfortunate interview, and so had not
witnessed both Delia and Darby swearing their official oaths of
loyalty under the peevish direction of Lady Margaret, or joined
the muted celebration that had followed. No one had commented
upon his absence, although Helen had caught Lady Margaret
watching the door throughout the evening. Now his lordship had
arrived before breakfast to start training, and with someone else
in tow. A firm message, it would seem, that they were to push on
as before with no acknowledgment of that energy that kept flaring between them. He wanted a focused, logical, nonsentimental
trainee. Well, he would have exactly that.

"Darby," she called.

"There, she's up now," her maid whispered. "And you've delivered your boxes, so off you go."

"Yes, Mistress Chide."

"Cheeky monkey," Darby said, but Geoffrey was already retreat-
ing down the staircase.

Helen heard the door closing, and then five measured steps
brought Darby to the dressing room doorway, a large rounded silhouette in the gloom.

"Good morning, my lady." She bobbed a curtsy and headed
to the window. "Geoffrey just delivered some bandboxes for you.
From his lordship." She gathered two handfuls of the heavy velvet curtains and drew them back. "Shall I bring them in, or do you
wish to have your chocolate first?" She folded back the shutters
and pressed them home with a soft clunk.

Helen blinked in the sudden morning light. "Bring them in,
please."

The long sleeve and bodice of Darby's dress—a refashioned

castoff from Helen's wardrobe—caught the sun in a show of chestnut pin tucks and pleats. It was her maid's best gown; she did not often bring it out for everyday wear.

"Are you by chance going into town with Mr. Quinn this morning?" Helen asked, keeping her tone bland.

Darby, bending to affix the shutter snib, twitched a shoulder. "As it happens, my lady, I am. He is teaching me to move expediently through a crowd." She lifted her head, cheeks pink. "He has also promised to take me for cake and tea after to celebrate my oath. If I have your permission?"

Helen nodded, and received a beaming smile.

"I'll get the boxes, my lady." She hurried from the room.

Helen flipped her plait over her shoulder and ran her fingers along its thick brown corrugations. The interest between Darby and Quinn was fast becoming fixed, but even with all the goodwill in the world, Helen could see no happy ending for her maid and the big Pacific Islander. They would always be the target of hateful words, and even foul physical missiles, slung at them by small-minded people outraged by a "brown savage" touching a white woman. More to the point, there would be a day, heading toward them at a great rate, when all the training was done and Lord Carlston returned to his real Reclaimer duties with his Terrene at his side. Darby, of course, would stay with her, the two of them expected to stand on their own.

Helen's fingers stopped their restless runs, the thought of being on her own bringing an instant of breathless immobility. At least that alarming future was still some way off. She also had Delia now, although his lordship had clearly not approved of her as an aide. Helen closed her hand around the end of her braid. It did not matter what he thought; he had said it was her decision.

"There is a note, too," Darby said, emerging from the dressing room with two large bandboxes stacked together.

"Put them here." Helen patted the blue silk coverlet.

Darby placed the boxes on the bed, and passed over the note.

"That one first." Helen pointed to the box closest to her leg.

Darby lifted the lid and pulled aside the packing paper. They both peered in. A pair of neatly folded pale buckskin breeches lay on top. As suspected, her male clothes. Now she would show his lordship *space* and *purpose*.

Darby pulled the breeches out and placed them on the bed. Next came a pair of white silk evening breeches, a pair of braces, three linen shirts with collars attached, ten fine linen cravats, stockings, and two waistcoats, one cream, the other striped in shades of burgundy. No metal buttons or hooks on anything, of course; metal was a deadly pathway for a Deceiver's energy.

Helen regarded the wide array of clothing spread out on the bed. A true Reclaimer's wardrobe. It was also a complete male wardrobe. Was Lord Carlston expecting her to live as a man? In truth, it would probably be more convenient for everyone; it was far easier to move around the world as a man than as a woman. Even more so for a Reclaimer. It seemed femininity was a definite disadvantage in this new and dangerous world.

She sat back against the pillows and broke the wax seal on the note from his lordship, spreading the paper. It was as curt as ever. She read it aloud:

> *We are in the salon and await your appearance*
> *in your new clothes.*
>
> *Yrs,*
> *C*

"Not a man to waste words, is he, my lady?" Darby remarked.

Neither words *nor* emotions. Helen refolded the note and laid it on the bed. "What is in the second box?"

Darby brought out a day jacket of good-quality fir-green broadcloth, followed by a black evening jacket. Finally, packed tightly into the bottom, there was a pair of slightly worn black Hessian boots, a dull gold tassel hanging from each curved front.

Darby picked up the top cravat from the pile and inspected the starched linen. "Mr. Quinn has explained the intricacies of dressing a gentleman, my lady, and I have practiced tying a number of cravat styles. I think we shall manage."

Helen threw back the clear side of the bedcovers and swung her legs to the ground. "Then let us get to it," she said in her best manly manner.

Twenty minutes later in the dressing room, Helen rolled her shoulders, trying to ease the compression of her breasts under the tight band of wrapped calico. It was even more uncomfortable than the long stays she had worn for her Court presentation.

Darby frowned. "I have bound you too tight. Shall I ease it?"

Helen shook her head. "I imagine it will give with movement." She looked down at her flattened chest. "I never thought to say this, but it is fortunate that I do not have much bosom."

Darby picked up a linen shirt and shook out its folds. "Mr. Quinn says I'd do well to get myself some men's clothes too, from the rag trader. But can you imagine trying to squash these flat?" She peered down at her generous curves. Helen winced in sympathy.

"Hold up your arms, my lady."

Helen obeyed, closing her eyes as the shirt was deftly thrown over her head, and her arms guided into the generous sleeves. Three decisive tugs on its tails rocked her back on her heels as Darby drew the shirt efficiently over her hips. She looked down;

the hem brushed her knees. Below, her shins and feet were as pale as the ivory linen.

"Now," Darby said, stepping back, "according to Mr. Quinn, the front goes back between a gentleman's legs to . . . well . . . hold in his . . ." She gestured at her crotch.

"His masculinity?" Helen supplied. She searched her new command of cant. "His plug tail? His sugar stick?"

They looked at one another, each with lips pressed together to hold back the rising hilarity.

Darby broke first, snorting a half-stifled giggle. "Sugar stick! That is a good one, my lady."

Helen, rather pleased with it herself, grinned and gathered up the linen. She pushed it between her legs, shifting her hips at the sensation of bulk and pressure. The only time she had anything in such a place was during her courses; how uncomfortable to have a wad of cloth there all the time.

"Do you think we should pad out the front, my lady?" Darby asked solemnly, although her eyes were still alight with laughter. "I have heard that some gentlemen assist nature with sawdust pouches."

"Truly?" Helen asked, fascinated. She took a sidestep to the mirror and viewed her reflection critically. The area was rather flat, but she did not fancy wearing a bag of sawdust. "I think if I bunch most of the shirt forward, it will be enough." She made the adjustment. "What do you think?"

Darby nodded her approval and readied the buckskin breeches. Helen stepped into them, grabbing the side of the bureau as Darby pulled the soft leather up over her hips and tucked the shirt into the waistband.

She lifted the square of cloth at the front. "How does this work?"

"We lace the waistband closed first," Darby said, matching

words to action, "and then lift the drop-front and button that up over it. See?"

Helen looked down at the buttoned flap. Very neat.

"They are very tight over the leg," she said, glancing in the mirror again. "Heavens!" All of her long thighs was on show, as was her newly enhanced groin.

Darby was busy at the back of her waist, buttoning something into the waistband. "Dip your shoulders, please, my lady."

Helen complied, and each arm was expertly threaded through the canvas braces. Darby adjusted them over her shoulders, their hold like a ramrod at her back. No wonder gentlemen had such excellent posture.

"All right," Darby said, drawing a deep breath. "We shall attempt the cravat." She held up the long length of starched muslin. "Mr. Quinn says that we must first wind it around your neck and pull very tight to achieve a smooth column of white cloth." She stepped up to Helen until they stood face-to-face. "Chin up, my lady."

Helen craned back her neck. All she could see was Darby's furrowed forehead as she slid the stiffened muslin inside the high points of the shirt collar. Her cool fingers smoothed the cloth against Helen's neck, wrapped it around twice, and, with a firm tug, brought the ends together. It felt as if a murderous hand had closed around her throat.

"Too tight," Helen whispered.

The pressure eased slightly, and Darby's earnest face bobbed up into Helen's line of sight. "I'm sorry, I dare not loosen it any more, my lady, or it will droop." She deftly tied the tails of the muslin, then stepped back, hands on hips. "It is done. I think it looks very well."

"Might I lower my chin?"

"A fraction."

Helen eased down her chin until she felt the stiff top of the column, her head still slightly cranked back. Now she understood that arrogant angle of chin found in most men of fashion. She looked in the mirror. A stylish bow nestled at the bottom of the column.

"It is marvelous, Darby. Well done."

An uneasy thought came hard upon the heels of her praise. Without Darby's expert help, how was she going to dress in these clothes again to meet Lowry?

The jacket came next: a feat of inching into the tightly tailored sleeves and shoulders. Helen felt the start of a prickling sweat under her arms. She would have to enlist Mr. Hammond's help if she was to wear the jacket to Lewes.

Finally her stockinged feet were levered into the boots, Darby brandishing the boot horn with brutal efficiency. Helen stood up, wriggling her toes. A good firm fit, although the long shaft of leather up to her knees and the small heel were unfamiliar.

She walked across to the mirror again and considered her reflection. Somehow she looked even taller than her five feet nine inches; perhaps due to the enforced military posture and pugnacious tilt of her chin. Her legs seemed very long, and very, very exposed. She felt her gaze shifting away from such immodesty and forced herself to look back at the pale length of buckskin. Could she really stride out with her thighs on show for the world to see . . . let alone the area above them that seemed to be framed for display under the cutaway front of her jacket?

She took a deep breath. All men wore breeches; no one would be focusing unduly upon the area. At least that cutaway front and the tails hid any curve of hip.

She raised her eyes. The M-style collar of the jacket certainly gave the illusion of wide shoulders, and the cravat covered the lack of Adam's apple and emphasized her strong jaw. It was only her long braid and the rather startled expression on her face that made her look feminine. She flipped the braid back over her shoulder, narrowed her eyes, and firmed her mouth into a harder line. There: a young man stood before her. A slim stripling perhaps, without beard or experience, but with enough height and clean features to pass as a young provincial mister. A resounding success. Yet she had to admit it was a little humiliating to shift into the masculine with such ease.

She shook off the thought. She should be glad that the costume worked so well. Here was something, at least, that his lordship or Lady Margaret could not criticize.

She turned to Darby and made a small bow. "Well?"

With an answering smile, her maid bobbed a curtsy. "I would not have warranted it, my lady, but you are a lad through and through."

Helen turned back to the elated young gentleman in the mirror. Maybe this would not be so difficult, after all.

⸺

As expected, it was far easier to take manly, purposeful strides in a pair of buckskins than in a gown. Helen descended the stairs to the salon three at a time, just to test the new freedom and feel the odd sensation of so much cloth around her nethers. No wonder gentlemen took such big steps and stood with their legs apart. She stifled a smile at the irreverent thought and approached the salon.

Geoffrey stood at his post outside the doors, his expression carefully neutral and his gaze fixed over her shoulder. Even so, Helen felt heat rise to her cheeks. He would surely have noted her thighs and graceless descent. Was he disgusted by her exposure or, even worse, delighted?

"My lady." He opened the door. His expression did not change, but she caught something behind his well-trained visage. A new kind of respect.

"Thank you," she murmured, not only for the opened door.

She squared her shoulders and stared into the room. No one was visible—just the opposite wall and its high-set window—but she could hear the murmur of voices. Inside was the real test of her transformation. Would Lord Carlston think she could pass as a man?

Only one way to find out. With a deep breath, she strode into the salon.

Since her last training session with Mr. Hammond, the empty room had acquired a few pieces of furniture and a strong smell of waxy sandalwood. It had also acquired six people, all of whom turned and stared as she entered.

Inevitably, she found Lord Carlston first. He stood with Lady Margaret by a table set along the back wall, arms crossed, his customary self-possession tensing into sudden surprise. She risked a glance at his face, locking for a breathless second into the hold of his eyes. Heat rose to her cheeks again, but this time it was not humiliation. He turned his head, breaking the moment, and she almost felt him step back behind his customary wall of cool evaluation.

Hurriedly she shifted her attention to Lady Margaret. Her chaperone was clearly astounded by her transformation. Helen fought back an uncharitable *Ha!*

Mr. Hammond and Delia stood near the front windows, both with their mouths agape. Behind them, Quinn was in the process of shifting a mirror atop a dressing table. He paused, a pleased smile dawning on his tattooed face, then returned to his task.

And in the corner, a small man with coiffed blond hair and a modish teal jacket regarded her with keen interest. Clearly the cove from London.

"Lud, Helen," Delia exclaimed, breaking the stunned silence. "Everyone can see your legs! Your . . . hips!"

Everyone's gaze dropped downward. Helen clenched her hands by her sides, fixing her expression into rigid indifference.

"Miss Cransdon," Lady Margaret said sharply, "I am sure it is hard enough for Lady Helen to find confidence in her disguise without you sabotaging the effort."

"I did not mean . . ." Delia started. "It was just such a shock to see . . ." She faltered and stopped.

"It is all right," Helen said. "I must become used to being so . . . displayed."

"You have done well," his lordship said. He walked around her, still, she noted, at a safe distance. "Very well."

"It was not all my doing." Now he was standing a good five feet from her, but she felt his gaze upon her as if his hands were sliding across her body. The sensation made her blink; she must stop these vivid imaginings. "Darby makes a very good valet."

"Indeed, Quinn could not have tied a better cravat."

His sidelong glance held only cool approval; he had himself back under control. Helen could not claim the same. That disturbing pulse beneath her heartbeat had intensified, leaping out toward him.

"I always knew you would make an excellent young man," Mr. Hammond said, striding forward. He bowed to her, a silent message in his relieved grin: *See, you can do it.*

Helen returned the bow, aware of his lordship crossing the room behind them. Her whole body felt attuned to him.

"Lady Helen, allow me to introduce Mr. Harrington," he said.

Helen turned to meet the low bow of the blond stranger. "How do you do, sir."

The man's whole attention seemed to be fixed upon the top of her head. "I am so very glad to see that you have thick hair, my lady. Much easier to work with."

Helen stared at him in bemusement. "Work with?"

"Mr. Harrington has come from London to cut your hair," his lordship said. "He is sworn to us so you need not monitor your conversation."

"Cut my hair?" Helen's hand went to her plait. When had this been decided? Her hair was her best feature. If she lost it, she would have nothing.

"You cannot lose your hair," Delia said, as if she had heard Helen's thought. "It is so pretty—" She clapped her hand over her mouth, her eyes on Lady Margaret.

"Young men do not wear queues or wigs anymore," Carlston said. "You cannot keep it at that length."

"But I will not be a young man all the time!"

Helen looked around for support. Mr. Hammond was pointedly studying the floor, and Delia had been subdued by a glare from Lady Margaret.

"Allow me to reassure you, my lady," Mr. Harrington said, bowing again. "I will crop your hair in such a manner as to suit both male and female guises. Then it is just a matter of dressing the hair with pomades and hairpieces."

"Crop?" Helen repeated, her voice rising. She turned back to Carlston. "You did not say that I would have to cut off all of my hair! You said nothing about hair."

His lordship frowned. "I cannot see the problem. This is part of your Reclaimer duties, Lady Helen. It is no great sacrifice: hair grows back. It is nothing compared to other sacrifices that we are called upon to make."

"Caroline Lamb wears her hair cropped," Lady Margaret said, her tone rallying. "It is a much admired and copied style."

Helen stared at her wordlessly. It was no use citing Caroline Lamb; she was a slim dainty thing well suited to the elfin quality of her famous coiffure. Helen knew no one could ever call her elfin; not with her height and the lean, angular features and physique that were the hallmarks of a Reclaimer.

"I will look awful." It was a weak objection, but it was the heart of the matter. She would look awful. In front of him.

"Lady Helen, I am sorry, but you cannot afford a woman's sensibilities, in this matter or any other," his lordship said. "You must act as a Reclaimer and do your duty."

She drew in a steadying breath. So the haircut was another test of her commitment. Another gauge of her progress as a Reclaimer, which apparently was not fast enough. She could not refuse.

"Of course," she said. "I see that it must be cut."

"Good." Lord Carlston signaled to Mr. Harrington.

"Please, come this way, my lady." The hairdresser gestured toward the dressing table.

With as much composure as she could muster, Helen sat down in front of the mirror. She saw nothing left of the elated young man who had been reflected in her dressing room glass. Now there was just a young woman in a costume holding back ridiculous, vain tears. She glanced at his lordship, but he was giving instructions to Quinn. The decision had been made and that, apparently, was that.

She clasped her hands tightly in her lap as Mr. Harrington arranged a drape of cloth across her shoulders and picked up his shears. The first snip cut off her plait in one long hank.

"For use in the hairpieces," Mr. Harrington remarked as he set it aside.

After that, her hair fell to the floor in a relentless rhythm of snip, snip, snip. All her softness carved away until only two inches of length was left upon her head.

Hideous.

"There," Mr. Harrington said, combing back the layers. "Arranged thus, it can be dressed with hairpieces and adornments into a modish young lady's style."

He paused, waiting for her response, but she could not even nod. Drawing a determined breath, he dipped his fingertips into a pot of pomade and quickly smoothed all her hair forward on a wave of thick sandalwood scent.

"And like this, it is a man's Brutus cut; or, if pushed to the side, even a short Windswept. Do you see how it changes?"

He looked hopefully into Helen's eyes in the mirror, but she had nothing to say.

"Some false side whiskers will complete the picture," he added encouragingly. "They are easily affixed with thespian gum. I will have them, together with the curls and Grecian knot for your woman's toilette, ready by tomorrow."

"It is very effective," Lady Margaret said.

Helen turned to Delia. Her friend was not quite quick enough to hide the stricken pity in her face. Nor, it seemed, could she find anything to say, merely conjuring a bracing smile and vigorous nod.

Helen smiled back. It must be worse than she thought.

She gathered her courage and looked back at her reflection. All she could see were sharp angled cheekbones, a square jaw, firm chin, and a nose on the long side—no feminine softness. Not quite as hideous as she had feared—she made a bold-faced boy—but not pretty, either.

In the corner of the mirror's reflection, she watched his lordship. He was studying her with such an odd expression. Did he think her ugly now? Unwomanly? Or was he relieved to see this stripping of her femininity?

She chewed the inside of her mouth. Yes, it was probably a

relief for him. A female Reclaimer brought too many complications that were his duty to solve. And of course there was the extra problem of the base attraction that leaped between them that even he could not fully quell. There, she had named it for what it was: *base attraction*. What else could it be, so anchored in the response of her body to his? She was just another fool caught in the thrall of his handsome features and physique. She must overcome it. He was still married, and such attraction was against the laws of God.

"It is a most artful cut, Harrington," his lordship said. "A successful transformation."

"Indeed," Mr. Hammond said. "In fact, so successful, I think Lady Helen is ready to start her field training."

That drew her attention from her shame. "Field training?" she queried, trying to catch his eye: *What are you doing?*

Ignoring her alarm, he turned to Carlston. "I propose a trip to a tavern. Lady Helen needs practice as a young man, and if Harrington has those side pieces finished by tomorrow night"— he raised a questioning brow at the hairdresser, who bowed his compliance—"I think we should go into Lewes."

Lud, he was bringing their expedition into the open. Helen forced an expression of enthusiasm. He should have told her he was going to do such a thing; she was the Reclaimer, after all. Not to mention the risk he was taking. What if his lordship said no, she was not ready? Yet beyond her own hesitancy, she could see the sense in it: they could meet Lowry under the guise of the training trip. No secret excursion to try to keep from the household—something that would be difficult, if not impossible.

Lady Margaret frowned at her brother. "For goodness' sake, Michael, do not rush her so. She needs—"

Carlston held up his hand, stopping her protest. She obeyed, but Helen saw her eyes flash.

"Why Lewes?" his lordship asked.

"The place is not fashionable. There will be almost no chance of meeting someone we know," Mr. Hammond said. "She can practice with impunity."

"What do you say, Lady Helen?" Lord Carlston asked. "Do you feel ready to go out into the world as a young man?"

"Yes, absolutely," she said. Even to her ears, she sounded confident. "The sooner the better."

Lord Carlston tilted his head, considering. "Tomorrow night you say, Hammond?"

"A Tuesday evening will be lively enough but not too unruly."

"True. And I am not otherwise engaged."

"You are, of course, very welcome to accompany us," Mr. Hammond said politely, but his true reply was deep in his steady gaze: *For her sake, do not come.*

Helen frowned. What did he mean, *for her sake?*

She saw his lordship's eyes narrow at the silent message, then cut to her in consternation: Had she seen it too? It was no use trying to hide the fact that she had, and on a rush of hot shame came the knowledge of Mr. Hammond's meaning. He knew about the energy between herself and Lord Carlston. Not only that, he had seen its effect upon her mind and body. Most likely on his lordship's mind and body too. Dear God, was it obvious to everyone?

The same thought had patently crossed his lordship's mind, for he closed his eyes for an appalled moment.

"No, I will not go this time," he said to Mr. Hammond, his voice clipped. "The two of you go alone, but keep this visit brief."

"A drink in a tavern and then we will return," Mr. Hammond said, a note of apology in his voice.

"It is settled, then," his lordship said. He walked to the doors, and Geoffrey opened them with a bow.

"Lord Carlston?" Lady Margaret called. "I thought we were to review Lady Helen's alchemy knowledge this morning?"

He turned back, his hand clenched at his side as he bowed. "You are quite right, but if you will excuse me, I must attend to other business." He directed a cold glance at Mr. Hammond; the apology, it seemed, was not accepted. "Use the time to prepare Lady Helen for her excursion tomorrow."

He bowed to Lady Margaret again, then strode from the salon, Geoffrey closing the doors behind him.

The room was silent.

"Is something amiss about your trip to Lewes?" Delia asked Helen. "His lordship seems displeased."

"You are mistaken," Helen said flatly. She aimed her own cold glance at Mr. Hammond. "Lord Carlston is not displeased."

She turned back to the mirror. Beneath her heartbeat she could still feel the other persistent pulse—that unbidden attunement to him. She dug her fingers into her new-waxed crop, driven by a sudden fierce impulse to push it back to how it had been before. But her hair was gone; she could not go back.

Slowly she lowered her hands, averting her eyes from the shorn, wretched girl in the mirror.

Seven

Tuesday, 7 July 1812

EVEN AT DUSK on a Tuesday evening, there were still a number of carriages on the road into Lewes. Mr. Hammond had neatly steered their gig past a stately landau, a post-chaise, and a sleek phaeton, but their quick progress came to an end as they drew up behind a farm dray, its wide berth and ambling progress forcing the chestnut to drop into a slow walk.

"What is the time?" Mr. Hammond asked, glaring at the broad back of the farmer. "Lowry said to meet him at nine."

Helen dug her fingers into the leather-lined fob pocket of her breeches and pulled out her touch watch. She squinted at the diamond arrow set in the center of the enameled case, but with no carriage lamps lit and only a sliver of rising moon, she could not make out the time. Still, that was the advantage of owning a touch watch. She drew her forefinger down the diamond arrow and slowly felt her way along the line of gems to the head. It pointed between the eighth and ninth emeralds set around the edge.

"Close on half past eight," she said, and returned the watch to her pocket. The weight of it against her hip was a comfort, as was the hidden Iceland spar lens inside. She would make sure to check the tavern with it before they entered. They were not there to chase out Deceivers, but it was always best to know if any were present.

"We are no more than ten minutes from the inn," Mr. Hammond said. "We should be well in time."

Helen sounded her agreement, but her attention was on the castle silhouetted on the hill to the left of the town. She had read about it in her guidebook: built in the eleventh century, and now a ruin of only two round towers and a gatehouse. Even so, it held a certain Gothic majesty, especially in the nominal moonlight. She was not one for omens, but the sight of it standing over the town seemed portentous.

She rubbed her hands along the soft buckskin on her thighs, trying to dry the dampness of her palms and quell the nervous jump of her leg. Lowry had almost the same strength as she did and knew how to disable a Reclaimer. She could think of no reason for him to attack—he wanted to sell the journal, after all—yet she had to be ready for all eventualities.

"Thank the Lord," he said as the dray made a ponderous turn into a side road. "We could have made better time on foot."

Helen glanced at him, surprised by the heat in his words. She was not the only nervous one. The thought was even more unsettling.

He urged the chestnut into a trot, and they were soon in the middle of the town, passing a neat post office, McLee's Circulating Library, and the White Hart Inn, a handsome Tudor posting house. Helen caught sight of a fine blue bonnet in a milliner's window, and then they were climbing School Hill and crossing a narrow bridge in a hollow thud of hooves and grind of wheels. The river Ouse, Helen remembered as she peered down at the dark water beneath them. Then Mr. Hammond called, "Hold on!" and she grabbed the edge of the gig as they swung into a right turn, drove under a low archway, and came to a clattering halt in the cobblestoned yard of the Bear Inn.

Three men in shirtsleeves and faded weskits—river men by their bare feet and muddied breeches—sat on blocks of stone near the tavern door, watching their arrival.

Mr. Hammond gathered the reins into one hand and said loudly, "I told you I'd get you here in under an hour, Amberley. Do you concede I am the better driver?"

The masquerade was on. Helen, in her guise as Charles Amberley, young buck about town, drew back her shoulders and climbed down from the gig, making a show of looking around. The yard was enclosed by a double-story tavern, a long wing of rooms for travelers, and a ramshackle assortment of outbuildings.

"I concede I owe you a bottle of claret, Hammond." She was pleased with the pitch of her voice: a good, manly tenor. It had been a hard road over the past weeks to modulate her feminine tones, but Lady Margaret's coaching had been most effective. "That is if we ever get a boy to take the horse," she added.

The snide comment was designed to carry, and a few moments later a shifty-eyed ostler appeared from the dingy stable. Hammond tossed him a coin, gave a few brief instructions for the mare's tenancy, then made his way toward the tavern.

Helen followed, glancing over her shoulder as the ostler led the mare and gig to a stall. It was clear from the tavern's shabby exterior and the lounging river men at the door that the Bear had lost the war for genteel custom to the more centrally located White Hart.

Helen pulled out her touch watch again as they passed the men and strode through the doorway. Better to be busy with a timepiece than try to outstare so much masculinity. Maintaining a bold gaze was one of the hardest parts of the masquerade.

"Hold a moment," she said softly in the dim foyer. Only one

sputtering candle in a dirty lamp lit the cramped, smoky area, the dull light catching the rich green enamel of the watch case, making it ripple. Ahead, the sound of male voices and shrill female laughter thrummed from the taproom. "Let me check for Deceivers."

Hammond stood at the inner door, shielding her as she clicked the three parts of the lens into place. She held it to her eye. Pale blue outlines shimmered around all of the bar patrons. Except one.

Her lens stopped on a sandy-haired man seated on a bench with a woman on his lap, most of her sagging breasts shockingly exposed, and another gent seated at his side. To all ordinary eyes, the sandy gent was a handsome middling sort, wearing a good coat and with a fine set of whiskers. Only Helen could see the bright blue energy around him and the obscene gray feeder tentacle that extended from his back. It curled around the bare shoulder of the woman lolling against his chest, its thick circumference pulsing as it drew on her energy.

Helen quelled a shudder. A Luxure Deceiver, if she were not mistaken, feeding on the drunken lust of the woman. The tentacle rose like the head of a cobra, then slid across the other man's hands as he squeezed the harlot's breasts, drawing on his energy too. The three of them laughed raucously, the woman thrusting her chest harder into the kneading hands. Helen felt her jaw lock with revulsion.

"There is one," she said, lowering the lens, "but it is skimming."

Therefore not her business, she reminded herself as she folded the three-part lens back into the body of the watch. A Reclaimer was to approach a Deceiver only if it was glutting upon one person, or its skim-feeding was causing obvious harm to its victims.

"Lowry is already here," Hammond said, tilting his chin at a man sitting alone at one of the plank tables set at the far wall. "Do you wish to stay for a moment more, or shall we go in?"

A candle in a sconce above Lowry cast his face into shadow, but Helen could sense his fixed stare upon the doorway. A wide space had been left around his table. It seemed the patrons of the Bear recognized a dangerous man when they saw one.

"I am ready," Helen said, ignoring the tightening of her gut. She kept the watch in her fist; a handy weapon. "I shall go first."

Hammond hesitated, then stood aside.

They entered the large room—intolerably humid from the press of people and an unnecessary fire in the hearth—and weaved their way around the crowded tables and benches. Helen took shallow breaths, her Reclaimer sense of smell revolted by the stink of malty ale, sour wine, and hot bodies all underpinned by a faint wash of urine. The sweat under her breast band itched almost as much as the false hair at her temples, yet she could not address either.

She focused on Lowry. He had straightened at their entrance and she saw a flash of pale tongue as he licked his lips. Was it nerves or anticipation?

"Oy!" Helen turned at the sharp protest. An old man in a drab suit glared up at her from a stool. "Watch where you're going, pup. You nearly had my drink over."

Helen lifted her chin and drew in a haughty breath, then froze. She had almost told him not to speak to her in such a way. A woman's words. No, a *lady's* words.

The man stared at her; what should she do? A raucous burst of laughter from a nearby table broke her indecision.

With a slight bow, she said, "My apologies, sir."

The man squinted at her, then nodded and turned back to his ale.

"That was close," Hammond murmured.

She glanced sharply at him; he had seen her falter. Well, she would not allow another mistake.

Ahead, the Deceiver had his hands under the woman's patched

skirts, the tentacle, no doubt, crawling across her private skin. Helen forced her eyes away from them. She could not challenge the creature, but maybe she could intervene. At Almack's, she had seen Lord Carlston use his touch watch to persuade a Deceiver to leave the ballroom. Perhaps she could do the same here. Show Mr. Hammond she was a true Reclaimer.

"This way," she said to him, and swerved around a table of soberly dressed tradesmen intent upon the words of one of their number who had come to his feet with the passion of his speech. She caught a snatch of his polemic: ". . . not at the current price of wheat. We must act!"

The Deceiver was at the next bench, his attention fully upon the harlot in his lap. Helen clutched her touch watch, feeling her palm dampen around the smooth enamel. Did she dare? What if the creature attacked? No, it was not likely in so crowded a public place.

She was almost upon him. It was now or never.

With heart thudding, she lurched into him and grabbed his meaty shoulder. The telltale itch of his recent feed crawled across her skin. With her other hand, she pressed hard upon the diamond arrow on the watch, deforming the Iceland spar inside to create a spark of energy. It passed through the circuit of her Reclaimer body: a slight tingle for her, but something far more brutal for him. His heavy muscles jerked under her grip as the mechanical charge delivered a dose of toxic energy. He swung around, his pained, outraged eyes meeting her own.

"My apologies, sir," she said, showing her teeth.

"I'm doing no harm," he hissed, pulling away.

"Harm enough," Helen said.

The woman smiled blearily in her direction. "Yer a pretty boy," she slurred. "Wanna join us, sweethe—" The invitation turned into a shriek as the Deceiver pushed her off his lap onto the filthy floor. "I thought we was having a night of it," she whined. "You said all night."

Helen moved on, leaving the harlot's protests behind.

"I take it that was the creature?" Hammond asked.

Helen nodded. Her hands were shaking.

"He's leaving," Hammond reported.

Holy heaven, she had just chased away her first Deceiver. "Good," she answered with a smile, riding the elation.

Ahead, Lowry was watching with interest; he had seen the confrontation. She fought the impulse to look over her shoulder to make sure the creature had gone. A real Reclaimer would not look back, and she had to appear strong in front of Lowry.

He stood as they reached his table, a jerk of his chin acknowledging the tussle. "A Luxure?"

Helen nodded.

"I hate Luxures," he said without heat, and waved over a wiry serving girl. "Three tankards, and don't dawdle."

The girl ducked her head and bustled off with the order.

Bartholomew Lowry was exactly as Helen remembered: not overly tall, but with a broad, powerful build and a fleshy face that was veined from drink. A line of sweat sat above his upper lip and in the cleft of his heavy chin, and stringy brown hair hung blunt on either side. His clothes were the usual low-middling mix of old and new: his burgundy weskit still had rich color and sheen, but the cravat at his neck was yellowed and limp, and the points of his linen shirt were grimed above the worn collar of his drab jacket. His eyes were green and pig-small, with a cunning intelligence that set the skin crawling. Especially, Helen thought, when they lingered insolently on her groin. She clenched her teeth; she would not flinch.

His pale tongue flicked out again. "You make a comely man. You should watch yourself around him." He nodded at Hammond.

"He might forget you're not a real boy and take you back-wise."

Helen froze at the profanity. But that was what he wanted, wasn't it? To shock her and enrage Hammond. She cleared her throat, sending a warning glance at her companion: *Do not rise to it.*

Hammond's blue eyes were dark with fury, but he gave a slight nod.

"Where are my manners?" Lowry said, and waved a mocking hand toward the benches. "I beg you, sit, Mr. . . . ?"

"Amberley," Helen said.

"Mr. *Amberley.*"

Helen stopped herself from saying thank you and stepped over the bench, remembering at the last minute to flick out her coattails as she sat. Hammond took the seat by her side. His face was rigid with dislike, but he had himself under control.

"You know why we are here," Helen began. "I have authority—"

She stopped as the serving girl approached with tankards clasped in her reddened hands.

"'Ere you go." The girl slid them onto the table, sending a small, gap-toothed smile in Helen's direction. "You want anyfing else?"

Lowry gave a yellowed leer. "My young friend here might be up for a tumble later," he said, raising his brows.

The girl eyed him waspishly. "I ain't no whore, sir."

"Well, then, he won't pay you," Lowry said, snorting a laugh.

Helen smiled at the girl. "That will be all, thank you."

The courtesy drew a shy sideways glance and a mottled blush.

Lowry dug inside his breeches pocket and tossed three grubby coins onto the table. "There, that's a penny over. Surely you'll spread your legs for that?"

The girl gathered up the coins. "Only to take a piss." She sent a last sliding glance at Helen, and was gone.

Lowry burst out laughing. "I'd like to take my whip to her—I reckon she'd kick and scream good."

From all that Hammond had told her, Lowry was not speaking euphemistically. He pushed a tankard across to Helen. She stopped its trajectory with a flat hand.

"I am not here to drink, Lowry. I am here for the journal."

He sobered immediately. "Just you and me." He turned a pugnacious smile upon Hammond. "You go wait outside like a good little lapdog." He tilted his head. "Or should that be arse dog." He snorted again.

"I'm not going anywhere," Hammond said.

"This is Reclaimer and Terrene business. Not for the likes of you." Lowry took another swig, his eyes on Helen. He wiped his mouth on his sleeve. "I know he's not your Terrene."

"No."

"I hear your maid is going to be your Terrene."

"How do you know that?"

"I still got a friend or two in the Dark Days Club." He gave another amused snort. "A girl Reclaimer and a girl Terrene. I can imagine Pike's view on that. You haven't done the bond ritual yet, eh?"

"No."

He smiled and leaned back, his eyes finding Hammond again. "Like I said, Reclaimer and Terrene business, and you ain't neither."

He was not going to deal until they were alone. "Wait in the yard," she told Hammond. "This will not take long."

He gave a small shake of his head. "I will not leave you with this man."

Helen clenched her fists on her thighs. He was making her look weak. "Go," she ordered.

He angled his face from her own, bracing against her insistence.

She leaned closer and whispered, "He will not bargain while you are here. Do you want us to fail?"

Hammond hissed out a breath, logic finally overcoming his

distrust. He stood, his eyes on Lowry. The former Terrene gave a contemptuous wave, then raised his tankard again and drank deeply.

Hammond stepped back over the bench, pausing for a moment near Helen's ear to whisper, "I will be at the doorway if you need me."

She nodded, although if Lowry did attack, it would be at Terrene speed. Hammond would have no chance of getting near her in time.

"Well, now," Lowry said as Hammond walked away, "that, there, is the crux of the problem."

He placed his emptied tankard on the table and pulled across Hammond's abandoned one, the ale slopping over the side. Helen watched him. No need to ask the question: he was going to tell her anyway.

"That's why female Reclaimers don't work," he pronounced. "A man wants to protect a woman, even when the chit in question could tear his head off with one hand."

Helen let the comment pass. "Pike wants the journal," she said steadily, her voice pitched for privacy, although no one sat close enough to hear in the babble of the room. "I have the authority to offer you five thousand pounds."

Lowry leaned his elbows on the rough plank table. "Straight to business." He pointed a forefinger at her chest, a crescent of dirt beneath the nail. "You have the black heart of a merchant, *Mr. Amberley.*"

"Five thousand," she repeated, ignoring the insult.

Lowry rested his chin on his hands. "Has he told you anything about it?"

"Enough," she said warily.

"Did he mention what it's written in?"

"What do you mean?"

Lowry smiled. "Benchley wrote the whole thing in blood. Real hard to read, in more ways than one. Makes you want to puke after looking at it awhile."

"Blood? Whatever for?"

He lifted a shoulder. "He never told me the whys and wherefores. We did do quite a bit of blood collecting, though."

Helen regarded him narrowly. Was he just trying to scare her or was the journal really written in blood? She could see no deception in his small eyes, only unholy enjoyment. From her reading, she knew that blood was one of the carrier elements of alchemy, just like hair. The *Colligat* that her mother had created—now in the hands of the Grand Deceiver—had been made out of hair, its power woven into the strands. Perhaps the journal had power woven into its blood ink? A disturbing thought.

"Want to know where we got the blood for the last bit?"

"I do not," Helen said curtly.

He grinned. "Ratcliffe Highway."

The name of the infamous murders brought a chill of horror. "Are you saying it is written in the blood of those people? That poor baby?"

"We were after the blood of the two Deceivers among them. But it got messy in there."

"You are disgusting."

"Well, then, you won't want to know what I copied out about your parents." He reached into his jacket pocket, pulled out a grimy, creased piece of paper, and placed it on the table. "Call it an enticement."

An enticement for what? Pike was already offering to buy the journal.

"How do I know what it says is real?"

He reached for the paper. "You don't have to read it if you don't believe me."

Helen snatched it up; she had to know what was on it. Ignoring his soft laugh, she angled the slip of paper toward the dim glow of the candle. The writing sprawled in an upward slant, the letters ill formed. Squinting, she slowly made out their meaning.

Lady C and Lord D boarded the Dolphin at Southampton 25 May 1802. VC told me they were intending to flee to France.

The sentence stopped. Helen turned the paper over; nothing written on the back. Was the information genuine? The twenty-fifth was the day before her parents had died, and the *Dolphin* was certainly their yacht. Moreover, no one had known her mother and father had decided to flee to France. It seemed likely it was real.

"Who is this VC?" she demanded. "You've read the rest of it, haven't you? Tell me what it said."

"If I told you everything, you wouldn't need the journal." He tilted his head to one side. "I'll tell you one thing, though: Benchley thought he and Carlston were the ones meant to fight the Grand Deceiver. Not you. He said you was just the bringer of evil."

"I'm not the one who kills babies and innocent people."

Lowry snorted. "Girl, you just wait a bit. You'll be killing like us in no time, or you'll be dead."

She ignored the vile prophecy and slid the scrap of paper into her jacket pocket. "I'm keeping this."

Lowry shrugged. "I've got the original, and five thousand ain't enough for it."

Pike had said fifteen thousand was the maximum offer, and

after that she had to make it clear that the Dark Days Club would take it by force. Would this man even care about such a threat?

"Fifteen thousand in gold. That is the most I can offer."

"Fifteen thousand in gold," he repeated. "Holy Mother of Christ." He looked around the smoky room and drew a deep breath through flared nostrils. "Well, that answers the question of how much Pike wants it. If you'd offered me that a week ago, I'd have taken it. But not now." He licked his lips. "Now there's something I want far more than just money, and it's the only thing I'll take for the journal."

What on earth could he want other than money? She did not have the authority to promise anything else.

"What is it?"

He leaned forward, his eyes fixed on her like the ravening hyena she had once seen at the Exeter. "Change. I don't want to lose my Terrene powers," he said softly. "The only way I can keep them is to bond with another Reclaimer—you. Tell Pike if he makes me your Terrene, he can have the journal."

"No!" She jerked back from the demand. "I already have a Terrene."

"You just said you ain't bonded yet. Easy for me to step in and take over."

"It is a ridiculous idea. You could never enter my world. You are too low."

"That won't wash in the Dark Days Club, *my lady*," he said, pitching his voice for Reclaimer ears only. "Pike was a butcher's son; now he's Second Secretary. I grew up in the Brighton work-house, and I rose to be Benchley's Terrene. It don't matter where you come from in our line of work. Besides, you're trying to place your own maid as your Terrene. She's got an estate and fine manners, has she?"

"At least she is civilized," Helen snapped. He had been in the workhouse? She almost felt a stab of pity. *Almost.* "Pike has already agreed to my choice. The matter is settled."

He regarded her with narrowed eyes. "Pike don't want two women doing what we do—it ain't natural." He sat back and crossed his arms. "I know he'd get rid of you if he was able, but he can't change the accident of your birth. Mark my words, he'll jump at the chance of getting rid of your maid and putting me in her place. Not only will he get the journal, he'll save his precious Home Office fifteen thousand pounds and get an experienced Terrene to keep you in line."

"No. Pike . . ." Helen's mouth dried around her words. He was right: Pike would take the offer in a heartbeat. And if she was to believe the scrap of paper in her pocket—which she did—the journal really did contain information about her parents and most probably Lord Carlston, too. Even so, she could not have this man as her Terrene. It was unthinkable.

"I don't want you." It was all she could manage to say.

He shrugged. "Did you take the oath?"

She pressed her lips together.

"Of course you did. You're bound by law to do what Pike says. Or will you go against your King and your word?"

"You have."

He squinted at her, sizing her up. "You wouldn't break an oath—far too noble and moral for that kind of thing." He wagged an admonishing forefinger. "You need to learn how the world really works. Go tell Pike he can have the journal as soon as you and me are bonded. We'll do the ritual on the twenty-fourth, the full moon—it makes the strongest bond. That means you got seventeen days to make the preparations. I'll tell you where we meet. And if you do as I say, like a good girl, I'll let you see what else Benchley wrote about your traitor mother."

Helen clenched her fists, every fiber in her body aching to reach across and close her hand around his throat. To force the information out of him. Force the whereabouts of the journal out of his swelling, blue face.

He gave a yip of laughter. "I can see the violence in your eyes, but you won't do it, will you? You can't. Don't worry, when we're bonded, I'll make a real Reclaimer out of you." He leaned across the table, fleshy lips wet, his voice only for Reclaimer ears. "And a real woman. I'll enjoy holding you down, grounding you to the earth like a good Terrene."

Abruptly she stood, the bench toppling over from the force.

The two men at the nearest table turned. Helen felt their interest spread to the group on the next table and the one after that, a cascade of unwanted curiosity. She bit back her words and stepped over the bench. Her body wanted to fight or run or scream, but all she could do was back away.

Lowry picked up his tankard again and gave her a lazy wink. "Good evening, Mr. Amberley. I'll be seeing you again."

She turned and made for the doorway, pursued by the image of Lowry lying across her body, his sweating weight pressing her against the earth. Like a good Terrene.

Eight

TEN MINUTES LATER, Helen was gripping the edge of the gig seat as the chestnut clattered back across the bridge. She had uttered only one word in the yard—"Go"—and had not spoken since, afraid that she would scream or weep if she opened her mouth. Not the kind of behavior expected from a young man. She stared ahead, mind churning, barely seeing Hammond's anxious glances as he steadied the horse into a trot down School Hill.

She could not take Lowry as her Terrene. She pressed her hand to her mouth. The man was foul. Yet she and Hammond had to retrieve Benchley's journal from him. How could it be done without sacrificing herself? She had to find a way, and be quick about it. They had less than three weeks before the full moon.

"Lady Helen, tell me what happened." The lamp at the side of the gig cast a weak light across Hammond's face, shading his eyes and mouth into dark pits of worry. "Please say something."

She held up her hand: *Not yet*. A glimmer of an idea was showing itself. She sat forward, gaze on the road ahead, but all her attention fixed upon the problem. For the moment, Pike only wanted the journal; he did not know of Lowry's demand. Did he know its contents had been written in such gruesome ink? She would wager he did. The journal's alchemical property was probably what he was hiding from them. Did it contain more than just information? Whatever the case, if she and Hammond found the book and delivered it to Pike, they had achieved their mission. They would be safe, and Pike would have no need to bargain with Lowry.

Yes, they had to find the journal and steal it. But how? Lowry could have hidden it anywhere.

Helen shook her head, the size of the task overwhelming her train of thought.

They passed the White Hart, its oil lamps and torches casting a yellow glow into the dark street. Three men departing through the front door stopped and watched them whisk past. Closing her eyes, Helen lifted her face into the breeze made from their speed, letting the cool air clear her panic.

Where would a man like Lowry hide the journal? She did not know enough about him even to make a guess. That would be the first step, then: to find out more about Bartholomew Lowry.

Of course, stealing the journal did not remove Lowry as a problem. If Pike came to know that the man wished to return to the Dark Days Club as her Terrene, he might see Lowry as a viable alternative to Darby, even if the journal was no longer in play. There was only one way to stop that terrible future: she had to bond with Darby as soon as her maid was ready. Perhaps even sooner.

"For God's sake, tell me what he said," Hammond entreated.

She opened her eyes. Yes, she could speak now. "Pull over."

He tightened the reins, drawing the mare into a walk and finally a stop at the grassy edge of the road. They were alongside the castle again, its ruined towers and gatehouse looming over them. In clipped sentences, Helen told him what had occurred in her interview with Lowry.

Hammond listened, his lips drawn back over his teeth in disgust. "Dear God, you say the book is written in blood?" He shook his head. "Benchley was mad as a hatful of snakes, and

Lowry is not much better. You cannot have him as your Terrene."
His flattened hand wiped the air, banishing the possibility. "I
cannot even think it. The bond is partly in mind as well as body.
A Reclaimer must trust their Terrene to protect them in their
most vulnerable moments. You have seen how Mr. Quinn must
inflict pain upon his lordship to draw him back from the edge
of madness."

Yes, she had seen it in Vauxhall Gardens. Mr. Quinn had drawn
a spike and stabbed his lordship through the hand to break the
thrall of the Deceiver energy in his lordship's body. It had been
the first time she had seen a Deceiver, and the first time she had
seen the violent bond between Reclaimer and Terrene. The shock
of both still prickled across her skin.

"Mr. Quinn knows how to inflict the minimum amount of force
to counter the Deceiver energy," Mr. Hammond continued. "But
you could never trust Lowry to be so careful. On the contrary, he
would take pleasure in hurting you. He would take advantage of
you at every possible opportunity, in every possible way."

Helen lifted her shoulders, trying to shift the too vivid imagining of Lowry's hands upon her body. "He has already indicated
such intimacies."

"He is a vile dog, and dangerous with it." Hammond stared up
at the castle and hissed out a breath. "He is right about one thing,
though: Pike will take his offer."

"As I see it," Helen said, "we must deliver the journal to Pike
or we will both be in peril, but we cannot tell him about Lowry's
demand."

"I agree. But how are we to deliver the journal?"

"We must find it ourselves."

What if he did not think it possible? That she was being a fool.
He regarded her solemnly. "How do you propose to do that?"

"Where would you hide something illicit and of infinite value?"

"If it was of infinite value, I would not let it leave my sight."

"True," Helen conceded. "But if you were someone like Lowry and wished to trade it, you could not carry it to a deal, in case it was forced from you."

Hammond nodded. "Then I would hide it somewhere secure. A bank, or Boodle's."

"I doubt Lowry is a member of Boodle's," Helen said dryly. "Would you not hide it in a place you knew well or with a person you trusted?"

"Well, I would trust Margaret with anything." He scratched his chin, considering. "You think he has placed it with a family member or a friend?"

"I am *hoping* he has done so."

"I would warrant he has no friends, or at least none that could be trusted. Does he have any family?"

"I do not know, but I think I have a way to find out." Helen leaned forward and, even though no one was around, lowered her voice. "While he was gloating, he let slip that he grew up in Brighton. Lord Carlston has said more than once that old Martha Gunn, the dipper, knows everything about everyone in the town. Surely she would know if Lowry has siblings or other family in the vicinity?"

"Perhaps." Hammond was silent for a moment, then nodded. "Yes, family would answer why he is in the area. If luck is on our side, this Gunn woman could point us in the right direction."

Helen sat back in the gig seat. Thank heavens he thought the plan had merit.

"I will make an appointment to take a dip in the sea with her in the next few days," she said.

He touched her arm, a fleeting gesture of camaraderie. "This meeting with Lowry may not have gone as we wished, but you rallied well."

"I ran from him—that is not rallying well."

"You beat a strategic retreat," he said, gathering the reins again. "Never underestimate the value of a good retreat."

She smiled at the quick rejoinder, but could not shake her growing sense of failure. They had no guarantee that her plan would yield a path to follow. And in all truth, her male disguise had not been much put to the test. She had frozen shamefully when the old man had spoken to her, and her interactions with the Deceiver and the serving girl had been so swift as to be negligible.

"I am not doing very well as a young man, am I?"

Hammond angled his face toward her, the lamplight gilding the draw of his brow. "Nonsense. Under the circumstances, you are doing splendidly."

He flicked the reins, urging the horse once more onto the road. Helen braced herself as the gig bumped back into motion, warmed by his vehemence. Even so, his belief did not drive away her own doubts. Or those of Lord Carlston.

"His lordship would not agree with you," she said over the grind of the wheels. "He does not think I am up to the task of being a Reclaimer."

"You are wrong." Hammond turned his attention from the shadowy road that stretched before them and regarded her, clearly weighing up his next words. "He is worried that you have lived the cloistered life of a young lady too long and will not be able to overcome your gentle upbringing."

"Is that what you think?"

He shook his head. "Not at all. You have the warrior within you—we all saw it when your full strength came at the Lamb Tavern—and I believe it will eventually conquer any feminine diffidence. I am sure his lordship believes the same. Besides, you chased off that Deceiver at the inn with great expediency."

True, but she had been afraid through the whole of the encounter. She looked up at the sliver of moon above the castle. So Lord Carlston feared she was too civilized, too feminine. She wet her lips, remembering the animal savagery she had felt on the arrival of her full Reclaimer strength. She had lost all precious reason, all control, and had tried to kill his lordship. It had been one of the most terrifying moments of her life. One that she did not want to repeat. Yet Lord Carlston was waiting—no, hoping—for that warrior to emerge again and carry her beyond the bounds of morality and reason.

⁓

THEY ARRIVED BACK at German Place just as the distant church bell marked eleven o'clock. Most of the houses were dark, but as they clattered past their own dwelling on the way to the mews, Helen noted the drawing room windows. Their shutters were still open, the room lit for occupancy.

"They are awaiting our return."

"There is nothing to worry about," Mr. Hammond said, his voice pitched low. He turned the gig into the narrow side lane that led to the stables. "We have our story prepared. Just stay with the truth except for anything to do with Lowry."

They handed the mare and gig to the young groom on duty and made their way to the house in silence. Garner collected their hats in the foyer, advising that they were expected in the drawing room. *Stay with the story*, Helen chanted to herself, and led the way upstairs. Yet the prospect of lying outright to his lordship dried her mouth and set her heart racing. Lud, she hoped Hammond was in a better state.

As they approached the doors, someone began playing the pianoforte—a Beethoven piece—and playing it well. Not Lady Margaret's usual choice of composer or her style of play, which sometimes had an unfortunate thumpety-thump rhythm. No, this was an elegant and sensitive rendering.

Geoffrey, stationed outside the room, opened the doors, but Helen stopped on the threshold, brought to a halt by the person at the pianoforte. Delia. Of course; how could she have forgotten that her friend was musical, although it seemed her skill had increased tenfold since their seminary days. She made a charming vision, too: the candelabrum set upon the instrument lit her loosely dressed hair into a celestial pale gold shimmer and brought a pearly glow to her skin. She was dressed in pristine white muslin, a row of glass beads around the low neckline catching the flickering light and drawing the eye to her creamy décolletage.

Lord Carlston sat on the sofa opposite, one elbow propped on the gilded arm, his chin cupped in his hand. All of his attention seemed to be upon Delia, the ever-present knit of pain between his brows for once eased. Helen felt her body lock. Right then, Delia was beautiful; she had conjured that alchemy that blended confidence and expertise into breathtaking transcendence. In the same instant, Helen knew that she, herself, stood in gentleman's garb, tall and awkward, with no expertise in anything.

She drew in a ragged breath. No, wait; his lordship's eyes were fixed upon Delia, but it was plain his thoughts were not. In his ease, she could read his expression, and it held such tenderness and sorrow that it could not have come from Delia's transfiguration or the music alone. Was he thinking about his missing wife? Surely such pining and regret could only belong to her memory.

"You are back," Lady Margaret said over the music, rising from the sofa.

Delia stopped playing.

His lordship turned, the effect of the piece still soft in his eyes.

So much sweet tenderness; how would it be to have such a look truly directed at one?

"Lady Helen!" He cleared his throat, a flush on his skin. "How went it?"

She could not answer, momentarily overwhelmed by the pulse that thundered in her blood. Lud, was she to be undone by a glance that belonged to a ghost?

"It went very well," Mr. Hammond said, ushering her further into the room. "A triumph, in fact."

Without further invitation, he launched into the abridged account of their excursion: the slow farmer's cart, the crowded inn, the heat, the confrontation with the Deceiver—

"I beg your pardon?" His lordship lifted his hand, stopping Mr. Hammond's flow. There was no tenderness in his face now. He addressed her abruptly. "Did Mr. Hammond just say you approached a Deceiver by yourself?"

Clearly she had done something wrong. "I saw him through my lens in the taproom," she said. "He was skimming, but taking energy from only two people, and I could see they were beginning to suffer. The woman particularly—she was quite inebriated."

"But he was skimming, not glutting?"

"Yes," she admitted. "But from only two people."

"Lady Helen managed it well," Hammond said hurriedly. "You would have been impressed by the way she used the watch to deliver a jolt of that electric energy." He gave a slightly nervous laugh. "He was out of there like a scalded—"

"Are you telling me that Lady Helen *engaged* the creature physically? By herself?"

Helen looked sideways at Mr. Hammond; he was rapidly digging a hole for them both. She saw him brace himself.

"Yes," he said. "But I was right behind her."

"Which would have amounted to nothing whatsoever if the

creature had decided to attack." His lordship paced across the room, still keeping his distance. "I cannot believe this, Hammond. How did 'take a drink in a tavern' translate to 'engage an unknown Deceiver'? I thought I could trust you to ensure Lady Helen's safety. Instead you urge her into premature danger."

Hammond turned his head as if his lordship's accusation were a physical blow. Still, he said, "You wanted her to take more initiative. To overcome her natural diffidence."

"Initiative is very different from recklessness. Or negligence, for that matter."

Hammond stiffened. "Do you imply that I have been negligent?"

Helen stepped forward. "No, it was my fault. I did not tell him what I was going to do. It was a spur-of-the-moment decision."

His lordship whirled around. "Which makes it even worse." He dug his fingers into the bone above his temple, the knit of pain back between his brows. "How many times have I said that you must always approach an unknown creature with caution? Did you have a strategy in mind if it decided to attack rather than run?"

She had not even given thought to the possibility, and he saw it in her face.

"God Almighty!"

Helen winced at the violent blasphemy. Nevertheless, he was not being fair. "You told me yourself that it is unlikely a Deceiver would attack a Reclaimer in a public place. Besides, I saw you chase out that Deceiver, Mr. Jessup, from Almack's in exactly the same manner. Your Terrene was not beside you then."

He waved away the defense. "It is not the same. I have known Mr. Jessup for years. We had our battle years ago, and he knows I am the stronger. He would not dare raise an energy whip against me."

"The Luxure in the tavern had not glutted; it had no whips," Helen said quickly.

"A Deceiver does not need energy whips to inflict damage upon us. Especially an untrained Reclaimer like yourself. As soon as you stepped out of that tavern, you were vulnerable. Was the stable yard full of people? The road to Brighton crowded with carriages?"

She stared down at the carpet; there had been many opportunities for an attack. "No."

"That Deceiver could have come at you in any of those places, and without the support of a Terrene, you could have been killed." He paced back across the room, the heel of his hand pressed against his forehead. "You could have been killed, and then where would we be?"

"Well, she was not killed, or even attacked," Lady Margaret said. "Surely we can be thankful for that." She walked over to him and laid her hand on his arm, her voice dropping. "The pain is back, isn't it?"

He drew in a deep breath. "It is nothing."

"Come, sit down," she urged. "I am sure my brother and Lady Helen now realize that their heedless behavior—"

"Do not apologize for me, Margaret," Mr. Hammond said tightly. He strode across to the sideboard and lifted the crystal stopper from the decanter. "Brandy, Lady Helen?"

"Thank you, no," Helen said.

"I do not appreciate that tone, Michael," Lady Margaret said.

He shrugged and poured himself a measure.

His sister regarded him for a long, unacknowledged moment, then turned back to his lordship. "Please, come and sit down."

"I am perfectly well. Thank you." Lord Carlston shrugged away her hand. "Lady Helen, tomorrow we will focus on defense techniques," he said curtly. "Wear your male garb again." He did not even wait for her nod but walked over to the pianoforte. "You play very well, Miss Cransdon," he said, patently trying to moderate his tone.

Delia, who still sat at the instrument, jumped at the sudden notice. "Thank you, Lord Carlston."

He bowed. "Would you favor us with another piece?"

"Of course."

She played the opening notes of a sweet ballad as he walked across to the hearth and frowned into the small fire that burned in the grate, one hand clasping the mantel.

Helen took a seat on the sofa, keeping him at the corner of her eye. His fingers were back against his temple. Mr. Hammond finished his brandy and poured another. Lady Margaret, stranded in the middle of the room, made her way to the armchair.

Helen listened to the heavy silence in the room that lay beneath the soaring music. She resisted the impulse to glance at Lord Carlston again, keeping her eyes on her hands clasped in her lap. Even so, she could feel his gaze upon her skin like a whisper touch. It seemed she could not please him whatever she did; either she was too much the warrior or too much the woman.

Nine

Wednesday, 8 July 1812

N EXT MORNING, BEFORE breakfast, Helen flicked back her coat-tails and took the seat at her secretaire to compose a note to Martha Gunn. *A dip, as soon as possible*, she requested, then signed the letter with her flourish, folded it into a packet, and sealed it with a damp wafer pressed flat with the heel of her hand.

She sat back in the gilded chair, considering the unhappy epilogue to last night's events. It had been humiliating to be scolded in front of everyone, but on reflection, his lordship had probably been right. Tackling the Deceiver by herself had been foolish. Although it had been a Luxure, and therefore not as vicious or unpredictable as a Cruor or Pavor, it could easily have attacked rather than fled. Even so, it had felt good to rout the creature, to have finally acted as a Reclaimer. Surely Lord Carlston would have to admit that she had, at least, managed the use of the touch watch very well.

She picked up her quill again, dipped it in the ink, and inscribed the East Street address on the front of the packet.

"Darby," she called.

Her maid emerged from the adjoining dressing room. In the short time that Helen had finished dressing and applied herself to the note, Darby had made some changes to her own toilette: an extra braid worked into her soft brown hair, and a new pin-tucked chemisette under the neckline of her second-best blue gown. No doubt all for the benefit of Mr. Quinn again.

"Will you deliver this, please, while we are at breakfast," Helen said, passing across the sealed packet. "I am seeking an appointment with Mrs. Gunn. You are to wait for an answer."

Darby read the address. "Yes, my lady." She hesitated, then added, "I've heard that she is booked up for a week in advance, my lady."

Helen beckoned Darby a step closer and lowered her voice. "Mrs. Gunn knows I am acquainted with Lord Carlston. Tell her my need is pressing. This is Dark Days business, and is to be kept between you and me for now, Reclaimer and Terrene."

"Do you not mean Terrene-in-training, my lady," Darby said lightly.

"No, I mean Terrene," Helen said with some force. She wanted no mistake made about her intent. "In my mind, our bond is already made."

"Of course, my lady. I meant no disrespect," Darby said earnestly. "I think of myself as your Terrene too."

Helen nodded. Lud, how she wished she could tell Darby about Lowry and Pike and the journal. But she could not, and the prohibition was a sore strain. She missed her maid's common sense and wise counsel.

"How goes your training?" she asked instead. "Has Mr. Quinn said when you will be ready for the bonding ritual?"

Darby's answer was lost to a loud knock on the door.

"Helen," Delia's voice called, "may I come in? I have something to show you."

For an instant Helen considered denying her friend, but the chance for private conversation with Darby had gone, particularly now that someone as *curious* as Delia stood outside the door.

"Yes, of course," she replied.

Delia bustled in, brandishing a letter. "Would you believe it? I have had an invitation from Pug Brompton to their gathering on Friday night."

"Indeed I believe it. Pug is a very amiable girl." Helen turned to Darby with a meaningful look. "You may go now."

Darby curtsied, the packet shifting from one hand to the other, out of Delia's line of sight, as she left the room.

Helen rose from her chair and adjusted the front of her jacket with a small tug; a male habit she was trying to cultivate. "As soon as Pug knew you were my guest, I am sure she thought to issue an invitation."

"It is a compliment to you," Delia said. "Her mother cut me at Donaldson's yesterday, looked right through me as if we had not met at least a dozen times during my seasons." She gathered her primrose muslin skirts and sat sidesaddle on the end of the bed, one satin-shod foot poking out from the ruffled hem and beating an agitated rhythm. "I will always be haunted by Mr. Trent, won't I? I will always be the ruined girl."

Helen kneeled on the royal blue bedcover, then tucked her legs up underneath herself; a much easier operation in a pair of buckskins. "You have a new calling now. Forget about the scandalmongers."

"Yes, of course, you are right. I will banish them." Delia wiped the air between them, expelling, it seemed, all scandalmongers from her mind, then took in Helen's relaxed pose. "I must say, you look very comfortable in your breeches and jacket." She regarded Helen with grave eyes. "How are you after last night? His lordship has no trouble expressing his disapproval, does he? The way he paced and that awful tone in his voice. Is he always so angry?"

Helen lifted one shoulder. "I probably deserved it."

Delia shook her head. "I cannot agree. It seems unfair to me. He says you must think for yourself, and yet when you do, you are admonished. He should be easier upon you while you are learning."

Helen opened her mouth to defend his lordship, then closed it again. Her friend had a point. His lordship had become far more hot-tempered since they had arrived in Brighton. A worrying situation, considering the vestige darkness within him.

"His lordship never promised me an easy time," she said dryly. "In fact, he promised me the opposite."

"It still does not seem fair to me. Even so, for all his bad temper, he is very handsome." She glanced sideways at Helen. "And an Earl."

Was Delia setting her cap at Lord Carlston? A flash of the previous night caught Helen in the chest: Delia dressed in white, playing for him.

"You do know that he is still considered to be married?" she said. "The law will not declare Lady Elise deceased for another three years."

Delia tilted her head, clearly perplexed. "Oh!" she said, coming to some realization. "You goose! I was not thinking of myself. I thought *you* were developing a tendresse for him. And he for you."

"No," Helen said quickly. "You are mistaken." So even Delia, a newcomer, could see the energy between them.

"Are you sure?"

"I am certain," Helen said firmly.

"Then I will say no more upon it." Delia folded Pug's invitation, pensively running the edge between her thumb and forefinger. "You know it is my dearest wish to help you as much as possible, but I must admit I am not sure what I am supposed to do as your aide. Do you wish me to report things that I have noted?"

"Noted about what?" Helen asked, still distracted by her visceral response to her friend's question about Lord Carlston. Clearly she was failing miserably to quell her attraction.

"Well . . ." Delia shifted, the bed creaking under the movement. "It is not so much noted as overheard."

That snapped Helen's attention back to her friend. "Delia! You have been eavesdropping again. You promised me you would stop!"

Her friend raised pale palms in contrition. "I know, and I *am* sorry, but I think you should hear what Lady Margaret said."

"I do not wish to hear what she said."

"I think you do."

The warning note in Delia's voice stopped Helen's next protest. She studied her friend's face, which was sincerely troubled. "If you must."

Delia looked over her shoulder at the closed door, then leaned closer. "Last night, Lady Margaret was talking to Lord Carlston in the drawing room before you returned from Lewes. She said that Darby and Mr. Quinn were 'becoming very close' and that Darby might not be the best choice of Terrene for you. She said a young maid of such low origin could not be relied upon to choose duty over love."

Helen drew back. "I can assure you, Darby is very mindful of her duty."

"It was not my remark, Helen. It was Lady Margaret's. And his lordship agreed."

"He agreed?"

"Yes."

Helen dug her fingertips into the silk bedcover. Did they intend to replace Darby? No, she would not allow it. Especially not with Lowry lurking in the background.

"I know that you think Darby very loyal, but is it possible that Lady Margaret is correct?" Delia asked. "From my own experience with Mr. Trent, I know when it came to a choice between love and duty, I chose love without hesitation. To my own detriment, of course." She pressed the back of her hand against her throat; a gesture of embarrassment that Helen recognized from their school days. "I could not see past him, even though I was heading to my own ruin. The Natural Philosophers tell us that finding a mate and producing offspring is the most basic drive among animals. Do you think that Darby and Mr. Quinn can resist that drive?"

Helen regarded her friend with narrowed eyes. "I hope you are not intimating that Darby's station in life or Mr. Quinn's race make them more like animals."

"Of course not!" Delia waved away the suggestion with a flap of her hand. "But if Darby decides she wants the comfort of family and wishes to marry Mr. Quinn, would you insist upon her staying with you?"

Helen wanted to say yes, but knew she could never countenance such a cruel separation. She sighed and settled for, "I don't know. Probably not."

"Of course it may all come to nothing," Delia said. "The course of love is never straight. I just thought it would be prudent for you to consider other possibilities before his lordship takes the decision out of your hands." She stared into the distance for a moment, lips pursed. "Mr. Hammond would be a good alternative, don't you think? He is steady and reliable, and although not large, he would be quick." She leaned over and squeezed Helen's hand. "Or even myself, although I know I would not be your first choice. Too thin and scrawny now. However, if it comes to it, do not hesitate to ask."

Helen forced herself to smile. "Thank you."

"You do not hold it against me for telling you?"

"Of course not."

"But you look so stricken."

Helen shook her head, her fingernails clawed deep into the silk cover, anchoring her panic. "As you say," she said calmly, "it may never happen."

———

MIDWAY THROUGH BREAKFAST, Garner entered the morning room and made his stately way to Lady Margaret's side.

"Lord Carlston has arrived," he reported. "He has elected to go directly to the salon to await Lady Helen's convenience."

Delia paused in buttering a roll and asked Helen, "Do you think he is still angry?"

"Lord Carlston does not nurse his anger," Mr. Hammond said. He glanced at his sister. "Unlike others."

Ignoring her brother, Lady Margaret asked, "Did you pass on my invitation for his lordship to take breakfast with us, Garner?"

Helen met Delia's eyes: *Something seems to have occurred between the siblings.* Delia drew her mouth down—*I do not know*—and returned to her buttering.

"His lordship declined the invitation with thanks, my lady," Garner answered.

Helen placed her teacup back onto its saucer and crammed the last bite of her third piece of seed cake into her mouth. His lordship might not hold on to his anger, but she did not want to irritate him all over again by making him wait. And she needed to settle the question of Darby's Terrene status as soon as possible.

"I'll go now," she said around the mouthful. "His lordship will want to start training as soon as possible."

Besides, when they were training, he could not keep his distance. The unbidden—and unwanted—thought stopped her mid-chew.

Lady Margaret wrinkled her nose. "Please, close your mouth, Lady Helen. You may need to eat as much as a man now, but you do not have to chew like one at our private table."

Helen swallowed the cake. "I do apologize. Excuse me."

She pushed back her chair and made for the door, abandoning Delia, Mr. Hammond, and Lady Margaret to each other's disgruntled company.

Upstairs, Geoffrey stood at his station outside the salon. He bowed as she approached and reached for the door handles, but Helen stopped him with a shake of her head. She needed a moment to prepare, to ensure her mind was upon the matter at hand—Darby and their bonding ritual—and not lurking with foolish thoughts about his lordship.

With a conspiratorial smile at the footman, she stepped closer to listen through the oak. Her Reclaimer hearing distinguished the thud of two pairs of feet on the floorboards at the far end of the room, the creak of a chain, and quick breathing. Even after only a few weeks of training she recognized the sounds: Darby and Mr. Quinn working on tackles using the stuffed Hessian bag that hung from the ceiling. Her maid must have already been to Martha Gunn and returned. Did that mean she had her appointment?

She stretched her Reclaimer hearing and found the breath of another person near the front windows. Yes, she recognized that slow, steady rhythm: Lord Carlston. And the rustle of thin paper, too: he was reading the *London Gazette*. Not the action of a man still angry from the previous night. Mr. Hammond was right: his lordship was not one for holding a grudge.

"Why don't you come in, Lady Helen?" It was his voice, pitched for her Reclaimer hearing.

She stepped back, surprise breaking into a smile. Although an oak door and half a room separated them, she had heard him as if he stood by her side. He must have been listening for her tread up the stairs.

"Thank you, I will," she murmured, knowing he, in turn, would hear it.

She nodded to Geoffrey, who opened the doors.

His lordship sat beside the window, legs stretched out before him, newspaper angled toward the sunlight. He had removed his jacket, the muscular length of his body enhanced by the unbroken line of plain buff waistcoat and buckskins. The light cast his profile into relief, the bold classical symmetry of straight nose and broad cheekbones softened by the curve of his lips that still held some of the smile that had been in his voice. His attention, rather pointedly, was on the paper, not on her entrance.

She studied him for a moment longer, something jarring about his apparent composure. A *tenseness* beyond his normal ready manner. She twitched her shoulders. Here she was again, her thoughts on an impure path, and as guilty as Lady Margaret of over-watching the man.

She walked into the room, remembering her male stride, and bowed. "Good morning, Lord Carlston."

Lord Carlston folded the paper and placed it on the small table at his side. "Mr. Amberley." He rose smoothly from his chair and executed his own bow. "You may be interested to know that the Committee for Secrecy has been elected."

It was one of his tests. Well, she would show him she was prepared.

"Indeed? And is Mr. Wilberforce among their number?" She strolled over to the paper and picked it up, every nerve abuzz with the sense of his eyes upon her, and glanced at the page. Twenty-one names listed, including Wilberforce and Mr. Canning. "Ah, I see it is the case. The Luddites do not stand a chance against his fervor."

He regarded her with his half smile. "Yes, nicely done. Manner and voice are excellent. I would have no trouble believing you to be a young gentleman with an interest in national security."

She placed the paper back on the table, returning his smile. She would take it as a conciliation of sorts. Perhaps he, too, felt he had been unfair last night.

At the corner of her eye, she saw that Darby and Mr. Quinn had broken from their exercise and were watching with interest. The stuffed Hessian sack swung gently from its creaking chain behind them. Mr. Quinn had built it to resemble the size and weight of a man, a heavy wooden cross embedded within the sawdust and wool stuffing to mimic bones and skull.

She faced their scrutiny, forcing some nonchalance into her voice. "How goes Darby's training, Mr. Quinn? Do you think she will be ready to make the Terrene bond soon?"

"I do, my lady," Quinn said with a bow. He brushed self-consciously at the dust on his jacket. "If Miss Darby keeps training this well, she should be ready in time for the next full moon."

"Surely we could bond sooner than that?" Helen smiled, trying to mask the urgency behind the question. "I am keen to get it done."

Carlston stretched his arms behind him, driving the sitting kinks from his long body. "Both of you need to be ready, Lady Helen." She flushed at the implication that she was even less ready than Darby. "There is, to a certain extent, a union of mind as well. A sense of each other's essential self that informs the partnership. It is best to perform the ritual during a full moon, when the earth's energies can be used to produce the strongest bond in both mind and body."

"Surely it can still be done without the full moon?" Helen persisted.

"It can, but the exchange of strength is not as complete,"

Carlston said. "I want Darby to have the best chance of a complete bond."

"Aye," Mr. Quinn agreed. "And Miss Darby still has a way to go. She'll need to have me down and tied before I let her go out into the world as your Terrene."

Helen bit down on her disappointment. There would be no gain in arguing the point; she did not want them to mark her desperation.

"Is that a usual method for subduing a Reclaimer, Mr. Quinn?" she asked instead, only half teasing. After all, she had seen him stab Lord Carlston.

The big man's slow smile appeared. "No, my lady. Just between me and Miss Darby."

"Nathaniel!" Darby's fair skin flushed. "Don't mind him, my lady. His blood's up is all."

"Quite," Carlston said. "I think it is time for both of you to take some air."

Quinn ducked his head, smile still in place. "As you wish, my lord."

"Were you able to complete your errand?" Helen asked Darby as she prepared to leave.

"Yes, my lady. Two days hence." She met Helen's eyes for an eloquent moment, then curtsied and took Quinn's offered arm.

Helen nodded. Martha Gunn had agreed to see her on Friday. The first part of her plan was in motion.

His lordship watched the door close behind the two servants, the nail of his forefinger flicking hard against his thumb. He had clearly not realized the extent of Quinn's and Darby's affection for one another, and it troubled him. Well, it troubled her, too. Perhaps here was the opportunity to use Delia's ill-gotten information.

"I believe Mr. Quinn and Darby are well on their way to a deep attachment," she said carefully.

"I had not realized it had gone so far." He picked up the paper, looked at it distractedly for a moment, then tossed it back onto the table. "Fool. He should know better."

"Know better?"

"He saw what I went through after my wife disappeared. I should have thought that by itself would have been an adequate deterrent." He glanced at her, the jut of his chin a challenge. "No doubt you have heard some version of the story."

"I have heard a number of versions."

"None to my advantage, I would wager," he said bitterly. "I did not kill my wife, Lady Helen, if that is what you are wondering. She disappeared, and from that day onward I have been under suspicion. Do you know how that feels?"

"My parents disappeared too, Lord Carlston. I know, at least, how that feels." She paused, remembering the overwhelming pain of those childhood days and the never-ending echo of it still tolling through her. "The helpless agony of not knowing what happened."

He nodded slowly. "Yes, helpless agony. You do understand."

For a moment they were both silent.

"Elise and I were at my seat in Carlston for Michaelmas," he said abruptly. "I had gone to visit a neighbor about a trifling matter. On my return home I found . . ." He stopped, lower teeth clamping for a moment upon his upper lip. "A large amount of blood in Elise's dressing room. Even then I had seen enough death to know the volume would have been almost the full complement of a human body. It was also still warm. Whatever had happened had occurred only minutes before. If I had returned just a little earlier, I would have . . ." He stopped and flexed his shoulders, as if pushing past the guilt. "To this day I do not know what actually happened in that room. Foolishly, I picked up the knife lying in the blood and raised the alarm. I had everyone searching the estate, but we found nothing—neither Elise nor a perpetrator.

Eventually, as the investigation fruitlessly continued, all eyes inevitably turned to me. That suspicion was compounded by one of the maids who claimed she saw me coming from the room with the knife. Which, of course, she did. I never found Elise or any trace of the other person involved. I searched England, and then, when the rumors turned into accusations, I was ordered to go to the Continent. So I took my search there, just in case she had somehow survived."

Helen realized her hand was pressed over her mouth. She pulled it away. "You thought she might still be alive?"

"No, I don't think I did, but it is hard to give up hope, isn't it? Almost as hard as having it." He rubbed his forehead as if the pain of that hope still lingered. "I suppose I knew even then she could not be alive. Not with all that blood."

"But why would someone murder a woman and carry her body away so that there was no trace?"

"Indeed. I could think of only one organization that could do that so efficiently. Which has done so in many cases before, and continues to do so."

Helen stared at him. "Are you saying the Dark Days Club killed your wife?"

"No. After the events at your ball, I now think Benchley killed my wife, and the Home Office cleaned up after him, as they did the Ratcliffe Highway murders. I will never know if that was truly the case, but it is my belief."

"Why would he kill your wife?"

"I did not know it at the time, but his paranoia was extreme even then. Six years had passed since he had dumped his darkness into your mother, and I believe he had tipped once again into vestige madness. I think he believed Elise was a Deceiver. Sir Jonathan, our Tracer, has told me that Benchley had in fact requested a Trace upon Elise."

"If you believe the Home Office cleaned up after him, how can you bear to work within that organization?"

"I gave my oath, Lady Helen. Besides, I have no proof, and if I abandon the Dark Days Club, I will never have a chance to find out the truth."

Would that proof be in the journal, alongside her own answers about the death of her parents? Yet she could not even hint at that possibility.

"This oath expects a lot from us," she said.

"It does, and one of those expectations is that we do not become attached. Quinn knows it is against the rules, as I am sure Darby does too. They must put an end to it."

Helen stared at him. Had she heard right? "What do you mean, against the rules? Are you saying the oath actually forbids them to fall in love?"

"Surely you are aware of the oath that you swore? Attachments in the Dark Days Club are forbidden, Lady Helen. We are an army, albeit a very small one. We cannot afford to be compromised by tender emotions."

Helen crossed her arms. "My mother and father loved each other, and they were both members of the Dark Days Club."

"Indeed, it was their tragedy, and my own, that forced the rule against attachments into existence. Pike instituted the ban, and it is not his worst decision."

"Does it apply to everyone?"

"Not everyone. Just Reclaimers and Terrenes."

She had a horrifying sense of a trap closing; one that she had stepped into willingly. "Even with someone outside the order?"

"Even outside." He looked at her sideways. "Even Dukes."

She ignored the jibe. "Banning love and marriage is absurd," she said hotly. "How does the Home Office plan to enforce such a rule?"

"It is not up to the Home Office to enforce it. We must control ourselves."

"*You* may find it easy to expel all emotion, but I do not want to live like that, and I am sure Darby—"

She stopped. He was looking at her with such an odd expression upon his face.

"Easy? You think that I do not feel anything?" For just a second the guard within his dark eyes dropped away, and she saw what lay behind: a silent howl of pain and guilt and, clawing through it all, desire for her. Savage and intense.

He turned from her shock and took a few steps away, placing some space between them. "There is nothing easy about putting one's duty above all else, in any way, but we have sworn to protect our country. Self-gratification is not part of our oath."

She drew in a shaking breath. He still felt it too, that wild pull toward each other. Yet he was saying they must control it.

She cleared her throat. "I do not think Darby knew she was swearing to forgo love and a husband and children."

"*I acknowledge that I am subject to its rule,*" he recited, turning to face her again. "*That I serve at the King's pleasure, and that I will never, by deed or word, place the Dark Days Club in jeopardy.*"

"I see." Helen looked down at her hands. She had laced her fingers without even knowing, the knuckles aching and white. "*Deed or word.* It is a very wide definition."

"It is in the regulations as well."

Ah, yes, the rules and regulations. She had tried to read through them all, but had been defeated by the endless paragraphs of tortuous legal language. Clearly she had missed some very important clauses. And poor Darby, who had her letters but did not read with any ease, would have had little chance of understanding the ramifications.

Carlston frowned. "In truth, I had not expected Pike to come to Brighton to swear you in—I had thought to give you more time to consider the gravity of that final step. Even so, Pike should have asked if you fully comprehended what you were undertaking before you took the oath. Did he not?"

Helen closed her eyes. Yes, he had asked, and she had reassured him—no, she had coldly *told* him—that she knew exactly what she was doing. Pike's manner had brought out all her prideful contrariness. Darby, too, had been asked the same question by Lady Margaret, and had given all reassurances that she understood. This time she could not lay the fault of her ignorance at his lordship's feet. This had been her own failing.

"Pike did his duty." She opened her eyes, rallying. "Nevertheless, it is a ridiculous and unfair rule. You are saying that we must live without the consolation of creating our own families. Without love and intimacy. Without tenderness."

"I am not saying it is fair. Plainly, it is not. But you must understand that the rule was writ for men, not women. Reclaimers and Terrenes are men. Usually." He rubbed at his temple. "Forgive me for being blunt, but there are ways for men to assuage their needs without emotional attachment."

What was he saying . . . *assuage their needs*? An instant later, his meaning burst upon her. He meant *lovers*. Or worse, harlots.

"That is hardly an avenue that Darby or I can take!" she said.

"I am aware—" He stopped and squeezed his eyes shut, his fist clenching. It was not in reaction to her words; something was wrong with him.

"Lord Carlston, are you unwell?"

He opened his eyes, clearly trying to focus. "No, I am perfectly well." Drawing a careful breath, he added, "Perhaps you should consider that you are no longer living a woman's life. That those ties that bind normal women no longer apply. You are young; it would indeed be cruel to sentence you to a life without intimacy.

Perhaps your needs . . . I mean your . . ." He cleared his throat. "Perhaps they could be met in a less formal manner."

"I beg your pardon?" She felt her skin heat. "Are you advising me to take a lov—" She stumbled over the idea. "To follow Lady Caroline Lamb's example?"

"Perhaps not so indiscreetly as Caro." His voice hardened. "And I advise that you do not go in Selburn's direction."

She held up her hands; the subject had to stop. "I am not going in anyone's direction."

He gave a short nod. "Perhaps that is for the best. Even such loveless attachments bring their problems."

"Lord Carlston, please stop!"

"I have shocked you." He gave a small bow. "My apologies. Even so, the ban still stands. I will speak to Quinn. You must speak to Darby. Make it clear that it can go no further."

"No, I do not want to have such a conversation. This rule is unfair and cruel."

Admittedly the refusal was somewhat ironic, since she did not want Darby to abandon her for Quinn. Nevertheless, she could not break Darby's heart.

She braced for his lordship's anger. It did not come. Instead, he sighed and dug his fingertips into his brow as if they could burrow right through to the bone.

"I, too, am not looking forward to the conversation. Quinn deserves more happiness than he can find at my side." His mouth pinched into regret. "Regardless, you and I are the Reclaimers in this equation, Lady Helen. We must lead our Terrenes. That duty is never-ending and never easy."

Their duty. He was right, although she wanted to deny it and run away. As he had said, she had sworn an oath to God and King, and had claimed to have a full understanding of that undertaking. There could be no backing out of such a solemn and binding vow. Besides, Mr. Hammond was relying upon her to help finish their task. She hated to admit it, but the love between two servants had to take second place to a man's survival and an oath made in God's name. Not to mention her own safety.

"There have been many times when I have wanted to walk away," Carlston said softly, as if he had read her mind. "But you and I have been brought up with the same immutable knowledge: without adherence to our word, we are worth nothing."

There was such pain in his voice. Too much pain perhaps for merely an unwanted task. His skin had paled too, and he pressed his hand over his eyes as if the light had suddenly become too much.

"I do not think you are well at all, Lord Carlston. Do you have the migraine?"

He dropped his hand from his brow as if she had caught him in an illicit act. "Of course not." Turning from her scrutiny, he added, "Come, let us begin training."

He was taking refuge in practicalities, and right then she did not have the wherewithal to pursue the subject. Her mind was reeling from the ramifications of the ban for herself—could she live her life without love?—and the prospect of speaking to Darby on such a painful subject.

His lordship walked to the long table set against the far wall and picked up two canes. "We will work on your defensive techniques first and then introduce some *canne chausson*. I want you to get over this squeamishness about hitting me. You must get used to making contact and withstanding blows."

"I am trying."

"I know." He waved at her garb. "The technique is based upon kicking, so keep your boots on, but remove your jacket for ease of movement."

Helen shifted her shoulders, the tight fit of the broadcloth bringing home an awkward problem. "I cannot take my coat off without aid."

"Ah, yes. Every fashionable man's problem," he said, trying for lightness. "It seems I have sent away your maid prematurely." He hesitated, then added, "I will assist you, if you allow."

She wet her lips. To be undressed by him, even just the removal of a jacket, was, at the very least, untoward. For decency's sake, she should insist that Darby be called back, particularly since she had just seen what lay beneath his iron will. Not to mention the scandalous conversation they had just had about lovers and needs. But in truth, the real reason—the shameful reason—was because any time they touched, her body felt alight. For her sake—for both their sakes—she should say no. Yet . . . she nodded.

"Yes," he said, unnecessarily. Was he, too, looking for the chance to touch? Maybe they both wanted to play with fire.

A few strides took him to the chair. He propped the canes against it and stood for a moment—watching her, she realized, for any hesitation.

There was still time to change her mind. To say no, and send for Darby.

She turned her back, every sense aware of his approach. One step, two, and then he was behind her, his body only inches from her own. She stared fiercely at the opposite wall, waiting for his touch. Her whole being was full of the sandalwood scent of his shaving soap, the draw of his breath, the heat of every exhalation upon the nape of her neck.

What were they doing? Had she not just railed against him and his order? Had he not just told her that this attraction was forbidden? It was as if he were the sun and she Icarus, ignoring the bright, hot danger ahead.

"May I begin?" His voice was at its most formal.

"Yes."

She braced herself. There, his hands upon her shoulders, fingertips working their way under the jacket collar. Knuckles brushed against the lobe of her ear. She curled her fingers at the sensation, hot energy coursing through her veins. His breath caught for a second. Had he felt it too?

He leaned in and firmly pulled back the shoulders of the jacket. The tightness of the fit drew her arms back too, as if he held her bound. She turned her head, his smooth shaven cheek so close to her lips. If she turned just a little more . . .

But she did not shift. Nor did he. The only motion, their breathing, two quickening rhythms blending into one.

"Step forward," he finally said, his voice ragged.

She obeyed, her arms coming free of the sleeves.

She turned, but he was already walking away, head bowed. He draped the jacket over the chair, picked up the canes, and slowly straightened, rolling back his shoulders.

"If you recall our last lesson," he said, facing her, voice still rough, "the *canne de combat* action is always circular." He passed her a cane. She stared at his hand; it was shaking. "Our stance is not that of a fencer, but more face-on, so that we may move in any direction with speed and use our feet to kick."

He walked toward the stuffed Hessian sack, but stopped and hunched as if caught by sudden pain.

"What is wrong?" She stepped forward.

"Nothing." He straightened. "Think of your hand as the turning point. The cane moves and the body follows."

"You are in pain."

He shook his head. "Watch carefully."

She heard him draw breath, then he pivoted across the wooden floor, the cane swinging above his head in a graceful arc. Yet there was something frenetic in his movements, a shivering tension within him like an overstrung bow. He lunged and brought the cane down in a fast low sweep that connected with a thud on the stuffed sack. It swung heavily on its chain, the force of the blow leaving an indentation across the rough cloth.

"Recover on the front foot." He drew breath again, an awful rasp within it. And she could see blood seeping from his nose.

She stepped forward. "Lord Carlston, you are bleeding!"

"Follow with a higher strike," he said, ignoring her alarm.

The veins and tendons on his neck had corded with strain. He swung the cane above his head, his movements blurring into sudden acceleration. Even with Reclaimer sight, Helen could barely follow the frightening speed of his body as he pivoted and lunged around the swinging sack. The cane struck it again and again and again, the hits so fast and heavy that the blunt wood sliced through the Hessian, ripping it apart. A cloud of sawdust and wool burst out, the sack spinning wildly. The huge wooden cross dropped out, but it never hit the floor. His lordship met it midair with a vicious round-kick that propelled it across the room, straight toward Helen's head.

She dived to one side, landing heavily on her knees and elbows, her cane flying from her grasp. The cross speared past her and smashed into the wall with an immense thud that seemed to shake the room. Plaster and wood exploded in a stinging hail of chunks and dust and splinters. Helen covered her head, curling up as clumps of wall pelted her body.

The salon doors burst open. "My lord!" Geoffrey called. "My lady?"

Almost as quickly as it had begun, everything was still again. Panting, Helen lifted her head. Plaster dust floated in the rays of sunlight, the floor littered with drifts of wool and sawdust and hunks of wall. The footman coughed, his forearm against his mouth.

Lord Carlston stood beneath the remnants of the Hessian sack on its chain, the broken end of the cane in his hand, blood still seeping from his nose.

"Did I harm you, Lady Helen?" he rasped.

"No." She sat up. "What happened?"

"It felt as if I had a sun within me. So much power . . ." He staggered and dropped to his knees.

"My lord!" Geoffrey ran to him.

"Get Quinn," Carlston ordered hoarsely. "I need to be against the earth. I need . . ."

He pitched forward, the footman sliding two hands beneath his head just before it slammed against the floor.

Ten

TWO HOURS LATER, Mr. Quinn stood before them in the drawing room. His frown and the tattoos that angled across his forehead and cheeks gave him a ferocious appearance, belied by the anxious twisting of his hands.

"None of the energy was in him," he said to Lady Margaret, who sat in the largest armchair as if in judgment. "When I pressed him upon the earth, there was no release of power into the ground. I can feel it when it goes out of him, and I swear, nothing went."

Helen, seated on the sofa with Delia, nodded her agreement. "I watched through my touch watch lens, and no energy passed from his lordship to the earth."

The support earned her a grateful smile from Darby, who stood mutely by Quinn's side.

The big Terrene had arrived in the salon moments after his lordship's collapse and had quickly carried his senseless master downstairs to the courtyard. The whole household had followed and witnessed Quinn grounding the Reclaimer, to no apparent effect. At that point, Lady Margaret had taken control and ordered Quinn to carry his lordship to Mr. Hammond's rooms. Carlston had roused once on the way up the stairs, grabbing Helen's hand, then his eyes had become eerily fixed and staring. The Reclaimer fugue, Mr. Quinn called it; he had seen his lordship heal in such a manner before, always awaking from the strange trance a few hours later, fully recuperated.

In the meantime, Lady Margaret had assembled everyone in the drawing room to determine exactly what had happened and why.

"It does not make sense," she mused, chewing on the end of her knuckle. "He said himself that it was an excess of power." She looked at Helen. "That is what he said, was it not?"

"As if he had a sun within him," Helen reported again.

She glanced around the circle of worried faces. It should have been her asking the questions—she was the Reclaimer—but in all honesty, it had been a relief when Lady Margaret had taken charge. The events of the day had shaken her more than she cared to admit. Lord Carlston had looked so vulnerable, so young, gathered in Quinn's arms, senseless and pale.

Beside her, Delia asked, "Is that a normal way of describing the power you experience? It seems very . . . big."

Helen shook her head. "I do not know. I have not had enough experience of it."

Mr. Hammond leaned his shoulders against the mantel ledge. "His lordship has had no encounters with a glutted Deceiver in the last week, or none that I know of?" He glanced questioningly at Quinn and received a nod of confirmation. "So where has the power come from?"

"Could it be the power that he absorbed from the Deceiver at my ball? The power I shared with him?" Helen asked, ignoring the memory of her body locked against his, the power thrumming between them. "We never released any of it into the earth. It seemed to dissipate, but perhaps it did not."

"Are *you* experiencing any such effects?" Mr. Hammond asked.

"No, not at all."

He shrugged. "Then I do not see how that could be the source.

Besides, if it were, Mr. Quinn's grounding would have had some result."

That was true.

"There is another explanation," Mr. Quinn said heavily. He glanced at Darby, who nodded encouragingly.

Helen knew what he meant, and, by the look upon Lady Margaret's face, so did she. But it was Mr. Hammond who voiced it.

"You think it is the vestige darkness within him," he said flatly.

Quinn nodded. "I do, sir." He looked at Helen. "I know you saw how much is in him when he reclaimed the boy in London."

"Yes," she said, "but I was under the impression he had years before it would have such a dire effect."

"I was too, my lady, and so was he."

Darby took Mr. Quinn's hand, the sweetness of the gesture bringing an ache to Helen's throat.

Mr. Hammond stubbed the toe of his boot into the hearth grate, every line of his body denying the possibility.

"What darkness in him?" Delia asked, her voice small in the silence.

No one else seemed inclined to answer, so Helen said, "It is the accumulation of the vestige, the little spark of Deceiver energy that Reclaimers absorb when we reclaim the soul of one of their offspring and bring it back to full humanity. We cannot rid ourselves of it in the earth like the normal Deceiver energy. It stays within the body and builds up, creating a dark energy that sickens us. Usually we retire from reclaiming before it causes problems, but if we do not draw back in time . . ." She stopped, not wanting to give utterance to the inevitable outcome.

"It sends the Reclaimer mad," Mr. Hammond finished.

"Is his lordship mad?" Delia asked.

"No!" Lady Margaret said forcefully. "He is not."

Delia looked around at them. "But he has stopped reclaiming, hasn't he?"

Mr. Hammond shook his head.

"He will not, Miss Cransdon," Quinn said. "I've tried over and over to reason with him, but he won't listen. He says he's on this earth to save souls and, God damn it . . ." He stopped, flushing. "I beg your pardon. He says he will save souls whatever the cost."

"Atonement," Helen muttered. He had been too late to save Lady Elise from whatever ghastly fate had occurred in that bedchamber.

Quinn looked at her oddly. "Yes, my lady."

Delia leaned forward. "Atonement for what? His wife?"

Helen gave a small shake of her head. It was not the time for such an exchange.

Mr. Hammond pushed himself from the mantel and paced across the room. "Maybe it is not the case, after all. Maybe there is another reason for this surge of power."

"And what would that be, Michael?" Lady Margaret asked. "A head cold? However much we may dislike it, the obvious reason is probably the correct one. He is being overcome by the vestige."

Mr. Hammond crossed his arms. "You are jumping to conclusions. There could be another explanation that we do not have the experience or records to understand."

"None of us wants it to be true, Michael," she said, a little more gently, "but we have to protect his lordship and the Dark Days Club. We must insist that he stop reclaiming, and try to find some way to alleviate the damage already done. Although it pains me to say it, I think we may have to consult Pike on the matter. He has access to historical records and rare alchemical texts that we do not."

"No!" Helen and Mr. Hammond exclaimed at the same time.

Lady Margaret blinked at the united onslaught.

Mr. Hammond glanced wildly at Helen: *I will handle this.*

"I think it is obvious that Pike is looking for a reason to ruin his lordship," he said. "Mentioning this would be handing him the gun and the powder."

"Besides," Helen said, ignoring his directive, "there is no way to rid a Reclaimer of the darkness except by shifting it to another Reclaimer and destroying them. Benchley offered Lord Carlston that solution, a way to pass all of his darkness to me, and he refused it."

"Of course he refused it," Lady Margaret said. "So, if we are not to consult Pike, then what are we to do?"

They were all silent again.

"We must stop him from reclaiming," Hammond said. "By force if necessary. Lady Helen, and you, Quinn, are the only two who can do that. Are you willing?"

"I am," Helen said. "Quinn?"

He sighed. "Yes."

A soft sound, the press of a hallway floorboard against another, caught at Helen's Reclaimer hearing. She turned just as the door opened. His lordship leaned against the doorjamb, face drained and eyes hooded. He wore Mr. Hammond's burgundy silk banyan over his shirt and breeches, the long quilted robe fitting close on his larger frame.

"By force?" he repeated, a sardonic glance taking in Helen and Quinn. "I doubt that would be possible or necessary. This sickness is not the vestige darkness."

Lady Margaret rose from her chair. "William, what are you doing out of bed? You should be resting."

Hammond crossed the room. "You look like death, my friend. Come, take my arm, sit down."

The Earl waved him away. "I am not an invalid." He walked slowly into the room and leaned his hands heavily on the back of the sofa, fixing on Helen. "Are you truly unharmed?"

"Yes. Thank you." She studied his face. Anyone could see the fatigue in the drawn pallor around his eyes, but he still snapped with energy deep within. "You are not fully recovered."

"Well on the way."

He smiled, and it held such an appeal for solidarity, such a heartfelt apology, that Helen found herself returning it.

Neither of them, it seemed, wanted to break the sweet accord. It was only Helen's sudden awareness that they were being watched by Delia that made her drop her gaze. Carlston must have realized the same, for he stepped away.

"If it is not the vestige darkness, your lordship," Delia asked, following him with that penetrating gaze, "what is it?"

"I do not have the answer to that, Miss Cransdon." He swept a thoughtful glance around the gathering. "I do, however, know someone who may."

"Who?" Hammond demanded. "We will consult them immediately."

"The Comte d'Antraigues."

The name meant nothing to Helen, but it obviously meant something to Mr. Hammond.

"You jest, don't you?" he demanded. "The Comte is a Deceiver."

"I am well aware that he is a Deceiver. Nevertheless, he and I have had dealings before and he is open to negotiation. If anyone will know about this type of energy surge in a Reclaimer, it will be him. He has seen over a hundred English and French Reclaimers live and die."

"Some of them by his hand," Lady Margaret said curtly.

"True. But then I have killed just as many of his kind," Carlston said. "Of course, if he does know, he will make us pay."

"He will want money?" Helen asked.

"No." Carlston leaned a hand upon the mantel; for actual support, Helen realized. He was weaker than he admitted. "The

Comte deals in secrets and information. He has been a spy for many countries. Currently he is supporting the Duc d'Orléans in his bid to overthrow Bonaparte. It is why he is tolerated here in England, but I would not rely upon him as an ally. Monsieur le Comte is a wily intriguer who has outlasted many enemies."

Lady Margaret crossed her arms. "And you propose to make a deal with him, a French Deceiver spy, in the middle of a war?"

"I do. He and his wife will be at Lady Dunwick's rout." He turned to Helen. "I will introduce you, and then you and I will make a deal with a devil."

Helen glanced at Mr. Hammond. Was he, too, thinking of Pike's suspicions? His lordship had just admitted that he had made deals with a French Deceiver—deals that involved secrets—and intended to do so again. Perhaps his loyalty had been compromised. Or if not his loyalty, then at least his judgment. There was the very real possibility that his lordship was wrong or deluded, and his collapse had, in fact, been caused by the vestige darkness and its creeping madness.

Mr. Hammond met her gaze, and she was startled to see her own unease mirrored in his eyes. He was one of Lord Carlston's most staunch supporters, and yet even he was beginning to have doubts.

"I hope the devil will give us the answers we need," Helen said, her reply as much for Mr. Hammond as it was for Lord Carlston.

Eleven

Friday, 10 July 1812

"EVER BEEN IN the sea afore, my lady?" Martha Gunn, the queen of the Brighton dippers, asked Helen.

The old woman was huge, in both girth and personality. She easily stood as tall as Helen, and had at least three times her heft, with burly shoulders that would have made any man proud. She stood braced on the shingles of the eastern beach—for female bathers only—her legs set wide beneath her rucked-up navy skirts, one hand on her hip, the other shielding her shrewd eyes from the glare of the hot midday sun.

"Never," Helen said, raising her voice above the squeals of delighted terror that came from the women already in the water. She surveyed the white-capped waves slapping the beach with broad foaming fingers that reached for her feet. The surf had seemed so small and manageable from the roadway above. Up close, it seemed larger and a great deal more wild.

"I did once bathe in a river," she offered.

"Not the same at all," Martha boomed. "But I don't think you'll have much of a worry"—she leaned forward and gave a conspiratorial nod, her voice dropping a few notches—"you being like his lordship an' all." She gestured to a wooden bathing machine set high on four large wheels and being drawn out of the water by a salt-encrusted black pony. A ruddy-skinned man urged the animal across the broken, sliding pebbles. "We'll just let the lady afore you dis-em-bark, and then you and yer maid can go in."

Darby observed the slowly approaching machine with a wary eye. "It doesn't look safe, my lady."

"There is no need for you to stay in it when it goes into the water, Darby."

"If you want me to stay, I will," her maid said stoutly.

"No, that is not necessary."

In fact, Helen thought, not wanted at all.

She looked back at Lady Margaret and Delia. They stood beneath their parasols next to a bank of rocks that was doing duty as a waiting area for those ladies who were not brave enough, or perhaps silly enough, to immerse their bodies. They were not in hailing distance, but still close enough for the eagle-eyed Lady Margaret to be curious about any intense conversation. Helen would need to wait until she was well in the water with Martha Gunn before she asked any questions.

Lord Carlston had insisted Lady Margaret accompany her to the beach, more, Helen thought, from the desire to be rid of his aide's fussing than from any fine sense of propriety. He claimed he had fully recovered, and it did seem as if the worrying effects of his collapse were all but gone.

The beachward door of the machine opened, and a slightly bedraggled lady draped in a violet shawl over a lemon muslin gown descended the wooden steps, her maid following with a stack of wet clothing and drying sheets in her arms.

"The same again tomorrow, Mrs. Cavendish?" Martha inquired.

The lady gave a quick nod, patted the limp curls that hung from under her bonnet, and headed toward the path to the road.

Helen gathered her own muslin skirts and picked her way

across the shingle to the machine, her feet feeling every jagged edge through the thin leather soles of her sandals.

"Careful, my lady, the steps are wet," Darby said behind her as they ascended.

Everything seemed to be wet: the plank floor inside the wooden box, the two small bench seats set on either side, and the walls to about halfway their height.

"Lordy, that is a stink," Darby said as she closed the door behind them.

Helen sniffed: a combination of wet wood, wet hair, and salt. Not wholly unpleasant, and it was a relief to be out of the midday heat.

A narrow window above each bench let in enough light to ameliorate the uncomfortable sensation that one was in a damp water closet on wheels, and to allow the management of buttons, clasps, and hooks. To that end, Helen undid the pearl button on her glove and began to peel it off her hand.

"Wait, my lady," Darby said. "Let me put something down on that seat for you." She pulled out one of the drying sheets in her arms and placed it along the bench. "There, now you can sit without getting wet."

"Yes, I wouldn't want to get wet in a bathing machine," Helen said with a smile.

Darby giggled, dumped the rest of the sheets and clothing on the other seat, and bent to the task of undoing the braid frogs on Helen's spencer. With her deft help, it did not take long for Helen to be out of her promenade ensemble and into her new yellow flannel bathing shift, her cropped hair covered by the ugly matching flannel cap.

Clanks and jingles told them that the horse had been walked back around the machine and harnessed to the seaward side, ready to haul it back into the water.

"Well, then," Helen said, scrunching her bare feet against the damp wood. "Go tell Mrs. Gunn that I am ready."

Darby departed the machine at its beachward end, a brief flash of sunlight dazzling Helen's eyes before the door closed again. She smiled; poor Darby couldn't get out fast enough. She turned and stood in the dim, cool box, her breath quickening a little in anticipation. Her mother and father had drowned at sea, either by accident or, if Pike was right, by ill deed. The prospect of stepping into such an expanse of water by choice seemed entirely mad.

A thump against the wall and a loud "Ahoy" from Martha heralded the first lurch forward. Helen pressed a hand on either wall, steadying herself as the machine rocked its way across the shingle. The weights sewn into the hem of her gown thudded against her ankle bones in a stinging rhythm that matched the slow, grinding progress.

"Steady," she heard Martha call, and then came the slap of the surf against the wooden walls. Cold water oozed through the planks beneath her feet.

"Orright!" Martha yelled. The machine stopped moving. The clank and jingle of the harness sounded again; the pony being walked around to the beachward side. Another thump, this time on the seaward door, and then Helen heard Martha call, "When you are ready, my lady."

Helen stepped across to the door and opened it, a spray of cold water wetting her face. She blinked in the bright sunlight. Below, Martha Gunn stood in the glinting surf, an unmoving anchor against the pound of the waves, her navy gown swirling around her sturdy body. They were a good twenty yards or so from the next bathing machine, where two young ladies clung to the steps, shrieking as their dippers tried to pry them from their safe hold. Beyond them, at least ten other machines were lined up, dippers and clients bobbing in the surf.

Martha beckoned to Helen. "Just come on down the steps, my lady. I'll be here to keep you up."

Helen stared down at the lapping water. Dear Lord, she could not see the bottom. At the next machine, the screaming ladies still clung to the step. She could understand their terror, but she would not allow her own fear to humiliate her in such a manner. Gathering her resolve, she stepped down onto the wet wood. Water enveloped her feet, and she drew in a startled breath. So cold! On the next step, the icy water rose up her legs and wrapped the weighted hem around her shins.

"Right you are," Martha said.

Helen felt the dipper's strong hands take her forearms. She yelped as her body plunged up to her neck into the freezing water. The gown billowed and then collapsed, the wet cloth dragging her down. For an instant, Helen felt dizzying panic as a wave washed over her head and filled her nose with salty water that stung the back of her throat, and then Martha's hold changed. One large hand gathered flannel at her back, while an arm circled her waist. Helen groped for the dipper and found a meaty shoulder. A few panicked kicks and her feet were free from the tangle of her hem. She felt the sandy bottom beneath her soles, thank God, and dug her toes in, bracing against the buffeting waves.

"Do you wish to go right under?" Martha's voice said near her ear.

Helen thought she had already done so. "No!" she gasped.

"We'll stay as we is, then."

With the bulwark of Martha at her side and her feet dug into the sand, Helen took a few deep breaths and looked back at the beach. At least thirty yards of rolling, foaming, depthless water away. Quelling a rise of panic, she forced her mind to the business at hand.

"Mrs. Gunn," she said, raising her voice above the screech of gulls and women, and the crash of waves, "Lord Carlston says you know everything there is to know about Brighton and its inhabitants."

"That be right," Martha said. "And all the whereabouts, too, from Shoreham to Eastbourne. It's why his lordship recruited me. Hold on now; here's a big one."

A harder wave hit, sending them staggering back a step. Martha laughed, the sheer joy of it bringing a smile to Helen's face. It seemed even after sixty-odd years of dipping, Martha still reveled in the sea and its caprices.

"We are looking for a man by the name of Lowry. Or for any of his people," Helen said, regaining her footing. The water no longer felt bone-chillingly cold, and, as long as she could touch the sand with her toes, it was not too frightening. "He grew up in the Brighton workhouse."

"Lowry?" Martha's wet wrinkled face furrowed into more lines as she pondered the name. "Nobody of that name in Brighton."

Helen licked her lips, the tang of sea salt seasoning her disappointment. Had Lowry lied? Perhaps she had remembered amiss, and it was not the Brighton workhouse.

She tried another tack. "He was Samuel Benchley's Terrene. You know what a Terrene is, don't you?"

"I do. His lordship told me all about hisself and the Deceivers. And yourself, too." She leaned closer, eyes solemn. "You and he be marvels to keep us protected from them creatures. What's it like to have such power, my lady? I've always wanted to ask his lordship, but it's not the kind of question you ask him, is it?"

Helen blinked. No one had ever asked her what it felt like to be a Reclaimer. "Well, it is . . . I mean, at times it is wonderful . . . and other times it is not."

Martha nodded. "Good and bad, like most gifts from the Almighty, and harder for you, I imagine, being a lass. It be like this job—only for them that's got the pluck. There's none braver than his lordship, but I seen the look that comes into his eye. Right haunted it is. You be careful not to get that look, my lady."

Haunted. Helen silently agreed with the old dipper's assessment of his lordship's eyes. Ever since he had collapsed there was a shadow upon his every look and gesture; perhaps the knowledge that he could no longer count upon his own control.

"Watch out now!" Martha called. She swung in front of Helen, taking the brunt of a sly wave against her broad shoulder, then said, "This man you want is Samuel Benchley's Terrene, eh?" Raising a dripping arm, she tapped her forehead as if urging a slow clock to turn. "Ah, I know who you mean. He came back here a year ago with Benchley. But his name weren't Lowry growing up. It was MacEvoy. Bartholomew MacEvoy."

"Bartholomew, yes, that is his Christian name." Helen looked up at the sky, sending a quick, fervent prayer of thanks. "Does he have any family in Brighton or somewhere nearby?"

"A sister, Katherine. Married a man by the name of Holt, right here in Brighton." Martha regarded Helen with a doubtful brow. "These ain't good folk, my lady."

"Where does she live?" Helen asked.

Martha rubbed her chin. "Well, now, like I said, Kate Holt ain't a respectable woman. What I got to say ain't for gentle ears. Maybe it'd be best if I tell his lordship."

"No," Helen said quickly. "Lord Carlston wants me to find Lowry's relatives. You must think of me as a Reclaimer, Mrs. Gunn, not a lady."

The old dipper nodded. "It's like I tell my Stephen: when I'm in me water dress, I'm more man than woman. Got to be if I'm to keep you ladies safe. Well, now, about Kate Holt. If you be forgiving my bluntness, she used to trade on her own bottom, and now she and her man run a bawdy house down in the Lanes. Have you an idea of what that is, my lady?"

Helen did, and she could not keep the shock from stiffening her face. Kate Holt was a bawd and kept a brothel. Dear God, was Lowry hiding the journal in a house of ill repute? How could she go into such a place?

Martha viewed an incoming wave with narrowed eyes. "Hold tight," she advised, then jumped, pulling Helen above its crest with practiced ease. They landed back on the sand, one side of Helen's gown puffing up around her.

"Brighton's got more whores and bawdy houses than you can shake a stick at, what with the army nearby," Martha continued. "And when you quality folk come to town, even more open their doors. Kate Holt's house does for those men who want a flogging or a bit of throat squeezing. I've heard tell too that she has rooms for those who like the boys, and that the Duke of Cumberland has even visited." She regarded Helen with a shrewd look in her dark, triangular eyes. "Understand what I'm saying?"

Helen nodded. It was rumored that the Duke of Cumberland, the Prince Regent's younger brother, had killed his Italian servant two years ago after the man had discovered him fornicating with his valet. An inquiry had found that the Italian had committed suicide, but many believed the man had been silenced.

Helen could feel the blush heating her face and willed herself not to look away. "Where is this place?"

"In the Old Town. Do you know the Quakers' Meeting House on Ship Street?"

"Yes, I have seen it."

"Kate Holt's is down the next lane, Union Street. At front it's a coffeehouse, but the real business is done out the back." She pursed her lips. "Kate's no saint, that's for sure, but she ain't the worse of them. She's got a son with a vestige in him—almost insane now, poor child—but she stands by him and won't put him in the madhouse."

Helen stared at Martha. "Her son is an *offspring*?"

"Aye. Not by her husband, Holt, mind you, but from one of her culls when she was whoring. When you London folk come down, so do the Deceivers. Kate's brother and Benchley tried to reclaim him a year back, but it didn't work. That's how I know your man Lowry is really Bart MacEvoy. Benchley told Kate that her son is one of them Unreclaimables. He was going to put the boy out of his misery, but MacEvoy—or should I say Lowry—wouldn't let him do it."

Helen frowned. As an Unreclaimable, Kate Holt's son came under the most troubling mandate of the Reclaimer oath: *To reclaim them back to humanity when possible, and when it is not, to save them from a life of torment.*

"Are you and his lordship going to try to reclaim him again, my lady?" Martha asked.

It was no doubt their duty, but she could not tell his lordship about the boy. It would mean telling him about Lowry's sister, and by that leading him to the journal. And if the boy was Unreclaimable, she did not want to be faced with the task of killing him.

"At present, all of our attention is on finding Lowry," she said. "Do you know if he has visited his sister recently?"

"Not that I know of, but I know a girl in Kate Holt's house, Binny—she'll keep a lookout if I ask. She wants to get out of whoring and learn how to dip. I'll give her the chance if she gives us the nod and keeps mum. My boys will hunt up information too."

"If he is found, could you send word to me immediately?"

"Of course, my lady."

Helen had a sudden opportunistic thought. "There is another man I am seeking too. His name is Philip. He used to be my footman. A tall, handsome fellow, over six foot, with red hair and freckles. Wears a gray beaver. Can your boys look out for him, too?"

Martha nodded. "Six foot, red hair, gray beaver."

Helen tightened her grip on the dipper's forearm, remembering to moderate her strength; she did not want to break the old woman's bones. "If you find either man, send word to me only. Any time of the day or night. It is of the utmost importance. I am at Twenty German Place."

"Yes, my lady. You have my word."

Helen had the feeling that Martha Gunn's word was inviolate. "Thank you." At least she and Hammond now had a way forward: an address where the journal might be hidden. And if Philip was located, possibly a way to retrieve the *Colligat*.

For a few moments, she and the dipper were silent, the sea rocking them on their feet. Helen squinted into the endless horizon, the warm blue of the sky meeting the cold navy of the water in a long hazy strip of light.

"It looks like it goes on forever," she said.

"She's a beautiful thing, the sea," Martha said. "But a right bitch too, if you be forgiving me language. Me mam always said, 'Never turn yer back on the sea, and remember what's hidden beneath her is always more deadly than what's in plain sight.'"

Helen looked down into the dark water. "Like the Deceivers."

"Like the Deceivers," Martha Gunn agreed. "And like people, too."

Twelve

LADY DUNWICK'S ROUT was set to start at nine o'clock, and by that time clouds had rolled over the sky, threatening the balmy evening. The original plan had been for the four of them to walk to the gathering in Marlborough Place—Lord Carlston was making his own way there—but Lady Margaret decided to bring the town coach around in case of rain. Nankeen boots were quickly untied and replaced by satin dancing slippers, the matching satin *pochettes* abandoned. There was no need for such protections when they were to be delivered to the Dunwicks' front door by carriage.

On the way out of the house, Helen managed to hang back with Mr. Hammond in the foyer. It was the first time she had been alone with him since she had spoken to Martha Gunn.

"Lowry has a sister," she whispered, pretending to fuss with her gold silk shawl. "A harlot who has a bawdy house in the Old Town Lanes."

Mr. Hammond's brows lifted. "A bawdy house?" He considered the news. "A clever place to find refuge."

Helen nodded. "I have told Martha Gunn to send word to me if Lowry is seen thereabouts. She knows a girl inside the house."

"Michael!" Lady Margaret called from the steps outside. "Where are you? Where is Lady Helen? You hold us up."

"I shall be there directly," he called, turning back to Helen with a frown. "Do we wait for that message, or should I go in and search?"

Helen felt a moment of raw relief; he did not expect her to go into such a vile place.

"I doubt that he would leave it there. Even if he did, we would not know where to look. I think we must wait until he makes an appearance."

"I agree. We do not want to tip him off too soon."

"For goodness' sake, hurry up," Lady Margaret said, peering in the doorway. "The sooner we go to this awful affair, the sooner we may return."

Helen sat next to Delia in the carriage, her friend eagerly pointing out various silhouetted landmarks on the seafront as they made their way toward the Steine.

Helen's sight, however, had turned more inward and was a great deal more critical. Since Monday and that disturbing conversation with Lord Carlston, she'd had at least three opportunities to speak to Darby about the rule forbidding love and had shrunk from them all. When had she become so weak-willed? She could not bear the thought of bringing Darby heartbreak; and perhaps, if she were honest, there was a little self-interest at play as well. Darby might very well leave her to serve his lordship in order to stay with Quinn. The possibility had only occurred to Helen after seeing Darby's silent staunch support of the Terrene in the drawing room.

And, of course, she was guilty of another kind of weakness as well. She could not find the steel within herself to quell her attraction to his lordship. Well, now she must. He had made it very clear that self-control was the duty of a Reclaimer.

The coach turned up South Parade and made its way toward Edward Street. On Helen's side, Donaldson's Library was bright with candles and lamps, and she could see an audience seated on rows of gilt chairs. One of their famous musical recitals.

On the next corner, three young gentlemen in evening wear stood outside Raggett's Club, and peered insolently in the coach windows as it passed. Helen drew back from their stares. Was the Duke inside the club? For all his vow of continued devotion, she had not seen him for a week. Perhaps he had finally realized the futility of his pursuit. Or perhaps he had been called back to London on Parliament business. Helen chewed the inside of her mouth. What was she going to do when her brother finally arrived? She could hardly ignore him in a town this size.

The line of waiting carriages outside the Dunwicks' caused some delay, but finally it was their turn to move up and alight. Geoffrey opened the door and let down the steps, handing out Lady Margaret first. Helen descended next, and stood for a moment to take in the handsome neoclassical frontage of the house. According to Pug, her father, the Earl of Dunwick, had secured the Brighton residence at the beginning of the Prince Regent's patronage of the seaside resort. A canny investment, for it now sat close to the ever-expanding Royal Pavilion, the Prince Regent's favorite palace and the venue of some of his most scandalous parties. In the shadow of such notoriety, the Dunwicks' house was a suitable location for her own intrigue, Helen thought wryly. And for her first proper *tête-à-tête* with a Deceiver.

She pressed her hand against her stomach, trying to ease the nervous fluttering that turned within. Somewhere inside that house she was going to stand beside his lordship and bargain for his sanity with one of their sworn enemies. She could see the necessity of dealing with the creature, but even so, his lordship was dragging her into questionable deeds and unholy alliances. All behavior that seemed to confirm Pike's allegations.

Delia stepped down beside her and clutched her arm. "It feels so long since I have danced. I do hope I am asked."

"You can be assured of Mr. Hammond," Helen said, glad to be diverted from her dark thoughts.

Inside the residence, a footman ushered them and Lady Margaret to a well-appointed library that was doing duty as the ladies' retiring room. They quickly deposited their wraps and returned to the foyer to greet their hostess. It did not take them long to move down the line of arrivals, and with a quick curtsy and "Good evening" to Lady Dunwick, and a delighted squeal of welcome from Pug, they were on the way up the staircase to the salon.

Lady Margaret was stopped at the top by an acquaintance, and she waved Helen and Delia onward.

"This is a much larger party than I was expecting," Helen whispered. "I thought it was to be a few select families."

Delia giggled. "The Dunwicks do *everything* on a large scale. I think the entire Brighton Barracks has been invited."

Helen stifled a smile. It was true, but Pug's generosity and kindness did not deserve such ridicule. "At least so many people will obscure our purpose. If there were fewer guests, an extended conversation with the Comte d'Antraigues would look rather particular."

Delia nodded. "Are you nervous about meeting him?"

"Not at all," Helen lied as they entered the long, noisy salon.

They both paused on the threshold, taking in the sea of red uniforms interspersed with pale gowns and the dark jackets of nonmilitary men. At least a hundred candles burned in white porcelain candelabra, their light reflected in large mirrors that doubled the sense of how many people milled in the room. The stink of beeswax and smoke, perfumes and heated bodies brought a rise of tears to Helen's eyes, her Reclaimer sense of smell momentarily overwhelmed. A group of musicians sat at the far end, waiting to play, the flutist in their midst trilling a soft sweet song that soared above the thrum of conversation.

A familiar stooped figure and sour face caught Helen's eye. Oh no: Mr. Pike. He was talking to a group of gentlemen, supercilious smile in place. He had not seen her, but she would wager he knew she would be attending tonight. At some stage he would come looking for a report about Lowry. She must warn Mr. Hammond. Another search of the room proved fruitless. Mr. Hammond was not yet among the throng.

"Delicious, isn't it?" Pug said, bustling up to them. She flicked open her *brisé* fan with a click and hid her mouth behind the ivory span. "So many handsome officers, and far more of them than ladies, for you cannot ask only some of the men from the barracks and not the others. Mama has released me from greeting the arrivals to start the dancing." She leaned closer to Helen, her white-satin-clad décolletage drawing a passing gentleman's gaze. "I do like your new coiffure," she whispered. "Very queenly."

Helen touched her carefully curled crop, threaded with a pale green riband that matched her muslin gown. "Thank you."

"I have something to confess." Pug raised the fan to conceal both of their faces, her protuberant eyes contrite. "I meant to warn you before tonight, but with all the preparations, I forgot. The Duke of Selburn is here. He is in the cardroom across the landing."

Involuntarily Helen looked over her shoulder. She could not see him, of course, but just knowing he was there sent a frisson of panic down her spine. There could be no doubt that he would at some stage seek her out, and since the goal of the evening was for her and Lord Carlston to meet with the Comte, the Duke would most likely find her at his lordship's side. Helen closed her eyes for a moment, seeing in her mind all too clearly the moment at her own ball when the two men had clashed, snarling at each other like wolves.

"We do not know His Grace very well," Pug continued, "but he acknowledged us in Edward Street and stopped to converse.

He has a house on the Steine, you know. He made it so clear he wished to attend tonight that Mama invited him there and then. Such a coup for her, you see. I could hardly stop her, could I?"

"I understand," Helen murmured, privately consigning Lady Dunwick to the devil. "Tell me, has Lord Carlston arrived?"

"Oh, yes," Pug said. "He is over there, by the front window."

Helen found him immediately. He stood a head's height above most of the other men, and was also set apart by the close cut of his dark hair amid all the more fashionably disheveled styles. He must have felt her gaze, for he looked around and gave a small nod, warmth springing to his eyes. Helen looked away lest he see her gratification. There, self-control.

"Mama told me about the old friction between His Grace and Lord Carlston over poor Lady Elise," Pug said cheerfully. "I think Mama hopes for some of their fireworks to liven up the party. It is so hard to make a memorable evening these days." She cupped Helen's elbow. "Come, I'll call the first dance. You both"—her glance took in Delia—"will be inundated with dance requests. Just you see."

And so it transpired. Helen and Delia were secured for the first set by two young officers from the Tenth amidst many offers from their comrades. Helen's partner was a dark-skinned young man by the name of Nesbitt, whose English relatives, Helen gathered from his conversation, had secured him his commission as a cornet despite his maternal Indian connections. He proved to be an excellent dancer and a charming companion with a ready flow of amusing anecdotes about his childhood in India and life in the Hussars. Helen, however, saw the habitual watchfulness behind his smiling demeanor. It must be very difficult, she thought, to be one of the few colored men in the officer ranks. Even as they danced, there were some side-glances that were not entirely friendly. Ignoring them, Helen focused all her energies upon her partner and the figures, finding some respite from her worries in the felicity of motion.

As the second dance, a robust reel, drew to an end, Helen caught a signal from Lord Carlston, who was watching from the edge of the dance floor: a tilt of his head toward the door. She curtsied to Cornet Nesbitt and, with a warm smile of farewell, turned her attention to the elderly couple who stood at the entrance. This, then, had to be the Comte and Comtesse d'Antraigues.

The Comte surveyed the room through a gold quizzing glass held up to his eye by an elegant hand. His superbly tailored blue jacket made the most of his tall build, and the crisp cravat between his stiffened shirt points was expertly arranged in the fiendishly difficult Waterfall, the same style that his lordship favored. The Comte's expression was one of delight, his small mobile mouth curled into an attractive smile. He had to be near sixty, Helen estimated, but had the straight bearing of someone half his age, and would be called a fine-looking man in any company. The benefits, perhaps, of leaching the life energy from those around him.

The Comtesse had not fared quite so well, but then she was not a Deceiver. She still had the remnants of what must have been a ferocious beauty, enhanced now with yellow hair dye and artful cosmetics. The fire in her eyes, however, was in no way diminished, nor was her commanding manner.

"J'ai besoin d'un peu de champagne, Louis," she said, her trained opera voice penetrating the hum of the crowded room.

The Comte waved over one of the footmen and procured the required glass, earning a brilliant smile from his wife that hinted at her famous passion.

"She prefers to speak French," Lord Carlston said quietly. Helen jumped; she had been concentrating so hard upon the d'Antraigues that she had not noticed his approach. "He is reasonably fluent in English, but will insist upon conversing with us in French to ensure he is at no disadvantage."

"Are you asking if my French is up to the task?"

"I have no doubt that you are fluent, Lady Helen, but this will be a serpentine conversation, and Monsieur le Comte is an erudite creature. One of the more refined Hedon Deceivers."

He held his touch watch cupped in his gloved palm. Did he have it out as a weapon or a lens?

"I shall be quite able to follow," she answered in French. "I may have had a female's education, but it was a good one. I can also speak Italian and read Latin."

"*Bene*," his lordship said.

"*Più che buono*," She turned her attention back to the Comte and Comtesse, but knew he had appreciated the pert reply. "Do we go to the Comte now?"

"No. He is most solicitous of Madame's comfort, and will see her settled with some admirers before he turns his attention elsewhere. But he has seen me and understands that I wish to speak to him."

Helen looked down at his touch watch. "Has he glutted?"

"No."

"Skimming, then?"

Carlston repressed a smile, but his eyes were alight with it. "Monsieur le Comte would never be so gauche as to skim a friend's gathering."

"Yes, of course, how gauche," Helen said, meeting his silent amusement.

It was such moments as these—the warm sense of camaraderie and collusion—that made her so weak-willed. Not to mention those other, warmer moments that lit such a fire within her body. She forced herself to look away from a curve of dark hair that refused to sit neatly over the scar that ran from his temple to sideburn, and clenched her fingers around her fan to stop the mad impulse to smooth it down.

"Are there any other Deceivers here?" she asked.

"One. That woman in ill-advised pea green near the orchestra. Mrs. Carrington-Hurst."

Smiling at the acerbic description, Helen located the Deceiver: a short blonde with a rather prunish face. She was watching them warily.

"She is a Hedon like the Comte. As you see, she is aware of us and will no doubt make her adieu to Lady Dunwick before long." He touched her elbow. "Half an hour, meet back here. We will make our compliments to the Comte."

She watched him move into the crowd, nodding now and then to an acquaintance. To the casual eye, he looked as self-possessed and vital as ever, but Helen saw the hidden exhaustion that dragged at his smooth walk, and the strange taut energy deep within him. He had not recovered as well as he claimed.

"I am ravenous," Pug said, arriving at her side, fan waving vigorously. "Come, let us get a bite to eat and a drink before the next set. Dear Mama is keeping a cold supper table throughout the evening. Some of the army men will have to leave before the hot supper, and she could not bear to think they would miss out entirely."

"Wait." Helen scanned the room for Delia. "I must find—"

"Miss Cransdon?" Pug snapped her fan closed and pointed it across the room. "She is over there."

Sure enough, Delia stood surrounded by three young officers, the small group laughing at some quip she had made. Her cheeks were pink from the heat of the room, a delicate rose upon the smooth alabaster of her skin, and her hurriedly altered cream gown made the most of her new silhouette. She looked like a slender lily set against the crimson backdrop of the men's uniforms.

"Miss Cransdon seems to have changed a lot since the"—Pug dropped her voice—"scandal. She has certainly found the way to be fascinating."

"What do you mean?"

Taking Helen's gloved hand, Pug led her toward the door. "She has the irresistible aura of scandal around her." A tilt of her head directed Helen's attention to an emaciated, hawk-nosed woman in purple who seemed to be watching Delia with some kind of malicious delight. "That is Mama's best friend, Mrs. Albridge, a nasty cat of a woman. One of the biggest gossips in England. She has been busily reminding everyone of your friend's disgrace—how she eloped and was never married—and so now the men think she is . . ." Pug let the sentence hang.

"She is not!" Helen protested.

"It does not matter if she is or she isn't," Pug said, linking her arm through Helen's. "Anyway, you and Lady Margaret have lent her the protection of your good names, and so she has moved from scandalous to fascinating." Pug surveyed Delia for a moment, then sighed. "She certainly looks fascinating. I wonder how she lost all that weight so quickly. Do you think it was the vinegar diet?"

"I think it was all the pain and anguish," Helen said dryly.

"Well, that is not a route I'd wish to take, even for such a figure," Pug said. "I would much rather be comfortable and eat what I like."

On that synchronous note, they reached the refreshment room. A large table ran down the center, filled with platters of cold delights for the army gentlemen or, indeed, anyone else who could not wait for the hot supper at midnight: jellies, tarts, carved meats, cheesecakes, nuts, meringues, and even a churn of ice cream. A huge silver epergne in the shape of a cornucopia stood in the middle of it all, overflowing with strawberries, nectarines, grapes, and three costly pineapples, one already cut into bite-size pieces for the delectation of the guests. Two footmen in blue and silver livery stood in attendance: one in charge of a tea service set upon a smaller table, and the other ready to help serve from the table. Yet underneath all the delicious smells, Helen could detect something tainted. She wrinkled her nose. Yes, something was definitely well into decay. She glanced at Pug; her friend did not seem to have noticed.

A few people were circling the largesse with plates in hand. One lone lady, in a slightly outmoded lavender gown, sat on the edge of a chair against the far wall, a glass of lemonade clasped in her hand. She did not look at all well, pasty skin, cracked lips, and deep lines of suffering etched across her forehead and between her brows. Even so, there was a sweetness about her heart-shaped face and large eyes, and a dignity in the straightness of her back.

Lady Dunwick swept into the room and cast a critical eye over the table. Her attention paused for a moment on the wan lady, then came to rest upon her daughter. "Ah, there you are." She waved them both over, the two heavy gold Egyptian bracelets about her wrist clinking together. "I am glad to have found you, Elizabeth. And you, Lady Helen." She lowered her voice, addressing her daughter. "Will you do me a favor, my dear? That lady over there is Mrs. Pike, the wife of the Second Secretary at the Home Office. She knows no one, and I fear she is not enjoying herself. Will you talk to her for a while? It will, I think, help Papa."

That was Pike's *wife*? Helen looked at the woman again. So Pike banned love, yet was married himself?

Lady Dunwick lowered her voice even further. "We had to invite her and her husband. They are not in our circle, of course— their lodgings are at the far end of Edward Street—but he has the ear of Lord Sidmouth, and now that the new Cabinet has been named, that is quite useful. Lady Helen, I would not presume to impose the acquaintance upon you. I am sure Elizabeth will not be long. Let me find an officer to escort you back to the salon."

She looked around the room as if searching for a lurking redcoat.

"That is not necessary, Lady Dunwick," Helen said quickly. She was not going to pass up the chance to meet Pike's wife. "I have no objection to making the lady's acquaintance."

"That is most gracious of you, my dear. Come, then."

They skirted the table—one of the meat dishes was definitely rancid—and advanced upon the little lady, who, seeing them approach, rose from her seat.

"Ah, Mrs. Pike," Lady Dunwick said warmly. "Allow me to present you to my daughter, the Lady Elizabeth Brompton, and her friend, the Lady Helen Wrexhall."

Mrs. Pike curtsied. "Honored," she murmured.

The smell was stronger around the woman, Helen noticed.

"Well, I shall leave you to converse," Lady Dunwick announced, and with a satisfied nod she abandoned them, bracelets click-clacking as she hurried from the room.

"Are you enjoying Brighton, Mrs. Pike?" Helen asked.

"Yes," she answered.

Pug smiled. "Have you seen much of the town?"

"Yes."

It seemed Mrs. Pike was not a woman inclined to chatter.

"Are you here for the Season or for your health?" Pug tried.

"My health." Mrs. Pike passed the lemonade glass from one slender hand to the other. "My husband insists I come every year. The seawater is very beneficial."

"Yes," Pug said, seizing upon the subject. "Lady Helen is here for her health as well."

"You are?" Mrs. Pike asked, a spark of interest entering her pretty hazel eyes. "Have you found much relief from the water?"

"I find it very invigorating," Helen said. "Have *you* found some relief?"

Mrs. Pike wet her cracked lips. "My ailment is long-standing, I'm afraid, but I do find that I am a little improved after a sojourn here."

Long-standing. Was she consumptive? But she did not cough. Perhaps a canker in her breast? Helen had seen similar symptoms in one of the maids at her uncle's estate. A startling realization dawned: the rancid smell in the room was Mrs. Pike. *Good Lord*, Helen thought, *I can smell disease!* Was this another Reclaimer talent?

"I am glad to hear you are improved," Pug said bracingly. "If you will excuse me, I must return to the salon to call the next dance." She glanced at Helen pointedly. "I believe you are promised for the next set as well?"

Helen was not promised, purposely so, but Pug clearly thought her in need of deliverance from Mrs. Pike. She was quite wrong.

"Thank you for the reminder," she said. "I will be in directly."

"Of course." With a nod to them both, Pug made her exit.

"I am acquainted with your husband," Helen said.

"Oh, really?" Mrs. Pike smiled, the expression taking years from her worn face. She could be no more than five years older than Helen herself. "He is Second Secretary, you know," she added. "And a most ardent servant of the country."

Clearly she was proud of her husband, but did she know of the Dark Days Club?

"Are you well acquainted with his duties?" Helen asked.

"Oh, no. I am afraid I am not interested in politics, and my husband does not want me bothered with his worries. He is such a good man. So careful of my health." Suddenly the smile upon her face deepened into delight. "Ignatious!"

Helen turned. Pike stood in the doorway, his face rigid. He forced himself to smile as he crossed the room to them. "Lady Helen." He bowed, his cold eyes wary.

Helen inclined her head. "Mr. Pike. I am delighted to meet your wife."

"Lady Helen is here for her health as well, Ignatious."

"Indeed." He smiled at his wife, the first time Helen had seen anything approaching warmth in the man. "I fear that you have overtaxed your strength, Isabella. It is time we departed."

She nodded. "You are quite right. I will get my shawl." She turned to Helen and made an elegant curtsy. "It has been an honor to make your acquaintance."

Pike touched his wife's shoulder, an unconscious, protective gesture. "I will join you directly, downstairs."

"Of course."

They both watched her deposit her glass with the footman and depart the room.

"Your wife is charming," Helen said.

Pike crossed his arms. "Have you made contact with Lowry?"

Helen closed her hand around her fan. "Yes."

Pike watched an army man pause in the doorway, calling jovially to a comrade to come view the provisions.

"We cannot talk in this room," he said. "There is a ladies' parlor on the next floor, directly to the left of the staircase. Wait a minute, and then make your way there. Unobtrusively."

How did he know about such a room?

He bowed and headed for the impromptu rendezvous. Helen kept her eyes fixed upon the gold carriage clock on the mantel. All Pike wanted was a report about Lowry. Well, she had her story ready, as close to the truth as possible. Moreover, she had her own questions. She felt her heart quicken, each beat thudding with the shift of the clock's gold hands.

⌒

THE LADIES' PARLOR had a chill in the air that was older than just one night, and no lingering smell of fire in the hearth or of the perfumes of female habitation. Plainly a secondary morning room, not often used. Pike had picked up a hall candelabrum on his way into the room and placed it on a sideboard. The three candles threw their shadows across the pink silk walls like huge silhouettes cut from gray paper.

"He will take fifteen thousand pounds in gold," Helen said, glad to have her lies masked in the dim light. "We are to make the exchange on the twenty-fourth, at a place of his choosing."

Pike regarded her for a long uncomfortable moment. "Why such a delay?"

For the full moon, Helen thought, quelling a shiver. "He did not explain his reasoning."

"You should have at least insisted upon the choice of place. He will have the advantage."

"He wants the gold. He will not jeopardize the exchange."

"Perhaps not." Pike drew a deep breath, a victorious gathering of air. "I will have the payment ready for you. Tell me the place he decides upon."

"I will." Helen clasped her fan more tightly. "Lowry showed me a line he had copied from the journal."

Pike's eyes narrowed, the flickering candlelight catching the flare of interest in his face. "Did he, now?"

"About my parents." She let that sit for a moment, but he did not react. "A scrap that mentioned them and someone with the initials VC. Do you know who that could be?"

"VC?" He shook his head. "I was not a member of the Dark Days Club when your parents were alive, Lady Helen. That was ten years ago. I joined six years ago, and the subject of your parents was never discussed."

Was he lying? It was hard to tell. She decided to prod in another direction. "According to Lowry, the whole journal is written in blood."

200 ~ Alison Goodman

No response from Pike whatsoever, no moue of disgust or shiver of horror. So he already knew about its gruesome ink. Perhaps he also knew why it had been written in such a medium.

"The journal has alchemical properties, doesn't it? That is what you were keeping from us at my oath."

"Ah." He walked across to the sideboard and stared into the tiny candle flames for a moment. "You are as clever as Lord Carlston claims you are."

Beneath her focus, she felt a fleeting satisfaction: Carlston thought her clever. "What is the real purpose of the journal?"

Pike turned to face her again. "I will tell you, but it will be under the purview of your oath and it goes no further than this room."

"You do not need to remind me of my oath." She could not resist driving home the fact of her word. "I have told no one about the journal, have I?"

He tilted his head, conceding her silence. "This time, not even Mr. Hammond can be privy to the information. His devotion to Lord Carlston is too compromising." He waited for her nod of agreement, then said, "The journal is not only full of sensitive Reclaimer information. It is also a *Ligatus*. Do you know what I mean by that?"

Oh yes, Helen knew what he meant. She felt the fear of it in her bowel. A *Ligatus* was one-third of the *Trinitas*: the three-part alchemical weapon that included her own lost *Colligat* and another part called a *Vis*. It was a weapon that could destroy all the Reclaimers if the three parts were brought together. Sweet heaven, Pike had set her and Hammond on the path of a weapon that could destroy all her kind across the world.

"I see that you understand the importance of it," Pike said. "I have to admit, I only came recently to the knowledge that the journal could be a *Ligatus*. It is the most difficult element of the *Trinitas* to create, almost impossible to do so by oneself. Both Deceiver and

Reclaimer blood are worked together into an irrevocable binding alchemy. It takes a great deal of alchemical knowledge and blood sacrifice—and by that I mean the collection of the vital fluid on the cusp of violent death."

"Like the Ratcliffe Highway murders."

"Among others. It must be destroyed, Lady Helen, as soon as possible."

Such a heinous thing must indeed be destroyed. Yet something did not make sense. Benchley had tried to steal her *Colligat*, and it seemed he had spent years building a *Ligatus*. The man had clearly been bent on creating a *Trinitas*.

"Why would a Reclaimer create a weapon that could kill all Reclaimers?" she asked.

Pike gave a small laugh; the kind that covered true fear. "Because it is not only a weapon. The *Trinitas* is said to have another use: it can open the door to the place where the Deceivers originate. Perhaps open a door to Hell, if, as many believe, that is where they come from. I think Benchley was set upon finding a way to destroy all the Deceivers at once."

Helen gasped, and Pike nodded his agreement. "Yes, true madness. A path that leads to the Deceivers will also lead back to us. Thankfully, there is only one *Vis*—the power source of the *Trinitas*—in existence and it is secure. Another cannot be manufactured."

"But what is it? Where is it held?" Helen asked.

Pike shook his head. "You do not need that information."

Clearly she was to be trusted only so far.

Pike continued. "What we must face is the fact that the other two parts of the *Trinitas* have now been created, and one of them is in the hands of the Deceivers."

Her fault. She had allowed the Deceivers to get a *Colligat*. And Philip was here in Brighton too, no doubt searching for the *Ligatus*.

"The Grand Deceiver must be piecing together a *Trinitas* as well," she said. The skeptical lift of Pike's brows drove her forward a step. "Do you still not believe that a Grand Deceiver is here?"

"Considering the source of that information is Lord Carlston, I do not. It seems clear that Benchley was the one attempting to create a *Trinitas*."

Helen stared at him, aghast. Men and their vendettas.

"Even if you do not believe it, you should have all the Reclaimers set upon retrieving the journal," she said. "Not just me."

"No," he said sharply. "I do not know who has been involved. You are the only one who could not possibly have had a hand in its creation."

"You think some of the other Reclaimers helped Benchley?" It took a moment, but Helen finally came to his true meaning. "You think Lord Carlston helped him make it. You think he is involved in this insane plan to open the doorway to the Deceivers?"

"It takes many years to build a *Ligatus*, and Lord Carlston was Benchley's protégé for at least five years before he was exiled under a murder charge." He paused, allowing that to sink in. "I also know Lord Carlston is suffering from some kind of mental decline. Maybe it is vestige madness, or maybe it is something else to do with the creation of a *Ligatus*." He raised his brows. "Perhaps you can tell me more about his state of mind?"

"What do you mean?" It was all she could manage through her shock. She could not—no, *would* not—believe his lordship had anything to do with building such a heinous creation.

"I think you know exactly what I mean, Lady Helen. Mr. Ryder, the former Home Secretary, was also at their recent meeting in London, and he recognized the signs: the strange energy, the change in temper, a certain looseness in judgment. He wrote to say he had seen the same behavior in Benchley at the start of his madness."

"He is mistaken."

"Has Lord Carlston shown any unreasonable violence? Any lack of judgment?"

Helen gripped her fan even more tightly. "I have seen none of that."

"I know you feel some kind of loyalty toward Lord Carlston." Helen clenched her teeth; the way he said it was so salacious. "But you must realize that the Dark Days Club cannot afford another Samuel Benchley. Nor can the world."

Helen shook her head, drawing outraged breath, but Pike held up a hand, stopping her protest.

"Yes, yes, I know, his lordship is nothing like Benchley. But neither was Benchley at the beginning. You met him at the end, Lady Helen, and you saw the depth of his insanity. His depravity."

Yes, Helen remembered the snake-whip madness in the old Reclaimer's eyes. She also remembered Lord Carlston's horror at his mentor's confessed involvement in the Ratcliffe murders.

"His lordship would never kill a person for some unholy alchemical ritual," she said. "He condemned Benchley for his murder of those poor people. Besides, Quinn would never stay by his side if he did such a thing."

"A diseased mind can warp duty into many strange shapes, Lady Helen. If Mr. Ryder is correct, then Lord Carlston is on his way to the same kind of decline as Benchley. Perhaps he started walking the path to such madness at the side of his mentor, before he took Mr. Quinn as his Terrene."

"I cannot believe such a thing," Helen said.

Yet Mr. Quinn had said his lordship's excessive reclaiming on the Continent had been some kind of atonement. Was it for creating a *Ligatus* and not for failing to save his wife?

"It does not matter what you believe. You are under order to inform me if he shows any further symptoms. Any aberrations in behavior. We will not allow another Benchley. Is that clear?"

"What will happen if he does show such signs?"

"A rabid dog must be put down, Lady Helen. For the safety of society."

He bowed and walked from the room, closing the door. The three candles flickered and jumped from the draft, making Helen's lone silhouette shiver on the wall. She groped for the back of the sofa and leaned against it, unable to breathe past the shock of his words. It felt as if she had been struck in the chest. The journal was a *Ligatus*, and Pike had just threatened to execute Lord Carlston.

What must she do?

Warn Lord Carlston; it was the first impulse. Yet if she did, it would be a slippery slope to telling him everything. Cold-blooded treason. And what if Lord Carlston did deteriorate into something like Mr. Benchley? It was a terrible thought, but the possibility had to be faced. Pike was right about one thing: the world could not afford another monster like Samuel Benchley. That must never happen again.

She straightened, the vow giving her some kind of anchor in the wild wash of dread and fear. There was no easy answer to any of this, no way forward that did not place someone at risk, including herself. For now, all she could do was fix a smile in place, return to the salon, and pray that the Deceiver that lived as the Comte d'Antraigues knew what really ailed Lord Carlston, and was willing to make a deal for the cure.

Thirteen

HELEN SCANNED THE crowded salon and found Lord Carlston near the orchestra talking to another gentleman, his eye on the doorway. She watched him note her arrival, bid his companion farewell, and start to thread his way across the room. Did he look more strained than he had before? Or was it Pike's horrifying aspersions conjuring her worst fear? Could Carlston really have been party to Benchley's mad plan?

"Lady Helen!"

She turned. The call had come from the middle of a group of young officers. One of them moved aside, and Delia came into view. She smiled and waved, disengaging herself from her admirers.

"Is this not a wonderful party?" she said, almost dancing up to Helen and taking her hands in an excited grip.

"Wonderful," Helen echoed hollowly. The horror of her interview with Pike still buzzed through her bones. She pulled her hands free from her friend's grasp in case she somehow transmitted her agitation. "Do you think we could sit down?"

"Lady Helen." The smooth deep voice stopped her mid-request, recognition of its owner feathering down her spine.

She turned to face the Duke of Selburn. "Your Grace."

Behind him, she saw Lord Carlston quicken his progress through the throng. It was all happening just as she had predicted—

two snarling wolves—but it was too late to try to stop it.

She curtsied to the Duke. "Allow me to introduce Miss Cransdon."

Delia curtsied. "Good evening, Your Grace."

The Duke bowed and turned his attention back to Helen. "It is marvelous to see you again. You are radiant, as ever. Would you do me the honor of the next two dances?"

At that moment Lord Carlston stepped in beside the Duke; a little too close for courtesy, but the perfect distance for threat. "You are too late, Selburn. Lady Helen has promised these next to me."

The Duke stood his ground. "Carlston. You look positively ill," he said with mock concern. "A reflection of the inner man perhaps? Are you sure you are up to dancing?"

Helen drew a sharp breath; the barb had more truth than Selburn realized.

Carlston gave an ironic bow. "Thank you for your solicitude, Duke, but I am quite well." He offered Helen his arm. "Shall we? I believe Lady Elizabeth is about to call the dance."

Helen flushed at his proprietary manner, but took his arm. "Please excuse me," she said to Selburn. "I am already promised to Lord Carlston."

The Duke regarded them for a moment, then turned to Delia. "Miss Cransdon, would you do me the honor of the next two dances?"

Delia's eyes darted to his lordship. "I am . . . I mean . . ."

Helen saw a young officer hovering nearby, clearly Delia's promised partner for the set and somewhat cowed by the Duke's presence.

With a drowning glance at Helen, and a small helpless shrug to the lurking officer, Delia took the Duke's proffered arm. "Thank you, Your Grace."

What was Delia thinking? She was lucky the officer did not dare confront a man of Selburn's rank.

"Ladies and gentlemen," Pug called loudly. "Pray take your partners for the Perigordine."

A murmur of surprise and delight surged through the company. The Perigordine was on the very edge of respectability, being French and slightly vulgar. Helen squeezed her eyes shut. Trust Pug to choose that particular dance. It was an old cutting-in jig that gave the gentlemen leave to swap partners at will.

She opened her eyes to find the Duke leading Delia to the dance floor but staring back at her, his intention clear in his eyes: he was going to wrest her from Carlston at the first opportunity. The last thing she needed was to be in the middle of this fight.

"I wish to sit down," she hissed at Carlston as they watched Pug and her partner take the position below the Duke and Delia to begin the dance. "I will not be the excuse that you and Selburn fight over."

The first notes of the music started.

"Too late, it has begun," his lordship whispered back.

She was caught now; one could not abandon the floor during a dance.

"Why do you encourage him?" Carlston added.

Helen glared at him. "I do not encourage him. Quite the opposite. He is determined to rescue me from your influence. It is *you* who are at the core of the problem."

It seemed he was at the core of all her problems.

The Duke and Delia, as first-ranked couple, set the series of steps: a skipping *chassé* to the right, then to the left, a full turn to the right and once again to the left, and finally a small leap into the finishing *jeté*. All four danced the steps again, then the Duke abandoned Delia and took Pug's hand, twirling her into the steps. It was time for the third-ranked couple to join: Helen and Carlston.

"This should be interesting," he said, taking her gloved hand in his own and leading her into the middle of the dance floor. Through his grip, Helen felt the tension in his body, the kind of tension she fancied was reserved for prebattle.

She skipped into the first *chassé*, her eyes on Selburn behind them. He had maneuvered Pug across the floor in a traveling step so they danced in striking distance of Helen and Carlston. The second *chassé* brought Helen back to stand in front of Carlston.

"It is customary to look at your partner, not another gentleman," he drawled as he took her offered right hand.

"He is behind us," Helen said as they turned.

"I am quite aware of his position."

They turned again, then made the leap into the elegant final *jeté*.

Two more couples joined the dance as the Duke passed Pug on to another man and crossed to Helen.

"Lady Helen?" he asked, claiming her hand before she could answer.

"You are nothing if not predictable, Selburn," Carlston said.

"You are allowing Miss Cransdon to stand without a partner," the Duke replied as he led Helen into the first *chassé*. "Come, let us quit this area."

Retaining his hold upon her hands, he swung her into three long traveling steps away from the Earl. They ended up on the other side of the dance floor. A young officer released his rather gawky partner and approached, ready to claim Helen.

"Stand down, Lieutenant," Selburn said, his smile akin to a snarl.

Startled, the young man bowed and backed away.

"That is not in the spirit of the dance, Duke," Helen said.

His smile relaxed into something more genuine. "True, but I have only just secured you."

She had to smile back; there was such complimentary delight in his face. They turned the first circle, hand in hand.

"Your brother joins me on Monday," he said. "He wishes to call upon you as soon as he arrives in the evening. I believe he has a proposal to discuss with you—one to your advantage. Will you be at home?"

They clasped hands for the opposite turn. A proposal to her advantage? She doubted Andrew would have come up with a plan himself; he was not one for thinking beyond his own needs. No, she would wager the Duke had put some idea for her protection into her brother's mind. She knew it was his regard speaking, but even so, the intrusion was unwelcome.

She composed her expression into polite regret. "I believe Lady Margaret has made plans to join the promenade on Monday evening." At least the excuse was true.

"I see. Then Andrew and I will meet you there. I am sure he will enjoy a walk after such a long journey."

Helen bit down on her chagrin. There was no escaping it. "That would be most agreeable."

The Duke observed her narrowly as they completed the *jeté*. "And yet I sense that it is far from being agreeable." He took her hand again for the new figure. "Forgive me if I am trespassing upon family affairs, but you do not seem overjoyed by the prospect of your brother's visit."

"I believe Andrew will wish me to leave Lady Margaret's house, but I have accepted her kind hospitality for the summer. I will not be persuaded otherwise."

Selburn glanced at Carlston, who had just taken the hand of a lady in blue and was steering her toward them. "I do not think you should stay in that house any longer. I feel I must tell you that there are serious concerns about Lord Carlston and his companions."

Another young man stepped up to them and bowed to Helen.

The Duke turned her away from the offered hand, ignoring the young man's splutter of indignation.

"What kind of concerns?" Helen said, forcing her voice into polite interest.

"A man of my rank has many friends in the government, Lady Helen, and I have made some inquiries about your new companions. Lady Margaret and Mr. Hammond have a dubious French past, to say the least—possibly criminal—and Carlston himself is, I believe, under suspicion for espionage."

Helen lost the beat and stopped in the middle of the floor. His information was too close for comfort. "That is a slanderous claim, Duke. I will not listen to gossip about my friends."

He took her hand again, guiding her into the left turn. "Please, you must listen," he said, his voice urgent. "I believe you are being deceived by these people."

Helen felt the shock of the word register on her face. She shook her head, more to dislodge her overreaction than to deny his accusation.

"Carlston is preying upon your naivety," he said. "I do not know why—perhaps your fortune, perhaps some other vile reason— but I will discover the reason, and I will unmask him. I know this man, Helen. You must be on your guard."

The music lengthened into the final chords. Helen curtsied to the Duke's bow, then turned to clap the musicians, hiding her agitation. From the corner of her eye, she saw Carlston approach.

"Lady Helen," he said, bowing. "I believe we have the next dance as well."

"Lady Helen will stay with me," Selburn said.

Carlston gave him a lazy smile. "Lady Helen has her own voice, Selburn."

The Duke crossed his arms. "She does not know what you are, Carlston, but I do."

"And pray, what am I?"

"You are a debaucher. Your tastes are for the innocent with only corruption in your mind."

Helen drew in her breath. Dear Mother of Heaven, those were words designed to force his lordship into a challenge. Nearby, another couple had stopped to listen, and the Duke's description brought a gasp from the lady.

Carlston gave a soft, dangerous laugh. "By your account, I am indeed a villain. Should I point out that our tastes coincided four years ago? I believe your intentions were just as impure as my own."

Selburn stepped forward, his fists clenched at his sides. "You destroyed Elise. I swear you will not have a chance to destroy another innocent girl."

"Lord Carlston, I really do wish to sit down," Helen interrupted, grabbing his arm.

She could feel the coiled readiness in his muscles. Lud, she seemed doomed to step in between these two men to stop them killing each other. Or more to the point, to stop Carlston from killing the Duke.

She turned to Selburn. "Your Grace, thank you for the dance."

Ingrained good manners made him acknowledge her curtsy. "It was my pleasure, Lady Helen." His eyes, however, were fixed upon Carlston.

The Earl inclined his head. "As always, a delight, Duke."

Helen pulled him from the floor as the music for a quadrille started up. The obvious standoff had garnered more onlookers, and she could feel their curiosity as she and Lord Carlston made their way toward the salon doors. No doubt Lady Dunwick would be pleased; the confrontation would be the talk of the rout and Donaldson's tomorrow.

"He is becoming annoyingly protective of you and inquisitive about our activities," Carlston said. "Something will have to be done."

Helen stopped, her hand tightening on his forearm. Of course; he had been listening to her conversation throughout the dance.

"I will make it clear that I do not need or want his protection," she said.

Carlston regarded her thoughtfully. "If he does not draw back soon, I will take action. Do you understand?"

Helen looked back at the Duke. He was leading Delia into the quadrille set with no idea of the danger he had just brought upon himself. Well, she would not allow any harm to come to him, not on her behalf.

"Just give me some time to persuade him of my disinterest," she said.

"Be swift about it," Carlston advised. "Selburn has an unfortunate tendency to think he is one of Scott's heroes."

They had reached the salon doors. The narrow landing had cleared somewhat, most guests having found their way to the cardroom, the cold supper, or the salon. His lordship indicated a room at the end of the corridor, its open door showing two fully lit candelabra set upon a Chinoiserie sideboard.

"The Comte has suggested we meet in the morning room." His voice dropped into the secret pitch for Reclaimer ears. "I want you to take careful note of his expressions. Look for those moments when he is lying. He is a consummate actor, like all of his kind, but do the best you can."

"Of course," Helen answered in the same low tone. "But you have known him for many years. I doubt I will be able to recognize his lies more successfully than you."

Something crossed his face, a quicksilver flash of fear, so fast she almost doubted she had seen it. She stopped walking, forcing him to halt too. He looked at her inquiringly, those heart-stopping features carefully composed into polite interest. He knew she had seen his slip.

"What is wrong?" she demanded. "There is something you have not told me about the Comte."

"I have no idea what you mean."

His eyes had flattened into his shark stare, but she was not going to be deflected. Not this time. Too much was at stake.

"I saw fear in your face, Lord Carlston. Do not deny it—you know my skill in that area. For once, you must tell me the whole story."

He drew a breath through his teeth, reluctance in every line of his body.

"I deserve to go into that room fully prepared," Helen insisted.

"Yes, you do," he finally conceded. "It is possible . . ." He shook his head, correcting himself. "No, it is certain that this malady, whatever it may be, is reducing the effectiveness of my abilities." For an instant, the careful distance in his eyes was gone, and she saw that awful hollow fear again. "Perhaps even my judgment. I am not convinced that I will be able to read him thoroughly." He pressed his fingers against his forehead. "There is a pain here that I cannot shift. I feel as if I am being boxed in behind my own eyes, getting smaller and smaller. It is as if I am . . . disappearing."

She reached for his hand, a reflex of compassion. They both looked down at their gloved fingers suddenly entwined. The pulse of energy thundered in Helen's ears.

"I will not let you disappear," she said, tightening her hold. "You kept me sane when my strength came upon me. I will do the same for you."

He smiled. "You will be my anchor." He withdrew his hand, as if breaking the illicit bond was as painful as the darkness he carried. "It is worse than Quinn and the others think, and it is coming upon me fast."

Helen nodded, the ominous admission momentarily robbing her of any sound. But in her mind, Pike's voice was loud and clear: *A rabid dog must be put down, for the safety of society.*

⁓

LADY DUNWICK HAD refashioned the morning room into a with-drawing space for those guests who sought respite from the noise and rigors of the rout. At the doorway, Lord Carlston stood aside and ushered Helen in first, the rise of his eyebrows urging her to stay alert. As if she could be anything else after his terrible admission. She could still feel the touch of his hand upon her own, that insistent shadow pulse.

Fashionable yellow-striped paper adorned the walls, clashing slightly with the blue-flowered curtains. The usual dining furniture had been removed and replaced by groups of chairs arranged in twos and threes to facilitate conversation. A footman stood ready to procure drinks or provide any other service required, and a wholly unnecessary fire burned in the marble grate. Two elderly ladies in feathered turbans had taken up a position near that warmth, their conversation sporadic and limited, it seemed, to comments on the ratafia they were drinking. Helen could smell the sickly peach-infused liquor, and the rather pungent onion aroma of their heated skin.

The only other inhabitant was the Comte, seated facing the door and as far from the ladies as possible. He smelled of a musky perfume, ambergris perhaps. Helen swallowed, trying to dredge up some wet within her mouth. She felt the energy quicken through her whole body; perhaps a Reclaimer response to the enemy. It was certainly an odd sensation to see the elegant old man before her and know that within that human shell was a creature that preyed upon humanity.

He stood as they approached, intelligent eyes searching Carlston's face. His mobile mouth pursed for a second, then quickly shifted into a warm smile. "Guillaume!"

Carlston bowed. "Comte, may I introduce the Lady Helen Wrexhall."

His lordship's French was impeccable, even his accent sounding genuine to Helen's ear.

"Your charming protégée," the Comte answered in his own tongue.

Helen curtsied, rising to find the old gentleman watching her intently.

"Please." His gloved hand waved to the two chairs set opposite his own.

Helen took the seat beside Carlston. The Comte seemed very friendly toward his lordship, and his lordship was surprisingly congenial in return. Was this man not the enemy?

As instructed, she concentrated on the Comte's face, trying to read what lay behind the air of bonhomie. It was like pulling back a curtain of trailing greenery and finding a stone wall. No wonder; he'd had centuries to practice hiding his truth.

He regarded Carlston soberly. "You are not well, Guillaume."

"Is it that obvious?"

"Perhaps just to me." The Comte flicked open a little Sèvres snuffbox painted with yellow roses and edged in gold and offered it to him. The scent of rich tobacco laced with an aniseed perfume rose into the air.

Carlston eyed the box warily. "I thank you, no."

The Comte's shoulders shook with silent laughter. "You are remembering Paris. I assure you there is no drug in this batch."

"Still," his lordship said dryly, "I will decline."

Helen glanced at him. Paris? Drugged snuff? There was certainly history between them.

The Comte sat back, his attention on Helen again. "I met your mama and papa in Paris too," he said, brown eyes half-closed in recollection. "In the truce of 1802, before their tragic demise. You are a little like both of them, yes? The beautiful Lady Catherine and the resolute Lord Douglas."

"I had thought I did not resemble either, Comte," Helen answered. "But I am happy for it to be thought otherwise."

Her accent, she knew, was not as deft as his lordship's, but she was pleased by the approval in the old Comte's eyes. She mentally shook herself; she did not need a Deceiver's approval. The man was too charming by half.

The elderly ladies, having finished the ratafia, rose from their chairs and departed the room, their conversation turned now toward the impending hot supper.

"Let us take the opportunity for some privacy," the Comte said, and, with a flick of his hand, dismissed the footman. The young man bowed and closed the door behind him.

They were alone.

The Comte settled back in his chair. "You asked for this meeting, Guillaume. What is it you want?"

"I have a question, Louis, and I think you may have the answer."

Helen shifted on her seat. They were on first-name acquaintance. Only family and the closest of friends used such intimate appellations. Surely such familiarity should not exist between a Reclaimer and a Deceiver?

"I know many answers," the Comte said smoothly. "None of them are free."

Carlston smiled. "I am well aware of that."

The Comte turned his snuffbox in his hand, seemingly transfixed by the flash of gold and painted porcelain. "As it happens," he said finally, "there is something that I require. Something that you may be able to obtain for me." He looked up, expression still inscrutable. Helen knew she was failing miserably in her task. "It is possible that we may come to an arrangement. What is it you wish to know?"

His lordship sat forward. "This sickness in me—I do not believe it is the accumulation of the vestige. You have seen many Reclaimers in your time. Do you know what it is and how I can be rid of it?"

The Comte's eyes narrowed as if he could see the darkness within his lordship. Perhaps he could, Helen thought, although none of her reading on the subject had reported such an ability. She found herself leaning a little forward too, her breath held. *Dear God*, she prayed, *let it be something that can be cured.*

"You are correct." The Comte paused. "And incorrect. The vestige is part of it—you have been snatching back too many of our offspring, my friend—but it is something else as well. Something far more interesting. I believe I know what it is, and, possibly, how it may be ameliorated."

Helen laid her hand against the base of her throat, holding back a sound of dismay. So his lordship's sickness was, in part, the vestige darkness.

The Comte glanced at her as if he had heard her distress. "Do you plan to follow in your mentor's fervent reclaiming footsteps?"

"Lady Helen's plans are not part of this discussion, Louis," Carlston said. "Are you willing to deal?"

"I am."

"What is it that you want?"

The Comte flicked open the snuffbox with his thumbnail and shut it again, flick and shut, flick and shut, his eyes never leaving Carlston. "I have heard that there is a journal available for sale, written by your former mentor, Benchley."

Helen drew a sharp breath. Sweet heaven, not the journal.

"I want that journal, Guillaume," the Comte continued. "It has some information in it about myself and my wife that I would not wish to come into the hands of your Home Office."

Helen clenched her hands, digging gloved fingernails into her palms. If his lordship went for the journal too . . . No, she could not even begin to imagine the ramifications of it. The lies upon lies she would have to tell. The betrayal.

"I know of no journal written by Benchley," Carlston said. "You have been misinformed."

"No, my friend, it exists and it is in the possession of a man called Lowry. A slippery fellow, I am told. Very hard to find."

"Lowry," Carlston said softly. "I know of him." He rubbed the back of his head, clearly perturbed. "Such a journal, if it exists, would be very dangerous. I could not pass it into your hands, Louis."

Helen eased out a breath. He knew about the journal now— there was nothing she could do about that—but at least he wasn't going to give it to a Deceiver. Did the Comte know it was a *Ligatus* as well?

The Comte inclined his head. "I understand."

"Would it suffice if you received just the information about you and the Comtesse?"

Carlston pointedly did not look her way. She knew his profile, every bold muscle and contour, and there was no mistaking the tightness along his jaw. He was clenching his teeth, forcing his way past his own conscience.

She understood the urgency of finding some way to stop the sickness within him, but even without the fact that the journal was a *Ligatus*, the deal was rapidly heading into territory that bordered upon treason. But then, who was she to point the finger?

"That would be acceptable," the Comte said. He set down the snuffbox on the small table by his side, his smooth bonhomie dropping away to expose something far more implacable. "I want something else as well."

"Go on."

"This is my last body, Guillaume."

Helen frowned. Did that mean what she thought it did? He had no offspring to shift into at the death of his current body and so would die. But she was sure he had a son.

Carlston regarded the Comte thoughtfully. "I take it you are going to spare Julien?"

Yes, Helen thought, that was the son's name. Comte Julien.

"You are correct," the old Comte said. "He is my only offspring, and it is my decision not to take his body."

"Decision!" Helen exclaimed. "I thought the shift was involuntary?"

"No, Lady Helen. It is indeed a very strong drive, but it can be overcome."

"Why?" Carlston asked.

"Antoinette," the Comte said simply. He looked at Helen. "My wife. She, of course, is of your kind. Her life will inevitably end, and frankly I do not wish to continue without her at my side. Nor do I wish to extinguish the talents she has bestowed upon our son by taking his flesh. He is a marvelous musician. You have heard him play, Guillaume?"

Carlston nodded. "I have. Still, I find this hard to believe. You are the great survivor, Louis. To give up your existence for another is not in your nature."

"It is because you do not believe my kind can love, Guillaume. I think you do not even believe your own kind can love." His keen eyes darted to Helen again. "Your mentor is a hard man, my dear. All of his passion reserved for his duty. But he was not always like that. Oh, no, not at all."

Carlston crossed his arms. "Get back to the point, Louis."

"I have existed within these flesh bodies for many centuries now. Is it so much of a surprise that I have been affected by the emotions that endlessly course through them? Some of my kind call it a taint. But there is a small group of others, like myself, who think of it as a gift. We have overcome our instinct for isolation and call ourselves the Society of Sensation. Amusing, *non*?" He closed his eyes, his fingers toying with the gold fob attached to his fob ribbon. "Your senses . . . *mon Dieu*. You humans do not appreciate the glory of your senses. To taste food, to touch skin, to hear music."

Helen sat forward. "Are you all affected so?"

The Comte nodded. "But most eschew the nobler sentiments and embrace the vile passions."

"Do your wife and son know what you are?"

He gave a small laugh. "Such good questions, Lady Helen. My wife does. Many times she has succored me with her life force. Her beautiful, vibrant life force. It is one of a kind, so strong."

Helen studied her fan for a moment. Her most important question—what would they face if the Deceiver door was ever opened?—could not be asked. Even so, she could go some way to obtaining an answer.

"Comte, can you tell me where you and your kind come from? Are you from Hell?"

He clapped his hands, a delighted smile lighting his face again. "Do you know, that is only the second time any of you have asked the question. Even you, Guillaume, have never asked the straight question. Always it is the intrigue or the killing." He regarded Helen fondly, like a pleased parent. "Do you remember your beginning, Lady Helen? Your conception? Your birth?"

"No, of course not."

He gave a very Gallic shrug. "Voilà! Nor do I remember my beginning here."

Helen released her breath. No clues, then, to what lay behind the door.

"But I will tell you this much, because you asked without guile," the Comte added. "I came to my first senses in the body of a small child in a very low household. It was the saving of me. Many of my kind were not so lucky. They awoke in adult bodies and failed to come to an understanding of the world before their intrusion was discovered. They were called mad, witches, evil spirits, demons. Many, many of them died."

"But so did the child that you possessed, and the many other children afterward," Helen pointed out curtly.

He sighed. "True. It is the tragedy of my kind."

"Of *your* kind? What about humankind?"

"Humans can propagate themselves, Lady Helen. They create more and more humans. We cannot do so; our number is finite. Thus we pass from generation to generation in the hope of finding a way to reproduce. Some think the answer lies in a union between Deceiver and Reclaimer; others seek an alchemical solution that would have us fundamentally changed. There is even a small misguided number who believe that the change will just occur over time."

"Frankly, I hope you do not find such a solution," Helen said with asperity. Just the thought of it was appalling.

The Comte gave a soft laugh.

"What else is it that you want, Louis?" Carlston asked, bringing the Comte back to the deal at hand.

"I think you may guess."

"Julien?"

"I want him protected." The Comte held up a finger, forestalling Carlston's comment. "*Not* reclaimed. I am convinced that it is, to a small degree, my vestige that gives him his creativity. I want him left alone to live out his human life. To play his music. I think he will be one of the greats."

Helen glanced at his lordship. He truly believed in reclaiming the souls of offspring. Surely he would not agree to protect one of them from salvation.

Yet there he was, giving a slow nod. "All I can guarantee is protection for the extent of my lifespan."

The Comte smiled. "I have great faith in your ability to survive, Guillaume."

"However," Carlston continued, "protecting Julien from my colleagues will be quite an undertaking. You will need to give me something more."

"What do you want?"

"Everything you know about the Grand Deceiver."

The two men stared at one another. Helen felt her heartbeat like a ticking clock, measuring the silent struggle. She concentrated fiercely upon the Comte's face. There was, as far as she could tell, conflict, even fear, but no deception.

Finally the old gentleman nodded. "I have some information that will lead you in the right direction. Is that enough?"

Carlston regarded him closely. "You do not have a name?"

"No." The Comte raised his hand. "I swear on Antoinette's soul."

It seemed that vow was sacred, for Carlston nodded. "Even so, Louis, if you want me to survive long enough to protect your son, you need to give me something now. Think of it as an investment in Julien's future."

"I will tell you this, Guillaume," the Comte said soberly. "Do not underestimate what is coming your way." He glanced at Helen, drawing her into his warning. "We, too, have our *lusus naturae*, our freaks of nature. What they can do is beyond even my comprehension. It will take both of you to defeat the Grand Deceiver."

Helen felt something primal tighten her spine.

"That is what you are giving me?" Carlston scoffed. "I could have told you that myself."

The Comte smiled, but the implacability was back in his voice. "You do not know anything, Guillaume. Bring me the journal and I will tell you what I know about you"—a glance gathered Helen into his statement—"and the Grand Deceiver."

He held out his hand. Carlston regarded him for a long moment, wariness back in his eyes, then he grasped it and shook.

"Now, shall we have champagne? To celebrate?" The Comte's bonhomie was back in place.

"I am afraid not," Carlston said, standing. "Lady Helen and I must return to the salon before our absence is noted."

Helen rose from her chair and laid her hand upon his offered arm, the magnitude of what had transpired gathering into a rolling, crashing avalanche through her mind. His lordship knew about Lowry. He knew about the journal. *He knew.*

The old Deceiver stood as well. "Before you go, Lady Helen, will you answer a question?"

She could barely focus upon what he said. "A question?"

"Would you say you are a person who follows her head or her heart?"

She stared at him, momentarily diverted. Such an odd thing to ask. "I am a rational person, sir. I believe I follow my head."

"I see." The Comte bowed. "Then I wish you good luck."

Fourteen

OUT IN THE hallway, Helen took her hand from Carlston's arm. From now on, he would be fixed upon finding the journal. Moreover, he would expect her and Mr. Hammond to help him. It was all getting worse and worse. She could not tell him about their involvement, yet it felt just as much of a betrayal to hide her knowledge from him.

He watched her with a questioning lift of brow. She offered a wan smile. There was no way around it; she had to keep the secret and pray that his lordship did not see through her lies. It was terrible to think it, but his sickness-dulled senses could work in her favor.

"That was quite a lot to comprehend," she started.

"Wait. Let us return to the salon."

He offered his arm again. She tucked her fingers into the crook of his elbow and allowed herself to be led through the throng milling on the landing and back into the salon, her mind rapidly turning over strategies. Should she take the offensive; deflect the subject; keep quiet?

The dancing had ceased for the while, only a fiddler and flutist providing music that was barely audible above the high hum of conversation in the large room. Most of the company had shifted to the supper room, or gathered into groups to chat and partake of the punch *à la romaine* offered on trays by the footmen. Carlston steered her toward a pair of empty chairs set in the corner of the far wall. He waved away a footman offering them the tall glasses of the milky, iced rum.

"Here," he said, "we can keep an eye on anyone approaching. I do not want us to be overheard."

Helen took a seat and busied herself with the arrangement of her gown. As Carlston took the other chair, she said, "If I did not know better, I would think the Comte to be one of your oldest and dearest friends." It seemed she was taking the offensive path.

"I beg your pardon?" He was plainly startled by the attack. "On the contrary: I do not trust the Comte, and he does not trust me. It is just that we have dealt with each other many times before and have a respect for each other's abilities. In the end, however, we both know that we will do what is in our own best interest. That is certainly not my definition of friendship."

Helen leaped upon his wording. "Do you not mean the interests of the Dark Days Club?"

Carlston frowned. "Of course. What did you think I meant?"

"Offering to supply pages of the journal. Promising to protect Comte Julien. That is stretching our oath, Lord Carlston."

"Ah." He rubbed his mouth. "Yes, it could be construed as such. But if we are to get any useful information as to the identity of the Grand Deceiver, that must be worth a step outside our purview. Do you not agree?"

"Surely the oath must be our guide to what is correct?"

"Nothing is clear-cut in this world of ours, Lady Helen. You should understand that by now."

"Certainly," she said stiffly. "Nevertheless, I do not think it has to be this"—she searched for an appropriate description—"murky."

He gave a wry laugh. "Wait until you start dealing directly with Pike and the Home Office."

Helen felt her cheeks heat and turned her face, pretending to

226 — Alison Goodman

survey the room to hide the telltale flush. Time to change the subject.

"The Comte was very difficult to read. As far as I could tell, he was sincere, particularly when speaking about his family."

"Yes, that part of the interview rang true. I hope you did not believe all that other information about the origin of the Deceivers. I can tell you from experience that any information Louis offers for free is either a lie or a half-truth at best."

She focused on the fan in her hands, her voice at its most non-committal. "Then perhaps the existence of Mr. Benchley's journal is a lie too."

"No, he would not make a bargain for the well-being of his wife and son built upon a lie that could be so easily discovered. He certainly believes that a journal exists."

Helen clutched the head of her fan. "Do *you* think it exists?"

"Benchley was always adamant that he did not commit any of his knowledge to paper, a ploy to make himself more valuable. Even so, it is just as possible that he did write such a journal. And if he did, then its content will not be limited to information about Deceivers."

"What do you mean?"

Did his lordship know it was a *Ligatus*? If he did, then surely that must support Pike's accusation that he had played a part in its manufacture?

"I guarantee there will be information about myself in it. And probably about you and the other Reclaimers as well."

He paused, waiting for her response. Belatedly, she nodded. He did not know. Or if he did, she could not see the lie. Holy heaven, she would go mad too with all this second-guessing.

"We must find Lowry and determine whether it exists or not," he added. "If it does, I want it safe in my hands. Lowry must either give it to me or be forced to do so. I *must* have d'Antraigues's information."

His hands were fists on his lap, the knuckles outlined under the thin silk of his gloves. She could almost feel his desperation.

"What then?" she asked. "Will you take the journal to Mr. Pike?"

Perhaps his lordship would acknowledge that it belonged with the Dark Days Club, and this nightmare would be over.

"Pike?" Carlston gave a short, bitter laugh. "I would rather hand it over to the Comte. Ignatious Pike has a vendetta against me, Lady Helen, and I must admit, I return the dislike with equal violence. He may not have been directly involved in my wife's disappearance, but I am sure he is complicit, if only by his silence. I would not place something in his hands that could be used to compromise or compel. Surely you have seen he is without honor."

Yes, she certainly had seen Pike's lack of honor. Still, that did not mean his dislike was not based upon a true injury.

"What is the cause of his animosity, Lord Carlston?"

The question was dismissed with a wave of his hand. "It does not matter."

It mattered to her, a great deal.

"Do you say that because he has good reason?"

"Good reason?" Carlston drew back and crossed his arms. "Exactly how low is your opinion of me?"

"What else am I to think?"

He regarded her for a narrowed-eyed moment. "He was a Terrene; did you know?" She nodded. "Four or so years ago, his Reclaimer, Sir Dennis Calloway, came to me for assistance in reclaiming a madwoman. Calloway knew she was an Unreclaimable, but for some reason he wanted to attempt it. I refused, told him to do his duty and put an end to her misery. Instead, he went ahead. The woman got hold of a weapon and killed him, then absconded. In Pike's mind, it is my fault that he lost his Reclaimer and his Terrene powers."

"That does not seem fair."

She felt absurdly indignant on his behalf, and more than a little relieved. There was no good reason.

"If you expect fairness, Lady Helen, you had best abandon normal society and join Mr. Owen's Utopian experiment." He turned his attention to the milling groups of people in the ballroom. "We must find Hammond. I think he may have a way of locating Lowry."

"Mr. Hammond?" Helen echoed, her body tensing.

"Yes, he pointed out Lowry as Benchley's new Terrene in Vauxhall Gardens. Named him as a low sort, if you recall. Perhaps he has some knowledge of the man's associates that will lead us in the right direction."

"A good thought," she managed. Sweet heaven, she had to get to Hammond and warn him. "Well," she said, feigning a thoughtful tone, "we cannot do more here, and people will start to talk if I am much more in your company."

"You are right." He fixed upon a group of laughing officers. "Miss Cransdon is over there, amidst a horde of redcoats. Allow me to take you to her."

Helen rose from her chair with alacrity and was duly delivered to Delia's side, his lordship quickly making his bow to both ladies.

"I shall leave you in the tender care of the army," he said dryly.

Helen watched him walk away, clearly searching for Hammond, then unfurled her fan and gathered Delia behind its cover.

"Do you know the whereabouts of Mr. Hammond?" she whispered.

"I believe he escorted Lady Margaret to the cardroom. Is something wrong?"

"I have a message for him." She clasped Delia's arm in farewell. "I shall see you soon, in the supper room."

"Wait, I will come with you," Delia said.

Before Helen could demur, her friend had curtsied to the officers, laughing at the men's exuberant protests, and started toward the salon doors, linking Helen's arm within her own.

"I thought I would never get away," she whispered. "Their conversation was becoming a little . . . *outré*."

Helen gave a tight smile. The last thing she wanted was company, but at least they were ahead of Lord Carlston.

⁓

THE CARDROOM, USUALLY a gentleman's study by the very masculine oak and burgundy walls, was almost as noisy as the salon. Most of the chatter, however, issued from the groups of people who watched the five card tables, not from the intent players.

Helen scanned the faces around the brightly lit room. Mrs. Carrington-Hurst was not in evidence, and hopefully no other Deceivers had arrived in the interim. She did not want this conversation to be overheard.

"There he is," Delia said, pointing to the compact form of Mr. Hammond. He stood behind his sister, who was seated at the far table with cards in hand.

"Wait here," Helen said to Delia, and began to thread her way through the spectators.

Mr. Hammond saw her approaching and gave a small wave of welcome. "Margaret is, as ever, making a tidy sum," he whispered as she stepped in beside him.

His sister glanced up, acknowledged Helen's arrival with a tilt of her glossy black head, then turned back to her cards.

"We need to speak privately," Helen murmured.

Hammond nodded, immediately alert, and followed her as she edged to the marble hearth. It was one of the few clear spaces, being too far away from the action of the card tables and over-heated by the fire in the grate.

"Keep smiling," she warned, her voice barely above a whisper. "The Comte knows about Lowry's journal. He has made it his price."

She briefly recounted the deal that had been struck and her subsequent conversation with his lordship, watching the full horror of it register in Hammond's eyes.

"God's blood," he swore through his teeth, although he kept his face valiantly fixed into a smile. "So his lordship is after the journal too?"

Helen nodded. Dear Lord, how she longed to tell him it was a *Ligatus*. Share the burden. Yet she could not. She must sit with the knowledge of it like a burning coal in her mind, alight with malevolence.

"Not only that, but his lordship is looking for you now, to speak to you about your knowledge of Lowry. You named him at Vauxhall Gardens, and his lordship thinks you may know his associates."

"And so now we must act directly against his lordship." Hammond pulled at the side of his cravat as if its folds had tightened, his eyes finding the doorway. "This is too much."

"Do you think we should tell him about Pike?"

"Break our oaths?" He rubbed at his forehead. "Dear God, I wish I had more courage, but I do not want to die by the rope, my name loathed by all decent men. If we tell him, it will be treason and we will both be ruined. Besides, if we lead Carlston to the journal, he will take it to the Comte—he thinks it is his only way to a cure."

"You do not sound certain of the Comte's cure."

"He is a Deceiver. I do not trust him on principle."

"Perhaps we could persuade his lordship just to take the relevant pages for the Comte and give the rest to Pike."

Even as she said it, she knew Pike would see that as an even greater treason. Not only to break their oath, but to allow part of a *Ligatus* to fall into the hands of a Deceiver.

"Do you really think his lordship would agree to that?" Hammond asked. "He will not let Pike have that journal."

True. And if his lordship knew it was a *Ligatus* as well, he would be even more set upon keeping it from Pike.

"Even worse," Hammond added, "I do not think his lordship would ever be able to forgive us for such a betrayal, especially in his present state. Right now I am not even sure he would not kill us himself."

"No! He would never do that."

Hammond regarded her gravely. "I saw Benchley's deterioration, and his lordship's decline is happening a great deal faster."

Helen turned her face away from the brutal assessment. His lordship had thought the speed of his deterioration had not been marked. He was clearly wrong.

The intensity of their conversation was drawing attention from a gentleman on the other side of the room. "Laugh," she ordered, and waved her fan coquettishly, sending warm air across them both. "We are under scrutiny."

Hammond obeyed, dredging up a reasonable facsimile of mirth. "What should we do? What is our plan?"

She heard the shift of responsibility in his voice. Sweet heaven, he was looking to her for answers.

"Why do you think I have a plan?" she hissed. "I have only just found this out myself."

"You are the Reclaimer, Lady Helen," he said through his ghastly smile. "You are Lord Carlston's equal. You can face Lowry with his extra Terrene strength, and you have the leverage of being one of only seven protectors in this land." He stared at her, desperation in his eyes. "In the end, Pike may not be able to cast you aside, but I am entirely expendable."

He was right. Yet she was hardly Lord Carlston's equal—in courage or experience—nor did she have any leverage other than her current usefulness to Pike. She stared at the floor, trying to calm the frantic darting of her thoughts and review their very limited options. She could see no other viable path than the one they were on.

"We must go ahead as before," she said. "Lord Carlston does not know Lowry is from Brighton. While he discovers that fact, it will give us time to find the journal. When we do, the two of us will offer the Comte the pages that he wants. Perhaps we can obtain the information about his lordship's malady and the Grand Deceiver and still deliver the journal to Pike."

"Will the Comte deal with us?"

"I am not sure, but I hope so. He wants to be sure the information is expunged from the journal. I expect it does not matter who hands it to him."

Hopefully she would be able to destroy the pages once the Comte had seen them and provided the information about Lord Carlston. Helen nodded, more to fix the feasibility of the plan within herself than with Mr. Hammond.

"When his lordship finds you, can you give him the names of some London associates that will send him in that direction?" she asked.

Hammond smiled again and nodded, his eyes pained. "All this lying to him grieves me more than anything else."

"It grieves me, too, but it must be done."

She felt the shame of it sliding like a Thames eel beneath the surface of her fear, waiting to rise as soon as she had a moment of reflection. But she could not let it overcome her now.

Hammond leaned in, as if to share an amusing story. "I am a very good liar, Lady Helen. My life has depended upon it many times. Even so, his lordship is a Reclaimer. What if he reads me and sees that I am lying?"

"It is my fear too. But this illness is creating doubt within him. We must use that." She saw the shock widen Hammond's eyes. "I know it is not honorable to use his misfortune, but none of this business has much honor, does it?"

She paused; should she tell him, at least, about Pike's discovery of Lord Carlston's illness? No, even that would be too much for him to hold back—it was almost too much for her as well. He would insist on warning Lord Carlston, and that would set disaster into motion: for him, for her, and possibly for the whole Dark Days Club.

She lifted her fan again, hiding the urgency of her next question. "Do you agree? Can you do this?"

"There is no choice, is there?"

"I must go before he finds you and sees us together." She snapped the fan shut and curtsied, ready to rejoin Delia.

"Lady Helen."

She turned back.

"We will finish this soon," Hammond said. It was half statement, half entreaty.

"We will," she said. "We must."

Fifteen

Saturday, 11 July 1812

HELEN AND HER companions did not depart the rout until three in the morning. Lady Margaret was on a winning streak and firmly refused to abandon her chair until her opponents were played out and their IOUs collected.

By four o'clock, all of the German Place household had found their beds, but Helen could not sleep. Her mind churned over the horror that was the *Ligatus*, Pike's threat against Lord Carlston, and the Comte's deal, until she felt almost suffocated by her fear, guilt, and fraught imaginings. She rose before dawn and sat at the gilt-edged writing desk wrapped in her bedcover, watching the sky turn from inky black into the torrid oranges and pinks of a summer dawn.

Two months ago, her biggest decisions had been about what gown to wear to which assembly or rout, and even those decisions had been moderated by her aunt. Now her every word and deed had deadly ramifications; and even more frightening, Mr. Hammond had begun to look to her for leadership. Every moment of every day she was having to pick her way through lies and secrets to find a pathway over a deadly and muddied morality. And it was never going to end. This was her life now. Right then, in the chill of the morning, she wondered if she might be crushed by so much doubt and responsibility.

She drew the soft edges of the silk cover around her shoulders. Two months ago, if she had been asked where her duty lay, she would have said to her family, to God and country. Now it was not so simple. Her family had abandoned her as much as she had them; and while she had taken the Dark Days Club oath in the name of King and God, she seriously doubted that their representative, Mr. Pike, worked on the side of the angels.

Then there was Lord Carlston. Ostensibly he served the same masters, but he was showing himself to be more . . . *unilateral* in his actions. Helen nodded at the word; she had read its meaning of *singular action* in one of her uncle's journals. Moreover, it was quite possible that his lordship's actions were coming from a place of . . . instability. She would not concede it was madness. Not yet. Even so, why did she feel more inclined to offer him her loyalty above all the other claims upon it?

She pressed the back of her hand to her flushed cheek. She had a fair idea of the reason, and it was not to her credit. Still, that was not the only reason she felt so guilty. Lord Carlston had finally trusted her enough to tell her the truth about Lady Elise and the extent of the darkness within him, and she was repaying that trust with monumental betrayal.

She arched back her head, stretching out the tense muscles in her neck. Betrayal versus treason: it was a wretched, sickening choice, and she had somehow landed in the middle of the two— on the one hand, lying to Lord Carlston; and on the other, not quite following Pike's orders. Even so, the slippery path that she and Mr. Hammond were treading was the only way forward. At least, the only way she could see that would not end in their execution or Lord Carlston's assassination.

Helen sighed. And now she must do something else wretched: break Darby's heart. It was her duty to explain the Dark Days Club's ban on love. The thought of it made her feel sick with fury—not just on Darby's behalf, but on her own. It felt as if they had been tricked, which of course was patently untrue. They had both been given the regulations and both taken the oath of their own free will. Nevertheless, the prospect of never having a husband or family was insupportable. Surely she could make a case for their exception.

That, however, would have to wait. Far more urgent was her bond with Darby. She must hasten the preparations for the Reclaimer/Terrene ritual. Only then could she count herself and Darby safe from the doubts of Pike and Lord Sidmouth, and the disgusting ambitions of Lowry.

All too soon Helen heard her maid enter the dressing room from the hallway door, click her tongue in exasperation, and murmur under her breath, "No fire! Where is that girl?"

Helen closed her eyes, hearing some early morning congestion in Darby's breath, and the rustle of her gown. She concentrated more closely. It was a stiff brush of *new* cotton against the carpet, which could only be the hem of her maid's navy round-gown, made from a dress length last week.

Lord Carlston had told her to practice building a mind-picture of the world through sound and smell and taste in preparation for when she must fight a Deceiver's invisible energy whips. She had seen him use only those three senses to intercept and sever the deadly whips from a Deceiver's back, and it had been a marvel to watch. Now that she was trying to do it herself, she understood just how hard it was to put those sensory pieces together into a whole without any reliance upon sight.

She followed the sounds in the dressing room—the weight of Darby's tread upon the carpet, the swish of her gown, the direction of her soft breath—and built a sense of size and mass in motion. She smelled the air, working her way through old hearth smoke and powder to find the newer scent of soap on warm skin. Slowly in her mind the smell resolved into the rounded planes of Darby's arms, throat, and face as she opened a drawer.

Now taste. Helen licked her lips. Nothing. She stuck out her tongue. No, not a thing. What on earth did Lord Carlston mean by taste?

She opened her eyes, the simulacrum slipping away. It was time to face the real woman and break her heart.

"Darby," she called.

Her maid appeared at the doorway, in the navy gown. Helen allowed herself a moment of congratulation.

"My lady, I did not know you were awake." She took in Helen's wrapped figure. "Are you chilled? Sally should have set the fires by now. If you get back into bed, I shall bring you a warming pan and tell her to do your room first."

"No, I am perfectly comfortable, thank you." She waved Darby into the room. "There is something we must discuss."

Obediently, her maid approached.

"So . . ." Helen cleared her throat. "I cannot help but notice . . . I mean, it is rather obvious . . . that you and Mr. Quinn have become quite close."

Darby regarded her steadily. "Yes, my lady."

"May I inquire how close?"

Darby drew back her shoulders. "Mr. Quinn has spoken of love, my lady, and I return his regard."

Quinn had spoken of love—it was tantamount to a promise of marriage. It was worse than she had imagined. Helen pressed her lips together, wishing she did not have to say the next. This, however, was her duty as a Reclaimer.

"Darby, are you aware that the oath we took does not allow such an attachment?"

Darby's gaze did not waver. "Of course, my lady."

"Oh . . ." Helen floundered. "You know?"

"Mr. Quinn made sure I was well aware of the meaning of the oath before I swore to it."

"I see." Helen nodded. More than Lord Carlston had done. "Very comprehensive of him."

"Yes, my lady." Darby smiled, and it was heartachingly tender. "He is a very good man."

"Quite." Helen rubbed her forehead. "So, although you know you cannot be together, you have still declared your love for one another?"

"The oath does not change the fact of our love, my lady. But we both know we cannot wed or truly be together, not if we wish to do our duty."

"And you still wish to do that duty?" Helen asked quickly. "With me?"

"Yes, of course, my lady. Nothing has changed there."

Although she knew it must pain Darby, Helen could not help feeling relieved.

"In the end," Darby continued, "my situation with Mr. Quinn is not so different from any other servant's. Except our duty lies not with just one mistress or master, but with all mankind."

"But what are you going to do with your love for one another?" Helen asked. "How will you exist knowing that he is there, but you cannot be with him?"

"That, I do not know." Darby bit her lip. "I would ask you the same question, my lady."

Helen stared at her maid. "Whatever for?"

"Lord Carlston," Darby said bluntly. "Forgive me, but you are in the same situation, are you not?"

Helen opened her mouth to deny the statement, then shut it again. Darby was right. Well, not exactly right, but close enough to the truth.

"You love him," Darby pressed. "I have seen it as plain as you have seen my regard for Mr. Quinn. What will you do with *your* love, my lady?"

Helen shifted on the chair. How had this come to be about herself and Lord Carlston?

"I have resolved to ignore my feelings for his lordship," she said. "He has made it clear that attachments are not possible for Reclaimers or Terrenes."

Darby regarded her with a slight frown. Skepticism. "Do you think that will work?"

"It must. He did offer me an alternative." She leaned forward and lowered her voice, glad to finally unburden herself of the disquieting advice. "You will be shocked, as I was. His lordship said that I was no longer living a woman's life and suggested I seek to 'assuage my needs,' as the male Reclaimers do."

Darby's eyes widened. "Did he really?"

"He did."

She shook her head. "Forgive me, my lady, but his lordship is wrong. You *are* a woman. You cannot live a man's life."

Helen nodded; she had known Darby would understand. "I think he would rather I did. I am sure he would prefer that I were a man. It would make things easier."

"May I speak plainly, my lady?"

"Of course."

"I do not think his lordship, like most men, can look beyond his own idea of a woman's life," Darby said carefully. "Indeed, I think that everyone is of the belief that a woman's world is always lesser and smaller than a man's. Perhaps they are right. It is what the Church teaches us, after all. But you, my lady, cannot abide by that belief. You must live the kind of woman's life that has never been lived before. As must I."

Helen frowned. Darby's plain speaking was dangerously close to heretical. "Are you saying we should abandon the Church?"

Darby raised a hand, warding off the suggestion. "No, my lady, of course not. But it cannot be denied that you are twice as strong as most men and have been called on to police a demon world. When I bond with you, I will be stronger than most men too, and I will be your last line of defense. Every day we will be facing danger and death, and just by that fact, we cannot be bound by the normal rules of womanhood. We cannot defer when we must act. We cannot follow when we must lead. We must make our own rules."

"But we cannot just make up our own rules," Helen protested. "We are not God, or Parliament."

"I know what the Reclaimer oath asks of you, my lady," Darby said softly. "I know what it asks of me. They are duties that do not sit well with the expectations of us as women. Or indeed what is expected of us as mistress and servant."

Helen gave an unsettled laugh. Her maid's startling eloquence held a relentless logic and truth. Yet it felt as if Darby had placed another weight upon her shoulders that would make every step on that slippery, muddy path toward right even more treacherous and unsteady.

"Have you been reading *A Vindication of the Rights of Woman*?" she asked lightly, trying to shift the discussion to a less personal direction. "Is this a revolution?"

Darby smiled, but she was not diverted. "No, my lady. This comes from the fact that I may have to stab you through the hand to bring you back from the Deceiver thrall. And the fact that you may have to kill an offspring, a human, who cannot be reclaimed."

Yes, Darby was right; it was always going to be personal. Helen looked down at her hands, an image of Mr. Lowry's fleshy veined face forcing its way into her mind.

"There is no one else in this world that I would trust to bring me back from the thrall." She looked up, intent. "Do you trust *me*, Darby?"

"Absolutely, my lady."

"I am glad you are so sure, because I am going to ask you to bond with me as soon as possible. In the next week, if we can."

"But his lordship and Mr. Quinn said we are not ready."

"We must bond, Darby, even without their blessing. I cannot tell you why—I promise I will soon—but it is important that our bond is a fait accompli. Do you think you can learn the ritual from Mr. Quinn without him suspecting that we plan to go ahead?"

Darby nodded, although Helen could see the reluctance in her eyes. "Mr. Quinn says it should be done during a full moon. The next is just under two weeks away, on the twenty-fourth. Should we not wait until then?"

The date that Lowry had nominated.

"No. We must bond as soon as we have the ritual prepared." She stood and threw off the bedcover, taking Darby's warm hands in her own. "I know it is not what is expected, but you said we must make our own rules. Will you do this with me? Are we agreed?"

To Helen's relief, Darby did not hesitate. "Yes. We are agreed."

⟶

A LITTLE LATER, as Helen descended the stairs to breakfast in the morning room, a sharp voice rose from the foyer—"You are both going to London?"—the protest quickly dropping into a vicious whisper. Helen stopped, hand on banister. She should not listen, of course; had she not admonished Delia for eavesdropping? Yet this was clearly about Lord Carlston and Lowry. Shaking off a creep of shame across her shoulders, she concentrated her Reclaimer hearing down the two flights.

"But why does he insist on going as well?" Lady Margaret's lowered voice demanded. "He is needed here, to train Lady Helen."

"I have argued the point over and over with him, Margaret," Mr. Hammond said.

Helen tightened her grip on the polished wood. That was a lie; she could hear it in the fast rhythm of Hammond's heart. He must have persuaded Lord Carlston that London held the key to Lowry's whereabouts. Thank heavens his sister could not hear the quick beat of his deception.

"He is adamant that his contacts in London will prove more fruitful than my own," Hammond added.

"I suppose they might," Margaret conceded, "but you are more than capable of tracking down Lowry. His lordship has said himself that Lady Helen's training must be our focus, and yet here he is leaving us for at least another two or three days. You have seen yourself how far she is from being ready for any real field experience."

Helen drew in a sharp breath. Yet could she really argue with that assessment?

"He has told Quinn to stay here and continue Lady Helen's combat training," Mr. Hammond said.

"What?" Lady Margaret's dismay cut through the air. "He is going to leave his Terrene behind?"

"I know."

Helen heard the floorboards creak: Lady Margaret pacing a few steps.

"These are not sound decisions, Michael." The floorboards creaked again. "Do you think . . ." Her voice hesitated. "Is this the vestige clouding his judgment?"

"No, I think his judgment is right in this matter. We must find

Lowry if we are to find the journal. The Comte has made it his price, or at least the information within it, and he is his lordship's best hope for a cure."

Silently Helen agreed.

Lady Margaret made a low sound of distrust. "The Comte . . . I would rather pin our hope on a snake."

"Do you see any other way?"

A few heavy moments passed, then Lady Margaret released a frustrated breath. "Only Pike, and I know that is exchanging one snake for another." An echo of his lordship's view. "When do you leave?"

"Within the hour."

"Be careful, then." Helen heard Margaret kiss her brother's cheek, a soft benediction. "Keep him safe."

Helen crept back up the stairs. She and Mr. Hammond *were* trying to keep Lord Carlston safe. Trying to keep them all safe. Surely such a noble purpose would cancel out the wickedness of so many lies?

Sixteen

Monday, 13 July 1812

TRAINING WITH QUINN proved to be a dour affair. The usually stolid Islander was furious at his master's decision to go to London without him, and channeled all of his anger into teaching Helen how to punch and kick with deadly effect. His sessions were long and hard, and his fighting mantra—*A still body is an easy target*—kept Helen constantly moving, so that by Monday evening, when Andrew was to arrive in Brighton, she felt both bone-tired and certain she had mastered the basics of *canne chausson*.

They had not received any letter of progress from Lord Carlston or Mr. Hammond; nor had Helen had a message from Martha Gunn regarding Lowry. It was perhaps too early to be so concerned—only three days had passed since she had spoken to the dipper—yet Helen could not shake a sense that disaster was snapping at their heels.

It was a feeling that dogged her as she strolled along the Steine's gravel path arm in arm with Delia and scanned the throng for the Duke of Selburn and Andrew. The gentle walk was lifting her exhaustion, but beneath it lay a nervous energy at the prospect of meeting her brother.

The day had been warm, but the evening was proving less conducive for the evening promenade, the sun slowly descending into a bank of thick cloud, and the cooling night breeze prone to gathering itself into capricious salty gusts. Many of the ladies had refused to bow to the weather's dictates and wore extravagant bonnets and thin silk spencers, the wind catching at straw brims and wrapping muslin skirts around white-stockinged legs. The gentlemen in their heavier evening jackets were faring better, and Helen had a moment of regret that she was once again in her impractical female clothing, even if that included a pretty purple short coat over an olive silk gown, topped by a matching olive beret. Still, the gentlemen were not escaping completely unscathed. A few beaver hats had already left their pomaded moorings and landed on the path, to the hilarity of those around.

Helen could not yet see two tall fair men among the crowd. She had a strong notion that Andrew was going to insist she accompany him back to London the next day, with the sweetener that they could set up house together as she had once proposed. That all felt so long ago now: another life and another Helen. She could not help thinking that Andrew was not going to like this new unbiddable sister and her adamant refusal to accompany him back to that old life.

"I read in the *Advertiser* that the Prince Regent is going to keep his birthday in London, but may honor Brighton with a visit later in the Season," Delia said. "Apparently he is most aggrieved that the troubles with America will keep him from most of his summer sojourn."

"It does not seem to have stopped anyone else coming here," Helen replied, rising for a moment onto her toes to see over the sea of heads. Still no sign of Andrew or the Duke.

"Oh no, it is that Dunwick woman," Lady Margaret said from behind them.

Indeed, progressing somewhat gingerly toward them along the center path were Lady Dunwick, her scandalmonger friend

Mrs. Albridge, and Pug. All three ladies were heavy eyed, pale, and somewhat peevish in expression. It would seem that Brighton's relentless schedule of delights was already wearing upon them.

Lady Margaret leaned in between Helen and Delia. "Have they seen us? Can we cross the road and—"

"Lady Helen!" Pug called, her usual volume somewhat subdued.

"Too late," Delia said behind her gloved hand.

The ladies, on meeting, all curtsied.

"Foul wind, is it not," Pug said. "I swear it has something particular against my bonnet."

If it did, Helen thought, she would not be surprised. The bonnet was a dreadful concoction of pink pearl silk and vibrant blue feathers.

"Will you walk with me for a while, Lady Helen?" Pug asked. "I have something particular to discuss."

"Of course." Helen cast an apologetic glance at Delia, who gracefully ceded her position and dropped back to walk with Pug's mother, Mrs. Albridge, and Lady Margaret.

Pug linked her arm though Helen's and pulled her into a brisk walk. "I've got a head full of wool," she declared. She looked up at the wheeling, diving seagulls, their raucous cries piercing the chatter around them and the grinding rumble of carriages along South Parade. "I do wish those devilish birds would stop that racket. Mother and I attended the Billings rout last night and 'pon my soul their punch was as rough as Vauxhall's." She pinched the bridge of her nose. "Guess where I have been invited. I shall give you a clue. Dominoes."

Helen shook her head, only half attending, her attention caught by a fracas ahead. A large brown poodle had issued a challenge to a spotted spaniel, and both dogs, along with their owners, were loudly voicing their opinions.

"Dominoes and masks," Pug urged. A gust of wind bent back the brim of her bonnet. She clapped her hand on it and grabbed at the streaming ribbons.

"A masquerade?" Helen ventured.

"Yes!" Pug exclaimed. "Lady Oliver is holding a costumed masquerade ball Tuesday next, the twenty-first. I know you are not well acquainted with the family, but I wrote to Lady Oliver—she is my cousin, you know—and asked if she would allow me to include you and your friends in the invitation. She has written back and said that she would be delighted to further her acquaintance with you. Mother is grumbling, of course, for she says the Olivers' estate is halfway back to London, and it will not be quite a full moon for the journey, but it will be such fun, and I thought we could all go together in one carriage."

Helen smiled, even though the last thing she needed was a masquerade ball. "That is kind of you, but I do not think Lady Ridgewell would agree, particularly since she is not acquainted with the family."

"Let Mama talk to her," Pug said. "She is very persuasive, and besides . . . oh!" She wrenched Helen's arm. "Look who is ahead."

Walking toward them was the elegant figure of the Duke of Selburn, dressed in shades of buff and tobacco and, it seemed, very much alone. Where was Andrew?

Helen scanned the oncoming crowd: a bun woman offering sweet wares from a basket, a black gentleman in clerical garb with a wide-brimmed hat that flapped in the wind, a sweet little family in a tight cluster, and the rotund owner of the poodle fussing over his outraged dog, but no sign of her brother. Had something happened?

The Duke had not yet seen her, but the long lines of his face held no tension, no bad news. Perhaps Andrew had stopped further back to speak to an acquaintance.

"What do you want to do?" Pug whispered. "Shall we turn around?"

"No. I'd like to speak to him." Helen squeezed Pug's arm. "I am being contrary, I know. If he should stop, will you make your excuses so that he and I may walk together?"

"Of course I will, but you know it will set everyone's tongue wagging again." Pug gestured to the assemblage of fashionables. "They will have the banns up before you get to the end of the path. Have you changed your mind? Is he renewing his efforts after our rout?" She cast Helen a sly look. "Perhaps prompted by Lord Carlston's attentions?"

"Perhaps," Helen whispered as the Duke saw them and, smiling, threaded his way to their side of the path.

"Lady Helen and Lady Elizabeth!" He bowed. "How delightful to meet you again."

Helen, still arm in arm with Pug, curtsied alongside her friend.

"Good evening, Duke," she said. "I see that you are walking *alone* this evening."

He acknowledged the loaded word with a swift glance of reassurance. "I am, but if you and Lady Elizabeth will do me the honor of taking my arm, that sad state of affairs can be quickly rectified."

"Thank you for the invitation, Your Grace, but I am afraid I must return to my mother," Pug said. "If you will excuse me." She curtsied again and, with one last widening of her eyes at Helen, left them.

"A most amenable girl," the Duke said, offering his arm.

Helen placed her fingers lightly on his bent elbow, glancing back at her little party a hundred yards or so behind them. Lady Margaret and Delia were questioning Pug, but she was shaking her head. Dear Pug: not one to give up a friend's secrets. Helen turned her back on them. She would not have much time alone with the

Duke. Lady Margaret would soon rid herself of Lady Dunwick and Pug and come to her aid, whether she wanted it or not.

"Has Andrew been delayed?" she asked as she and the Duke started along the path.

"You might say that," he replied.

"What do you mean? Has something happened?"

"No, I assure you all is well."

He placed his hand over her own. A passing lady in a feathered turban raised her lorgnette upon its ribbon and observed the unexpected intimacy, whispering a comment to her companion. Helen caught the answering gasp. Old cats. Even so, she shifted her grip. The Duke took the hint and lifted his own hand.

"So where is he, Your Grace?"

"Andrew is still in London."

A reprieve. Yet it was not like her brother to fail a friend.

"London?" she prompted.

"Yes."

Good Lord, it was like drawing teeth. "Why is he still in London?"

An elderly gentleman coming in the opposite direction lifted his cane in greeting. The Duke returned a gracious nod, then said, "After Lady Dunwick's rout, I wrote to your brother and told him not to come to Brighton, after all."

Helen stared at him. Had she heard that correctly? "You told him not to come? Why would you do that?"

"Because I could see that you did not wish to be pressed into leaving Lady Margaret's house. I flatter myself that I know you, Lady Helen. If Andrew had come and insisted that you return to London as he had intended, you would have refused. Is that not true?"

"Yes, but—"

"I know your brother, too. Under normal circumstances, he is the most easygoing of men, but in this matter, he is as stubborn as yourself. The two of you would have ended up at grievous loggerheads. So, to avoid any further estrangement between you, I sent a messenger to Andrew with the suggestion that he stay in London and allow you to have your summer in Brighton with Lady Margaret under my protective eye."

Helen walked in silence, unable to form a coherent thought through the maelstrom of emotion: relief that she would not need to face Andrew, astonishment at what the Duke had done, and dread of Lord Carlston's reaction if he ever found out. And beneath all that, her own growing sense of anger. Such interference went well beyond propriety. It proclaimed possession.

"You seem to have a great deal of influence upon my brother," she finally managed to say.

"Yes, I believe Andrew does hold my opinion in high esteem." The Duke smiled at her, the expression in his eyes far too tender. "And very soon, I intend to offer him my advice as his brother as well as his friend."

Lud, he *was* renewing his attentions with alacrity. Helen withdrew her hand from his arm.

"Your Grace, you have already received my answer to that particular question." She stared fiercely at the bank of clouds across the horizon, trying to find the words that would make him abandon his hopes and retreat back into the safety of his own world. "We do not have an understanding. I did not ask you to do this. Forgive me, but I cannot thank you for such high-handed intervention. You are not my guardian, and nor is my brother. My uncle is my guardian, and he has offered no objection to my sojourn with Lady Margaret and Mr. Hammond."

He regarded her gravely. "As I understand it, your uncle no longer concerns himself in your affairs at all. I merely wanted to be of service to you. To show you that I will always protect you and your interests."

She shook her head, trying to ignore the hurt that had settled deep in his kind blue eyes. She must stand firm. "You take too much upon yourself, Duke. I am in no need of a protector."

"You know my thoughts on that matter, and your brother trusts my instincts. He has asked me to watch over you while you are in Brighton, and I have given my word to do so."

Helen drew a frustrated breath. Andrew had, more or less, handed her over to the Duke. It was just like him to duck out of any responsibility.

Selburn reached inside his tan linen coat and drew out a packet tied with a blue ribbon. "Andrew sent this back with my messenger: a letter to you; and there is also one from your aunt. I am sure his missive will agree with what I have said."

She took the offered bundle, seeing her brother's scrawl across the front. Andrew did not know it, but he had asked his friend to stand against Lord Carlston and the Dark Days Club.

"Your Grace, please listen to me. I do not want your protection."

"I have given my word, Lady Helen. But more than that, I know that you are in need of protection. Whatever you may think, you are not safe. My interest in your welfare, and my continued presence will, I believe, be enough to hold Lord Carlston's designs at bay, whatever they may be. He is not a fool; he will not make any move under such scrutiny."

They had walked almost the whole length of the western path and were now opposite the Castle Tavern, the handsome dome of the Marine Pavilion just visible beyond. Helen focused on the promenading people ahead, desperate to find some other argument to persuade the Duke from his purpose. It was a useless exercise. She could find nothing that would convince him to break his word to her brother.

It was at that defeated moment that Philip, the Deceiver, walked into view, this time near the opposite corner of Pavilion Parade.

Helen gasped. There could be no mistake: it *was* him. And he had seen her too, insolently tipping his gray beaver hat to her, a sly smile on his freckled face.

She stopped in the middle of the path, uncertain what to do. Run after him? But then the Duke, even now regarding her with concern, would surely follow, and she could not place him in the path of a Deceiver. Not to mention the scandal that would rise at the sight of a young lady running through the Steine with the Duke of Selburn in pursuit.

She looked back at Lady Margaret and Delia, but they were caught in an exchange with the decrepit Lady Staves.

She found Philip again. He was heading toward the corner at some speed.

The Duke followed her gaze. "Is that an acquaintance?"

She could not let him just walk away. He was their only link to the *Colligat* and the Grand Deceiver.

She gathered up her skirts, crushing silk and letters into a tight grip, and ran into the oncoming crowd. Startled gasps met her headlong dash, gentlemen pulling ladies out of the way. Suddenly her path was obstructed by two couples who had stopped to converse. She darted to the right, but found no clear route; the rotund man and his hysterical poodle were blocking the way. She darted to the other side. No way there, either. There was only one thing for it. Gathering her resolve, she pushed past the ladies.

"I say, what do you think you are doing?" one of their male companions called out.

Helen looked back. "My apologies!"

"Lady Helen, wait!" the Duke called, closing in behind.

She shook her head, waving him away for all the good that it would do. He was going to follow her, come what may. She threaded her way through a party of sober-clad gentlemen, all her attention on Pavilion Parade. Black top hats, army tricorns, and a variety of caps, but no shabby gray beaver. Where was he?

She stopped and scanned the street. He had disappeared again. Was he taunting her?

The Duke reached her side, his eyes alight with the chase. "Stay here," he said. "I will find him for you." He pressed his hat down more firmly, clearly intending to pursue the Deceiver.

"No!" She caught his arm, realizing too late she had done so with her full strength. He stared down at her iron grip, astonishment quickly turning into a grimace of pain. She snatched back her hand. "Please do not concern yourself, Your Grace. It is nothing."

He stared at her, rubbing his forearm. "Nothing?" He lowered his voice, casting a glance around the crowd that had gathered to watch such odd behavior. "Forgive me, but it is clearly *something*. You did the same thing at Hyde Park: suddenly you were running toward the runaway horse as if to stop it. Now you are running toward a man in a public place. What is going on?"

"It is nothing," she repeated. "Just a foolish notion."

"No, you are in some kind of trouble," he said slowly. "My dear, can you not trust me?"

A commotion parted the curious crowd.

"Let me through," Lady Margaret demanded. "Oh, Lady Helen, you poor child," she said loudly, "you are overcome." She pressed a hand against Helen's forehead. "Yes, too much sun and excitement, I fear. We must return home immediately. Miss Cransdon, would you please help me take Lady Helen to a sedan chair?" She turned a dazzling smile upon the Duke. "Thank you for your kind concern, Your Grace. Lady Helen is still not fully recovered from her riding accident."

Sensing an end to the excitement, many of the onlookers began to move away. It was a well-known fact, Helen heard someone murmur, that too much sun was indeed dangerous to a weakened constitution.

Lady Margaret and Delia each took one of Helen's arms. "For God's sake, pretend you are ill," Lady Margaret hissed as they steered her toward the waiting sedan chairs outside the Castle Tavern.

Helen looked back at the Duke, standing alone on the path. He was still holding his forearm, a perplexed frown upon his face.

———

I<small>T WAS NOT</small> a happy return to the German Place drawing room. Although Helen explained that she had seen Philip again, that the Deceiver had actually tipped his hat to her in some kind of sly taunt, Lady Margaret was not diverted from her wrath. Apparently she'd had her own plan to meet a trusted informer at the promenade, which had been ruined by Helen's bad judgment and reckless behavior. Not only that: Helen had drawn attention to herself in exactly the way that his lordship had ordered them to avoid.

Delia attempted a staunch defense, arguing that surely the retrieval of the *Colligat* was of the utmost importance, but in the end Lady Margaret's accusations were more or less true. Helen waited out the harangue, then escaped to her bedchamber with the packet of letters still crumpled in her hand.

The worst of it, she thought, as she carried her night candle to the writing desk, was the Duke's involvement. He was now convinced something was amiss, and she knew he would not give up until he discovered the truth. All her attempts to keep him safe had just placed him in more danger—from Lord Carlston, and possibly now the Deceiver world. On top of that, she had accidentally injured him.

She bowed her head. *Dear God, please let his arm be only bruised and not broken.*

The sound of footsteps in the next room lifted her head.

"Do you need anything, my lady?" Darby asked from the dressing room doorway, her voice soft with sympathy. Bad news traveled very fast in the house. "Did you wish to undress for bed now?"

Helen shook her head. "Not yet."

Darby curtsied and withdrew.

Helen took a seat at the desk and picked up the packet from Andrew. She drew a fortifying breath and worked her thumbnail under the wax seal, breaking it with a snap. Two letters were folded within: a thin missive with her name across the front in her brother's slanted scrawl, and a fatter packet in her aunt's neat hand.

The angriest first. She broke the seal on her brother's letter and unfolded it. One paragraph, and another paper tucked inside. She slid the enclosure onto the desk and angled the letter to the candlelight.

The Albany, Sunday, 12 July 1812

Dear Helen,

I have taken Selburn's advice and will not visit you in Brighton. I urge you, however, to note his careful protection of your well-being and to reconsider your decision regarding his proposal. He is still keen—God knows why after your treatment of him—and he has my and, more importantly, Uncle's blessing. Frankly, sprite, you are a fool if you do not take him. Enclosed is a draft on my bank account until September. Aunt has writ too, against Uncle's wishes, so don't write back. He'll just burn it and she'll have the devil to pay.

Your brother,
Andrew

Helen bit her lip. Andrew disliked putting pen to paper, and for him to actually set down his disgust in ink meant he was very angry indeed.

She picked up the bank draft: authorized for three months. A clear message that she was to come to her senses by the end of summer. Well, she could not afford to refuse the offering. She had left London with only pin money in her purse, and that was almost gone.

She turned her attention to the other packet. As she unfolded it, two ten-pound notes dropped onto the desk, bringing a sudden sob into her throat. Dear Aunt, so brave to have written a letter and enclosed money against Uncle's orders.

The missive was full of lighthearted gossip, not a word of reproof, and Helen could almost feel herself back at Half Moon Street, listening to her aunt in the drawing room, each at their sewing. There was nothing of great consequence in the closely written lines until she came to a paragraph near the end:

> I do not know if the news has yet reached Brighton, but your dear friend Millicent Gardwell is betrothed to Lord Holbridge. Such an excellent match, but then she does have enough countenance and connection to overcome her lack of fortune. They are, I believe, planning a winter wedding and she has asked if she may send a letter to you in Brighton. Have you not written to her, my dear? Do so directly, for I am sure she would wish you to witness the nuptials.

Helen pressed the heels of her hands against her wet eyes. Such happy news. Millicent and the Viscount would do well together; her decisive nature would complement his easy good humor. Sniffing back her ridiculous sentimentality, Helen opened the secretaire drawer, searching for paper. Millicent had always wanted to marry quickly and well, and now she had got her wish. Helen paused in her search, remembering their conversations about marriage: their adamant agreement that they must at least *like* their husbands, that a house in London was absolutely essential, and that if a son came first, three children were enough.

The warm recollection shifted abruptly into a stark realization. Unlike Millicent, she would never have a husband or the chance of children. Of course she had known that before she'd read Aunt's letter, but now it felt brutally real. She had signed a different kind of vow, and there could be no place for a family within it.

Helen scrubbed at her eyes. There was no value in self-pity. Best to forge onward. She pulled out a clean piece of paper and reached for the inkwell, then stopped again, an even worse realization hollowing her heart.

She could write to Millicent and wish her well, but that was all. She could not risk attending her friend's wedding, or even visiting. If the day's events had shown her anything, it was that wherever she went, the danger of the Deceivers followed. She would not expose Millicent, or anyone else she loved, to that world. Even if that meant never seeing them again.

Seventeen

Tuesday, 14 July 1812

THE NEXT DAY at breakfast, two letters arrived in the morning post: one from London for Lady Margaret; and the other, hand delivered, for Helen. For a heart-stopping instant, Helen thought the thrice-folded note on Garner's silver salver might be from Martha Gunn. Then the butler bowed and offered her the slim packet, and she recognized the writing across the front: the Duke of Selburn's hand. It would seem Lowry had decided to stay away from Brighton until the full moon; or perhaps he was just better at hiding from them than they were at finding him.

She picked up the Duke's letter and broke the seal. If he was writing, then at least his arm was not broken, she thought gratefully as she unfolded the single page.

Grand Parade, Brighton.
Tuesday, 14 July 1812

Dear Lady Helen,

After yesterday's events, I feel I must speak to you.

Please, do me the honor of driving with me this afternoon. I would be most obliged.

Yrs, etc,
Selburn

Helen folded the note again, ignoring the unabashed curiosity on Delia's face. The Duke's persistence was far too dangerous. She had tried polite refusal and blunt request. It was time for blatant discourtesy. A curt note, then, and if ever they met, she would have to deliver a cut direct: pretend he did not even exist. It would hurt him greatly, and her, too, but it had to be done. For his own protection.

"Lowry is here," Lady Margaret said, looking up from her own letter. She passed it across the breakfast table to Helen. "From my brother."

St. James's Square.
Monday, 13 July 1812

Dear Margaret,

According to his lordship's sources, Lowry is in the vicinity of Brighton. A most frustrating outcome, but at least we now have information to follow. His lordship asks that you instruct our informants in the area to search out any clues as to his location. We return with every expediency.

Yr affectionate brother,
Michael

Helen kept her eyes on the note, composing her expression. She had hoped Mr. Hammond would have been able to hold Lord Carlston in London until the following week.

"A strange coincidence that Lowry is hereabouts," she said, looking up with a careful frown.

"The coincidence, I think, lies in Mr. Pike and Mr. Stokes being here as well, and I would wager that is no coincidence at all," Lady Margaret said. "They are after the journal too."

Helen nodded thoughtfully, her heart beating harder. Lady Margaret was too clever by half; and his lordship would have come to the same conclusion.

Delia put down her teacup. "How annoying for Lord Carlston and Mr. Hammond to go all the way to London just to discover that."

"Indeed," Lady Margaret replied, her voice clipped.

"I will send a note to Martha Gunn," Helen said quickly. "To keep a lookout for Lowry." Not to mention to cover the fact that the old dipper already knew they were looking for him.

Lady Margaret nodded. "Good idea. I will contact my people too."

"I know I am very new among you," Delia said hesitantly, "but there is something that puzzles me."

"What is it?" Helen asked.

"If his lordship does find the journal, is it really the best course of action to take it to a Deceiver?" Delia looked from Helen to Lady Margaret, her fine brows lifted in inquiry. "From what you have told me, deception is an integral part of a Deceiver's nature. His lordship seems to be relying upon the word of the Comte d'Antraigues that his sickness is not just the vestige madness. He is also relying upon the Comte for the cure. I know this is an awful question, but is it possible that his lordship is in fact suffering from the vestige madness, and the Comte is using his lordship's desperation to obtain the journal for his own purposes?"

The clock in the breakfast room ticked through the silence. Helen chewed her lip. Delia had voiced Lady Margaret's doubts, and her own dread.

Lady Margaret smoothed out her brother's note, the plane of her fingers across the paper like the switch of a cat's tail. "His lordship has dealt with the Comte d'Antraigues for many years, Miss Cransdon. He is well able to judge if the Comte will keep his word."

Helen looked down at her plate, remembering that flash of desperate fear in Lord Carlston's eyes before they had met with the Comte.

"But is he?" Delia pressed. "If he is suffering the vestige madness, can you be sure his judgment is unimpaired? Surely it would be a dire situation if the journal fell into the hands of a Deceiver? If Mr. Pike and Mr. Stokes are also here to obtain it, should it not be given to them?"

"You have no idea what you are talking about," Lady Margaret said coldly. "I have been his lordship's aide for many years, and his judgment is as sound and brilliant as ever. If he does not think the journal should go to Pike, then it should not. He will have his reasons. He always has his reasons."

Not the opinion she had whispered to her brother in the foyer, Helen thought. Was she lying to herself now as well as to them?

"I did not mean to impugn—" Delia began, but Helen shook her head a fraction, stopping her.

Lady Margaret signaled to Garner, who pulled out her chair as she stood. "The Dark Days Club is a small group facing an overwhelming enemy, Miss Cransdon. We do not need doubt or dissension within our ranks." She picked up her brother's letter.

"The Dark Days Club is not just Lord Carlston," Helen said. Her own confused loyalties speaking perhaps, but it was the truth.

"No, Lord Carlston *is* the Dark Days Club, Lady Helen. Without him, it is little more than a disparate group of thugs under the control of a bitter and power-hungry bureaucrat." Lady Margaret's usual composure was replaced by sudden heat. "The only other honorable man among them is Stokes, and he does not have the subtlety or vision to lead such a group. Look what happened when his lordship was in exile." She jabbed the air between them, punctuating each word. "Benchley: that is what happened! What is more, he happened under Pike's watch."

That was true, and now Pike was adamant that it would not happen again.

"But what if his lordship is heading the same way as Benchley?" Helen demanded. There, she had said it. "What if Delia is right, and the Comte is lying about a cure?"

"The seeds of Benchley's savagery were sown well before he descended into madness, Lady Helen. To even think his lordship could become such a thing is"—Lady Margaret paused and shook her head in disbelief—"a heinous suggestion."

"I must think it, if only to stop any possibility of it coming about," Helen said.

"If you truly knew him like I do, you would not even think it a possibility. You would *know* he was incapable of that kind of mindless violence. You may be a Reclaimer like him, and perhaps his eyes do follow you, but he knows it is I who will always stand by him. He knows it!"

On that, she turned, her brother's letter crushed in her hand. Garner quickly opened the door, and she walked out, her usual gliding step locked into a stiff march. The butler closed the door again, his face carefully blank.

"Lud!" Delia said, slumping back in her chair. "She is in a vile mood. Did you hear her say his lordship's eyes follow you? Maybe that is what has made her so angry."

Helen had indeed heard the comment, but Delia was missing the truth of Lady Margaret's outburst.

"I do not think she is angry," she said slowly. "I think she is afraid."

❧

IT TOOK FAR longer for Helen to write her reply to the Duke than she had expected. Writing a polite letter was easy; writing a purposely rude letter designed to end a friendship was a far more difficult proposition. In the end, her note was as brief as his own: a refusal of his invitation to drive, a request to no longer importune her with invitations or correspondence, and a very abrupt final statement: *I do not wish to further our acquaintance.*

She bowed her head over the completed letter. It was as rude and ugly as the fear that hammered in her heart for him.

"Stay away," she whispered over it. "For your own good."

She sealed it, and rang for Geoffrey.

"Deliver it immediately," she said. "I do not require an answer."

❧

A FEW HOURS later, Delia stood in the doorway of the drawing room, swinging her closed parasol by its bamboo handle. She had changed into a walking gown—pale blue muslin with the shorter hem trimmed with red bows—and a straw-chip hat that she had tied jauntily over one eye with its matching red ribbons.

"Are you sure you will not come?" she asked Helen. "At this time of morning, Donaldson's is quite abuzz."

Helen shook her head. "I really must study." She shifted her legs beneath the heavy edition of *Elements of Alchemy in a New*

Systematic Order, Containing All the Modern Discoveries. It was crushing her own muslin gown. The weight of knowledge, she thought wryly.

"Please, Helen"—Delia dropped her voice—"do not leave me alone with Lady Margaret. She is like a bear with a sore head."

"You may stay here with me." It was not what she wanted, but she had to make the offer.

"No, I can see you are set upon your books." Delia sighed. "Perhaps Lady Margaret's informer will have news and improve her mood."

Alone again, Helen returned to her reading. In a canon of boring texts, this had to be one of the worst. Nevertheless, she had to understand the interactions between alchemical elements, and it was a relief of sorts to step away from the turmoil of her mind to focus upon the stolid text.

As she read, she heard Delia and Lady Margaret leave the house; the creak of the hanging Hessian sack and the murmur of voices as Darby and Quinn trained in the salon above; and the return of Geoffrey from his errand. The footman's cheery hail to the kitchen girls brought Helen's head up from the book, and she found herself watching the drawing room door, waiting to see if there was in fact an answer from the Duke. No footsteps ascended the staircase and the door did not open.

She forced herself to return to the grim description of the combustible nature of phosphorus, otherwise known as the Devil's Element. Apparently, when ignited and in contact with skin, it burned without end. Like lies, Helen thought, searing an ever-bright sore through the soul. Burning even when in the service of a sacred oath.

Two chapters later, a loud rap of the front knocker interrupted her concentration. She extended her hearing to the foyer as Garner opened the door.

"Mr. Stokes, to see Lady Helen," a deep Cambridgeshire voice said. "I am not expected."

Indeed, he was not. It could be no accident that he had timed his visit to coincide with one of the rare times she was alone.

She shifted from the armchair to the sofa, which offered a better view of the door, and waited for Garner to present the Reclaimer's card. It duly arrived, set upon the silver salver. Helen picked up the printed introduction: as unembellished as the man himself.

"Yes, I am at home," she instructed the butler.

Garner bowed. "Would you like me to call for Mr. Quinn, my lady?"

"Whatever for?" She saw something deepen beneath the butler's polite expression: suspicion. He did not like the unexpected visit. Should she be wary too? She could see no reason for it. "I am sure I will be quite safe, Garner. Thank you."

"As you wish, my lady." He bowed and left to retrieve Mr. Stokes.

Helen straightened the pleats on the bodice of her cream gown and touched the blue riband threaded through her hair. Apart from Lord Carlston and Mr. Benchley—who, frankly, could not be counted—Mr. Stokes was the only other Reclaimer she had met. Perhaps here was a chance to discover more about their strange occupation. Maybe even find some sort of ally in the murky recesses of the Dark Days Club.

Before long, her visitor was seated opposite her, shaking his head at the offer of tea. "No, thank you, Lady Helen. I am afraid my visit must be brief."

She dismissed the waiting butler with a wave of her hand. "That will be all for now. Thank you."

Garner bowed and closed the doors behind him. Mr. Stokes sat still with his blond head tilted—listening to the butler descend the staircase, Helen realized—then he gave a nod of satisfaction and smiled, his eyes crinkling into disarming warmth.

"Your butler does not trust me."

"No," Helen said baldly, earning a wider smile from the Reclaimer.

"I am glad your household is so well primed for your safety." He gestured to the window with one long hand, and Helen noticed an old jagged scar that started between his thumb and finger and disappeared under his jacket cuff. A Reclaimer injury? "Are they, however, aware that your house is being watched?"

"Watched? Are you sure?" Helen rose from her chair and crossed to the window. A scan of the quiet street showed only a maid sweeping a front doorstep. "A Deceiver?"

"Not that my lens could determine," Stokes said, patting the fob pocket in his buckskins. "The man is wearing a coat, but beneath I saw livery colors. The Duke of Selburn's, I believe."

Oh no. At least his lordship had not been the one to discover it.

"I would hazard the surveillance has nothing to do with Deceivers," Mr. Stokes added, a sly slant to his voice.

Was he teasing her?

"It is the talk of Brighton," he continued. "There is a book being taken on the date of the announcement."

Helen gave one last glance out of the window, then returned to her chair. "Brighton is wrong. There will be no announcement."

Mr. Stokes cupped a hand to his ear. "Did you hear that? All of the society mamas in England sighing with relief."

Helen stifled a smile. "His attentions are proving difficult, Mr. Stokes," she said.

He sobered. "I know. He has been inquiring about Lord Carlston and your companions at Whitehall. Did you want some assistance in the matter?"

Helen held up her hand. "That will not be necessary."

She certainly did not want another member of the Dark Days

Club set against the Duke, and her harsh reply to his letter would, hopefully, settle the matter once and for all.

Stokes nodded. "Of course." He pulled a letter from inside his burgundy jacket. "I have this for you, from Mr. Pike."

Helen took the proffered packet; it was surprisingly heavy. The fold was sealed with wax, and she felt a hard familiar shape beneath her thumb: a key. Ah, he was here to deliver the promised gold for Lowry. Fifteen thousand pounds' worth, which would be almost the same weight as an average man. Not an easy thing to carry around, even for a Reclaimer.

"Good Lord, you haven't brought it here, have you?" she asked. How was she to hide a stack of gold bullion that was never to be used?

"I brought nothing other than that packet. Were you expecting something else?"

"No." She waved away her comment. "I misremembered the arrangement. That is all."

It seemed he was not in Pike's confidence. Of course he would not be, Helen chastised herself. Pike had made it dangerously clear that he did not want any of the other Reclaimers to know about the journal nor the horrifying fact that it was a *Ligatus*. Another reason to keep his lordship's search for it a secret. Pike's packet, then, must hold the location of the gold.

Stokes looked around the drawing room, his attention coming to rest upon her books on the side table between them. "I have interrupted your studies." He leaned across and opened *Elements of Alchemy*. "Carlston is not making you read this ghastly stuff, is he?"

She laughed. "He is. Did you have to read it too?"

"I certainly did, but my mentor quickly discovered that my forte was fighting, not alchemy." He kept his eyes upon the book, turning pages. "How is Lord Carlston?"

Although his tone was as congenial as ever, the question was far more than just polite inquiry. Helen felt her spine stiffen. Beneath his easy manners, Mr. Stokes was still very much a hunter. He might not be in Pike's confidence about the journal, but he certainly knew about Lord Carlston's state of mind.

"He is very well, thank you."

Stokes let the book's cover slap back into place. "You know that is not what I am asking, Lady Helen." He looked up, his hazel eyes intent. "Has he shown any deterioration?"

Helen rose from her chair and walked to the hearth. "You can tell Pike that he is unchanged."

Stokes regarded her for a long moment, patently searching her face for lies. He smiled. "Ah, I see."

Helen turned her back, her heart beating her dismay. He had seen her true feelings for the Earl. She placed Pike's instruction on the mantel to be read later, although she had no intention of using the gold. Right now, she had a decision to make. Did she end this interview, or take a chance and play a dangerous card, gambling that the man before her was as honorable as Lady Margaret claimed?

She faced him again. "Mr. Pike seems convinced Lord Carlston is on the same path as Mr. Benchley."

"Yes, he does."

At least he did not pretend it was not so. She ground her palms together. "Do *you* think Lord Carlston is going mad?"

"I have seen him only once since his return to England. He did not seem . . . himself."

She regarded him for a long moment; he was playing his own close game. She could only trust her instincts. With a wordless prayer, she turned her card. "I think Mr. Pike intends to kill him."

In the quiet elegance of the drawing room, it sounded absurdly melodramatic.

Stokes crossed his arms. "Mr. Pike may be a bureaucrat born from the shop, but he acts within the bounds of his position and for the good of the Dark Days Club and England."

"Do you really believe that?"

"Lady Helen, you must understand that at present, Mr. Pike is, for all intents and purposes, our commanding officer. He has the authority of the King and of Parliament, and so we must obey his orders. I can see you may not have had much experience with the sanctity of chain of command, but I am sure you recognize the sanctity of our oath."

"Of course I do." Lately it felt as if she could think of nothing else.

"Mr. Pike does not act alone. If such a dire order were issued, it would be ratified by the highest sources in the land."

Helen swallowed; her mouth felt parched. "Is it going to be issued, Mr. Stokes?"

"We must pray to God that Lord Carlston can hold his own against the darkness."

Hardly a resounding denial. Helen paced across the hearthstone.

"I spent my youth in the army," Stokes added. "I have seen what happens on the battlefield when orders are disobeyed, or those above break under pressure. Campaigns can hinge on the delivery of a message or the removal of one person. We in the middle of the battle cannot see the whole, Lady Helen. We must trust those who can."

"And you think Mr. Pike can see the whole?"

"He may only have been Sir Dennis Calloway's Terrene, and a butcher's son at that, but he has the kind of devious mind required for the intrigues of our world."

"I do not know how you can say that. He does not even believe that a Grand Deceiver is in England."

Stokes sat forward. "Do you truly think you are here to battle a Grand Deceiver?"

Helen paused, taken aback by the sudden shift of subject to herself. "Yes. I do. The evidence points to it." She counted off on her fingers. "I am a direct inheritor. I have seen Deceivers working together. Two of them have actually told me that a Grand Deceiver is among us and that he is coming for me. I know deception is their nature, but I believe it."

Stokes sat forward. "I believe it too, Lady Helen."

"You do?" She smiled, the sudden rush of relief making her sway upon her feet. "I was beginning to think that we had no allies in the Dark Days Club. That it is totally corrupt."

"Corrupt?" Stokes seemed genuinely startled. "In what way?"

"The things that people are doing . . ." She circled her hand, trying to find the right words. "There does not seem to be any morality."

His mouth quirked; not in amusement, Helen decided, but in a kind of sad sympathy. "My dear girl, here is a truth that every soldier must understand: an army at war has its own morality, made of necessity. This tiny army of ours must do whatever is in its power to protect England. I suggest you come to peace with that as soon as you can."

He regarded her gravely, patently expecting a response. Yet how was she to come to terms with an idea that opposed everything she had been taught throughout her life? Surely there was only one morality in the world?

Stokes broke the awkward silence. "Let me reassure you that you do have allies, although we are not great in number. All of the Reclaimers believe a Grand Deceiver is approaching. We who walk in that world among the Deceivers cannot deny these new signs that herald such a creature. It is true Mr. Pike is yet to be convinced—he is a cautious man—but he will soon come to the same conclusion. Among the Reclaimers, it is only myself and Jacob Hallifax who agree with Lord Carlston's assessment of your role. The other Reclaimers cannot believe, or will not believe, that you are the warrior sent to destroy a Grand Deceiver. For them it is impossible to imagine that a young woman nobly born and barely beyond the schoolroom could defeat such a foe."

Helen crossed her arms. "How, then, do they explain the fact that I am a direct inheritor?"

"They have decided that you are here to take the vestige darkness from a true warrior in order to save him for the battle. In their minds, Lord Carlston is that warrior. He is the highest ranked among us and the most experienced, the best chance to lead us to victory."

Helen stared at him. "They want me to take his darkness into my soul?" She lifted her chin. "Why do they not offer to take his lordship's darkness upon themselves? Why do they not volunteer to encase their essence in a black abyss, to lose all compassion and tenderness, to hasten their own descent into madness?"

"Because it is a woman's place to make such a sacrifice," he said dryly. "Your mother took Benchley's darkness, and it gave him ten more years of sanity. Why not the daughter?"

"She did not take it willingly," Helen said, her voice rising. "He forced his darkness upon her without her knowledge."

"I know," Stokes said, a flash of his raised palms acknowledging the injustice. "Yet all they see is that Benchley proved it could be done. That it could save Lord Carlston."

"He would not want such a cure. He would never accept it."

"You are quite right. Lord Carlston, in his right mind, would never seek such a cure. However, the prospect of homicidal insanity could make even the most staunch man waver in his beliefs."

He rubbed the back of his head wearily, ruffling the blond curls. "All Reclaimers suffer, to some degree, from the vestige darkness. I have it lodged in me, bringing its torments. You will have it soon enough, once you start fighting and reclaiming. Even if we stop reclaiming before madness sets in, there is still a weight always upon the soul. It is part of the payment for such gifts."

"How do you keep fighting with the knowledge that you are harming your soul?"

He smiled. "I have never thought it good enough to lead just a blameless life, Lady Helen. It has always been important to me to have a purpose beyond my own small concerns. You and I, and the other Reclaimers, have been given the tools for *great* purpose. In my experience, life is always a question of courage. Which way do we run when we see danger: away from it, or toward it?"

"It depends on what the danger is," Helen said.

"No. It depends on what is at stake. And for us, it is the highest stake of all. The safety of mankind." He rose from his chair. "You have allies in the Dark Days Club, Lady Helen. People who believe in your great purpose. I am one of them. If you should ever need me, I am lodging at Twelve Church Street, just beyond the Brooks Chapel."

"Thank you," Helen said, surprised to find that her voice cracked upon the words.

He bowed. "I bid you good day, Lady Helen." He walked to the door and opened it, then turned back. "Lord Carlston told me that you have courage in abundance. I see now that he is right."

The door closed behind him.

Helen steadied herself with a hand upon the mantel. She had an ally, albeit one who believed rather too uncritically in the Dark Days Club and Mr. Pike. She clenched her fist. How dare those other Reclaimers think she was useful only as a dump for Lord Carlston's vestige darkness. She was much more than that; she was a direct inheritor! At least Mr. Stokes and Mr. Hallifax did not subscribe to the idea.

Helen rubbed her forehead. The whole business was a labyrinth, and she could only see one thing clearly: the *Ligatus* journal. It held the way to Lord Carlston's cure, her own safety, and the protection of England. She could no longer wait for Lowry to appear. She must act.

Eighteen

Wednesday, 15 July 1812

Helen smoothed down the front of her breeches and sat on the edge of her bed, regarding her Hessian boots. Their close fit made them the devil to put on by herself, particularly with Reclaimer strength; it was far too easy to misjudge a tug or pull and rip a garment apart. She had already destroyed one shirt. However, she could hardly call in Darby to help, not when she meant to creep out of the house unnoticed. With a rallying breath, she picked up the right boot and worked her stockinged foot into the long shaft.

The sound of departure rose from the foyer downstairs. She listened, finding the squeak of carriage springs and the jingle of the harness as Lady Margaret and Delia stepped into the carriage. They were headed for the Devil's Dyke, a nearby picturesque place of interest, and a rendezvous with another informer. Helen had excused herself from attending the expedition, claiming a sick headache from her courses. In fact, she intended to visit Kate Holt's bawdy house to find Martha Gunn's informer, Binny, and ask her if Lowry had visited recently—perhaps to hide the journal— or if Philip had been seen in the area. After all, she had seen the Deceiver herself twice near the Steine, and Kate Holt's house stood in the nest of lanes in the Old Town, just west of it.

Helen had to admit she was daunted by the idea of setting foot in such a depraved place. From what Martha had said, it was a den of perversions. Lud, they probably fornicated in front of one another, counting it as one of the attractions. She certainly did not want to witness the carnal act again. As it was, she could not rid herself of the memory of seeing it for the first time in Vauxhall Gardens—the horror of the Deceiver thrusting into his victim against a wall as he drained away her life force. Helen shuddered. How was she to walk into a fleshpot that sold the most private parts of a woman for the use of any man and still maintain a complacent face, as if fornication were nothing more than sport? And what if her disguise was not good enough, and she was unmasked as a woman? Would she have to fight her way out? Lowry would certainly hear of such a commotion, and would abandon any plan to take refuge in the house.

Even so, Helen knew she had to act before Lord Carlston returned from London. She and Mr. Hammond had to retrieve the journal before his lordship discovered it, then she must secure the *Ligatus* and hand it over to Pike. If that meant braving the bawdy house, she must put aside her sensibilities and get it done.

She yanked the tight instep over her foot and blew out a relieved breath. Boot and foot still intact. She picked up the other Hessian and worked her foot down to the instep, pulling hard. A closer sound—Darby's familiar tread across the dressing room carpet and the opening of the clothes press—swung her around to face the adjoining door.

"Do not come in, Darby. I am not well."

Yet the door opened. Darby stood at the threshold, Helen's green gentleman's jacket in her arms.

"I told you not to come in," Helen said.

"Forgive me, my lady, but I thought you might need some help getting ready." Darby lifted the jacket.

Helen busied herself with her boot. Her maid was too percep-tive. "Getting ready for what?" She finally felt her foot slide into place.

"Going out on your own, my lady. Testing yourself. Mr. Quinn has been wondering when you would finally come to it. He thought you might not do so at all, but I knew you would." She regarded Helen's frown. "It is what you intend, isn't it?"

It was close enough. "You were expecting it?"

"Mr. Quinn says that all this training is nothing without the confidence to use it. At some point, he said, you would have to prove to yourself that you can do what the Dark Days Club demands of you." She walked across to Helen and held out the jacket. "Shall I help you into it, my lady?"

Helen crossed her arms. "It would seem that my progress, or lack of it, is the subject of much speculation in this house."

Darby's hands dropped a little, the jacket sagging between them. "It was not meant with any meanness of spirit, my lady."

Helen relented. Darby only had her well-being at heart. "I'm sure it was not. Your Mr. Quinn is the least mean-spirited man I know." She stood and held out her arms for the jacket. "Have you spoken to him about the Terrene ritual?"

"I have," Darby said, her voice dropping into a whisper as she threaded Helen's arm expertly into the tight-fitting sleeve. "It is a blood-bonding, my lady. He explained the basics of it—a mix of blood and milk and burned hair, drunk by Reclaimer and Terrene—but he was adamant that the intricacies were best left for Lord Carlston to explain. I pressed him, but he became a little suspicious. I did not want to alert him to our plan, so I turned the conversation to other matters." She threaded Helen's other arm into its sleeve and, with a hoist that had all her weight behind it, fitted the jacket over Helen's shoulders. The force sent Helen for-ward a step. "I am sorry I could not find out more, my lady."

"I understand." Helen squeezed her maid's shoulder in reassurance. "We must find another source of the ritual."

It must be recorded in a book somewhere. She would make a thorough search of the alchemy books that Lord Carlston had left for her perusal.

"There," Darby said, smoothing a last crease out of the wool. "You look very fine. What do you plan to do, my lady?"

Helen rolled her shoulders into the tight fit. "I am not sure yet."

"You should do something *very* male," Darby said. She smiled tentatively. "You could go to Raggett's Club, or drive the gig down the main street by yourself." At Helen's smile, she gathered momentum. "You could even eat your lunch at a chophouse. At a bench!"

Helen placed her hat upon her head. *Or I could visit a bawdy house*, she thought dryly. There was nothing more male than that.

Half an hour later, she strolled along Union Street, a dingy laneway in the Old Town, with a red apple in hand, still smiling from the few moments she had spent conversing with the apple boy on the corner. She had passed him the coin, and the boy, with a lift of his sandy brows, had called, "Catch it, sir?" Helen had nodded, and her neat grab of the apple high in the air had earned her a grin of admiration from the lad before he turned to his next customer.

She could not, of course, bite into the fruit—even gentlemen did not eat in the street—but she lifted it to her nose as she weaved her way around the other pedestrians. Its fresh green scent was the sweetest she had ever inhaled.

She nearly walked past her goal: the sign above Holt's Coffeehouse was blackened with grime. It stood in a row of close-built shops, each three stories tall and in some disrepair. The draper's next door was open, a basket of cheap cloth set outside to tempt buyers inside and a display of sprigged dress lengths in its window. Holt's, however, looked ominously deserted.

Helen tried the stout red door. Locked. The view through one of the window's small panes showed a dark room. A single shaft of sunlight caught the curve of a roughly made stool and the corner of a table.

"Ain't open, mister," a young voice said. "Not till after midday."

Helen turned to find a girl of perhaps ten years watching her from beneath a rough knot of brown hair, one dirty hand clutching the bricks that quoined the corner of the building. She wore the bedraggled remnants of a woman's dress, its flowered print faded into ghostly roses and vines.

"You lookin' for the whores?" she asked, hoisting up the gaping neckline.

Her voice was very loud for such a small girl. Helen checked the street before answering. A man in fisherman's trousers and a smock strode by, intent upon his own thoughts; and a dark-skinned couple dressed in sober blues, Quakers perhaps, on their way to the Meeting House, hurried past, their chins tucked to their chests. Outside a butcher shop, a group of filthy children were floating sticks in a puddle reddened by drained blood, their squabbling like the sound of agitated geese. No one was heeding her at all. It was rather thrilling to be standing in a street by herself without a chaperone.

"I am looking for one girl in particular," she said.

"They all be asleep," her informer offered. "We opens the same time as the coffee-'ouse."

"I want to speak to Binny. Do you know her?" Helen asked.

The girl nodded, her watery blue eyes as wary as those of a kicked dog.

"Would you please fetch her for me?"

"The girls don't like to be woked, mister."

"Oh." Helen looked in the window again, at a loss. She had not expected the child to refuse her request.

The girl edged a step closer, hand still gripping the bricked edge of the building. "Give us a penny an' I'll do it."

Of course, everything here was a commercial transaction. Helen juggled the apple into her other hand and dug two fingers into her breeches pocket. She pulled out a penny.

"I will give you this now. And a sixpence, too, if you go and tell Binny that Martha's friend is here, and bring her back to me without disturbing anyone else."

The girl drew in a breath. "A sixpence? You gullin' me?"

"No, I am telling the truth. But you only get the sixpence if you bring me Binny *quietly.*"

The girl held out her hand. Helen dropped the penny into the cupped palm. The girl tapped the coin against a crooked front tooth. It seemed that it, and Helen, passed assessment, for she jerked her pointed chin toward a sliver of dirt path that ran up the side of the coffeehouse. "Follar me."

"What is your name?" Helen asked as they edged along the narrow space between drapery and coffeehouse. It was overhung with cords strung with grayed washing. The dank smell of human urine caught at the back of her throat, and she coughed, hearing the sound bounce off the close-set stucco walls.

"They calls me Sprat." The girl skirted a pile of old rope with practiced ease. "Course when I start swivin' next year, I'm gunna call meself Janey." She climbed over a small pile of broken bricks, her bare feet seemingly immune to the jagged edges, then squinted back at Helen. "Pretty name, ain't it? You'd like that if you was lookin' for a ladybird, wouldn't you?"

Helen translated the girl's words, steadying herself against the wall as she came to their awful meaning. "But you are a child."

Sprat stopped, pale brows furrowing into a frown of indignation. "I'm near twelve."

Heaven forfend; only twelve. "What do you do now?"

"Fetchin' and cleanin', and sometimes I'm allowed to keep the times and knock on the doors. Not for the floggin' rooms, though, 'cause them's the spesh-ee-al-itee." She sniffed back a nose full of mucus. "I can tell the time by a clock, and count up to a hundred."

A side-glance checked that Helen was impressed. Helen was appalled, but she nodded and smiled.

They had arrived at the back of the coffeehouse. Along the length of a small yard, yellowed drying cloths hung from cord strung between two wooden stakes that leaned inward from the burden. Behind the line of laundry, Helen could see a solid white-washed outbuilding, fairly new by the look of it, that formed the opposite wall of the yard. The back door of the bawdy house stood open and a greasy smell of roasted mutton turned Helen's stomach.

"Best stay 'ere," Sprat said. "Binny ain't gunna like being woked at all." She regarded Helen for a moment. "What's yer name?"

"Tell her it's Martha's friend."

Sprat gave a nod and headed into the kitchen, batting the washing on her way past.

Helen surveyed the quiet yard. A selection of long birch rods had been propped against the outbuilding wall, a wet circle on the cobbles beneath them. Newly washed, Helen surmised, and set into a patch of sun to dry. She eyed them uneasily, remembering Sprat's description of the house specialty. A tabby cat observed her discomfort from its position on the opposite roof, then yawned as she took the few steps across the rough cobbles and parted a curtain of limp linen to look at the outbuilding.

It was a solid wooden box, the only apparent source of light and air obtained from a rectangle cut high into the door and lined with six wide-set iron bars. A cell, then. Helen hesitated; perhaps it was something to do with one of the bawdy house perversions.

She wrinkled her nose: a rancid smell, like rotting flesh, emanated from within.

Hand pressed against her nostrils, she edged closer, peering through the bars into the dim interior. A straw pallet had been shoved up against the back wall, a jumble of blankets bunched at its end. A bucket, stained and buzzing with flies, stood in the corner. Nearby, an array of gnawed bones—no doubt the source of the rancid stink—lay piled carefully on the dirt floor, their own collection of flies weaving lazily above. A long chain snaked across the floor, the dirt around it swept smooth except for a churn of footprints to the left that clearly showed the chain's extent stopped well short of the side wall and the wooden chest pushed against it.

Suddenly the chain rattled and pulled tight. A face reared up at the bars, yellowed teeth bared.

"Sweet heaven!" Helen yelped, and jumped back.

"You got somethin' for Lester? You got somethin' for Lester?"

A filthy hand curled around a bar, and a pair of green eyes, the corners red and inflamed, blinked rapidly. The bared teeth, Helen realized, were a smile.

She straightened. Somehow she had ended up in a combat crouch three feet away. This must be Kate Holt's mad son. The Unreclaimable.

"You got somethin' for Lester?" The hopeful voice turned a little mournful, as if many times there had been nothing for Lester.

She could see now that underneath all the filth was a young man of about twenty-five, with thick black hair matted into hanks and a strong cleft chin. Lord Carlston had said that the vestige energy could sometimes overburden an offspring's mind and manifest itself in fits of extreme violence, promiscuity, or, as it seemed in Lester's case, a descent into pitiful madness. Would Lord Carlston end up in such a state if they could not find a cure? Helen pushed away the awful thought.

"Hello, Lester," she said gently, then realized she did have something to offer. She held out the apple. "Would you like some of this?"

A female voice answered, "I'm not rightly sure he's ever had one."

Helen spun around. A girl stood just outside the kitchen door, a broad hand clutching an old pink-flowered banyan robe around her plump body. Sprat stood at her side. They both flinched at Helen's sudden turn.

"Are you Binny?" Helen asked.

"Course she is," Sprat said, rallying. "You got my sixpence?"

Helen retrieved the coin and held it out. "Here."

Sprat darted forward and collected it. "See, told ya," she said to Binny. She scuttled off to the gate, treasure closed tight in her hand.

Binny picked her way across the yard. Her pair of high wooden pattens, designed to raise the wearer above the muck, clunked against the cobbles.

"You really gunna give it him?" she asked, nodding at the apple.

"Yes, of course. If he wants it."

"You gotta go up nice an' easy," Sprat advised from the gate. "Some of the girls tease 'im and snatch stuff away, so he's a bit grabby. If he gets yer hand, he won't let go."

"He likes to spit too," Binny added.

"Spit," Lester echoed.

Helen approached the door carefully and held out the apple. A hand, the wrist painfully thin and ingrained with dirt, shot out and grabbed the fruit.

"Ta, ta, ta, ta," Lester called.

He disappeared from view. Helen heard a loud crunch of apple flesh and a low hum of delight.

"Sprat says you're Martha's friend," Binny said softly.

Just as Helen nodded, a man's voice, high-pitched and vicious, rang out from the kitchen. "For Chrissakes, girl, take the man's money and get in 'ere. He don't want to be standin' in all that shite."

Helen peered down the yard, glad that the brim of her beaver shaded her face from view. A dim figure stood in the doorway, then moved away again. Kate Holt's husband?

The order sent Binny across the small distance between them. She clutched the banyan tighter, creasing the front of it around an ample bosom. She was perhaps a few years older than Helen, with a ruddy country complexion sprinkled with freckles. Her eyes were round, a pretty dove gray, and, at that moment, wide with fright.

"Pretend you're havin' a fumble," she whispered, and pulled aside the front of the banyan to expose one heavy breast. She grabbed Helen's hand and pressed it against her warm flesh, squeezing her fingers around the soft weight.

Helen froze. Dear God Almighty! She felt locked in place, her eyes fixed upon the girl's chest.

"Mrs. Gunn says I was to speak only to a lady. No one else. You seem like a decent cove, sir, but Mrs. Gunn was real particular. Only a lady, so I can't tell you nothin'." She stopped, watching Helen's face. "Ain't you never touched one afore?" She bit her lip, trying to hide a smile.

Face hot with horror, Helen pulled her hand free.

"Lordy, you never been with a girl, have you?" Binny said.

Helen squeezed her eyes shut. How could she act as if such casual obscenity did not matter? Yet she had vowed she would put aside her sensibilities and be a Reclaimer.

Pushing past her shock, she whispered, "I *am* the lady."

"What?"

Helen opened her eyes. "I am not a man. I am the lady Mrs. Gunn told you about."

Gritting her teeth, she caught Binny's hand and pressed it against her own chest, pushing the girl's fingers around the small curve that the breast band could not fully disguise.

Binny gasped. "Glory!" She patted Helen's chest again. "Dressed in men's clobber. Like them actresses."

"Yes."

Binny glanced over her shoulder. "Come with me."

She bent and ducked under the linen, pulling Helen after her with surprising strength. They landed side by side against the wall of Lester's cell. Binny pressed her finger against her lips.

"I'll tell Mr. Holt you just wanted a knee-trembler," she whispered. "But you'll need to give me the coin so's I don't get a hidin'." Deal?"

Although not quite sure what Binny had said, Helen nodded. The core of it was clear: she needed money to avoid a beating.

"Sorry 'bout stickin' yer hand on me pap. I didn't know," Binny continued.

"No, of course not," Helen said, feeling fresh heat rise to her face.

"I never sent you a message, my lady. I ain't seen no sign of the cove you want—Mrs. Holt's brother, MacEvoy."

"You do know what he looks like, though?"

"That I do." She grimaced. "Last time I saw him was about a month back. Mrs. Holt give him little Lizzie." Her voice dropped to an even softer whisper, barely more than a breath. "He cut her up bad and did things to her here." She tapped her head. "She still screams at night. He's real bad folk."

Helen sounded her agreement; Lowry was the worst folk. At least her suspicion that he would come here to take refuge with his sister was right.

"Have you seen Mrs. Holt hide anything special, or has she told you to stay away from some place?"

Binny shook her head. "We ain't allowed in her particular room, nor where she and Mr. Holt live, but that's always been so."

"Where are those rooms?"

She pointed up. "On the second floor. At the back."

Helen studied the small window that Binny had indicated. "Did her brother stay up there too when he was last here?"

"He spent his time down below, past the molly rooms. Him and poor Lizzie."

"Have you seen anyone else watching the house?"

"I 'ave," Sprat said, peeking around the corner of the building.

Binny glared at the girl. "What have I told you about sneakin' round, watchin' us?"

Sprat lifted a bony, truculent shoulder.

"Who have you seen?" Helen asked. Perhaps Philip was watching the place too. "A tall redheaded man?" She touched her own hat, searching for the right cant word. "Wearing a gray nab like this?"

"No. A go-by-ground, black hair. Looked real smoky."

Helen translated, a short man with dark hair who looked suspicious. So not Philip, but perhaps the swarthy companion she had seen at his side near Edward Street.

"Did he come inside?"

Sprat shook her head. "Never. Just stayed in the daffy house opposite, watchin'."

Helen floundered for a moment. *Daffy house.* Ah, gin house.

"I knows where 'e lives," Sprat added. "I follared 'im one day."

Binny clicked her tongue. "Mrs. Holt told you not to fork no more. Leastways, nothin' that could be traced back here."

Fork: Sprat was a pickpocket, too.

"Will you show me where he lives?" Helen asked.

Sprat regarded her expectantly, crooked teeth showing in a sly grin of encouragement.

Helen stifled a smile at the girl's cheerful venality. "Yes, all right, for another sixpence." She gripped Binny's arm for a moment in thanks. "You know where to send a message if MacEvoy comes back?"

"Twenty German Place," Binny said.

"Yes. As *soon* as he comes back."

"Soon as," Binny promised. "And you'll tell Mrs. Gunn that I done what she said? She's gunna teach me how to dip ladies."

Helen nodded. She pulled out more coins. "How much?"

Binny stared down at the money for a moment, clearly at war with herself, then said quickly, "Just a crown."

Helen handed her the coin. "Thank you."

Binny stepped aside, aiming an admonishing finger at Sprat. "Don't you do nothin' on the way. Go straight. Got it?"

Sprat nodded her agreement and pushed open the gate. It chewed along the broken cobbles in a harsh grind. "Come on, then."

The walkway at the back of the bawdy house was even narrower than the one at the side. Helen followed Sprat apace and found herself squeezing through a twitten, the passage between the two buildings so tight that the bungaroosh walls scraped at her back and belly and left her coat smeared with a fine sandy dust. They emerged into the middle of busy Black Lion Street, their sudden appearance causing no interest whatsoever from the other pedestrians intent upon their own business.

Helen brushed down her jacket and adjusted the set of her hat, and then they were on their way again, Sprat leading the way past the Free School and up to North Street. They took the downward incline of this steep and very busy road, passing the Chapel Royal and the General Coach Office, the front of which was blocked by the ten o'clock stage preparing to leave for London. Passengers called out directions to the coachmen for the placement of their luggage atop—mostly ignored—and milled around waiting to climb into the large carriage. Helen saw Sprat eyeing a few of the gentlemen whose coats were agape, but the girl resisted temptation and forged onward down the hill.

A left turn brought them onto the Steine beside the Castle Tavern. Helen wondered how much further they were to go. Apparently past the Marine Pavilion, for Sprat marched alongside the carefully planted green that fronted the Prince Regent's favorite home, not even looking at its splendor. Helen, however, snatched a moment to admire the classical circular building that formed the center of the residence—its high dome supported by graceful pillars—and the two large wings that extended elegantly on either side of it. There was, she decided, a very beautiful symmetry to the whole. The Prince Regent might not be the most sensible of monarchs, but he did have excellent taste in architecture.

Leaving the Pavilion behind, they crossed the road to Grand Parade, dodging through what seemed an endless stream of wagons, gigs, phaetons, and carts. Finally, Sprat stopped beside a grand house and hoisted up her dress again with an air of finality.

"Is this it?" Helen asked, looking up at the four-story town house.

"Across the way," Sprat said, jerking her head to the handsome row of houses on the road opposite: Marlborough Row. "The one with the green door." She considered Helen for a moment, then said, "I thought you was a man. You really a girl?"

There was no use denying it; Sprat had plainly heard all her conversation with Binny.

"I am." She couldn't resist asking, "Did you *really* think I was a man?"

"Yep." Sprat squinted up at her, watery eyes earnest. "Are you gunna kill Mrs. Holt's brother?"

"Good Lord, no," Helen said.

Sprat's mouth bunched sideways into disappointment. "If I was a man, I'd kill 'im."

"You do know that killing is wrong, don't you?"

Sprat regarded her for a long moment. "There's some people don't deserve to breathe. Not wiv what they does." She held out her cupped hand. "You're 'ere now. All done."

Helen dug in her pocket again and brought out the promised sixpence. "One last thing," she said, holding up the coin. "Do you know who lives there?"

Sprat shrugged. "A swell. That's all I know."

Helen dropped the coin into the girl's cupped hand. "Thank you."

"Bye, *mister*." Sprat gave a sly giggle and was off, darting back across busy Grand Parade.

Helen pulled her touch watch out of her fob pocket and flicked it open, clicking the three lenses into place. She settled in to wait, leaning against the corner of the end house with her arms crossed in as manly a manner as she could manage.

Thirty-five minutes later, the green door opened. Helen straightened. The little dark-haired man that she had seen at Philip's side emerged holding a cane. He opened the front gate and stood waiting, his attention fixed upon the doorway. So he was a manservant of some kind—a valet most likely by the good cut of his brown jacket—waiting for his master. She lifted her lens to her eye: the glow around him was bright blue, and a long bruise-black feeder tentacle extended from his back, weaving through the air like a sightless snake. As suspected, another Deceiver.

For a moment, Helen lost sight of him behind a particularly high-set phaeton making its way along Grand Parade, and then she saw the tentacle reaching for the paler life force of a youth walking past the house. It curled for a second across the young man's belly, unseen by all except Helen, then slid across the top of his thighs and groin. The youth dipped his hat to the Deceiver, never suspecting that some of his life force had just been stolen.

Helen lowered the lens, nauseated. She would never get used to seeing those feeder tentacles. There was something so inherently disgusting about the sickly color and serpentine weave of them.

The Deceiver's relaxed posture suddenly stiffened into obeisance. She squinted, making out another man in the town house doorway. It was too dim to see the features of his face below the brim of his fashionable beaver, but he was clearly speaking to the Deceiver, for the creature bowed. Helen strained to hear the words above the grind of the passing gigs and carriages.

"I am dining with the Murrays this evening, Lawrence. The new blue waistcoat, I think?"

She knew that smooth voice, even before the elegant gentleman stepped into the sunlight and full view. Helen's heart clenched into a hard beat. Philip's dark companion served the Comte d'Antraigues.

In reflex, she stepped back against the safety of the wall and watched the Deceiver—Lawrence—hand the Comte his cane. What did the association mean? She had seen Lawrence in Philip's company, and she knew Philip served the Grand Deceiver. Did that mean Lawrence did also?

She pressed her hand to her mouth, stifling a very female gasp that brought a startled look from a man walking past. Helen turned her face and pretended to cough. Holy heaven, was the Comte d'Antraigues the Grand Deceiver? It was possible, of course; yet somehow it did not seem likely. Not after their interview with him at Lady Dunwick's rout. Then again, Helen thought, as she watched the Comte stroll out of the gate, he had set Lord Carlston upon the search for the journal, and his man was watching the bawdy house.

Whatever the case, there was one very sobering truth that could not be denied: the Grand Deceiver, whoever he may be, knew that Lowry had the journal. But did he also know it was a *Ligatus*?

Nineteen

HELEN'S SUSPICIONS ABOUT the Comte d'Antraigues and his valet occupied her as she walked back to German Place. She took Marine Parade, alongside the beachfront, but hardly noticed the sun's warmth and was only momentarily diverted by the amusing sight of two squealing ladies run aground on a pair of cantankerous penny-a-ride donkeys.

There seemed to be enough evidence to suggest that the Comte could be the Grand Deceiver, yet Helen was not convinced. Not that she could say why. Perhaps she had been affected by his charm more than she cared to admit. And that, she realized, was another mark against the Comte: charm was one of the purported traits of a Grand Deceiver. The Comte had also admitted to a lowly start: another characteristic. Still, every Deceiver in the world had been shifting from generation to generation for centuries. Most of them would have started their earthly existence among the lower orders.

By the time she turned the corner into German Place, Helen felt even more tangled. Her mind insisted that the Comte was the Grand Deceiver—just look at all the evidence—but her gut instinct shook its head and stood firm, although it offered no support for its spurious claim.

The argument was going around in frustrating circles, so she abandoned it for the moment and instead surveyed the street for any sign of a spy in the employ of the Duke. The stretch of four- and five-story town houses stood quietly in the midday sun, only the dipping, wheeling gulls above providing any movement. No footman or groom watched the house. Her letter seemed to have had the required effect.

The real test, of course, would be when she and the Duke next met in public. She sighed. The cut direct—ignoring someone so deliberately and so completely—was the height of incivility, but it would make clear that she did not want any further association. Hopefully it would also sever any attachment he imagined he still felt.

Ignoring the sense of loss that followed that plan, she walked up the side lane to the mews. They gave access to the rear door of the house—a precaution in case anyone noticed that a young gentleman seemed to have joined the household at number 20. As she neared the stables, a groom led out a big chestnut gelding, one of a curricle pair that she knew belonged to Lord Carlston. Sweat dulled its usually gleaming coat. His lordship had returned. Was he inside or had he returned to his own lodgings?

Helen felt her step quicken and forcibly slowed herself again as she passed the groom and horse. She must control this compulsion to see him.

Geoffrey stood in the rear yard, gathering up two portmanteaus. He frowned at Helen's approach, squaring his big shoulders, then recognized her and dipped his head.

"Good day, sir," he said.

"Good day. Has Mr. Hammond returned?"

The footman glanced down at the cases. "He and Lord Carlston have just this minute gone up to the drawing room. I believe they are waiting for your return."

Waiting for her return: she could not stop a smile. Even so, she must order her thoughts. There were too many secrets and too much at stake to just give in to her desire to run willy-nilly upstairs. Everything had become ten times more dangerous: the *Ligatus* and Pike's dangerous belief that his lordship had helped make it, Stokes's warning, the Comte, and of course the threat to put his lordship down like a rabid dog. She had not seen Lord Carlston for four days; what if his mental state had declined further? She kneaded one fist within the other hand. *Dear God*, she prayed, *don't let him be worse.* If he were, could she really report it to Pike?

She continued through the kitchen door, acknowledged the curtsies from the cook and her girls, and took the stairs two at a time, arriving at the drawing room door with heart hammering. He would probably have heard her ascent. She hoped he had heard it; that would mean he had been listening for her approach. She stopped at the door, focusing her own Reclaimer hearing.

"There is no reason to think that Canning would be swayed in that direction," she heard him say, "particularly if Castlereagh favors it." She raised her head: was that a smile dawning in his voice? "Ah, Lady Helen has returned."

She pressed steepled fingertips to her lips for a moment, trying to contain her elation. She might have decided to quell her attraction to Lord Carlston, but it seemed her body had not.

The door opened. Mr. Hammond, face pale from fatigue, peered out. No wonder he looked exhausted; he and Lord Carlston must have left London before dawn to have reached Brighton by this time of day.

"Good morning," he said, and in just one glance his blue eyes passed a wealth of information: an apology for not keeping his lordship in London, concern for her, and not least, a question: *Lowry?*

She gave a slight shake of her head, covering them all, and walked into the drawing room. Lady Margaret and Delia were seated on the sofa. She had not expected them to be back as well.

Delia smiled a greeting, but Lady Margaret's eyes were fixed upon his lordship. Her smile was filled with the same kind of exhilaration that Helen felt.

"Good morning," Lord Carlston said, bowing.

He stood by the window, the sunlight catching the ebony shine of his hair and modeling the angles of his cheekbone and jaw, their stern symmetry softened only by the welcoming curve of his lips. Helen felt herself take too many steps toward him; how mortifying that a happy mix of shape and contour should have such an ungovernable effect upon her body. She stopped and rocked back on her heels, concentrating upon the whole of him, not just his lips. He seemed more at ease, the strain and deep snapping energy subdued, and that awful knit of pain between his brows gone. No doubt part of the reason for Lady Margaret's jubilation.

"You appear much improved, Lord Carlston," she said.

"I am, thank you." He walked across to the table, where a long black leather case had been set. It looked like a box from Rundell's, but was far too large for jewelry. His lordship placed his fingers upon the top as if calming what lay inside. "Mr. Quinn told me you have been visiting the town by yourself?"

Clearly the subject of his sickness was not to be discussed.

"I have. It seemed the right time do so," Helen said, keeping her voice determinedly nonchalant.

Lady Margaret leaned forward. "I do not see why you felt the need to hide your expedition." The statement bordered on the accusatory.

Helen stood silent. Any answer would be wrong.

"It was foolhardy," Lady Margaret added. "You need to apprise someone of your whereabouts."

"Lady Helen is a Reclaimer, Lady Margaret," his lordship said, turning away from the box. "She does not need to apprise anyone of her whereabouts."

Delia made a sound that was suspiciously close to a snort, turning it quickly into a small cough.

Lady Margaret stiffened. "I thought you believed she was not yet ready to go out on her own, Lord Carlston."

"She must be ready." He regarded Helen thoughtfully. "Was it a successful venture?"

"Yes, I believe it was." Helen paused; every step hereon was treacherous. She saw Mr. Hammond shift from one foot to the other. Yes, he felt the danger too. How much could she say? "I went into the Lanes. To a bawdy house."

"A bawdy house?" Delia exclaimed, blonde curls bobbing with shock.

"I did not go in," Helen said.

"Oh, of course not." Delia smiled her relief.

"Kate Holt's house?" his lordship asked. "Lowry's sister," he added for the benefit of the room.

Ah, he knew. His London informer must have told him.

"Yes." Helen caught a sidelong warning from Hammond as he crossed to the hearth into her line of sight. She forged onward. "I have asked Mrs. Gunn and her people to inform us if he should appear there or in town again, but I decided to go there myself and ask some discreet questions."

At least most of it was the truth.

"Did you find anything?" Hammond asked. He was doing a good job of hiding his nerves, but his hand had closed into a white-knuckled grip around the marble edge of the mantel.

"I saw a man watching the house. He was, I think, the same man I saw in Philip's company, so I followed him back to his residence. He is the Comte d'Antraigues's valet." She addressed the last to Lord Carlston.

The Earl's eyes narrowed as he turned over the news. "Ah. Now that is interesting. Well done."

Lady Margaret looked across at her brother. "The Comte," she said, as if it were a conclusion. "He must be the Grand Deceiver."

"Do you think it is possible?" Mr. Hammond asked Lord Carlston.

"Anything is possible," his lordship said. "It is not extraordinary to think the Comte would be seeking the journal himself, as well as setting me upon its path. That does not immediately make him the Grand Deceiver." He stopped, frowning as he considered the proposition. Finally he hissed out a breath. "I certainly hope he is not the Grand Deceiver—I doubt I would receive any cure from him if that were the case. My gut, however"—he slapped his hand against his green striped waistcoat, over the flat of his stomach—"says he is not. Granted, he is a Deceiver and deception is their nature, but I cannot see it."

Helen nodded her agreement. Or was it just hopeful thinking on both their parts?

"I cannot claim any logic to that feeling, just years of experience dealing with the Comte," his lordship added. "Even so, we cannot ignore the connection between his valet and Philip. Lady Helen, are you are sure it was the same man in Philip's company?"

Helen hesitated; she could not be absolutely certain. "I saw only a glimpse of him that first time, but I believe it is the same man."

His lordship rubbed his chin. "It is possible the Comte is not aware of the connection between his man and Philip. Either way, it does not change our goal. We must still obtain the journal before anyone else—the Comte, Pike, and the Grand Deceiver, if he is in play too. Whoever possesses it has the power."

More power than he knew, Helen thought.

"Press your informers," he said to Hammond and Lady Margaret. "For now, I wish to speak to Lady Helen alone. If you would all leave us, please."

The abrupt dismissal caught everyone by surprise. Helen

directed a wild glance at Hammond—*What does this mean?*—but it was plain he knew nothing.

Delia rose briskly from the sofa, her alacrity forcing Lady Margaret to stand as well.

"Please, do not overtax yourself, Lord Carlston," Lady Margaret began, then stopped when she saw his lordship's forbidding expression. She drew herself up. "I am pleased to see you so well."

He gave a small bow. "Thank you, Lady Margaret."

The three of them filed out, Mr. Hammond the last to depart. He sent Helen a worried frown before closing the door.

His lordship waited a moment, listening for the sounds of descent, then picked up the black box from the table.

"Foolish of me to ask them to leave, I know," he said, one broad shoulder lifting with self-derision, "but I have something for you and I wanted to give it to you alone. I have been waiting for it to be finished, and it was delivered while I was in London."

A gift from him, delivered alone? The intimacy of it took her breath away. By all rights, a lady should not accept a gift from a gentleman, especially a gentleman who was still considered married. Still, she had already accepted the touch watch from him.

He walked over and handed her the box. "One Reclaimer to another," he said firmly. He must have seen her discomfort.

It was heavier than she had expected. "Most kind of you, Lord Carlston."

"I do not know if you should call it kind. Perhaps expedient would be more appropriate."

It was definitely not jewelry, then. She dug her fingernail beneath the gold catch and flicked it free. With a glance at him—both of them smiling at nothing apart from anticipation, it seemed—she lifted the lid.

"Oh," she breathed.

A curved knife, the blade made from glass and the handle

carved in ivory, lay upon a bed of royal blue velvet. The knife's blade and handle were etched with scrolling leafwork and flowers entwined around the words *Deus in vitro est.* God is in the glass.

"You will find its leather scabbard under the velvet," Carlston said.

She touched the etched surface of the knife, feeling the velvety corrugations of the foliage. "It is so beautiful."

"Mr. Wedgwood made it for you."

"The gentleman who makes the dinner sets and vases?"

"Indeed. Like his father before him, Josiah Wedgwood is quite an alchemist in his own right. He creates our knives to be almost unbreakable and able to withstand Deceiver energy."

He moved to her side and leaned closer, tracing the Latin with his fingertip. "This has also been worked with a protection talisman for you." He cast her a mock-guilty glance. "I have to confess I saved some of your hair from the hairdresser for the alchemy."

He had saved her hair?

"What does the talisman do?" she asked.

"The knife can never be turned against you. If someone tries, it will always miss its mark."

Helen shook her head in wonder. Alchemy was the most troubling aspect of her duties—she had always considered the practice a sham at best and irreligious at worst—and yet here was alchemy woven into a battle cry that invoked God's name.

"It is hard to believe, I know," he said. "Shall I show you?"

"What do you propose? To stab me?"

"It will miss you. I guarantee it."

She regarded him, startled. "No, thank you. I do not wish to be stabbed!"

"Do you not trust me?"

One part of her did, but another part had seen the darkness in him, and the violence.

"I do not trust the alchemy." A side step of the question.

"This will change your mind." He tilted his head, considering her hesitation. "At some point, Lady Helen, you must make your peace with the mysteries of alchemy. It is not inherently evil or godless. It is but one more tool for us to use in our battle."

He gestured to the knife—a request for permission to gather the weapon from its velvet bed. It was, she realized, another Reclaimer test: Could she place her faith in alchemy? She had to admit it was not only worked into horrific weapons by madmen. She had seen it save a child's soul; and her mother's miniature, the lost *Colligat*, had enabled her to view the Deceivers without a lens.

"I suppose if it fails, it will not take my Reclaimer power long to heal me," she said dryly, offering him the box.

He smiled at that, and picked up the knife, weighing it in his hand. "Beautifully balanced." He gripped the handle in a business-like manner and nodded toward the table. "Palm down."

Helen pushed up the sleeve of her jacket and gingerly placed her hand on the polished tabletop, the wood cool against her skin. The danger of the position was like a long scream through her body; every instinct commanded that she snatch her hand away.

"Do not move," he instructed.

Easy for him to say; he was not about to be stabbed. She pressed her hand more firmly against the wood.

Without another word, he plunged the knife down at Reclaimer speed, the tip aimed between her knuckles. Her Reclaimer sight followed its blistering acceleration. His aim was straight and true and had his full strength behind it, but a mere inch from the soft flesh between her bones, the tip veered to the left, sliding past her hand as if caught upon another surface. With a loud thud, the blade hit the table beside her little finger, the force of the blow gouging its tip into the wood at least two inches deep.

She let out her breath.

"I have tested other Reclaimer knives, of course, but it is still such an odd sensation," Carlston said. "I felt sure I was on target, and then it felt as if I had hit something and I could not hold the course. The pull of it was remarkable. Mr. Wedgwood has certainly excelled himself this time." He wrenched the knife from the wood, and inspected the damage to the table. "You can see how deep it went; I was not holding back. Are you convinced now?"

"Quite," Helen said, a little shakily.

"Here." He held out the knife. "Test its balance."

She closed her hand around the offered handle, its deeply etched pattern of tight swirls and flowers rough against her palm. Designed, she realized, to stop it from slipping in her grip. She raised the knife and sliced the air in a series of crosses. Weight and balance perfect, with enough heft to give each cut of the blade maximum purpose.

Ha, she thought, smiling; now she was assessing a deadly weapon as if she were an expert.

"It is a marvelous thing," she said. "Thank you, Lord Carlston."

"Call me Carlston." He paused, his half smile appearing. "Amberley."

An invitation for Mr. Amberley to address him without title. Clearly he meant it as a gesture of friendship between two *men*.

She bowed, trying to hide the heat that had come to her face. "Most kind of you, sir."

"And when you are Lady Helen, I hope I will also be Carlston."

The change in his voice was so slight that she may have imagined it: a deepening that sent a charge through her body. She busied herself placing the knife back upon its velvet bed.

"Thank you . . . Carlston." It felt overwhelmingly intimate.

"Quinn tells me that Mr. Stokes visited you while I was away."

Through her delight, she felt a bright flare of self-preservation. She must concentrate. He knew about Stokes, and he knew the man would not have visited for tea and polite conversation. The impulse to tell him the whole was so strong, but she could not. Must not.

An unwelcome thought occurred. Were the gift and invitation, and indeed his charm, designed to weaken her defenses?

The suspicion was not only unwelcome, but unworthy. She was painting everyone and everything with her own subterfuge.

"Yes," she said carefully. "He came to give me a warning."

"Warning?" His voice had sharpened.

"He told me that some of the other Reclaimers believe I should absorb the vestige darkness from you. They think you are the warrior meant to battle the Grand Deceiver. Not I."

Carlston cursed beneath his breath, in Italian and using words she had never heard before. "Stokes should not have told you that. It is not a solution I would ever take." He fixed his dark eyes upon her, his voice taking on more force. "*Ever!* I would never do that to you."

"I did not think you would, nor does Mr. Stokes." Even so, it was a relief to hear him say it so emphatically.

"I will make that very clear to those Reclaimers who think it is a viable proposition." He rubbed his forefinger between his brows, frowning at some new thought. "Besides, we do not know the role you will take against the Grand Deceiver. You must be at your strongest, and taking any vestige will weaken you. I think perhaps you should refrain from reclaiming as well."

He smiled. "For now, let us start work on how to use that knife to best advantage."

Helen nodded, but her whole focus was upon his fingers pressing hard against his forehead. The awful knit of pain was back between his brows.

Twenty

Saturday, 18 July 1812

"NO, DO NOT lunge wildly for the whip, Lady Helen. You must anticipate the position of it," Lord Carlston said again. "Listen for the draw of the leather, feel the way it is moving through the air. Build the picture of it in your mind."

Helen, blindfolded with glass knife in hand, heard the impatience in his voice. Over the past three days they had been training in the salon for hours at a time, and she could still not picture the whip moving through the air or catch the damnable thing. All she could *feel* was the sweat crawling down her back and the sting of the last ill-judged grab for the coach whip across her leather-gloved hand.

"I am trying," she said.

"Try harder," he snapped.

She lowered her head at his tone.

He hissed out a breath. "Forgive me. Of course you are trying. Take a moment to refocus."

"It has been such a hot day. Dusk is almost upon us; perhaps we should all take a few minutes relief," Lady Margaret said.

Helen placed her near the windows.

"Margaret, do not interfere," Mr. Hammond murmured.

It sounded as if he stood only a few steps away from his sister. He, Lady Margaret, Darby, and Mr. Quinn were all in the room to provide distraction—sound and movement to unsettle her senses—and they were managing the task far too well.

Helen rolled her shoulders, easing the damp cling of her shirt beneath her waistcoat. She longed to rip away the blindfold, too, but settled for hooking a finger into the top and tugging against its firm hold.

"Lady Helen was much closer with that last one, my lord," Mr. Quinn's voice said.

"Yes, you are making excellent progress, my lady," Darby added, near the north wall.

Loyal words, as ever, but Helen knew she was not making excellent progress at all. Even more worrying than her own failure was the ever-increasing edge in his lordship's voice. The taut, deep energy within him had returned in abundance, and Helen could almost feel his strain as he fought to keep himself under control. The elusiveness of the journal was not helping either. Everyone was on edge, waiting for some news of Lowry to emerge from one of the informers.

"When you have conquered this exercise, sensing an actual Deceiver whip will be far more straightforward," his lordship said. "You will not be blindfolded when you face a Deceiver, so you will also be able to use his or her body as a cue to help build the shape and action of any weapons the creature has built."

"Then why must I do this blindfolded?" Helen asked, unable to keep the surly tone from her voice. She twisted her wrists, trying to ease the itch of sweat beneath the leather guards strapped around her forearms.

"You must walk all the sensory pathways that build the picture," Quinn said. Helen swung her head around to face him. He had moved from the back of the salon to the door in an impressively silent manner for such a big man. "If you are not blindfolded, you will still rely upon sight."

"Why not put the Iceland spar lenses into a pair of spectacles?" she said, airing the thought she'd had during another sleepless night. "We could even tie them on."

And then this torment would not be necessary, she added silently.

"Do you think we have not tried that?" his lordship demanded. "The Deceivers are not mindless animals; they saw the vulnerability of such a device immediately. The first Reclaimer who wore it ended up with the lenses smashed into his eyes. He died almost immediately. A Reclaimer's power can heal many injuries, Lady Helen, but not a shard of crystal straight into the brain. God's blood, girl, use your intelligence." His voice had deepened into a snarl.

"Lord Carlston!" Lady Margaret protested.

Helen could hear the anxiety in her voice. No doubt the same anxiety that she felt; he was definitely getting worse. By all rights she should report it to Pike, but she could not. He was not violent, not irrational, just increasingly impatient. Perhaps it was her failure that was prompting such bad temper.

Silence, and then she heard the Earl take a steadying breath. "We will go again," he said, his tone once again measured. "Remember, Lady Helen, move as soon as you have the image. At present you are taking too long to respond."

She heard a step, unmistakably his lordship's long stride, and turned her head, following his progress toward the right wall. Frowning with concentration, she forced her way past her physical discomforts and the distractions of the other four bodies zigzagging across the room. Every sense focused upon the whip in Lord Carlston's hand. She held her breath, hearing the thin sound of the long whiptail rising in the air, the smell of the leather stretching as it flicked back, the small crack as it folded in on itself, disrupting the currents of air against her skin. A sudden picture formed in her mind: the thin length hurtling toward her chest, its trajectory as clear as if she could see it. She jumped to the right, grabbing for the end point of its reach, but her hand closed on air.

"Better," his lordship said. "At least you avoided being hit."

Helen bent over, hands on hips, and pulled in a deep breath. She had only jumped to the left or right all evening, yet she felt exhausted.

With her hearing so exercised, she could not help but hear the knock on the kitchen door two floors down. She straightened and pulled off her blindfold, blinking in the golden light of the sunset through the windows. At this hour, only an informer would be knocking on the door.

"There is—" she began, drawing the attention of Mr. Hammond and Lady Margaret.

His lordship, however, was staring at the floor. He raised his hand for silence. He had heard the knock too.

"I got a message for the young lady," Helen heard a child's voice say. It was Sprat.

"Well, let me have it, girl," Garner's voice said.

"Sorry, mister. Binny says I'm to give it to the lady, and you ain't her. Binny says if I get any clapper-claw from the likes of you at the door, to say that it's from Mrs. Gunn."

"Clapper-claw?" Garner repeated icily. "You'd best come in, then."

Helen glanced at his lordship. He smiled, but there was no mirth in it, just a hunter's anticipation.

"It would seem Lowry has finally made an appearance," he said, and tossed the whip to Quinn. "Bring the glass knife and my leather armor. I am certain we will not be the only interested parties after the man." He opened the salon doors. "Come, let us receive your visitor."

Sprat had been well coached in the delivery of her message. She stood with filthy bare feet braced upon the foyer floor and both hands clenched into fists of concentration as she recited, "Binny says Mrs. Holt's brother, the one you call Lowry, has come back. He snucked in, but Binny saw 'im go into one of the molly rooms. He's usin' it as his hideout. She says she reckons he'll be there for a few hours leastways."

"Thank you, Sprat," Helen said.

She looked at the earnest faces that circled the girl. Carlston, of course, was fiercely jubilant. Quinn, a more cautious version of his master. Mr. Hammond's eyes held apprehension. He fleetingly met her gaze, and she glimpsed hope, too. Perhaps they would soon have the journal. Lady Margaret was attempting to hide her fear under a frown. And dear Darby, sweet mouth pressed into firm courage, had placed her hand lightly, protectively, on Quinn's forearm.

"We should move immediately, my lord," Quinn said.

Sprat nodded, turning worried eyes to Helen. "He's got Lizzie again, mister." She stopped and corrected herself, "I mean, my lady. He took her wiv him for sport an' Mrs. Holt let him do it. If you're gunna get him, quicker would be real good."

"I understand," Helen said. "We will do what we can for Lizzie."

Carlston glanced across at her, brows lifted in query.

"Lizzie is one of Holt's girls. Lowry has a penchant for cruelty," she said shortly.

"A harlot?" Lady Margaret asked, her tone dismissive.

"A girl," Helen said firmly. "In the hands of a monster."

Sprat nodded at that assessment, then held out her cupped hand.

"Sixpence," Helen prompted Carlston.

He gave her another questioning look, but dug into his breeches pocket and dropped the coin into the girl's grubby hand.

"I think you should stay away from Mrs. Holt's for a few hours, Sprat," Helen said. "Would you like something to eat?" At her wary nod, Helen motioned to Garner. "Take her to the kitchen and ask Cook to give her a good solid meal."

"Come on, girl," Garner said.

Sprat chewed on her lip, then said, "Lizzie ain't got more than a few hours left in her, my lady." She looked back as Garner ushered her to the stairs down to the kitchens.

"Has something happened?" Delia asked, peering over the first-floor banister.

"We know Lowry's whereabouts," Helen said.

"Finally," Delia said. She disappeared from view, reappearing a few moments later descending the stairs.

"How are we to go about it, sir?" Mr. Hammond asked.

"We need to corner him in the bawdy house," Carlston said. "Lowry grew up in the Old Town Lanes and is as cunning as a fox. If he gets into those, we will lose him." He rolled up his shirt-sleeves and held out his arm to Quinn. The Terrene fitted one of the guards over his forearm and began to tighten the laces. "I'll go in as a customer—try to maintain that essential element of surprise. Quinn, you are to keep an eye on the back."

"What am I to do?" Helen asked.

"You are to stay here."

"No! I must come!" Helen stopped, her urgency far too strong for the moment. She glanced at Hammond, saw the alarm in his eyes. They both needed to be at the bawdy house to secure the journal. She tried again. "You know I need experience in the world. Surely this is one such opportunity."

His lordship motioned to the glass knife still in her hand. "You do not yet have the necessary combat skills, or the protection of a Terrene."

Darby nodded her agreement. "It is too dangerous, my lady."

"We are facing a fading Terrene, not a Deceiver," Helen said. "How else am I to gain experience?"

"A Deceiver will make an appearance, you can be sure of that," Carlston said. "Most likely Philip, and possibly the Comte's man."

"She does need the experience, sir," Mr. Hammond said.

"If they or any other Deceiver do come, I will not engage," Helen added. "I promise."

Quinn cleared his throat and looked up from lacing the guard. "Forgive me, my lord, but you heard young Sprat. Lowry's hiding out in the molly rooms. It might be easier if you and Lady Helen do go in together, if you catch my meaning. He won't be able to stand against two Reclaimers, and with the both of you, it will be easier to get into those back rooms unremarked."

Helen heard an odd note in the Terrene's voice, and it was not just due to the untoward subject under discussion. No, Quinn was communicating something else to Carlston. Helen concentrated on the Islander's expression beneath the swirl of tattoos across his face. He did not think his master had enough strength and control left to face Lowry alone.

Lord Carlston stared at his man. "I see your point," he said.

Sweet heaven; Carlston agreed with him.

"What do you mean, molly rooms?" Delia asked.

Quinn looked around the group, but no one else offered to answer. "The bawdy house caters for many tastes, miss, including . . ." He paused, plainly searching for an unalarming way of expressing it. "Those who seek the Greek love."

Delia pressed her hand to her mouth. "Helen, you cannot visit a place like that!"

Beside her, Darby nodded. "My lady, you cannot see such . . . It is not for your . . . My lady, it will sully you!"

"It is not I who will be visiting it." Helen met Lord Carlston's eyes. "It will be Mr. Amberley."

She saw the dawn of his half smile. "Well, Mr. Amberley, you must do everything I say, without question and immediately. If I tell you to get out, you do not even look back. Agreed?"

"Yes. Agreed."

"Where am I to go, sir?" Hammond asked Carlston. "Front?"

"Yes, but on no account enter."

Lord Carlston raised his hand, stopping his protest. "Lowry may no longer be a Terrene, but he still has Terrene strength. If the Deceivers make an appearance as expected, I do not want to have to worry about you as well as Lady Helen."

Mr. Hammond gave a reluctant nod.

Helen watched Carlston check the lacing of the armguard. Somehow, she and Hammond needed to get to the journal first, although how they would keep it from his lordship was not clear. None of it was clear except a deepening sense of foreboding.

A rather apt line from Walter Scott's poem *Marmion* came to her mind: *O, what a tangled web we weave, When first we practice to deceive!*

At least they now had the whereabouts of Lowry; with him came a possible way to the journal and maybe even his lordship's cure and an end to this wretched business.

Twenty-One

HELEN FOLLOWED CARLSTON into Holt's Coffeehouse, edging her way past two men in the doorway engaged in vigorous debate. She heard the words *capital game* and *three notches to the Weald Coast*, and then she was inside the dimly lit, hot room. No more than thirty men sat at the small tables—at just past nine o'clock it was too early for the evening to be fully under way—but the air was still heavy with the smell of coffee and ale and the sour stink of male sweat. Every now and again the thunkety-thunk of a sea shanty, played upon an inferior instrument in another room, punched through the thrum of conversation.

She looked back out of the doorway to the lane. Mr. Hammond leaned against the wall of the daffy house opposite, the light from its oil lamps falling across his bowed head. She could not see his eyes beneath the brim of his beaver, but the line of his shoulders showed his tension. They had not had much time to make their own plan to retrieve the journal. If Helen did manage to capture it first, she was to pass it to Hammond, who would then take it to the nearby Raggett's Club and wait for her arrival. Admittedly it was under-conceived and relying upon luck and prayer, but it was the best they could do. God willing, they would get the journal first, but if they did not . . . Helen shook her head. No, they must.

"That is the entrance to the bawdy house," Carlston said near her ear, drawing her attention back inside the coffee room to a low-set doorway at the far end with a heavy red curtain drawn across it. He placed his hand upon her shoulder; to other eyes a friendly gesture, but to Helen it meant the hunt had begun. *Corner Lowry in the molly rooms and get the journal.*

Her heart quickened, her Reclaimer senses sharpening the rank smells, overheated air, and chatter within the room into a roar of sensation. She drew a resolute breath, steadying her way through the sensory onslaught, and followed Carlston between the tables and groups of conversing men toward the curtain. She flexed her wrists back, surreptitiously checking the leather guards beneath her jacket sleeves. Her glass knife was hidden down the side of her boot. Carlston had shown her how to wax the inside of the leather scabbard to ensure a smooth draw. Good Lord, what if she *did* need to draw it?

They had reached the curtain. Carlston pulled back the patchy velvet. The rattle of the curtain rings seemed unnaturally loud, but none of the men nearby took any notice as she and Carlston stepped across the threshold into the bawdy house.

It was somewhat of an anticlimax. They were in a corridor, its short length lit by candles set into plain iron sconces along a dingy wall. The air stank of old perfume and another more animal smell that made Helen wrinkle her nose. The pianoforte music had increased in volume, originating, it seemed, from a brightly lit room at the end of the hall.

A doorway to their right suddenly filled with a large body. Helen flinched. Carlston's hand closed upon her shoulder again, this time heavy with caution. A bruiser of a man in a patched shirt and gaudy blue waistcoat stood in their way, regarding them through narrowed bloodshot eyes.

"Go on, then," he said, stepping aside and jerking his heavy chin toward the far room.

Carlston steered her forward, hand still on her shoulder. "Follow my lead," he whispered.

Helen was not sure what she expected a bawdy house to look like. She had thought red and pink would feature in the color scheme, but the room they entered was decidedly blue and brown, and rather like a shabby drawing room. Of course, she had never been in a drawing room with so many half-clad women lounging around it.

A girl wearing yellow feathers in her brown curls sat at the pianoforte playing the shanty, her small breasts exposed above a loosely laced red stomacher. She looked up from the keys at their arrival and smiled, one black tooth marring the pretty effect. At a round table nearby, three more girls sat playing cards. All Helen registered were more breasts, smooth shoulders, and pale thighs before she hurriedly looked away. Her gaze landed upon a familiar plump body and pink banyan curled on a chaise longue. Binny! The girl sat up and gave a tight smile of acknowledgment.

"Evening, gentlemen." An older woman bustled toward them, set apart from the others by the fact that she was fully dressed and had a decided air of command. If that were not enough to place her as Kate Holt, procuress, her face clearly announced her kinship to Lowry: the same florid complexion, small piggy eyes, and cleft chin. Unlike her brother, however, Kate Holt had a head of clean luxuriant black hair and a rather pleasant smile.

"Jessie, their hats and gloves," she said.

The music stopped, and the girl at the pianoforte rose from her stool. Helen quickly removed her hat and passed it across, keeping her eyes away from the girl's freckled chest, then handed over her gloves. They were placed alongside Carlston's on a nearby bureau, with only one other hat, a set of gloves, and a silver-topped cane in residence. A slow night indeed.

"Can I offer you wine or some ale? Some meat?" Kate Holt asked.

"Claret," Carlston said.

With a jerk of her head, Kate Holt sent Jessie to a cabinet to draw out a bottle. "And what else can we offer you?"

"I hear you have rooms out back," Carlston said.

"Mollies," one of the girls at the table whispered to her neighbor, and picked up her cards again.

Kate Holt regarded Carlston's hand once again upon Helen's shoulder. "Who told you that?"

"I heard it about."

Kate Holt crossed her arms beneath her broad bosom, suspicion dawning in her small eyes. "Nothing like that here," she said briskly. "And you can bloody well tell your friends in the new Watch the same. It's all girls here."

Carlston smiled. "We are not Watchmen."

"Well, you ain't mollies, neither, are you? I'll thank you to get out of my house," the woman said flatly.

"They don't look like the Watch, Mrs. Holt," Binny said, rising from the chaise longue.

"You be quiet," Kate Holt ordered.

Helen glanced at Carlston. What should they do?

He took out a sovereign and held it up. "My good woman, all we want is a private room. We are not here to raid you."

Kate Holt regarded the coin for a long moment. She sniffed. "If you are mollies, show me." She nodded at Helen. "Go on, buss him."

Buss?

Shrugging, Carlston put the sovereign back into his pocket and turned Helen to face him. She looked up into his eyes and saw their message: *Stay calm.* Calm? Her heart was already thundering. Surely the whole room could hear it. At the corner of her eye she saw Kate Holt watching, mouth pursed in disbelief.

She forced herself to smile and saw the answering warmth in his eyes. He cupped the back of her head in the long span of his hand and drew her closer, leaning down to brush his lips against her temple. She felt a word breathed soft against her ear—*baciami*—Italian for *kiss me*. Ah, that was what buss meant.

The moment of relief disappeared. She had never kissed a man before. Not intimately. She did not know what to do, how to act. She felt his lips slide featherlike across her cheek toward her mouth. The memory of lying atop him in her bedchamber, their bodies pressed against one another, flashed hot through her blood. Yes, they had kissed then, but it had been life and death, and a product of the Deceiver energy. Hadn't it?

She smelled the clean, male scent of him, felt the rougher texture of his skin against her cheek, and drew a shaking breath. That pulse she had so brutally suppressed hammered into every part of her body, her fingers bunching with the sensation. She found herself turning her face to meet his careful progress, her lips finding the soft curve of his mouth. They both paused, breath mingling, and then she felt the warm pressure of his tongue against her own, the taste of him, salt and wine, merging with the clean smell of his skin. It was startling and soft and tender . . . and then it changed. Something wild crashed through her, a wave of throbbing energy that drove her up against his body, her fingers winding hard into the short crop of his hair. She felt him sway back, his breath catching into a gasp. She opened her eyes and saw the shock in his face flare into something more primal. She wrested him back to her mouth, any tenderness subsumed by animal need. He wrapped his arms around her, drawing her hard onto his chest, both of them locked into the dizzying sensation of their mouths and tongues and bodies pressed against each other. She felt as if she wanted to crawl into his skin, taste him, touch him, fill herself with him.

"Lordy," a girl's voice said. "Look at 'em go."

Carlston wrenched his mouth from hers, breath short and hot against her cheek. She caught the astonishment in his eyes before he stepped away. Bereft, she rocked back; the sudden loss of sensation as if she had been stripped to her nerves and left open to the world. She touched her lips, swollen and raw.

"I reckon that be real, Mrs. Holt," Binny said dryly. She was standing beside the procuress. "I'll take 'em downstairs if you want."

Kate Holt gave a short nod. "All right." She eyed Carlston. "I'll have that sovereign now. You got a room for an hour."

Carlston shook his head. "Two hours, undisturbed," he said, his voice little more than a rasp, "and two more bottles of claret."

Kate Holt smiled. "Two hours. One more bottle of claret."

Carlston nodded and passed the coin.

Helen stared at the patched carpet on the floor, mortified. Whatever had risen within her had called something within him, and the savagery of it had been exhilarating. And terrifying. It had been just like the moment her Reclaimer strength had arrived, and when she had flung herself atop him. He had felt it too—it had been in his response—yet he had not looked at her since they had stepped apart. Was he shocked by her wantonness? Of course he was. Even she was shocked by it. Yet all she could feel was that pulse in her marrow still hammering its beat of need.

With both bottles in hand, Binny motioned to the door at the other side of the room. Helen led the way, face hot, not daring to look at the other girls as she passed. Giggles and a low whistle followed her and Carlston out of the room.

They stepped into another hallway, lit again by candles in iron wall sconces. In an effort to force her mind back to their task, Helen counted the rooms: two each side with doors shut fast, and another room at the end, door ajar. The clatter of pans and the lingering stink of boiled meat marked it as the kitchen, and, if she recalled correctly, a way out to the backyard.

Before it stood a stair alcove. Helen caught a glimpse of steps heading up to the next floor, and down to the cellar. Down to Lowry.

Binny closed the door behind them, the draft setting the candle flames flickering.

"He's still here." She edged past, motioning them to follow. "Come wiv me, quick."

"No," Carlston said. "Just tell us which room." He broke off and doubled over, his knuckles pressed hard into his forehead. "Sweet Jesus!"

Helen and Binny stared at his hunched body.

"What's wrong wiv him?"

Helen ducked down. Dark blood seeped from his nose. It was the same as in the salon. She tentatively touched his arm. "Carlston, you are bleeding."

His hand went to his nose. "It is nothing."

"You are bleeding like before. What if the same thing happens?"

"It will not." He grasped her forearm with his other hand. She could feel the desperation in his tight grip. "We have to get this done. I have it under control."

He did not have it under control; she knew it, and it was clear he knew it too. Yet neither of them wanted to give up their chance at the journal. They were so close.

Helen pulled her arm free. If he lost control, maybe she could get to the journal first. She stood up, appalled by the ruthless thought.

"Are you sure?" she asked.

"Yes." He drew a deep, shaking breath and tentatively lifted his head to address Binny. "Lowry?"

"In the cellar, last room." She motioned to the stairs with one of the bottles. "Past the ale kegs."

"Go back inside with the others," he ordered. She turned to go.

"Wait." He took the bottles from her, hefting one like a weapon and passing the other to Helen. "All right. Go."

Binny gave Helen one last anxious look, then ran back to the door.

Helen gripped the bottle by the neck, the glass already slippery in her damp palm. She followed Carlston to the staircase. The blood still seeped from his nose; she saw the dark track of it in the yellow glow of the single wall lamp that lit their way. His breath was coming in short gasps, the pain almost palpable. She should make him go back. But how?

The worn wooden steps creaked beneath their progress, the air cooling as they descended. The earthier odors of damp stone and old wood replaced the noxious smell of boiled meat from above. Helen extended her hearing. Beyond their own respiration she heard two more sets of breathing, straight ahead, at the end of the dim vaulted passage.

"Lowry!" Carlston suddenly yelled and began to run.

What was he doing? He had just lost them their advantage.

She lunged after him, pressing herself into as much speed as she could gather in the short length of corridor, catching flashes of rooms on either side: beds, armchairs, and another stacked with kegs.

Carlston reached the end of the corridor. He spun around and kicked at an iron-bound door, roaring. It was the same way he had kicked the stuffed Hessian bag in the salon—barely in control. Beneath the crack of the blow, Helen heard wood splintering and the rattle of a crossbar. A man's voice cursed—Lowry—and then came the shriek of rusty metal and the clunk of wood thudding against stone. Oh no! She knew that sound. Lowry was in an old coal room, and he was opening the coal hatch.

"He's getting out!" she yelled.

Carlston roared again—an animal rage—and aimed another

kick. The door came off its hinges, slamming into the room beyond with a shrieking scrape of iron across stone. Carlston ran in, Helen a moment behind.

The room still held traces of its former use, a tide of black coal dust embedded halfway up the brick walls. Single candles stood alight in tin holders on the stone floor, casting a dim light across an iron bed with a thin woman curled upon it. Bloody welts on fair skin, torn chemise, and matted hair. Lizzie. Was she alive? Helen saw the shallow rise of the girl's thin chest. Alive, but insensible.

Carlston leaped onto a table set beneath the hatch: a ladder to the lane above. They both saw the flash of Lowry's florid face peering down, a leather post bag strapped across the grayed linen of his shirt. The journal!

Carlston threw the bottle. Helen heard the smash of glass on stone—target missed—and the sound of receding footsteps on the cobbles above. Grabbing either side of the hatch, Carlston pulled himself through in one smooth movement. A sound of scrabbling across the flags and then a scream. Had he brought down Lowry?

Helen dropped the bottle on the bed and climbed onto the table, sending up a silent prayer for Lizzie. The girl needed help, but she had to follow Carlston. Right now, he could tear the narrow street apart. More to the point, she had to follow the journal.

She clamped her hands on the stone flags above and pulled herself up into the lane, landing in a squat in front of the coffee-house. The ease of the movement brought a moment of elation, and then the full force of the situation burst upon her. Less than a yard away, a blur of bodies rolled and smashed into the wall of the coffeehouse at an unearthly speed, punching a hole through the wood. In the dim lamplight, Helen's Reclaimer sight separated the blur into two men: Carlston on his knees, clawing for the journal bag strapped to Lowry's body, and the former Terrene kicking viciously at Carlston's head as he scrambled backward, splintered wood flying into the air.

Two young fashionable bucks watched from the doorway of the daffy house opposite, their mouths agape at the blurred battle. Beyond them, Hammond stood holding someone back by the arm—a tall, fair man. Helen felt her breath lock in her chest. The Duke. What was he doing here?

He had seen her. His perplexed frown shifted into horrified recognition. It was just like the hanging, only tenfold worse. This time she was dressed as a man and coming out of a bawdy house cellar.

He wrested his arm from Hammond's hold, turning on the smaller man. "Is that Lady Helen?" she heard him yell. "For Christ's sake, man, is that Lady Helen?"

The fight between Lowry and Carlston erupted upward, and her sight shifted to follow their speed. Lowry was back on his feet, a vicious kick connecting with Carlston's head. The Earl slumped back onto his knees, blood running into his eyes from a gash across his forehead. Lowry staggered across the lane and grabbed one of the wooden stools outside the coffeehouse, swinging it wildly as Carlston lunged for him again. The first swing missed. The second caught Carlston across his shoulder and back. Helen winced at the impact, but the Earl ignored it and grabbed for the journal, hauling on the strap across Lowry's body. She could see the madness in Carlston's face, his mouth drawn back in a snarl, the blood from the gash and his nose smeared across his face. He had more strength than Lowry, but the mania had overtaken his mind. He was fighting without care and without strategy.

Gathering all her resolve, Helen launched herself at the two struggling men, Quinn's training like a litany in her head: *Find the range, transfer weight,* chassé, *connect, pivot.* She aimed the *chassé* kick at Lowry's gut, all the strength of her lower body behind the blow. He dodged, and her foot glanced off his meaty side, the impetus slamming her into his body. They staggered, holding on to each other's jackets as if in some ghastly drunken jig.

"You stupid bitch," he hissed, spraying her with bloodied spittle. He grabbed her wrist, twisting her hand from his lapel. "Everyone could have gotten what they wanted."

She saw his fist a second before it slammed into her face. Pain exploded across her mouth and cheek. She stumbled back, tasting a flood of warm metallic blood. It felt as if she had been hit in the face by a carriage, and the shock of it made her sway and gulp for air.

Lowry turned to run. He took only two steps before Carlston lunged and grabbed his ankles, bringing him down hard on the stones. They rolled away from Helen.

"It's a fight!" The call, stretched into long vowels, came from within the daffy house and was echoed in Holt's opposite.

Helen heard the scrape of stools and yells as the men inside pushed their way out to watch the spectacle, their movements slow and languorous as if they moved through water. She felt her sight shift back, their bodies jerking into normal velocity. They spilled into the lane in a ragged circle, taking a moment to register the unnatural speed of the fighters, and then the men who had surged out in front reeled backward, pushing those behind into the walls and against the windows.

"Devils!" someone shrieked.

"God preserve us!" another screamed. "It's devils fighting."

The yells sparked a stampede, some men pushing forward to see, others punching their way back into the safety of the buildings. The panic spread. Helen could almost feel it like a huge wave pounding across the lane. People ran, screaming, bringing more curious men and women out into the lane. The Home Office was not going to be pleased.

She scrambled to her feet. She needed help. Where was Hammond? She found him and the Duke still pressed up against the wall of the daffy house, hemmed in by the mob. Hammond was trying to follow the fight on the ground, all his focus upon Carlston and Lowry. The Duke, however, had his eyes fixed upon Helen, clearly horrified by her uncanny speed and bruised, bleeding mouth. He started forward, as if to wade through the panicked crowd to her side.

No, no! She shook her head, jabbing her finger wildly toward Hammond and then at herself.

His outrage disappeared into a searching frown, and then he nodded. Thank heavens he was a man of quick understanding and even quicker action. He yelled something in Hammond's ear. The smaller man straightened and looked across.

"Hammond, get Quinn," she bellowed. "Round the back."

He gestured to his ears—he could not hear her above the yelling and screams. She jabbed her finger toward the back of the bawdy house. "Quinn!" she yelled again. "Quinn!"

Finally he nodded, and leaned in to the Duke, yelling something in his ear. She strained her hearing and caught the end of his words: ". . . part of the Home Office. Stay where you are."

Hammond plunged into the tumult, the Duke staring after him, astounded.

Now he knew. *Damn it.* The last thing she had wanted was the Duke involved.

Another stool came flying through the air past Helen's head. She ducked, her Reclaimer sight finding Carlston and Lowry up against the daffy house wall, Carlston punching wildly, only half his blows connecting. Should she try to pull him off? But that might give Lowry the chance to bolt into the crowd.

Something forced itself into her fierce focus—a strong, familiar smell like the charged air after a lightning strike. She knew that smell: Deceiver whips. She swung around.

The Comte's small, wiry valet, Lawrence, stood barely two yards away. He held up a finger as if warning her to stay back, and then in a blur even to her Reclaimer eyes, he was standing above Carlston and Lowry.

"Carlston!" Helen yelled.

He must have already sensed the Deceiver coming, for he wrenched Lowry to the left and they rolled as one. The cobbles beside them exploded into dust and debris. Both men scrabbled back as the whip punched down again, smashing up another burst of stone.

Helen groped for her touch watch, hands shaking as she flicked it open and snapped the lenses into place. She knew she should not be using it—too much metal—but she could not trust herself to build a mind-image. She had barely managed it in training; how could she do it here?

She lifted the lens to her eye. The laneway blossomed into blue glows, the shifting life forces dazzling her for a moment. Her eyes fixed upon the vibrant blue around Lawrence and the pulsing ultramarine whip curving from his back and poised for another strike. Only one whip. She reached down to her boot and found the handle of her glass knife, yanking it free from its tight fit. She must not let Lawrence get the journal. Better that Lowry have it than the instrument of the Grand Deceiver.

The whip plunged down again, this time clipping Lowry on the shoulder, slicing through linen and flesh. He screamed, blood blooming on the pale cloth of his shirt.

Carlston hauled himself to his feet, shaking his head as if try-ing to focus. She saw the whip hover, then line him up for another strike. She had to stop it.

"Lawrence!" she yelled.

The Deceiver whirled to face her, his whip snaking around as if it, too, heard her call.

"*Voi sapete il mio nome?*" he said. *You know my name?*

With knife in hand, she edged forward, keeping her eyes fixed upon the weaving weapon through the lens. She should drop the lens, but she could not bear to lose sight of that whip. The bright blue end of it flicked out at her; another warning. Helen jumped back. Lawrence did not seem willing to attack her, just like Philip in her bedchamber. Why? She had no answer, but his reticence did not mean she could not attack.

His whip glowed in her lens. But she could not hold the glass to her eye and make any kind of approach. She would have to rely upon her senses. She pushed the watch back into her pocket, pray-ing that all her training would resolve into some sort of skill.

The air was charged with energy—she could taste it, smell it, feel the itching buzz on her skin. She strained, trying to find the image of the whip, but nothing formed in her mind.

Beyond the Italian Deceiver, Lowry was scrabbling back, his hand clasping his injured shoulder. Dear God, he was going to run, and he still had the journal. He hauled himself up and plunged into the crowd of onlookers at an unearthly speed, punching a pathway through them, their yells and curses following him.

"Get Lowry!" Helen yelled to Carlston.

It was no good; he was still lost in his mania. She could see it in the bloodshot heat of his eyes. He lunged at Lawrence, drag-ging the Deceiver down, the two of them hitting the cobbles. For a second they rolled and punched, and then Carlston screamed.

His shoulder peeled open, flesh and muscle coming apart as if by ghastly magic to the normal eye, his blood smearing across the stones as the two of them slid into the scraggly circle of horrified onlookers.

Helen ran, pure instinct driving her between the two men on the ground.

"No!" The Duke's voice whirled the Deceiver around.

She sliced blindly above Lawrence's back with her knife, connecting with air.

The Deceiver twisted to face her, lashing out with an arm. She jumped back, feeling the prickling sense of energy across her skin. His whip. She grabbed, finding air again, but for a glorious second she saw its outline in her mind. It was enough. Her hand connected with the pulsing weapon.

She gasped, feeling the whip's bright energy collapse into her body, flowing into her blood, her marrow, her muscles, the meat of her mind. It felt like the moment she had wrested Carlston back to her mouth: a soaring, fierce, violent, animal delight. Around her, the whole laneway was alive with the glow of blue energy. She could see every life force without the lens, the same as when she had held the *Colligat*.

She laughed, dropped her knife, and slammed her palm against the Deceiver's chest, seeking more energy, more sublime sensation.

Lawrence screamed, struggling against the touch of her hand. *"Cosa state facendo a me?" What are you doing to me?*

She could feel all his energy flowing into her hand, bringing so much strength, the ultramarine of his body fading into a pale, sickly blue.

"Lady Helen! Let him go. You will die!" Quinn's voice broke into her thrall.

She felt Lawrence wrenched from her hold. Gone.

She gasped, the loss of the connection like a thousand lamps in her mind suddenly extinguished. Quinn's strong arms circled her body, then slammed her against the ground, the stone hard and cold against her cheek. Through the blur of her vision, she saw Lawrence staggering through the crowd. Escaping.

"Lady Helen, let the energy go. Please!"

She would never let it go. It was part of her now, gloriously embedded within her body. Couldn't he understand that? She punched him, knuckles connecting painfully against his jaw. He grunted but did not loosen his grip.

"Hold her down!" he yelled. "Lady Helen, let the energy go into the ground."

"You're not her Terrene. It won't work," Hammond said.

"I have to try, don't I?" Quinn snarled. "He'll kill me if I don't try."

She felt Quinn's weight and other hands pinning her flat against the flags. It didn't matter. The energy was hers, and she could hold it.

"It's not going. It's not going," she heard Quinn sob.

"It's mine," she whispered. "It's mine!"

"We are well past twenty seconds, Quinn," Hammond said urgently.

"What does that mean?" The Duke's voice. Frantic.

"It means she's not going to die," Quinn said, husky with wonderment. "If a Reclaimer holds on to the energy too long, it usually kills them."

"Kills them?" The Duke again. Horrified.

Helen shifted. "Quinn, let me up."

She felt the man's heavy weight lift off her body. She took a deep breath. The bright blue life force glows had gone, and the laneway was once more dim and dingy, its narrow width blocked by stunned people watching them in silence. The glorious sensation had gone too. Even so, she could feel the Deceiver energy inside her like a bright heat.

She could not bring herself to look at the Duke. She focused on Quinn, who was crawling across the stones to the prone body of his master. Helen rolled onto her hands and knees and followed, her body feeling strange with so much energy: heavy, but as if it was lifting into the air with lightness. How was she able to hold on to so much Deceiver power?

Quinn pulled Carlston onto his back. "My lord?"

Carlston groaned, bringing a huff of relief from Quinn.

"Journal?" the Earl rasped.

Quinn shook his head. "Gone, my lord, with Lowry."

Carlston released a pained breath, a curse hissed within it. "Lady Helen safe?"

"I am here." Helen leaned over him. He was a mess of cuts and gashes, but his eyes were sane again.

"Ah." His smile shifted into concern. "You are hurt."

He lifted his hand to her face. As his fingers touched her cheek, a bright crackling charge of energy arced between them, the effect slamming them both backward.

Helen felt herself hit the ground, her heart heaving in pain. The bone-jarring impact punched all the air out of her lungs and cracked her head against the cobblestones in a sickening ache.

"What the hell was that?" Hammond's voice.

She gulped for breath, heard the scrabble of feet. The Duke's face appeared above her, his voice saying her name over and over again.

She turned her head and saw Carlston in a crumpled heap across the lane, eyes closed and face ashen white, his breath coming in ominously short gasps.

Good God, what had just happened? She had felt his hand touch her cheek and then all that power like lightning between them. Just one touch, and now he was barely breathing.

One touch. Her touch.

The dawning realization brought another kind of pain slamming through her heart. They had kissed, and his madness had come hard behind it. And in the salon, before he had lost control, he had touched her cheek too. She had been hurting him all along. Perhaps even causing his madness.

Twenty-Two

Sunday, 19 July 1812

THE NEXT MORNING, Helen sat at the secretaire in her bedchamber, her eyes fixed upon the lesson in her Book of Common Prayer but seeing none of the words. All her sight was turned inward, reliving the fight with Lowry blow by blow, as if she were still in the squalid lane. Could she have made another move, another decision, that would have stopped him escaping with the journal?

Of course she could have. She had been too slow; she had hesitated. Everything she had done had led to the loss of the *Ligatus* and Lord Carlston's incapacitation. It was all her fault, and when his lordship finally woke—*please, let him wake*—everyone would think through the events of the last few weeks and arrive at the conclusion that now seemed obvious to her: she was the cause of Lord Carlston's madness. The Comte had probably known it all along, and now the cure he had offered had disappeared along with Lowry and the journal.

She stretched out her left hand, the long sleeve of her gown just covering a ring of deep bruising around her wrist. The energy she had pulled from Lawrence was still a throbbing presence in her veins, a faint echo of its fierce violence curling her fingers. How had she absorbed the whip and not been destroyed by it? Perhaps a new direct inheritor power, but to what end? It seemed she could do nothing with it except harm Lord Carlston. Another thought came, hunching her shoulders: maybe Benchley had been right all along and she was, in fact, a bringer of evil.

She glanced at her glass knife on the desk. Thankfully, Mr. Hammond had retrieved it from the lane. *God is in the glass.* Perhaps; but did she still have God's grace?

She bowed her head, the tip of her steepled hands against her lips—half in prayer, half in fear—the press of her fingers bringing a small jab of pain. Another reminder of Lowry. Even so, she was lucky; by the time they had made their hurried exit from the narrow battlefield, her Reclaimer power had relieved most of the pain and swelling.

Lord Carlston's healing capacity had not been so efficient. He did not rouse from his unconscious state, and so Quinn had picked up his limp, bleeding body and forced a way out of the crowded lane, Helen and Mr. Hammond close behind, with the Duke determinedly following their retreat. They had emerged on the Castle Tavern corner, disheveled and attracting far too much attention from the fashionables on the Steine.

To Helen's horror, the Duke had immediately taken charge, hailing a hackney coach to take them back to German Place, and quelling the alarmed driver's protest with the flash of a guinea.

He had asked only two things in the carriage on the short journey up Marine Parade.

"Are you badly injured, Lady Helen?"

"It is nothing."

She had glanced at Mr. Hammond seated opposite. A frown on his stricken face had warned her from making any more comment.

"This is his fault, isn't it?" the Duke had then said, jerking his chin toward the senseless form of Lord Carlston propped against Quinn's sturdy shoulder. The Terrene had also been wounded: a deep, bloody gash across his tattooed cheekbone that his own healing ability had already started to close.

Helen shook her head at the accusation, but it was Hammond who answered. "I am sorry, Your Grace, but we are unable to explain anything. We must all abide by an oath of secrecy to the Home Office."

"It is better that you do not get involved," Helen said. "Please."

"Too late for that," he had said curtly, but had tempered his frustration with a small smile.

Even under such circumstances, the Duke held on to the manners of a true gentleman.

Helen closed her prayer book, abandoning all attempt at reading it. At some point, the Duke would come for an explanation. He was not a man to quietly step back, even when the authority of the Home Office had been invoked. And of course Pike would come too, as soon as he heard what had happened.

Helen closed her eyes. How was she to explain her failure to buy the journal as arranged, or Lord Carlston's pursuit of Lowry? As soon as Pike knew Carlston was involved, he would assume she and Mr. Hammond had broken their oaths and told him about the journal. Treason.

"Dear Lord," she whispered. "What are we to do?"

A knock on the door lifted her head. "Yes?"

"My lady, may I enter with Mr. Quinn?" Darby called.

Had his lordship finally awoken? She reached with her Reclaimer hearing and found his breathing: shallow and regular. Still unconscious. *Still.*

She rose from the gilt chair. "Of course."

They entered with an air of great purpose. Mr. Quinn carefully held a rolled piece of parchment in his big hand.

"Has his lordship shown *any* progress?" Helen asked.

"A little, my lady," Quinn said, rising from his bow. Although he was trying not to show it, his anxiety was writ into every move. "The shoulder wound has started to heal, and that must mean the Reclaimer fugue is doing its job. It's just taking a bit longer this time. You'll see. Lady Margaret is watching over him."

Helen nodded. Last night, Lady Margaret had ordered Quinn to carry his lordship upstairs to her brother's bedchamber again, and neither she nor the Terrene had left Carlston's side the whole night. Helen, agonized by guilt and worry, had stood outside the door for hours, but had not dared enter. What if she harmed him even more? All she could do was listen to his breathing and pray that she had not irreparably damaged him.

Darby swiftly closed the door and made her curtsy. "We have come on another matter, my lady. Go on," she urged Quinn.

"My lady, I told Miss Darby everything that happened last night—about the danger you were in, and the power that passed between you and his lordship. We think the two of you need to bond as soon as possible, even without the full moon and his lordship's direction. You need the protection of a Terrene. . . ." He faltered, the anguish in his deep voice pulling Darby a step closer. "Forgive me, my lady. I could not help you when you took the Deceiver's power. I tried, but I'm not your Terrene, and now his lordship is—"

"It is not your fault, Mr. Quinn," Helen said quickly. Quite the contrary, but she could not say so yet. Not until she had explained the terrible truth to Mr. Hammond and Lady Margaret, and, God willing, Lord Carlston. "I agree that we must complete the ritual as soon as possible." She met her maid's patent relief with a smile. "When can we do it?"

"Tomorrow night," Darby said. "It will take us a little time to obtain all the elements, and you, my lady, need to learn the ritual."

With a dip of his head, Quinn passed her the parchment. "You need to say the words perfect, my lady. They are in Latin."

Helen unrolled the thick paper. She recognized the writing upon it immediately. "His lordship wrote this?"

"Aye," Quinn said, and gave a small smile. "I'll catch an earful when he knows I've given it to you without his say-so."

She found herself touching the written words as if they held a direct link to him; a foolish fancy. The directions for the ritual were brief: a rather gruesome exchange of blood collected from a cross cut into the hand by the other party, then mixed with other alarming elements, including fresh goat's blood, milk, and sanctified water. All drunk in a form that promised to be foul. The Latin that accompanied it—uncomfortably close to an incantation—was quite complicated. Even so, she had memorized far longer poems for recitation. And this task was not a schoolgirl chore; it had the impetus of desperate necessity.

"Tomorrow night," she said. "I will be ready."

⌒

AFTER BREAKING HER fast, Helen set herself at the table in the drawing room—where the light was best in the house—to study the bonding ritual. The wording of the incantation was, to say the very least, disturbing. She had translated the Latin, although she knew it was not perfect. It began:

Forge this bond of earth and air, ground and sky.
Forge this bond of mind and body, strength and soul.
Bind these two with blood made one, blood made whole.
Bind these two to lives in battle, torn asunder as
they die.

It went on in much the same heathen manner for another three verses until the final two lines:

This bond must be forged in love and trust,
For suspicion and hate can ne'er be just.

That, at least, Helen thought, was based in godly truth.

She had just finished committing the first two verses to memory, when a knock announced Garner.

"My lady, there is another child at the door insisting that he has a message for you."

Helen rose from her chair. Could this be news about Lowry's new hiding place? If so, Martha Gunn had worked a miracle.

The child was a boy of about eleven standing on the front portico in bare feet with a wary gaze and a letter clutched in his hand.

"You Lady Helen?" he asked.

"I am."

"'Ere you go, then." He passed her the note. It was on rough paper and sealed with a grubby wafer. "Mrs. Gunn said to put it into yer 'ands." He bobbed a bow and ran down the steps.

Clutching the note to her chest, Helen returned swiftly to the drawing room and closed the door. She broke the wafer and unfolded the page.

My lady,

Last night a man matching your footman's looks took the 9 o'clock night coach to London. Please forgive the lateness of this message, but my boy went to tell you right after he saw the coach leave, but you was out. He said he waited, but then a hackney arrived and brought a lot of commotion. He took affright and hopped it, and didn't dare tell me he hadn't passed you the message till now.

Martha Gunn

Not Lowry, then, but Philip. The slight disappointment was quickly eclipsed by the new information. It seemed the Deceiver had left Brighton before she and Carlston had even encountered Lowry last night. Yet that made no sense. If Philip was working with Lawrence, why had he not stayed to help his comrade obtain the journal? She folded the note and slipped it into her morning gown sleeve. Perhaps she had been mistaken, and they were not working together at all. No, surely they had some connection. Maybe Mr. Hammond would have more insight when he returned from gathering intelligence in town.

She took her seat once again and picked up the incantation, intent upon learning the final verses.

By three o'clock, when Delia came in and suggested they take some restorative tea, she finally felt confident that she had committed the Latin and the disturbing ritual to memory.

"You need to rest, Helen," Delia said. "Lady Margaret is burning herself to a frazzle watching over Lord Carlston. I cannot even get her to take some broth. You must not do the same."

Helen put down the parchment. "I should be with Mr. Hammond."

"You know that is not possible. In your male guise you could be recognized as one of the perpetrators of last night; and you cannot go into company as yourself, not with that bruise on your poor mouth. You look as if you have been engaged in fisticuffs."

"I have been engaged in fisticuffs," Helen said dryly.

"Exactly. And we cannot have anyone making that connection,

can we? Mr. Hammond will return soon, and I am sure he will bring news."

Helen frowned. "I should have thought he would be back by now."

"He said he would attend church, and then make his way to Donaldson's and Raggett's to listen to the gossip." She leaned over and squeezed Helen's hand. "I think he is just wishing to be busy until Lord Carlston wakes."

What if Lord Carlston never wakes?

Helen fought back the fearsome question and rose from the sofa, needing to move herself away from her dark thoughts. Delia, for all her firm optimism, could offer no real comfort. She did not know that Helen was trapped in a web of lies that could, very soon, unravel into a hangman's noose. At least, a noose for Mr. Hammond. For her, a noblewoman, it would be the executioner's block.

With a shudder at the thought, Helen walked across the room and sorted through the sounds upstairs—the snap of a sheet as a maid aired a bed, a footman prising spent candles from their holders, Lady Margaret's weary footsteps pacing across the bedchamber—until she found the shallow breathing of Lord Carlston. *No change.*

"Sit down, Helen," Delia urged. "I know you hardly slept last night. There can be no gain in exhausting yourself with worry." She reached over and picked up a pack of cards. "Come, you need a break from your studies. Shall we play a hand?"

Helen smiled wanly. Delia could offer no counsel, but she did, at least, offer some distraction.

A game of piquet later, Helen heard the sounds of arrival at the front door. Two men, their voices and footsteps identifying them immediately. She placed her cards down on the table.

"What is it?" Delia asked, looking up from making her play.

"Mr. Pike. And the Duke of Selburn."

"Oh," Delia breathed. "Together? Do you think it is a coincidence?"

That hope was quickly banished as Helen stretched her hearing to the conversation at the front door.

"Take me to Carlston," Pike demanded. "I know he is here."

"*Lord* Carlston is not seeing visitors at this time," Garner said, his voice at its most dignified and polite.

"He will see me," Pike said.

"His lordship has not yet regained his senses, sir. He is—"

"If the man is unconscious," the Duke interjected, "what on earth can you gain by seeing him, Pike?"

"I can make *sure* he is insensible."

Helen rose from her chair and crossed to the doors.

"What are you doing?" Delia asked.

"I do not think we need to wait upon their visiting cards," Helen said dryly. "This is not a formal call."

Delia hurriedly pushed back her chair and joined her at the doors. They both leaned closer, listening to the approach of the visitors through the heavy wood.

"What is going on?" Lady Margaret's voice called, sharp and urgent, from the floor above.

"Mr. Pike is demanding to see Lord Carlston, my lady," Garner replied.

"His lordship is in no state to receive visitors."

"Stand back," Helen whispered, then opened the doors.

The two men were halfway up the staircase: Pike first, like a tall, hunched crow, and then the Duke, impeccably dressed in bottle green and self-possessed as ever. Lady Margaret peered down from the landing above, her dark hair hanging in loose curls around her tired and angry face.

Mr. Pike stopped, halting the Duke behind him. "Lady Helen," he acknowledged tightly. "Allow me to inform you that the Duke has been sworn in to the Dark Days Club." She saw the silently furious *And you are to blame* in the jut of his chin.

She gripped the doorjamb. "Sworn in?"

All her attempts to keep the Duke safe had been for nothing. Here he was, following her into the Deceivers' world.

"Sworn in," the Duke said, "and set to be your aide if you will have me, Lady Helen." He bowed, then inclined his head toward Delia. "Always a pleasure, Miss Cransdon."

Pike looked over his shoulder at Selburn. "Your Grace, would you please escort Lady Helen and her friend back into the drawing room. I will be down directly." His tone was as close to command as the Duke's rank allowed.

"Of course," the Duke said amicably.

Helen and Delia retreated into the drawing room. Pike sent Helen a hard look as he passed the doorway on his way toward the next set of stairs.

"I do not want Lord Carlston disturbed," they heard Lady Margaret begin.

"I don't give a damn what you want," Pike snarled. "Where is he?"

"Mr. Pike is somewhat discomposed," the Duke said, entering the drawing room and closing the doors. He turned and regarded Helen. "I see that you are discomposed too. I imagine my appearance alongside Mr. Pike has come as a surprise."

Helen gave a brittle laugh. Surprise did not even come close to describing the dizzying collision of worlds within her head.

"How did you even know to go to Mr. Pike?" she asked.

"Your Grace, would you like to take a seat?" Delia interposed, gesturing to the armchair. She glanced at Helen, adding sotto voce, "Sit down, dear. You look as if you may faint."

Delia was right; she did feel light-headed. She grasped the back

338 — Alison Goodman

of the sofa and edged her way around to its seat. Selburn took the armchair, flicking out his jacket tails. A rather fine double-breasted Weston, she noted, then had to fight the irresistible—no, hysterical—urge to laugh at the absurd observation. She gathered her muslin skirts and sat beside Delia on the sofa, the simple action bringing a return of equilibrium.

"If you recall," the Duke said, "Mr. Hammond told me that you were all under oath to the Home Office. I know Mr. Pike serves the new Home Secretary, my good friend Lord Sidmouth. Ergo, I visited Mr. Pike and demanded an explanation of last night's events." He smiled tentatively at Helen. "I could not believe what you did in that lane. Your courage—it was remarkable."

Helen clasped her hands together, forcing her tone to stay measured. "Pike told you about the Dark Days Club? Just like that?"

"No, not at all. He adamantly refused to do so until I suggested I would return to London and discuss the matter in Parliament. He quite sensibly, if not graciously, decided it was more expedient to swear me to silence than risk that kind of exposure."

"I wish he had not," Helen said.

He drew back. "Am I not welcome as a comrade in arms?"

"It is exactly what I did not want to happen. This is a dangerous world, Duke. I did not want you dragged into it."

He bowed his head, but Helen could see the corner of his smile. "Ah." He looked up, blue eyes warm. "You are worried for my safety."

"Of course I am. Have you any idea of what we face?"

"Indeed. I saw what you faced last night. I also saw that you faced it more or less alone. As far as I could tell, Lord Carlston was more a danger to you than the leader he is meant to be. I am also aware that Miss Cransdon has newly joined you as your aide." He nodded to Delia. "But with all due respect, Lady Helen, I think you need the help of a man who can offer you real and practical support and protection. Mr. Pike agrees with me."

Of course Mr. Pike agreed with him. Helen pressed her hand to her forehead. Carlston hated the Duke, and vice versa. They would never be able to work together. If Carlston ever woke up.

"View it this way," the Duke added. "You know I have been watching over you since your arrival here in Brighton. Now I have merely formalized my own inclination and cemented my promise to your brother."

"I told you I did not want such protection."

"I know, because you did not want me to be at risk." He leaned forward, casting a glance at Delia, who took the hint and turned away, busying herself with the fringe of her pink silk shawl. "I do not care if I am at risk if I can protect you. That is why I hired a room in the town house opposite and set a man to watch you and report back on your activities. I am glad I did, or I would not have been on hand last night." He smiled, a little gleam of mischief in his eyes. "Mind you, I did not know that the young man in the company of Lord Carlston was in fact you."

Helen felt her skin heat. "It is part of what I must do as a Reclaimer."

"So I understand. Nevertheless, Lord Carlston should have taken more care with your safety."

"It is not Lord Carlston's fault."

Selburn's mouth quirked into disbelief. "Come now, the man was out of control. You saw it yourself. You were injured because of it."

Helen sat up, apprehension stiffening her spine. "You did not say that to Mr. Pike, did you?"

"Of course I did. I told him Carlston was like a berserker. He put you in danger."

No doubt Pike had leaped upon that part of the report.

"You do not understand," Helen started.

"Perhaps not, but I hope to learn."

He leaned forward and took her hand, lifting it to his lips and brushing a soft kiss across her skin. Delia pointedly looked away from the intimacy.

"There will be no more secrets, Helen," the Duke added, still holding her hand. "No need to try to protect me. I am in this world with you now, by your side. I will help you in any way you demand. You just have to ask."

The door suddenly opened to admit Pike. Helen snatched back her hand.

"How is Lord Carlston?" she asked, ignoring the Duke's frown of irritation.

"Unconscious," Pike said, his voice hard and somewhat pleased. "Come with me." He addressed Selburn. "If you will excuse us, Your Grace, I have Reclaimer business with Lady Helen. I am sure Miss Cransdon will be able to answer any further questions you have about your new role as a Reclaimer aide."

Delia looked at him in alarm. "I am not sure I know that much, sir."

Pike observed her for a heavy, dismissive second, then bowed to the Duke.

Helen rose from the sofa. "Your Grace." She curtsied, but could not quite meet his eyes. He was so ardent in his desire to protect her against all dangers. Surely she should be glad to have such a man by her side, yet all she could feel was a heavy sense of dread. She would bring harm to him; it felt as inevitable as her next breath.

In silence, she followed Pike out of the room, one hand pressed over the back of the other where the Duke's kiss still warmed her skin.

Twenty-Three

"CLOSE THE DOOR, Lady Helen," Pike ordered.

He stood in the middle of the morning room, a shaft of afternoon light through the front window catching a shiny wear patch on the sleeve of his black jacket and showing the wilt of his shirt points. The slight shabbiness, however, did nothing to detract from the menace of the man. He continued to observe her silently, seconds ticking by into an agonizing minute. Just a tactic, Helen told herself, and yet her clasped hands were becoming decidedly clammy.

"Hammond claims neither he nor you informed Lord Carlston about the journal," Pike finally said. "Is this true?"

"You have spoken to Mr. Hammond?" A sense of foreboding pushed Helen forward a step. "Where is he?"

"Currently in the custody of Mr. Stokes on the charge of treason."

He said it with such mildness. Helen pressed her hand to her chest. *Custody. Treason.*

"Well?" he prompted. "Is it true?"

"We did not tell him."

"How did he know about it, then?" Pike's voice was still deceptively mild.

There was no place to go now. Mr. Hammond was in custody. She had to tell the truth. God help them.

"He believes the Comte d'Antraigues knows the way to cure him of his . . ." She paused, still not wanting to say "madness" to Pike. "Malady. The Comte made some of the journal pages—those about himself and his family—the price for the information. He also has information about the Grand Deceiver."

"And both of you chose not to tell me this?" The mildness had snapped into a tight snarl.

"We thought we could get the journal before Lord Carlston."

Pike drew in a deep breath. "He has made a deal with a Deceiver, a deal that promises a cure for something that cannot be cured and information about a myth, and you still think his judgment is unimpaired?" His voice rose. "You are blinded—you and Hammond—by your feelings, by your carnal *desires*." He spat out the word. "Your misguided loyalty has lost us the journal. I should have you in chains as well."

Mr. Hammond was in chains?

Pike stalked across the space between them and stood a bare foot from her, the fury in his face drying up any defense on her tongue. She fought the impulse to step back. She must not give up her ground.

"Carlston is trying to retrieve his *Ligatus*," he said, his voice pitched low but still fierce.

"No!" Pike might think her blinded by desire, but he was blinded by hate. "I assure you he did not know it existed until the Comte told him about it. He does not know it is a *Ligatus*."

"How can you believe he would not know such a thing existed?"

"He has been out of the country for three years. You said yourself you did not know it existed until recently."

"Yes, but then I did not make it, did I? I think Lord Carlston is almost as good at deception as our foes."

He paced a few steps away. Helen gulped a breath as if his

absence had suddenly allowed air into her vicinity again. How could she fight such willful pig-headedness?

He rounded on her again. "You let Lowry get away with the *Ligatus*."

This time she did step back. "I had no choice. Either Lowry got it or the Deceiver." She crossed her arms. "Would you rather the Deceiver had it now?"

"Of course not. Even so, your actions—and Hammond's—are treasonous. You have disobeyed orders. You have withheld vital information from me."

"It was all my fault," she said. "I decided to try to take the journal. I told Mr. Hammond to keep quiet. He was following my orders." She swallowed; her mouth felt so dry. "All is not lost, I assure you. Lowry will still want to make a deal. Nothing has changed."

"Don't be naive. He will not trust you now. For God's sake, I don't trust you. He will sell it elsewhere, perhaps even to the Deceivers."

Helen felt herself sway as if she stood on the edge of a very deep chasm. A lie would buy her more time to retrieve the journal; and the truth . . . Well, the truth would bring a cruel brute into her mind and soul. There would be no bond with dear Darby, no safety, no trust. Yet Mr. Hammond was charged with treason, and the *Ligatus* had to be retrieved.

She wet her lips. "Lowry does not want money."

"What does he want, then?" Pike studied her, a glimmer of comprehension dawning in his face. "What does he want, Lady Helen?"

It felt as if someone else was saying the irretrievable words. "He wants to be my Terrene. He wants his powers back."

"Ah." Pike gave a dry laugh. "Now it makes sense. Why you have not made the exchange." He shook his head. "A woman's mind. You would endanger the whole world because you are too fine to take Lowry as your Terrene."

"You know what he is." She touched the bruise on her mouth.

Pike's stare did not falter. "He is an experienced Terrene, and he has the *Ligatus*. I know he is a foul man, but then this is a foul world and you have chosen to serve it. Make the deal, Lady Helen. Redeem yourself as a Reclaimer. Save yourself and Hammond." He leaned in, his face so close that she could see the red tracing of vessels in his narrowed eyes. "Make no mistake: a Reclaimer who cannot be trusted to carry out his *or her* duties, who has no loyalty to King and country, is worth nothing to the Dark Days Club. Less than nothing. They are a liability."

The thought of bonding with Lowry, joined by alchemy, made Helen ill to her very core. Her mind would be polluted by his violent depravity, her body molested at her most vulnerable moments. She pushed away a sudden vision of poor Lizzie.

"If I take Lowry, I want something in return," she said, forcing steadiness into her voice. "I want Mr. Hammond's release." Pike's hard expression gave no indication of agreement or refusal. "I also want those pages for the Comte d'Antraigues. Even if there is only a chance that the Comte knows how to cure Lord Carlston—"

"No." He sliced the air with a flat hand. "I cannot let a Deceiver have any part of the *Ligatus*. You are a fool to think one of those creatures would know such a thing anyway."

"I believe he knows that I am the cause of Carlston's madness."

There, she had said it.

Pike frowned. "You are causing it?"

"I think that something in me is quickening his deterioration." Pike drew back, his skepticism palpable, but Helen forged on. "I am sure the Duke told you about the charge of strange energy that passed between me and Carlston last night."

"He did, but by his account it did not come solely from you, but from both you and Carlston. Nor did it make Carlston mad. He was already in some kind of berserk state, and the charge merely stopped him from destroying even more of the lane."

"Listen to me! When I touch Lord Carlston, skin to skin"—she flushed at the admission of such intimate contact—"it brings on fits of violence. And when he is not near me, he improves."

"Improves?" Pike shook his head. "You are mistaken. When he went up to London to see Lord Sidmouth—far from your presence—he was in no way improved, Lady Helen. On the contrary, Mr. Ryder saw the signs of the madness in him immediately. You are overwrought and imagining things. You are not responsible for his deterioration."

"I am; I am certain of it." She clasped her hands together to stop herself from shaking the man. "The Comte may have a cure. You cannot be certain he does not. I will take Lowry as my Terrene if you release Hammond and give me the chance to find a way to help Lord Carlston."

"We are not striking a bargain, Lady Helen. I am ordering you to obey your King's command."

"Please, Mr. Pike. Grant me these two things. Please. I will do everything as you say."

"You will do everything as I say anyway. It is your duty." He regarded her from under hooded eyes. "I suppose I should not be surprised that you have allowed your emotions to rule your actions. I will release Hammond, but be assured I will not be so forgiving if it should happen again. As to the other, bring me the *Ligatus* and I will consider it."

"Thank you."

"This is still between us, however," he added. "None of the others may know it is a *Ligatus*—"

They both heard the smash of an upstairs door slamming hard against a wall.

Pike looked up at the ceiling. "What is that?"

A second later, a voice shouted, "Carlston, what—" The Duke's voice, cut off.

He was awake.

A scream rang out. Lady Margaret. Then Delia shrieked, "Let him go!" and Darby yelled, "No, Miss Cransdon, you will be hurt."

A yelp of pain followed—Delia again.

Helen ran to the morning room doors, wrenched them open, and took the stairs three at a time, her hem bunched high in her hands. She heard Quinn's voice yell, "My lord, no!" and then she shouldered her way through the drawing room doors.

It took a moment for the scene to make sense. The armchair had toppled backward with Selburn in it. Carlston, clad only in buckskins and shirt, had his knee braced against the Duke's chest, pinning him down, both hands around his throat. The Earl's teeth were bared, the mad savagery in his face making him almost unrecognizable. The Duke's hands were locked against Carlston's chest, straining against the deadly force, his face red, eyes bulging from the choking hold.

Quinn leaped forward and wrapped his arm around Carlston's throat, trying to heave him off the Duke.

"Help Quinn, my lady!" Darby yelled. She and Lady Margaret were holding up a dazed Delia.

Behind her, Helen heard Pike order, "For Christ's sake, Lady Helen, get him off Selburn!"

She ran forward. Carlston had to be pulled off the Duke, but if she touched him . . . The Duke's desperate bloodshot eyes rolled to her, his blue lips mouthing her name. She grabbed Carlston's shoulder. There was no charge of energy between them like last time, but it was like taking hold of a brick wall. Immovable.

Beside her, Quinn released his necklock. "I can't shift him."

"Together," Helen said. "Now!"

Quinn grabbed Carlston's other shoulder and they hauled backward. He strained against them, muscles rigid under Helen's grip, but his stranglehold on the Duke shifted for a second. The Duke gasped, drawing at the sudden pathway to air, but the Earl pressed in again.

"William!" she yelled in his ear. "Let go!"

Carlston lifted his head—a fleeting beat of recognition. It was enough. She and Quinn heaved Carlston back again, their momentum ripping his hands from the Duke's throat and wrenching him abruptly into their bodies. An elbow slammed into Helen's stomach as she crashed to the floor, punching out all her air.

Quinn rolled away, his hands to his face. She saw Darby run to Quinn and Delia stagger to the Duke, and then a blur of movement as Carlston hauled himself up again, his face even more savage. She must have touched his skin. He launched himself at Selburn again.

Gulping for air, Helen grabbed at his leg, her hands closing around his ankle. Bare skin did not matter now. She felt herself dragged across the carpet, his forward impetus slowing. His eyes turned upon her, no recognition in their fevered depths. Only fury. He was not going to stop.

Helen launched herself upward, all of her weight behind her fist. Her knuckles connected with his chin and mouth, the heavy blow knocking him sideways and sending searing pain jarring up her arm. She swung into a round-kick, hampered somewhat by her skirts but still with enough force to hit him hard in the temple. He staggered and dropped to his knees. For a moment he looked up at her, puzzled, the question clear in his face—*Why did you kick me?*—then he crumpled to the floor.

Helen clasped her aching, bleeding fist to her chest, rocking with the pain. The room was silent except for her jagged breathing and Selburn's wheezing gasps. Quinn hauled himself onto his knees and crawled across to his inert master. Gently he pulled back one of Carlston's eyelids, showing the white. Dear God, she had hit him so hard, Reclaimer-hard; his mouth was bleeding. Was everything in this world answered with violence?

"Is he . . . ?" Helen whispered. She could not say it.

"Breathing." Quinn smiled grimly through his own bloodied mouth. "Two well-placed, clean blows. He is not seriously hurt, but he will be out again for a while."

"My lady, let me look at your hand," Darby said softly.

Helen jumped; she had not heard her maid come to her side. She straightened her fingers, hissing at the sharp jab of pain, and offered the hand for inspection. Darby took it gently in her own, clicking her tongue.

"Duke, are you injured?" Delia asked. A nasty blue bruise was forming on her cheekbone.

Selburn shook his head, although he held his hand ringed around his reddened throat.

Pike leaned over Carlston's unconscious body. "This seems to be the safest state for him—and everyone around him—at present." He turned to Lady Margaret. "What happened?"

"He woke and went looking for Lady Helen. The three of us couldn't stop him—Quinn, Darby, or I." Her eyes darted to Helen as if it were her fault. It probably was, Helen thought. "When he arrived here, he attacked the Duke."

"I see." Pike straightened. "I think your theory is somewhat flawed, Lady Helen. This violence did not start with you touching him."

"Theory?" Lady Margaret asked.

Helen shook her head; this was not the time.

Pike bowed to Selburn. "I think it would be best if you left with me now, Your Grace. Who knows how long Carlston will be insensible, and you seem to be his target."

"We cannot leave the ladies here alone with him," the Duke protested.

"I am sure Mr. Hammond will be here within the half hour," Pike replied, sending a pointed glance in Helen's direction. The deal was in play: Hammond for her obedience. He offered his hand to the Duke. "Besides, Lady Helen and Mr. Quinn are the best equipped to control him."

The Duke nodded reluctantly and gripped Pike's hand, rising stiffly from the floor. He looked down at Carlston, his desire to kick the Earl's prostrate body as clear to Helen as if he had declared it.

"You should not let him regain his senses," he said to the company at large. "Dose him with laudanum."

"We are not going to drug him," Lady Margaret said, stepping closer to Carlston.

Quinn hauled himself up from the floor. "Laudanum doesn't work on a Reclaimer, Your Grace. The workings of their bodies are too fast."

The Duke glanced at Pike. "Is that true?"

Pike nodded.

"Nevertheless, you must find some way to restrain him," the Duke said. "Before he kills someone." He made a small bow to Helen, then made his way to the door.

"His Grace has a point," Pike said, regarding Carlston with a look of satisfaction that chilled Helen to the bone. "Find a way to keep him under control until it is decided what can be done with a man who has lost his mind and has the strength to tear apart entire streets."

He turned and stalked from the room.

PIKE WAS TRUE to his word: half an hour later, Mr. Hammond arrived back at German Place. Apart from a slight dishevelment of his usual neat attire, he seemed composed as he helped himself to a glass of claret in the drawing room. Yet Helen could smell the sharp stink of fear on him, and his hand shook as he poured, spilling some of the ruby wine down the side of the glass.

". . . and now Pike has ordered us to keep his lordship insensible," his sister said, concluding her account. "It is unthinkable. Why did you take so long in town, Michael?"

Her fingers plucked at the fringed ends of her royal blue turban. She had abandoned her usual elaborate coiffure, confining her hair instead beneath the makeshift headdress, the blue silk accentuating the dark shadows under her eyes. After Pike and the Duke had departed, Quinn had carried his lordship back up to the bedchamber and was now watching over him alone, but only because Delia had insisted Lady Margaret take some respite from her vigil. Even so, she sat on the edge of the sofa next to Delia as if ready to fly up the stairs at any sign of consciousness from the Earl.

"I am sorry, Margaret," Hammond said. He placed his hand for a moment upon her shoulder, then walked to the window where Helen stood, the late sun warming her back. "I was delayed in Donaldson's."

He took a sip of wine, his eyes meeting Helen's for a moment over the rim of the glass, the flash of raw fear in his face hidden from his twin and Delia.

"Continuing to batter him into an unconscious state is unthinkable," Lady Margaret repeated, her defiance aimed at Helen.

"I agree." Helen closed her hand and felt the painful pull upon her scabbed and bruised knuckles. She had already come to the necessity of another solution. Whatever that might be.

"You do?" Lady Margaret's fingers stopped their agitated picking at the fringe. "Good."

"What did you find out in town, Mr. Hammond?" Delia asked, breaking the strained silence.

He tipped back his glass and finished the wine in one gulp. "Last night is being explained by a case of St. Anthony's fire—a bakery in the lane selling bad rye bread, and the flour contaminating the air, causing hallucinations. People seem to be believing it. A few are even leaving town. The Comte and Comtesse d'Antraigues are returning to London."

"London?" Helen repeated.

"Yes," Hammond said, walking across to the wine jug again. "It would seem the Comte has given up on his lordship obtaining the journal."

"I've had word that Philip has left for London too," Helen said. "Perhaps they think Lowry is now heading to the city."

Did the Comte and Philip know something about Lowry that they did not? Or was their defection to London for another reason entirely? After all, Philip had left Brighton before the events at the bawdy house. Perhaps his departure had been mere coincidence.

"It is possible Lowry is on his way to London," Mr. Hammond replied, "but it is just as possible he is still in Brighton. I could find no confirmation either way." He addressed his sister. "I have some other information that is for Lady Helen only. Would you and Miss Cransdon leave us, please?"

Delia immediately rose from the sofa, but Lady Margaret frowned at her brother's tone, which had been more command than request.

"If this is to do with Lord Carlston's well-being, I shall stay," she said, and crossed her arms.

"Margaret, please go," Hammond said. He lifted the jug and poured another generous measure. Hand still shaking, Helen noted.

"Do not order me about, Michael. If this is—"

Mr. Hammond slammed the jug down onto the silver tray in a ringing clang of glass against metal. "Devil's sake, Margaret. Just do as I ask."

She flinched upright in her seat, back straight and face rigid. Hammond turned and walked back to the window. Helen watched him drain the glass again; two full glasses in a matter of five minutes.

"Lady Margaret," Delia said softly, "it would be best, I think, if we go to the morning room."

With a fierce glance at her brother's back, Lady Margaret stood and followed Delia from the room. Mr. Hammond waited until the door closed behind them, then walked once again to the decanter. This time his gait was not so easy; a small limp, favoring his right side.

"Are they gone?" he asked, pouring another full glass.

Helen listened to the two pairs of footsteps descending the staircase. No conversation between the two women, but she separated out Lady Margaret's breathing: hard and quick.

"They are entering the morning room," she said. "Your sister is quite agitated."

"My sister is furious and frightened." He took a large mouthful of wine, then turned to face Helen. "Stokes found me in Donaldson's. It was all done very discreetly, of course. Then we got back to his lodgings."

He put down his glass and pulled back his right coat sleeve. Raw abrasions ringed his wrist.

"He bound you?"

"Manacles; he was most apologetic." He retrieved his glass, the next mouthful taking half its contents. "Then I was *questioned*. Pike was certain we had told Lord Carlston about the journal."

Helen frowned at his intonation. "Do you mean he had you beaten? By Stokes?"

She could not believe that Stokes, a Reclaimer, would hit a normal, bound man. Surely he had more honor?

An image of Carlston's hands around Selburn's throat flashed into her mind. He could have snapped the Duke's neck in a second, and yet he had not. Proof, perhaps, that he still held enough rationality to hold back from pure savagery. It was a glimmer of hope. Then again, perhaps the arc of power between them had somehow diminished his Reclaimer strength.

"No, it was not Stokes." Hammond swirled the remainder of wine in the glass. "Two other ruffians. Pike sent Stokes away."

Of course, Helen reminded herself, Pike did not want any of the other Reclaimers to know about the journal.

"Did they hurt you badly? Do you need a physician?" She crossed over to him, sweeping an assessing glance over his body.

"No." His smile of reassurance was too tight. "They knew how to deliver just enough but not too much."

"But why would Pike do that? You are one of his own people."

"His own people?" He gave a light, rather ghastly laugh. "He knows my loyalty is to Lord Carlston, not the Dark Days Club. He did this to remind me that he could, at any time, imprison me. To remind me that I am a coward."

Helen opened her mouth to reject his harsh assessment—he was no coward—but he raised his hand, refusing her protest.

"More importantly, Lady Helen, he did this to show *you* that he is in control." He drained the glass.

"He arrested you to show me?"

Hammond gripped her shoulder. "Pike cannot control Lord Carlston. He has never been able to control him. But he knows he can control you. He said as much to me. A girl. A novice. A gentlewoman brought up to believe in God, country, and duty." He drew back, wincing at the action. "He is right."

"What do you mean?"

"Before he let me go, he told me you offered to take Lowry as your Terrene in exchange for my release."

"Of course I did. I had no other—" Helen stopped; she had just proved his point.

"As long as you care about the people around you, as long as he is more ruthless than you, more willing to hurt them—and he is—he controls you." He stared down into his empty glass. "It will not stop here, with the journal. He has his claws in you. In us."

She had known that deep down, and yet his bald statement of it brought a new sense of despair. *To always be Pike's creature.*

"What do we do?" she said. "Stop caring for people? Stop doing our duty?"

She ground her palms together. It was impossible.

"When Margaret and I were ten years old, we were caught up in the Terror." He turned back to the jug. "French father, noble, and English mother. Both met Madame Guillotine. We were smuggled away in time by servants, but we ended up in the hands of a"—he tilted his head—"*connard.*" Helen had not heard the word before, but his tone made the meaning all too clear. "After many years under his control, we ran as far from him as possible and lived by our wits."

"Is that what you think we should do? Run?"

"I think Lord Carlston is in grave danger."

More than he imagined, Helen thought. From Pike and from her unwilling drain upon his sanity.

"He won't run," she said.

He would not leave her; she was certain of it. It was no longer just about duty. Something stronger connected them. They had both felt it in the kiss in the bawdy house.

Hammond bowed his head in agreement. "So neither will I nor Margaret."

"Pike said he would consider offering the Comte d'Antraigues the information he seeks in return for Carlston's cure."

Hammond gave a small pained laugh. "He will not."

"He kept his word and released you."

"To show you his power."

He lifted the claret jug; it was all but empty. He replaced it and picked up the decanter of brandy instead and tilted it toward her, brows raised. She nodded. Perhaps brandy would deaden the despair and futile rage that burned at her innards.

He hooked two glasses and slid them across the silver tray. "Pike will never allow the journal anywhere near Lord Carlston or a Deceiver."

He was right, even without the knowledge that the journal was also a *Ligatus*. Pike would never contemplate a deal with the Comte.

Helen turned and walked to the window, hearing the liquor splash into a glass. Its rich fruity fumes reminded her of Vauxhall Gardens and the brandy Hammond had pressed upon her after Lord Carlston had shown her the Pavor Deceiver and told her she was a Reclaimer. A direct inheritor.

She drew back her shoulders. There was only one path ahead that held any honor and any chance of success. It would not keep her safe from Pike, but it could keep Hammond and the others safe, and maybe—just maybe—stop his lordship's deterioration.

She had to leave this house, leave her friends, and most of all she had to leave Lord Carlston.

Twenty-Four

Monday, 20 July 1812

I N CONTRAST TO the last time Helen had visited Union Street alone, the narrow lane was eerily quiet. No Quakers on the way to their Meeting House. No shrieking children hunkered down beside the butcher's playing in the puddles. The door of the draper's next door to Holt's Coffeehouse was closed fast, as were all the doors along the site of the battle. Boards covered the broken windows of the gin house and the hole in the front of the coffeehouse. Only one person hurried past Helen: a man in the sober garb of a clerk, who dipped his head to the slim young gentleman standing outside the coffee shop. Helen nodded back. It seemed that the story of contaminated air had, for the moment, discouraged most people from using the thoroughfare.

She waited until the clerk had turned into Ship Street, then edged her way along the side of Holt's, the same way Sprat had led her less than a week ago. Then, she had been so elated by the novelty of walking alone through the streets. Now there was no elation, only a sense of loneliness and deep foreboding.

She stepped over the coiled rope and peered around the corner of the building into the rear yard. Empty, although she could hear Mad Lester humming to himself, and the clink of his chain. The bawdy house was still occupied. Beyond the walls were the sounds of feet upon carpet, the low murmur of voices, a scrape of spoon against pot. It stood to reason; Kate Holt and her girls had nowhere else to go.

Helen smoothed the packet in her hand. A message to Lowry. One of two notes she had written that morning: the first sent by footman to the Duke, asking for the favor that would help Carlston; and this one to Lowry, offering to reinstate the deal. She truly was Pike's creature. Helen twitched her shoulders under the weight of the thought.

Her instincts told her that Lowry's sister would still be in contact with him. On the other hand, if Kate Holt had no way of delivering a message to her brother . . . She pushed away the useless anxiety. Time to find out if her intuition was correct.

Five long strides took her to the kitchen door. The greasy woman standing over the pots looked up, mouth forming into a gummy circle of surprise. Helen did not wait to hear any protest. She barged through to the corridor and headed past the staircase to the parlor where Kate Holt's pleasant voice issued instructions to a deeper male bass. Her husband, or the bruiser in his gaudy waistcoat? It did not matter, Helen told herself. She would not allow anyone to stand in her way.

The door stood ajar. Helen flung it back and stepped into the room, her blood thundering through her veins. Kate Holt and the bruiser turned almost as one, any surprise replaced by wary readiness. They'd clearly had practice dealing with sudden appearances.

"You!" the bawd spat. She gestured to the bruiser. "Henry, get him."

Helen caught a wild flash of what was to come—the clash of the present and the violent immediate future making her falter.

Henry lunged for her, aiming a punch at her face. The room suddenly felt still, everything expanding but at the same time sharpening into close focus, detail crowding into her mind. The smell of suffocating perfume, the sound of breathing—hers, theirs—like bellows in her ears, the scratch of her linen shirt. Henry moved as if he were wading through water, heavy and ponderous. Like the onlookers in the laneway.

Ah, now she understood: she had shifted into Reclaimer speed. She had more than enough time to lift her hand and catch his fist as it inched closer. She twisted it sharply to one side. The snap of bone was slow too, the sound stretched out. The pain registered in his eyes, his lips drawing back in a sluggish grimace of pain as he slowly flinched backward. The encounter was unfair, to say the least. Even so, she thrust him away by his damaged wrist, his arms and legs flailing in slow rotations as he lifted into the air and sailed past Kate. He finally landed against the opposite wall, the sound of the impact like a cannon shot in Helen's ears.

Carlston had explained that this window into the future, like their speed, was held in the rush of their blood and could be controlled with training. Another skill she had not yet mastered. She staggered back and took a deep breath, trying to steady the beat of her heart and bring the world back to its normal pace. It took three more deep inhalations before the overwhelming smells and sounds dropped back to their muted everyday levels.

"'Pon my soul, you're one of them," Kate Holt said, looking up from her fallen man. She stepped forward, both fists clenched, fear overtaken by something more primal. "You here for my Lester? I won't let you kill him. He's not doing no harm to no one."

"I am not here for Lester," Helen said. "I am not going to kill your son."

Kate Holt regarded her, stiff with tension. "You swear?"

"I do not kill poor unfortunates. Lester is safe."

The bawd studied her for a moment more, still wary. Finally she nodded. "What then? My brother? He ain't here. You and the other one saw to that."

"I want you to give him a message."

"You got a nerve." She peered more closely at Helen, recognition dawning in the small dark eyes that were so like Lowry's. "Ah, now I see what's for. You ain't no man. You're the girl he told me about. His way back to all that ungodly strength."

Helen stepped forward, raising her palms in truce as Kate Holt flinched back. "Do you know about the journal?"

Kate frowned. "Journal?" She snorted. "My brother don't keep no journal. He never liked making his letters."

If she did know, she was a masterly liar.

"Is he still in Brighton? Can you get a message to him?" Helen asked.

"Maybe."

Helen held out the packet. "I am offering him another chance at all that ungodly strength. The deal is the same. We'll meet here. On the full moon, the twenty-fourth, like he wanted."

"He won't trust you."

"Tell him I'll be alone. My word on it."

Kate took the offered packet. "I'll tell him." She studied Helen again. "And let me tell *you* something, girl, on account of your mercy to Lester. Get as far away from my brother as you can. He will eat you alive." She tapped her temple. "He gets in here, and you won't ever be the same. Nothing soft survives around him, and you got too much soft in you."

Helen backed away, feeling her skin crawl with the truth of the woman's words. "Just give him the message," she said, and turned on her heel.

Halfway down the corridor she heard an urgent hiss, and stopped. A pair of watery blue eyes under a mess of brown tangled hair peered around the stairwell balustrade. Sprat. The girl sat crouched on the top step, skinny arms hugging her knees, the oversized dress slipping off one knobbled shoulder.

"What you doin' back?" she demanded. "Mrs. Holt is furious wiv you an' the gent. No one's comin' in 'cause of what you did."

"Are you all right, Sprat?"

She nodded. "All's bob. Wiv Binny, too." She uncurled herself and climbed the few steps, her eyes on the doorway into the parlor. "What about you? What was that thump?"

"Henry, hitting the wall."

"Really?" Sprat grinned, but it quickly faded. "Did Mrs. Holt tell you Lizzie's gone to Kingdom come?"

Kingdom come. Lizzie was dead; God have mercy upon her soul. Helen drew a shaking breath. Perhaps if she had stopped and tended to Lizzie that night. Done something . . .

"You couldn't do nothin'," Sprat whispered, as if Helen's heart had been laid bare. "Lizzie was dead soon as she took his fancy." She reached across and patted Helen's arm: a grimy-fingered absolution. "It's how it is."

She withdrew her hand and cleared her throat—too much emotion, it seemed—and hoisted the gaping neck of her dress over her shoulder.

They both turned at a stream of loud cursing from the parlor.

"Henry," Sprat said. "You best get goin'. Me too." She stood and with one last small smile ran down the steps into the cold gloom of the cellar.

Helen made her way quickly out through the kitchen and around the side of the bawdy house again to Union Street. She checked both ways before stepping out into the lane—still deserted—and started in the direction of Black Lion Street, her boots ringing eerily against the flags in the quiet. Now she had the task of explaining the cause of Lord Carlston's madness to those waiting at German Place, and then the grim moment of leaving them all—the only people who understood this dangerous world and her place in it. The only people she could call her friends.

She had just passed the butcher's when she heard another set of boots upon the stone. Behind her and accelerating. She turned her head slightly, seeing a tall figure at the corner of her eye moving too fast for a normal man. *Deceiver!* She felt the pulse of her blood quicken.

Gathering her Reclaimer speed, she ducked down, pulled the glass knife from her boot, and whirled around, every sense focused upon the . . . Her hand stopped, forearm caught in an iron grip, her vision full of a tall, very thin, blond man.

"Good try," the deep Cambridgeshire voice said. "But you went for your knife before you spun. It was like a town crier yelling your intention."

"Mr. Stokes!" Helen dropped back onto her heels and fought down the race of blood and violence in her veins. "I could have stabbed you!" She wrenched her forearm from his hand.

"Not with that move, you couldn't."

He stepped back, regarding the still raised knife. Helen lowered it. She could feel a tremor of unused energy in her hand.

"What are you doing here? Did you follow me?"

"I did." He smiled, although there was none of his usual bonhomie within it. "You are doing well with your masquerade. I did not immediately recognize you when you left German Place."

"You have been watching me?"

"Watching *for* you." He tilted his head toward the end of the lane. "Come, keep walking."

Helen stooped, slid the knife back down into the scabbard in her boot, then skipped a few steps to catch up with his long pace. His normally warm hazel eyes were fixed upon the passing ground in a bleak stare, his lips pursed.

"What is it, Mr. Stokes?" she prompted.

He scanned the buildings around them, then said, "While this is not expressly against my orders, it is definitely not within the spirit of them." He stopped beside a dry goods shop. "Can you hear anyone nearby?"

Helen focused her hearing: a soft scritching in the cellar below them, probably rats; a creak of a roof in the wind; the low rumble of carriages and voices upon nearby Black Lion Street. "No one, as far as I can tell."

He gave a nod of agreement. "This must not be overheard. I have come to warn you that Pike has dispatched a letter to Lord Sidmouth requesting permission to proceed with the control of Lord Carlston."

Helen lifted her hand to her throat as if she could hold down the fear that leaped through her body. "Control means kill, doesn't it?"

"It does. Pike says Lord Carlston has made a deal with a French Deceiver, fought a former Terrene in the middle of a crowded street, and attacked the Duke of Selburn. He said you had to knock him senseless to stop him from killing the Duke. Is that true?"

"Yes," Helen said, her reluctance drawing the word out. "But it is not his fault. It is mine." She tapped her chest. "I am causing his madness."

"Pike does not believe that, and I must say I find it hard to believe too," Stokes said. Helen opened her mouth to explain, but he shook his head. "It does not matter even if it is the case. Pike is convinced Carlston is too far gone: irretrievable, like Benchley. A danger to those around him, and a danger to the security of the Dark Days Club."

"He is not irretrievable."

"Do you know that for certain?"

She wrapped her arms around her body. "No."

Stokes gripped her shoulder. "It will take at least five days for the decision to be made and ratified, and then for the messenger to get back here. I would wager my estate that the response will be a signed warrant. Lord Sidmouth will take Pike's direction in the matter. Carlston has five days."

"Who will Pike send?"

"Another Reclaimer," Stokes said, releasing her shoulder. "Someone who knows him and whom he trusts. Someone like me." He regarded her somberly. "Five days, and if there is another public show of insanity, I don't think Pike will wait for the warrant."

With that, he turned and walked toward Black Lion Street, the sound of his quick footsteps beating out the hard rhythm of Helen's heart.

Twenty-Five

IN HER NOTE Helen had asked the Duke to arrive at two o'clock, but by the time she made her way back to German Place at just on half past one, he was already standing at the hearth in the drawing room. The positioning, Helen realized, was no accident. He faced the door with solid marble at his back and two sofas between himself and any direct line of attack. Understandable, considering what had happened during his last visit to the room. He also held his silver-capped cane, usually relinquished at the front door with his gloves and hat. He had come armed—again understandable, if not very polite.

She tried to smile as she returned his bow. His early arrival was inopportune, to say the least. Now that he was here, she could not risk telling Mr. Hammond and Lady Margaret about the warrant. The Duke would probably greet the news with pleasure, and she was not sure Mr. Hammond would maintain his composure under such provocation. More importantly, the Duke's loyalties were not yet known. It was entirely possible that he would pass on their knowledge to Pike. News of the warrant would have to wait until she found a moment alone with the twins, or if that did not occur, then by letter once she had left the house.

"The Duke says you requested that he come here," Lady Margaret said. She and Delia sat on the furthermost sofa, inadvertently making a charming contrast: black hair and blonde, red gown and white. Lady Margaret's expression, however, was not so charming. "What is this about?"

"It is about Lord Carlston," Helen said. "Is he . . . ?"

"Still in the fugue," Mr. Hammond answered.

"Glad to hear it," the Duke said coolly, earning a savage stare from Lady Margaret. He smiled at Helen. "You make a convincing young man, Lady Helen. Please be assured that I am happy to oblige you in every one of your requests."

"Thank you, Your Grace."

Mr. Hammond shot her a curious glance. "Requests?"

Helen paced across the room, rubbing her palms together. She should wait until his lordship awoke—it was he who needed to know the truth about her effect upon him—but she could no longer afford to be in the same house with him. Or more to the point, he could not afford it.

"I asked you all to gather because I believe I know what is causing Lord Carlston's madness," she said. "It is not just the vestige—"

The doors suddenly opened again, drawing everyone's attention.

"Helen?" Lord Carlston stood upon the threshold, fully clad this time, eyes sweeping the room with fierce urgency until they found her at the window. Sane eyes, thank God.

Quinn stood behind him, face stiff with tension, plainly ready to intervene if his master made any violent move. And beside Quinn, Darby stood just as ready.

"Carlston!" Helen took a step toward him.

Twice now he had woken with Selburn in the house. Coincidence? Or could hate penetrate the fugue state?

"Stay back," the Duke ordered, his cane raised into a club.

Helen held up her hand. "Put that down, please, Your Grace. Lord Carlston is himself. I can see it."

Carlston stared at her for a moment—such an agony of relief

and regret—then turned his attention to Selburn. "What are you doing here?"

The Duke watched him, cane still raised. "I am here for Lady Helen. I am a member of the Dark Days Club now, Carlston. A sworn member."

"Is that true?" The snarled question was aimed at Mr. Hammond.

His aide nodded. "He saw us outside the bawdy house. Forced Pike to explain." He glanced at Helen, alarm in the brief connection. "My lord, perhaps you should step outside."

Carlston strode into the room, shadowed by Quinn and Darby. The Duke braced his feet into the carpet, his hand flexing around the cane handle.

"Please, Your Grace, there is no need for alarm," Helen said, hoping she was right.

Warily, he lowered the cane.

Carlston stopped at the sideboard, his hand finding the edge. The quick, commanding entrance had cost him. Helen saw the flare of his nostrils as he fought to keep his breathing smooth, and the tiny slump of relief as he leaned into the support of the solid mahogany.

"You should return to your bed, Lord Carlston," Lady Margaret said, rising from the sofa. "You are still not well."

He waved her back. "I am completely recovered, thank you."

Even the most obtuse observer could see that for a lie, Helen thought. He had none of his usual grace, his skin was drained of color, and the broad width of his shoulders rounded. That same observer, however, would not see what was so apparent to Helen: the Deceiver energy still snapped within him, barely under his control. The energy that she had unknowingly forced upon him.

Lady Margaret cast an agonized glance at her brother and sank back onto the sofa.

Carlston regarded the Duke. "Sworn or not, you are unwelcome here, Selburn."

"You made that quite clear during my last visit," the Duke said, his hand reflexively ringing his throat. "Nevertheless—"

"What visit?" Carlston snapped.

"He does not know," Delia whispered to Lady Margaret.

"Lord Carlston, you attacked His Grace yesterday," Lady Margaret said. "In this room. You nearly killed him. Lady Helen and Quinn barely stopped you in time."

Carlston glanced at Helen. She nodded.

"The last thing I recall is the lane . . . losing the journal." He gave a dry laugh aimed at the Duke. "I attacked you? Even divorced from rationality, it seems I have good instincts. Lady Helen does not need your protection."

The Duke smiled coldly. "Lady Helen asked me to come here. She has asked for my help."

Carlston frowned. "Is that true, Helen?"

She felt her bare name hang in the silence: a statement to her and a challenge to the Duke. Caught again between these two men. A deep ache opened in her chest, like a claw raking across her heart.

"Yes, it is true, Lord Carlston."

The use of his title caught in her throat, but it had to be done—for his own safety. She saw his eyes flicker: a pained acknowledgment of her formality.

He jerked his chin at Selburn. "What help can he possibly give you?"

"His Grace has kindly agreed to allow me to take up residence at his house in Grand Parade."

The statement locked everyone into shocked silence.

Finally Delia said, "Helen, you can't do that! What will people say?"

"Why would you leave this house?" Lady Margaret demanded. "You are not even close to finishing your training."

Helen ignored both women, her attention solely on the shock in Carlston's eyes. "I am causing your illness, Lord Carlston."

"What makes you think that?" He rapped out the question.

"I think it started at my ball when I took half of the whip energy that you absorbed from Philip. Neither of us released it into the earth, yet it seemed to dissipate. I do not believe it did. Somehow the energy has stayed within us. Over the past month I think it has been quickening the madness in you."

"Why is it not quickening in you, then?" he demanded.

"God's blood," Hammond said, the logic of her words plainly dawning upon him. "She has never reclaimed. She has no vestige darkness in her soul."

Helen nodded. "But I still have the whip energy within me. I think that I, particularly, store it like . . . like . . ." How could she explain such a concept?

"Like a Voltaic pile," Hammond supplied in wonderment.

"What are you talking about, Michael?" Lady Margaret said sharply.

"An experiment I saw in London a few years ago, conducted by Mr. Volta. He created energy in stacks of different metals." He addressed Helen. "It would make sense. The energy stays within you, until somehow, by some mechanism, it is passed to his lordship. The energy that is within him attracts that which is in you."

Helen nodded, relieved that Hammond, at least, understood. "If I am near you, Lord Carlston, just in your vicinity, the energy slowly increases the spread of darkness in your soul." She drew a steadying breath. "But if we touch, skin to skin, that is like a connection that brings on the rages, as if there is some kind of immediate transfer from me to you."

The Duke's head turned at that. "Skin to skin?"

Carlston pressed his fingertips to his mouth. She knew what he was remembering. She could feel the kiss upon her own lips: the heat, the dizzying exhilaration. The savage need.

"Did you touch in the salon, the first time it happened?" Lady Margaret asked tightly.

Helen looked at Carlston. "My jacket," she said.

His jaw shifted. "It was *barely* a touch."

"And the arc of power between you in the lane," Hammond said. "You took that Deceiver's energy, Lady Helen, and then when his lordship touched you—" He slapped his hands together, making Delia jump. *"Bam!"*

Carlston rubbed his forehead. "That, I remember."

"If all this is true, my lady," Darby said, "then it is even more important that we make the Terrene bond today."

Carlston rounded on her. "Today?"

Quinn stepped in front of Darby. "After what happened in the lane, my lord, we thought it would be best if Lady Helen made the bond with her Terrene as soon as could be arranged."

Carlston eyed Quinn's blatant stance of protection. "I see."

"Perhaps if you and I could earth this energy within you, my lady . . ." Darby began.

"No, I will not bond with you," Helen said.

The harsh refusal pushed Darby backward a step, her sturdy body swaying as if she had been hit. "But, my lady—"

"It is no longer possible."

Darby's face was so stricken, it was almost as hard as denying Carlston. She looked at Quinn, a moment of shared bewilderment.

"But we must bond, my lady," she said. "You must have a Terrene."

Helen curled her fists into balls of resolve. She could not give the real reason for her refusal—her deal with Pike. "I want you to stay with Lord Carlston and Quinn. That is my decision. Stay with Quinn. You and he should be together."

Darby drew herself up. "My lady, I go where you go."

"Not this time, Darby. I do not wish you to accompany me." She looked away from the brimming hurt in Darby's blue eyes. "I go to the Duke's house as Mr. Amberley. I do not need a maid."

"Then I will dress as a man and go as your valet!"

"I said no, Darby. Do as you are told."

She heard Darby's breath catch, the sob hastily quelled, but she dared not look into her maid's face.

"You cannot go *alone* to his house," Carlston said.

"Do not ascribe your base impulses to me," the Duke said. "Lady Helen will be in no danger. She will be safer in my house than here."

"I must not be near you, Lord Carlston," Helen said.

"You do not have to go. I will go. I have my own lodgings."

"You can barely walk," Helen said. "You need time to recover— far away from me, with those who can help you."

The reason did not hold up under scrutiny—he could, after all, recover in his own lodgings—but she could not stay in the house with those who might stop her from her purpose.

Carlston plainly saw the reason for what it was: an excuse. He glanced at Selburn, his mouth tightening. Faith, he thought she was doing this to be with the Duke. Helen knitted her fingers together, fighting the impulse to correct the sordid assumption.

"Lady Helen is right," Lady Margaret said. "You need to recover properly."

"If you are intent upon going, Lady Helen, allow me to accompany you," Mr. Hammond said. "It will be my honor."

"You cannot go, Michael," Lady Margaret said. "Lord Carlston needs you here."

"Do not make yourself anxious, Lady Margaret," the Duke said coolly. "My invitation does not extend to your brother, or you, for that matter. I have heard about you from Mr. Pike and you must excuse me if I do not invite thieves and"—he paused and shrugged—"into my house."

Hammond stiffened. "Thieves?"

"Michael," Lady Margaret warned. "This is not the time."

"Surely you cannot object to me, Your Grace?" Delia said hurriedly. "I am Lady Helen's aide, after all."

The Duke bowed. "Miss Cransdon, you are of course welcome." He addressed Helen. "At present, I do not have a suitable chaperone in my house for a young lady. If you wish, I can make those arrangements, but it will take some time. Or perhaps Miss Cransdon can also take up a male guise?"

Helen looked away from Delia's determined face. "It will not be necessary."

She did not want her friend anywhere near Lowry, or the danger that would come with the *Ligatus* once she had retrieved it. And if she were brutally honest, Delia was, at present, more liability than asset.

Carlston straightened, tentatively releasing his grip upon the sideboard. "This is all predicated upon your suspicions being correct, Lady Helen, but I am not convinced. I insist we put it to the test."

"No!" Lady Margaret rose abruptly from the sofa again. "It is too dangerous!"

"My sister is correct, sir," Hammond said, crossing to Carlston's side. "I believe Lady Helen has hit upon the truth and you will put yourself, and all of us, in danger."

"We will go to the salon, then," Carlston replied. "Just Lady Helen, Quinn, and myself. At this moment, they will have no trouble containing me if this theory is correct."

"I will go too," the Duke said.

"No, Your Grace!" Delia said. "If Lord Carlston attacks anyone in that room, it will be you."

"Miss Cransdon is right," Carlston said. "Come into that room, Selburn, and I'll attack you. Whether I am affected or not."

The two men stared at one another.

Carlston drew back his shoulders, his eyes moving to Helen. Entreating. "I need to know. Surely you do as well? I ask you as a fellow Reclaimer. Let us know the truth."

Helen nodded. She knew she should leave with the Duke immediately, but she could not ignore Carlston's plea.

⌒

THE SALON WAS lit by a mellow wash of afternoon sunlight, a glitter of dust motes rising as Helen and Carlston made their way into the center of the long room.

"This will do," Carlston said. He turned slowly in a circle. "Enough empty space for . . . whatever happens."

Helen looked away from the cut on his lip, the bruise upon his jaw. The damage that she had already inflicted.

"Do you remember how I stopped you attacking the Duke?" she asked.

"No, I do not."

She held up her fist. "It seems the only way is to render you unconscious. You *will* lose control, and I do not want to hit you again. Please, Lord Carlston, let us return to the drawing room."

"Just Carlston," he corrected gently. He touched the bruise upon his jaw. "We do what we have to do."

A clatter from the weapons table drew their attention. Quinn grimaced an apology and picked up the dropped knife to pass it to Hammond—the last weapon to be collected.

"I will be outside," Hammond said. He gave one last look at

Helen, his unhappiness echoing her own, then left the room. Quinn shut the doors behind him, the stiff line of his shoulders registering his disapproval of the whole affair.

"Lock the doors, Quinn," Carlston ordered.

The Terrene obeyed, then turned to join them, but Helen lifted her hand, stopping him. "Wait." She had to tell Carlston about her visit from Stokes. He had to be warned.

She turned away from Quinn, the move drawing Carlston around too. "I did not want to say this in front of the Duke," she said, her voice pitched for privacy. "He does not have your best interests at heart."

"Quite," Carlston said, matching her dry tone.

"Stokes found me today. Pike has written to Lord Sidmouth to request a warrant. For your death."

Carlston hissed out a breath. "Already? The man is irritatingly efficient."

"He believes you are irretrievable. Like Benchley."

"I am not quite there, yet."

"You should leave," Helen said. "You and Quinn. Maybe even Lady Margaret and Mr. Hammond. Go back to the Continent."

"You would have me run away?"

"To save your life—your sanity—yes. Stokes believes Lord Sidmouth will give his approval; and the further you are away from me, the better chance you have of retaining some sanity."

He shook his head. "I do not believe that; and I will not allow Pike to force me out of England again. Sidmouth would never sign such a dishonorable warrant."

Helen stared at him. Was that his true belief, or was it the madness speaking? Perhaps she should tell him about the deal with Lowry. She would have the journal soon enough and, by God, she would make Pike bargain for the cure from the Comte. Yes, if Carlston knew there was hope, perhaps he would agree at least to hide from Pike. She swayed toward him, drawn forward by the relief of the decision.

"I will not leave you to Pike's machinations," Carlston said. "He refuses to see the importance of you, and he does not understand what is coming toward us."

She closed her eyes. He would never allow her to put herself in such danger, especially not at Pike's order. Moreover, she knew he would do everything in his power to stop her from bonding with Lowry, even if it was at cost to himself. Yet she had the best chance of obtaining the journal; she had what Lowry wanted. She could not tell Carlston and risk him ruining the plan. Not like last time.

"I will not leave, Helen."

She opened her eyes. She knew that fervent tone in his voice: he was already losing control. They were standing far too close to each other; her point would soon be proved.

"And I do not want you to leave," he continued. "Even if this test proves your theory, you must not go. It is a foolhardy plan, especially without the support of aides or a Terrene."

I will have a Terrene soon enough, she thought grimly. "The Duke wishes to be my aide."

Carlston pressed his fingertips hard into his forehead. "Dear God, do not make him your aide."

"Why? Because you hate him?"

"That is not the reason." He dropped his hand away from his brow. "He is not the man to help you become what you need to be, Helen. He cannot see past the fact that you are a woman. All he wants to do is protect you."

"What is wrong with that? Surely it is the role of an aide."

"Helen, *you* are the protector. That is your sworn duty and birthright. Do you really think Selburn will obey your orders? Can you see him standing aside so that you may lead in the way that you must?"

He had a point. The Duke had tried to pursue Philip, and he had taken charge of their escape after the laneway battle. Even so, she had to go somewhere, and he had her interests at heart.

"It is my right to choose my own aides." She hesitated; he must let her go and she must use whatever means possible to make it happen. "But that is not the real reason, is it? This is about Lady Elise. You and he are playing out your battle again. You cannot bear to think that he will win this time."

"It is not about Elise. It is about you." He averted his face, strong jaw and cheekbone angled as if he had just been hit. Or was maybe preparing to be hit. "Is he going to win?"

"He has offered to help me, and right now I need his help."

"Is it just his help, or are you going because you wish to be with him?" He leaned closer, face fierce. "Do you love him? Is that it?"

"You, of all people, have no right to ask me that."

"Maybe not, but I ask it anyway. Do you love him?"

"Love him?" Helen's voice rose. "Apparently I am not allowed to love in this godforsaken world!"

"Apparently neither am I," he said through his teeth. "Yet . . ."

Yet what? His face, his body, were so close. So dangerously close.

"Stay," he breathed.

She shook her head.

He stepped away, the sudden distance between them full of pain.

"Quinn!" he snapped.

"My lord, this is a bad idea all round," Quinn said gruffly as he joined them in the center of the room. "I think her ladyship is right about the energy."

"I did not ask for your opinion," Carlston said. He held his arms out. "Make sure I cannot move."

Quinn stepped behind him and hooked his arms over Carlston's, pulling his master's arms back and securing them in a lock hold. Carlston rocked forward, testing his man's grasp.

"Good," he said. "Lady Helen?"

She stepped forward. Now she could touch him, and it tore at her heart.

"Do it," he ordered.

Behind him, Quinn braced.

Helen lifted her fingers to Carlston's face. His dark eyes followed her hand as it reached toward his cheek. Her throat ached, choked with unsaid words. She cupped his jaw, his breath warm against her fingers. Slowly he turned into the curve of her palm, cut lip pressed against her skin. She heard two whispered words, felt them kissed into her flesh: *amore mio. My love.* Two words: the shock of them held her still.

He looked up at her and she saw the longing in his eyes harden into savage madness. With a sob she pulled her hand back, closing it into a fist.

———

HELEN WRENCHED AT the salon door handles, the blood on her hands making her grip slide off the metal. Locked; Quinn had locked them. She turned the key, her hand shaking, then twisted the bloodied handles again, finally stumbling out onto the landing. She had to get away from what she had done.

"Lady Helen!"

Mr. Hammond, standing at the top of the stairs. She could barely see him through the blur of tears. She tried to take another step, but her legs buckled. She sank to her knees and felt his strong hands catch her forearms before she fell forward.

"My God, your knuckles," he said, on his own knees and bracing her against his chest. "They are split open." He shifted to look over her shoulder into the salon, and she felt his slim body stiffen. "Sweet heaven."

"I had to keep hitting," she gasped. "Quinn could hardly hold him. His eyes, they were . . ." She shook her head; could not stop shaking it. "He called me his love. I hit him. Over and over, Hammond. I hurt him so much. I cannot be this thing they want me to be."

"Lady Helen!" He caught her jaw in his hand and held her head still, his stricken blue eyes fixed upon her own. How could he bear to look at her? She was a monster. "Stop it!" he said. "You did what you had to do."

"He said I was his love. '*Amore mio.*'"

"Did he?" Hammond gave an odd pained laugh. "Well, that is not such a surprise. Your destiny is bound with his; it is plain to see. Do not torment yourself. He knows you are trying to help him." He pulled her upright, his tight grip steadying her on her feet. "You are the only one who *can* help him."

She drew a shivering breath. And another. Mr. Hammond was right. She had the way to help him: Lowry and the journal. She pushed the heels of her hands into her eyes, pressing away the image of Carlston's bleeding, battered face, forcing out the sensation of her knuckles slamming against his flesh and bone.

"Stokes told me Pike has sent a dispatch to Lord Sidmouth for a warrant," she said, dropping her hands. She saw the significance register on Hammond's face: the flash of fear. "We only have five days at the most—until Saturday—before the decision is made and the government messenger arrives. I am going to bond with Lowry and get the journal on Friday." She paused; *please, God, let it be Friday.* "But if something goes wrong, you need to be ready to get Carlston out of England.

He will not go willingly; he has said as much. You will have to make him."

Hammond nodded. "Pike won't give you those pages for the Comte." It was more question than statement.

Helen knew he was right. She had tried to bargain for them. Plead for them. But Pike did not want Carlston cured.

"I know. I am going to take them," she said.

"You know what he will do to you. To us!"

"I no longer care. Do you?"

He squared his shoulders. "No. Pike and his blackmail can go to the devil."

"I will leave with the Duke now. Do not speak about Lowry to anyone. This is the last chance, Hammond. Nothing can go wrong."

"I understand." He gripped her shoulder, the trust within his eyes almost breaking her barely held control. "Good luck."

⁓

THE INTERIOR OF the Duke's town carriage was upholstered in pale blue silk woven with the Selburn coat of arms across the backs of the two bench seats. Helen stared at the dark arc of her blood smeared over the *lion passant*.

"I am so sorry, Your Grace, I have ruined your seat," she said, cradling her bleeding hand. Every time she stretched her fingers, the wounds split open again.

"Do not concern yourself about the seat," Selburn said.

He rapped the silver cap of his cane against the blue silk wall behind him. The coach immediately lurched into motion.

Helen could not help but look back at the town house as they pulled away. A face appeared at the morning room window. Darby, her eyes swollen and red. Helen drew a ragged breath, the sob within it making the Duke reach across the footwell and take her hand in his own.

"Does it pain you?" he asked, inspecting the injury with a frown. "You should not have to bear this."

"It will heal in a day or so." At least her hand would, she thought. "Thank you, for . . ." She gestured to the carriage with her other hand. "All this."

"I think you know that I would do a lot more for you."

She withdrew her hand and smiled, somewhat watery and forced, but at least it showed him her gratitude.

The Duke stared out the carriage window for a moment, his finger tapping the cane's silver cap. Then he sat forward, his long face set into ardent lines.

"You must forgive me for raising this subject now, my dear—I do not wish to seem inopportune—but I feel I must say that none of this has changed my feelings toward you. My proposal still stands. Even more so now that I know the truth. If we were to wed, Helen, I could be of great help to you. You would have the protection of my name and rank, and I could perhaps even take on this role of Terrene. It would make me so much easier if I could be sure that you were safe. Not only that, you would be reunited with your family. They would embrace our marriage—"

"Your Grace, please stop." It was plain that he had only her interests at heart, but she could not listen to his avowal. Not now.

"I understand, this is not the time. Forgive me. It is my concern for you speaking. When you are ready, we can discuss it."

Beyond the curtained window, dark clouds had bleached the blue sea into a dull gray. The bathing boxes were all back on the

beach and lined up well beyond the tide line, ponies and atten-
dants gone. A storm must be on the way, Helen thought.

"You are well out of there," the Duke said, drawing her attention back to his sympathetic face. "You will see how easy it will be
for you in my house. Everything will be as you wish it. You will
be safe."

Safe? Helen smiled again. He was so kind. And so very, very
wrong.

Twenty-Six

Tuesday, 21 July 1812

THE DUKE OF Selburn's butler entered the candlelit dining room with the silent tread of the well-trained servant, and waited stolidly for his master to finish speaking to his young guest.

"That may be, but I do not see how he can expect you to take on so much in such a short time," the Duke said, answering Helen's defense of Carlston's training regimen. He cracked open a walnut in his long hand and picked out the meat. "How long did it take him to learn these things himself? He would surely have studied fencing from childhood. As I did. He cannot expect you to master it in a month." He noticed his servant. "What is it, Fairwood?"

"There is a *woman* to see Mr. Amberley, Your Grace." The butler's intonation indicated the dubiousness of the visitor.

Helen looked up sharply from peeling a peach. "Woman?"

The Duke glanced at the gold clock on the mantel. "It is past ten," he protested. "Has she given a name?"

"No, Your Grace. She says she is known to Mr. Amberley."

Helen straightened in her chair. It must be Kate Holt, finally bringing word from her brother. But was it a yes or a no? On one hand, she desperately wanted Lowry to agree to the deal; on the other, the idea of bonding with him—in mind as well as power—brought a fear that had made her retch into the silver gilt washbasin the night before.

The idea of killing the man had, of course, occurred to her, the savage desire bringing its own wave of sickness. It was hard enough to live with what she had done to Carlston. To kill a man in cold blood was a step that could never be reconciled with her conscience. It would bring its own black mark upon her soul, born not from the Deceivers, but from the dark recesses of the human heart. Besides, Lowry still had Terrene strength and far more experience with violence than she did. If she attacked him, it was more than possible that she would end up at his mercy. A situation she most fervently wanted to avoid.

Nevertheless, she had dressed that morning with her glass knife down the side of one boot, and a small dagger down the side of the other, both scabbards well waxed. They were now part of her toilette.

"Thank you, Fairwood," she said, rising from her chair. "I shall come directly."

"Good Lord, you must not go to her," the Duke said. "She must come to you." He addressed his butler. "Mr. Amberley will receive his visitor in the library."

It was his house, of course, and his right to arrange such things. The last night and day had been full of numb misery—reliving those terrible, violent minutes in the salon; seeing over and over again the betrayal in Darby's eyes—and she had to admit that it had been rather comforting to have her well-being so masterfully managed. Even so, Carlston's warning echoed softly in her ear. The Duke was indeed used to command.

The thought of Carlston brought an ache into her throat. *Amore mio.* She closed her hand around the words he had pressed into her skin. Precious words, but he was not free to make such a declaration. It must have been the madness speaking. In his right mind, he would never have abandoned his oath or his vow to his missing wife. Although the words felt like the truth in her heart, she could not accept them. For her own sanity.

"Is this whom you have been waiting for?" the Duke asked.

She had not said she had been waiting at all; the man was too astute.

"An informer," she said.

"Ah." He let the remains of the walnut drop onto his plate in a tiny clatter of crushed shell. "Allow me to accompany you."

"Thank you, but no," Helen said quickly. "She will not talk with a man present."

He sat back. "As you wish."

He was not happy, but then he would be even less happy if he knew that she intended to bond with a man like Lowry.

⌒

The Duke's library smelled of leather, beeswax, and that peculiarly calming scent of ink and paper. Three walls were lined with books: a fortune's worth of knowledge. The fourth wall was reserved for a magnificent view of the Steine through two large sash windows. Helen stood by the elegant writing desk, the top inlaid with the Selburn arms in satinwood, and watched the night activity that swirled around the town green under the light of the bright gibbous moon. Fashionables taking the air along the lamplit paths; groups of men heading toward the Old Town; and a procession of carriages on their way to evening entertainments, the grind of wheels and clack of hooves barely audible through the solid stone front of the house.

A knock on the door turned her from the view.

"Enter," she said.

Fairwood opened the door and announced, "Your visitor, sir."

Kate Holt swept past him into the room, her small eyes darting over its rich appointments. Helen could almost see her mind calculating the prices of the large blue-and-white Chinoiserie vases, the vibrant Aubusson carpet, and the inkwell set upon the desk that caught the candlelight in a flash of gold and glass.

The bawd had clearly chosen her best ensemble for the interview: a red-and-blue-striped pelisse atop a mustard gown adorned at the hem with garish red bows. A smart chip hat sat atop her thick black hair, the ribands tied loosely under her cleft chin.

"You can go now," she said to the butler. "This gent and I want to be alone."

Fairwood eyed her for a long, chilly moment, then turned to Helen. "Do you wish for anything further, sir?"

"No. Thank you."

He bowed and closed the doors.

"Well, now," Kate Holt said, "this is all very grand." She walked over to one of the vases and tapped it, the porcelain ringing its pure tone. "I've come with word from my brother."

Helen clasped her hands behind her back and dug her thumbnail into her palm. She must not show her eagerness.

"Does he agree?" she asked, keeping her voice measured.

"He does."

Helen drew a deep breath, easing her thumbnail from her skin. The journal was in sight.

"But not on the twenty-fourth, like you said," Kate added.

"But that is when he wanted to meet." It could not be later: Stokes had said five days. Only five days. "What night, then?"

"It seems to me that this information is worth something to you," Kate said, folding her arms under the bulk of her bosom.

"Are you asking for money?" The last two days of anguish boiled up within her, a bright fury taking hold. She stepped forward.

"You stupid woman. You saw what I did to your man. Do you think I would not do the same to you in a second?"

It was no empty threat. Helen felt ready to throw the woman across the room. To tear the message from her body.

Kate backed away, all bravado gone. "You got me wrong. I don't want no money. Bartholomew says you're special. That you got more power than any of the others. I want you to help my boy, Lester. Mr. Benchley—the other one like you—said he couldn't be saved, but maybe you can do something."

God pity her, she was bargaining for her son's sanity. Helen felt her fury collapse into a sudden image of Carlston's eyes shifting into savagery. Wasn't she doing the same: bargaining for a man's mind?

"I've seen your son," she said. "I don't think he can be saved."

"You could try, though, couldn't you?"

"Give me the message."

Kate chewed her lip. "He wants to do it tonight. You're to come with me now, so he knows you ain't planning anything like last time. He's got everything that is needed for the ritual. He said for me to say, 'Just bring your own sweet self, girly.'"

Helen drew back. The man was foul even through a reported message. "Right now?"

"Yes. He's watching. If you talk to anyone else, it's all over." Her hand cut through the air. "He's gone, along with that book you want."

Helen looked out of the window at the passing carriages, their lamplights flashing across the spiked fence railings that guarded the house. Lowry was out there somewhere, waiting. The thought sent a shiver across her skin. Whatever happened, she would have the journal—the *Ligatus*—by the end of the night. Nothing else mattered.

"'My boy?" Kate Holt asked.

"He'll get his chance," Helen said.

Kate nodded. "Thank you."

They waited in silence until Helen heard Fairwood's soft tread climb the stairs in response to a summons from the dining room bell.

"Now," she said to Kate Holt.

She led the way out of the library and across the large foyer, holding her breath at the sound of their steps on the marble floor. She collected her hat from the sideboard and gestured to the footman to open the door. He bowed as they passed.

Out on the busy street, Helen looked up at the shuttered dining room window. It would not be long before the Duke discovered her absence, but by then she would be in the Old Town, just another young man heading into the stews for a night of drinking and gambling. She pulled her hat brim lower over her eyes. She was heading into a night of drinking one man's blood and gambling for the sanity of another.

⁓

UNION STREET WAS still bare of company compared to the bustle of nearby Black Lion Street, but a small number of men had returned to the night establishments along the narrow lane. Two of those brave souls grinned up at the first floor of Holt's Coffeehouse.

Helen craned her neck back. Four girls leaned out the windows, calling enticements and offering flashes of pale breasts and thighs in the bright moonlight. Among the lewd winks and false smiles, an earnest freckled face with round blue eyes peered down: Binny. She lifted her hand as if to warn Helen to turn back, her lower lip caught between her teeth.

"Give us a smile, Freckles," one of the grinners called. "I can get frowns like that at home."

"Are you coming?" Kate demanded from the doorway, her thick body silhouetted by the lamplight within.

Helen nodded. There could be no turning back. She rolled her shoulders within her jacket, easing the cling of her damp shirt. Kate had set a fast pace across the Steine and into the Lanes, but the sweat was not from exertion. Helen could feel the fear oozing from her skin, gathering in the small of her back and behind her knees.

They passed quickly to the back of the sparsely populated coffee room and through the red curtain. Kate waved back the new bruiser standing on the other side with a curt, "It's me, Tom."

"Your man Henry?" Helen ventured as they made their way along the dingy corridor that smelled this time of cheap lavender perfume and beef tallow.

"Got no use for a man with a busted hand," Kate said.

Helen felt a moment of guilt, then reminded herself that the man was a thug.

Their entrance into the parlor halted the low conversation of the three girls seated around the card table. Helen remembered one of them from her last visit: Jessie the pianoforte player. No sign of Binny. She must be still at the windows.

Jessie and the other two girls watched as Helen placed her hat on the bureau and followed Kate through the room, their silent stares crawling across her back.

The sense of being watched intensified as Kate led the way to the staircase. Helen looked over her shoulder and caught a glimpse of a pinched white face peering around the edge of the bedchamber doorway at the end of the corridor. Sprat.

The girl shook her head, filthy topknot slipping to one side, her eyes squinting with the urgency of her message. *Don't go down there.*

"Sprat, clean that room," Kate ordered.

The girl drew back, disappearing from view; no doubt thinking of what Lowry had done to her friend.

Helen shifted her jaw, the click of bone in its socket loud in her ear. The image of Lizzie curled up on that bed, dying, preyed upon her mind too. Once Lowry was her Terrene, she would always have to be on guard. And if she should be incapacitated, vulnerable . . . She gripped the wooden banister, anchoring herself in the here and now. No use conjuring terrors when she was about to face one.

They descended the wooden steps into the dim cellar. Helen shivered as the cooler air chilled the sweat on her skin. She slid her finger between the cravat and her throat, easing the damp choke of the fine muslin.

"He's set up all the doings in the old coal room," Kate whispered, ushering her into the stone corridor. "He thought it would be funny."

Helen's shoulders lifted. A room where he had tortured and killed a girl; very funny, she thought savagely.

Kate regarded her owlishly in the gloom. "Remember, he likes to get in your head"—she tapped her temple—"likes to find the weakness." She dropped her voice to a bare breath. "Don't let him find it."

Kate, it seemed, was trying to protect her son's chance at sanity. Not exactly an ally, but not totally loyal to her brother either.

Helen focused past her own hard heartbeat and Kate's phlegmy breath. Yes, Lowry was here already, his respiration slow and steady. The breathing of a confident man.

At the end of the corridor, a narrow rectangle of light cut across the stone floor from the coal room. The bright glow cast a halo of light that gave shape to the stack of kegs ahead and the dark doorways of the molly rooms.

"He's told me not to let anyone else down here," Kate said, leading the way past the wall of barrels. She stopped a few feet from the sharp edge of light. "Bartholomew, she's here."

"Well, send her in, then."

The words were nonchalant, but Helen heard the note of anticipation like a coiled snake in his voice. His breathing placed him in the center of the room, away from the doorway.

Kate waved her forward, her hand lifting to tap her temple—a final warning—before she turned to retrace their steps.

Helen ground her palms together. The door had not been replaced; the stone jamb was pocked with ragged holes where Carlston had ripped out the former hinges. No locked door, then. Did he have the journal with him?

"If you are wondering, the journal is not here," he said lazily. *He likes to get in your head.* "Once the ritual is done, I'll tell you where it is."

She stretched out her fingers, trying to loosen the tight fear in her body. The healing scabs on her knuckles pulled under the strain. A tiny pain, but it focused her mind. She stepped into the coal room.

Candles; a fortune of them arranged around the room in tin holders and glass lamps and one large iron candelabrum set upon the table in the center of the room. No wonder the light was so bright. Their flames brought an airless waxy heat into the room that seemed to stick to Helen's skin.

Lowry stood before the table, one hand leaned back upon it, head tilted in sly regard, lank black hair tied back. His florid complexion showed signs of strain: pale blue pouches beneath the narrow eyes, lines cut deeper between nose and mouth, and a bristle of beard across his cleft chin. The smell of him—old sweat and a fusty maleness that she now understood—brought a gagging swallow into her throat.

The bed had been pushed up against the wall. Helen angled her face from it and the memory curled upon its bare straw mattress.

"I was surprised that you and Carlston tried for the journal the other night," he said. "You're not as honorable as I thought." He made it sound like a compliment. "Carlston's well on his way to bedlam, ain't he?"

Carlston; his name pushed Helen further into the room. "Let us get this done," she said.

Lowry straightened, green eyes narrowing even further into wariness. For a second it startled her; but of course, she was as strong and fast as him. Probably more so.

"Didn't think you'd be so eager." He waved her over to the table. He was an inch or so shorter than she, but twice as broad, with a bull neck and shoulders. The weight behind one of his fists would be devastatingly heavy. "Do you know the words to be said?"

"Yes."

She studied the ghastly implements. One blue ceramic bowl full of thick red liquid already beginning to congeal: goat's blood. One empty blue porcelain bowl to collect their own blood from the crosses cut into their flesh. Sweet heaven, he would be cutting into her hand. She curled her fingers over her palms, her eyes fixed upon the dagger. So sharp. She forced her eyes to move to the other items. Water in a long thin glass vial, presumably sanctified; long pieces of cloth; a thin wooden yew switch; and a pitcher of milk with a yellow skin across the top, exuding a faint sourness.

Lowry hooked a finger around the lip of the empty bowl and dragged it closer to the edge of the table. Helen flinched at the scrape of porcelain against wood, the reflex bringing a small smile to his lips.

"For our blood," he said.

"I know."

He picked up the knife. Helen tensed, but with a flick of his wrist he turned it, offering her the leather handle.

"My lady," he said, the smile widening into a show of yellow teeth. He held out his left hand, palm up. "In the shape of a cross. We only need a few drops."

She stepped closer. His eyes held a challenge; he did not think she could do it. She shifted her grip, positioning the point over the hollow in his palm. Could she cut into another person's flesh? Even flesh as repulsive as Lowry's?

"If you want the journal," he said softly, like a caress, "there's going to be pain. Mine and yours."

She drew a deep breath through her nose—she would not be cowed by his creeping words—and pressed the knife into his hand. The tip met the slight resistance of skin, then bit into his flesh. She heard him hiss as she drew the blade down, blood welling around the quick vertical slice. She lifted the tip again, swallowing a sour taste of revulsion.

"Don't stop," he said.

She positioned the tip again. One swift slice finished the bloodied cross. He curled his hand into a fist and held it over the bowl, the trickle of blood hitting the bottom with a soft patter. He snagged one of the cloths and wrapped it around his hand.

"My turn," he said, and held out his right hand for the knife.

Helen picked up the other cloth and wiped the blade. Delaying the inevitable, but she did not want him to see the tremor in her hands.

"Are you afraid?" His voice was silky.

He likes to get in your head.

She tossed the cloth back onto the table and met his strangely eager eyes. "I am not."

She passed him the knife and lifted her hand. Only a slight shake. She turned it over, palm out.

He licked his lips—a flash of that foul, pale tongue—then reached over and took her wrist in a tight grip, bracing it.

"What are you doing?"

"You're too squeamish. You'll pull away."

"I will not."

"We'll see."

He placed the knife tip against her palm and pressed it into her flesh. It slid through skin and flesh, a sting. But it did not stop. He pushed it deeper. His eyes were not on the knife, but on her face. Watching, savoring, as he drew the blade down her palm in a slow, burning line of agony.

She gasped and wrenched her hand from his hold, the knife ripping out of her flesh.

"See," he said. "No stomach."

"I did not go slowly, like that," she said, cradling her hand, blood pooling in her cupped palm.

"We should finish, or you'll start healing and we'll have to start all over again."

Sweat crawled under her breast band and down her back. Although every instinct screamed against it, she held out her hand. "Make it fast."

He lifted the blade and brought it down for the crossbar, the slash quicker but just as deep, sending a jag of pain through her again.

Gritting her teeth, Helen snatched back her hand and closed it in a fist over the bowl. Her blood was brighter than his, the quick run of it sliding down the blue porcelain and pooling around his smaller offering. She grabbed the other cloth and wrapped it tight around the searing, wet sting.

He tossed the knife back onto the table. "Start saying the words," he ordered, and picked up the bowl of goat's blood.

Helen squeezed her eyes shut for a moment, past the pain, and found the Latin.

"*Procude vinculum ex terra ac aere,*" she recited. He poured the viscous fluid into the bowl. "*Ex tellure ac caelo. . . .*"

As she continued to chant the words, Lowry poured in the sanctified water, then the milk, and stirred them with the switch, his heavy brow furrowed with concentration. The obscene amusement was gone, his mouth set into a tight line of determination.

"*Hoc vinculum in amore fideque procudendum est, Nam neque suspicio neque odium umquam approbantur,*" Helen finished. *This bond must be forged in love and trust, For suspicion and hate can ne'er be just.*

There was no love and trust here; perhaps the ritual would not work.

Dear God, she prayed, *let it work, or I will never find the journal.*

He drew out the switch from the bowl. They both regarded the pale pink liquid, still swirling. The meaty, sour stink of it reminded Helen of the tanneries near Newgate Prison. She swallowed, her throat closing in anticipation.

"Cross to cross," he said.

He unwrapped his hand and held it up, the carved symbol still oozing blood. She had to touch him again.

Helen unwound her own makeshift bandage. The two intersecting wounds sent jabs of agony through her as she held up her hand. He slapped his palm against her own, locking his fingers between hers, grinding the raw cuts together. She drew a startled breath, panting with the new influx of pain. He smiled, although his own breathing was short and shallow.

"You first," he said.

She lifted the bowl, holding her breath. Two large mouthfuls. It was not so much the warm, sour, metallic taste that made her gag, but the thick, almost gelatinous feel of it around her tongue and along her throat. She coughed, caught between the reflex to retch and the determination to swallow. Her hand throbbed under Lowry's brutal hold, the delight in his eyes bringing its own gag of revulsion. Every part of her wanted to spit out the liquid, wrench her hand free from Lowry. No, she must swallow it. She must have the journal. She must cure Carlston.

It took all her will, but the liquid went down. She felt it hit her stomach, bringing another heaving reflex. Heat flashed through her body, pushing out a fresh ooze of sweat. Was this how it should feel?

"Give it to me," he said.

She held out the bowl. He cupped it in his free hand, lifted it to his lips, and took a long draft, the muscles in his throat jumping as he fought the mixture down. He lowered the bowl, his eyes fixed upon hers in triumph.

The heat within her flared, as if a new coal had been thrown upon a fire. An oily weight squirmed across her consciousness: a swollen, crawling presence that left a slick of loathsome urges darkening the edge of her mind. A whispering rattle clicked and clacked in her head like dry bones.

Lowry laughed, head back, mouth open wide with the salacious sound. "You are so bright," he said, gripping her hand harder, squeezing more pain into their union. "So new."

Helen shook her head. The rattle was in her bones. Her dry bones. A parched death rale clattered through her body, building into a high-pitched screech. Was this the bond?

Behind the screech, a deeper roar of obliterating heat, rushing through her veins and sinew. A deluge in her blood, forging its way through the breach of flesh and skin carved into her palm.

She felt the torrent of energy slam from her hand into Lowry, the shock flinging him back against the edge of the bed, the iron frame lifting and crashing against the stone wall. She staggered to one side, dropping heavily to her knees, the impact jarring through her thighs. The roar and dry clatter still surged in her veins, but muted like a storm heard in the distance.

Lowry groaned, his hand reaching for his throat. The large jugulars were swelling, thick and blue. He clawed at his neck, eyes widening beyond their lids, bulging from their sockets. The web of veins across his cheeks expanded into thick blue ridges stretching the skin. She heard an obscene wet pop, and one of the swollen ridges burst in a spray of blood, peeling back the layers of flesh. He screamed, the sound suddenly cut off as he gulped wetly for air.

Helen scrabbled backward, her shoulders hitting the firm hold of the wall. She had seen this before. Deceiver energy. It was the way Benchley had died.

Lowry writhed across the stone floor, ripping at his chest, his mouth open in a silent scream. Blood seeped from his nose and eyes. His heels drummed upon the stone floor, a quicker beat beneath the sound of his shoulders and head slamming over and over against the stone. She heard the sound of teeth cracking under the locking spasm of his jaw. His whole body stiffened and lifted into an arched convulsion that snapped bone. He dropped back on the ground, eyes fixed, his final agony frozen into a death snarl upon his ruined face.

Helen gasped into the abrupt silence. The Deceiver energy had killed him. She had killed him. How?

She turned her hand. The cross was gone, her palm as smooth as if the blade had never met it. Hammond was right: she stored Deceiver energy like Mr. Volta's stacks. But why had the energy forced its way out? Helen drew a shaking breath: the blood ritual. There was no other explanation.

She curled her knees up to her chest. Dear Mother of Mercy, if she had tried to make the blood bond with Darby instead of

Lowry . . . No, she must not think of it. As it stood, it was bad enough. Lowry was dead and she did not know where he had put the journal. What if she could not find it?

She stared at his twisted body, her gaze sliding away from the peeled flesh. Perhaps he had lied. Perhaps it was hidden upon him somewhere.

She crawled across the floor, keeping her focus upon the opening of his jacket, away from the bulging eyes. The mix of blood and piss and hot split innards rose in a sickeningly acrid stink. Carefully she reached over his clawed hands and flicked back his blood-soaked jacket. There were no pockets in the sodden cloth. She clenched her teeth, trying to stop herself from retching. No journal. No bargain.

"Glory!" a voice said.

She spun around in a crouch.

Sprat stood in the doorway, eyes fixed upon Lowry's corpse. The girl edged into the room, thin arms wrapped around her body, the faded dress bunched up past her bare ankles.

"Did you do that?" she asked.

Helen tried to say yes, but her voice was gone, lost within quick, shallow breaths that brought no air.

Sprat squatted in front of her, eyes solemn. "You all right?" She reached across and patted Helen's shoulder with one dirty hand. "All yer bits an' bobs together?"

Helen gasped at the touch—God forfend, the energy!—but no torrent boiled up to fling the small girl across the room. She could still feel the Deceiver power within her, its distant click and moan, but it seemed to need a path of blood.

"Don't give his worthless carcass no thought, my lady. He deserved it." Sprat regarded Lowry with satisfaction, then wrinkled her nose. "Lordy, he reeks, don't he." She scratched her grimy neck. "Looks like it hurt him. A lot."

"Yes," Helen finally managed.

"Good." Sprat clambered to her feet, hitching her dress. "You lookin' for what he stashed, ain't ya? The book."

Helen lurched forward. "You know where it is?"

"Saw him put somethin' in with Mad Lester afore you came."

Helen bowed her head, almost overcome by the giddy wash of relief. Thank the Lord for small, inquisitive girls.

"I need to get it, Sprat." She climbed to her feet. Shaky, but firm enough.

Sprat nodded. "Come on, then." She snagged one of the lamps and led the way to the door. "I'll get you past Lester. He's all riled up right now, but he won't hurt me. "

Shyly she held out her other hand. Helen took it in her own, the wrap of small sticky warmth fighting back the horror of the room behind them.

Twenty-Seven

Mad Lester was indeed riled up. Helen watched through the bars of his cell door as the wild-haired, dirt-encrusted young man paced back and forth, the chain attached to his thin ankle slithering and chinking along the dirt floor. He punched the air around him, both hands balled into fists. One eye was swollen half shut, the other wide and darting to all corners of his gloomy enclosure. Helen pressed her hand to her nose. Wafts of foul air—rancid meat and excrement—exuded from the shed, stirred up by the poor creature's frantic perambulations and intensified by the warmth of the night.

Sprat lifted her lamp and stood on her tiptoes to see through the bars. She clicked her tongue. "Glimflashy, ain't he?"

Helen searched her cant. *Glimflashy*: angry.

"Always gets this way when his uncle goes in there. Looks like the blasted louse hit 'im in the face again."

For a moment Helen did not know whom Sprat meant, then realized Lester's uncle was Lowry. Or had been Lowry.

"Where is the book, Sprat?"

"In that box o'er there," she said, waving the lamp toward the chest pushed up against the far wall. "Hey, Lester," she called, her voice lilting into a gentle singsong. "It's all right. Go sit yerself down." She held up the hunk of bread she had filched on their way through the dark, deserted kitchen. "Got this for ya."

Lester kept pacing and punching, his breath wheezing gasps.

Helen looked back at the bawdy house. The shutters of the two bedchambers above the kitchen were still open, the soft light from within reaching out across the yard and bringing a ghostly glow to the hanging laundry. Shadows flickered across the slice of wall visible through one window. The room was occupied. Someone could look out at any moment and see them.

Sprat dropped back onto her heels and glanced up at the windows that still held Helen's attention. "It's all right, my lady. No one will go near Lowry's bolt-hole—we was all told to stay away. He won't be found for hours, so no one's gunna be lookin' for yer." She gave a reassuring grin. "'Sides, no one'll be able to see us when we're inside wiv Lester. It's where I hide all the time."

"Let us go in, then," Helen said. "Out of sight."

"You keep behind me, my lady. I knows you could kill 'im with one hand, but he's all bovvered, and he might try you. I'll get 'im to sit down and be real quiet. He always listens to me."

Helen lifted the heavy metal bar that secured the cell door and swung it around upon its hinge, the iron grinding into a soft screech. She held her breath, but no one came to the windows. Lester, however, stopped pacing.

Sprat held out the lamp. "You take this, my lady. He don't like light. Keep to that side"—she gestured to the left—"and move real slow."

Helen hooked her fingers around the tin handle on the side of the lamp, the metal still warm from Sprat's grip. The candle within was little more than a stump, the flame close to its end.

Sprat stepped into the dark, stinking cell. "Lookee, Lester. I got some bread."

Helen followed, shielding the light from the panting young man.

Sprat inched closer, holding out the bread. "You gotta sit down if you want it."

Slowly Helen sidestepped to the chest, the lamp casting long shadows of Sprat and Lester upon the back wall. The chain clinked.

Helen stopped, muscles tensing, ready to pull the girl out of harm's way. "Be careful!"

"Don't worry, my lady. Me an' Lester is good friends. I do this all the time," Sprat said as Lester sank down onto his haunches. "There you go." She passed him a piece broken off the bread.

Helen crouched beside the chest. Made of cheap wood and no lock. Apparently a madman was guard enough. She placed the lamp on the floor and, with a formless prayer made of hope and need, lifted the lid. The lamplight caught flashes of silver poking out from dirty calico wrappings—a spout and the dome of a sugar shaker. Someone's treasures. Or more likely, their haul. But where was the journal?

She shifted the wrapped teapot, and a gilt candlestick below it. Ah, something encased in leather, slotted between the wrapped flat shape of a tray and the side of the chest. She slid her fingers down the narrow space, hooked them around a leather thong, and pulled out a book. No larger than her own hand and bound in stained green leather.

"I've got it," she said.

Sprat looked over her shoulder again. "Are yer sure, my lady? Yer don't wanna nab the wrong thing."

Good point, Helen thought. She had never actually seen the journal, only the post bag that Lowry had carried it in. She had to check. There was time—no one knew they were in the cell—and if it was the journal then she could rip out the precious pages about the Comte. *Please let them be there,* she prayed. She untied the thong and opened the book, turning the front page to the lamplight. The scrawled words were written in a pale rusty ink.

Even as she thought *blood*, a deep, roiling nausea hit her, like one of Martha Gunn's waves, slamming her onto her knees and hunching her around a hard retch.

"My lady!"

She forced her head up.

"What's wrong?" Sprat was slowly backing away from Lester. Coming to her aid.

"Do not come any nearer," Helen gasped. "It is alchemy."

Now she remembered. In the Lewes tavern, Lowry had told her that reading the journal had made him puke. But this was way beyond mere sickness. She felt as if her innards were being ripped from their moorings.

Sprat stopped her slow creep. "Alchemy? Ain't that magic?"

"In a way. It is written with murdered people's blood." And, if Lowry had been telling the truth, the blood of Deceivers. "It is making me sick."

"Dead'uns' blood?" Sprat gave a sniff of disgust. "I'd reckon so."

Helen slowly straightened. It did not matter if she vomited out her internals; she must find the information about the Comte. She drew a shaking breath and, squinting through the mounting pain, turned the pages. Each had a title at the top: a person's name or a notation like *Rumor* or *Myth*. Benchley had method in his madness. Although one page seemed to indicate nothing more than madness: it was entirely filled with the legend *GD2*, over and over again. Was it someone's initials?

Her stomach heaved again, sour bile burning her throat. She would have to be quicker. She flipped more pages. The names were written clearly, but the rusty scrawl below them was in some kind of code. Initials and abbreviations and . . .

She retched, again and again, the spasms deep and unforgiving. Her heartbeat thundered from the strain, the power of the blood alchemy scritch-scratching in her mind like a nest of rats.

She heard the chain shift and rattle.

"It's all right, Lester," Sprat sang. "It's all right." She looked over her shoulder. "You all right, my lady?"

Helen nodded and wiped her mouth, her chest and diaphragm aching. Maybe she was flipping too fast through the pages. She slowly turned the next page: *Hallifax.* Another: *Dempsey.* She felt a sudden heaving lurch, her vision blurring from the violence of the convulsion. One more: *Pike.*

She blinked, clearing the blur from her eyes. Holy star! Benchley had written about Pike. She had to read that entry, whatever it cost. Taking a deep, stomach-steadying breath, she held the pale writing up to the lamp again.

> *12 March 1807. Messenger came 7 of evening: I. Pike killed Sir D in botched reclaim. Fool desperate to cover up. Obliged. Told him one day I would call in the vowels.*

As she finished reading the last word, the spasms slammed through her body, the journal falling from her grasp. There was nothing left in her guts to bring up. Every wrenching gasp was dry and deep, pushing her onto her hands and knees.

"My lady, stop readin' it!" Sprat pleaded. "I think it's doin' some-thin' bad to Lester, an' it's makin' me feel sick too."

"Not too much longer," Helen said. She slowly drew herself upright, back onto her knees, as stiff as an old woman.

Lester's one good eye was fixed upon the journal, his thin body rocking, fingers shredding the bread into tiny crumbs. Sprat was right: the book clearly disturbed him, too. It seemed the blood alchemy affected everybody, but especially any kind of Reclaimer or Deceiver energy, be it Lester's vestige or Lowry's fading Terrene power. And for a full Reclaimer like herself, it was like poison.

She shook her head, trying to bring what she had read about Pike back into focus. He had killed his own Reclaimer and enlisted Benchley to help hide the fact. No wonder he had been desperate to find the journal: he knew Benchley would have recorded such a damning piece of information. Even so, Benchley had written a *botched* reclaim. Surely that meant it had been an accident. Why did Pike feel compelled to hide it? He had clearly placed himself at Benchley's mercy by doing so: the phrase *the vowels* meant IOU. Without a doubt, Benchley would have called in that debt many times over.

Helen gasped: the Ratcliffe Highway murders. Benchley must have forced Pike to hide his crime. Did Pike realize the man had been collecting blood for this very journal? For a *Ligatus*? Helen allowed herself a grim smile. All along, Pike had been accusing Lord Carlston of helping Benchley make this godforsaken book, when in fact it had been himself.

The journal lay on the filthy floor, still open at the entry for Pike. In there somewhere must be a page for the Comte d'Antraigues. For her parents, too. But she could only look in the journal once again; she did not have the strength for more than that. It had to be the Comte. Bracing herself, she picked up the heinous book and flipped the pages, feeling the impending violence build in her body. She passed *Stokes, Ball,* and then . . . *Comte d'Antraigues*. She gave a hoarse, sobbing laugh. It was there; the information was there. The Comte would have his bargain, and Carlston would have his cure. She dared not read it. Instead she ran her finger down the roughly sewn binding; the page should come out easily enough.

She gripped the paper close to the spine and tugged. It did not tear. Rather, the page was strangely immovable, and every drag upon it sent a sickening stab through her body as if she were ripping at her own innards. She doubled over, vomiting bright red blood, gasping with pain.

She tried again, wrenching at the paper, agony building through bone and flesh as she pulled. Understanding finally penetrated the heaving pain: the book was protected by its alchemy, irrevocably bound together, the pages never to be torn from the spine. She would come apart before it did. Her body convulsed, expelling more blood, the tears that streamed from her eyes not only from the pain of the grinding retches that rocked her body. *No bargain. No cure.* The pages could not be pulled from the journal, and she could not give the whole journal—a *Ligatus*—to a Deceiver.

Distantly, she heard Lester's chain chinking, Sprat talking, but her vision was gray, her body under siege, unable to do anything other than ride the pain through to its end.

She came to herself lying flat on the floor, panting, the closed journal a few feet away.

"My lady," Sprat whispered, "Lester ain't takin' notice of me no more."

Slowly Helen looked up. The madman was rocking to and fro on his haunches, all of his attention fixed on the journal between them. His lips curled back in a wet, yellowed snarl. He looked up at Helen. She saw the intent lock in his eye a second before he leaped.

She sprang, hearing Lester's chain snap tight and Sprat's yelp as he lunged. Filthy hands groped for the book, Lester's swollen face a blur of scream and spittle an inch from her own. He slammed into her side and they rolled, arms and legs and chain entangled, the book sliding from the madman's desperate grasp.

Helen snatched up the journal, the scratching energy surging through her mind as her hand closed around the soft green leather binding. Lester's clawed fingers clamped over her own, their hands locked around the journal. He screamed, a deafening, rancid-meat screech in Helen's ear. A sickly yellow light enveloped him, his flesh-and-bone body a shadow shape beneath it.

Helen gasped. The alchemy had conjured Lester's sick soul. She had seen this kind of bilious light before, around the boy reclaimed in London. But that had been through a ritual; this power was coming from the journal. She could feel the loathsome energy stirring within it, using her as a pathway to reclaim the vestige in Lester. It howled and chattered against her mind as if called by the oily, dark nugget of Deceiver energy rooted deep within the light that surrounded Lester's crown. Thick trailing tentacles writhed tightly through the glow of his soul, choking and warping him into madness.

Helen's pulse pounded in her ears, every throb of heart and blood aligning Lester's beat with her own. She pushed against his rigid body atop her, trying to throw his weight off, but it was as if they had been fused together. The howling grew louder in her head, built of blood and death, Deceiver and Reclaimer, innocence and murder. A dank metallic taste flooded her tongue, and then the blood power rose: a roaring, blinding, searing light that swept from the journal through her and over Lester. A ravening force, boiling across his soul, consuming the dark mass of the vestige and its obscene tentacles, claiming the foul dark energy.

The power slammed back through Helen, back into the journal, ripping at her screaming soul, her mind loosening beneath the gibbering madness caught within it. She could feel the journal's darkness clawing at her own sanity, dragging her into the howling blood and suffering of its pale, rusty ink.

⌒

SPRAT'S FACE ABOVE. Cracked lips. Watery blue eyes, all the whites showing. "My lady?" A hand on her arm, shaking it gently.

In her mind, she formed the words *Do not worry, Sprat*, but nothing happened. Her mouth did not open, the sounds did not issue. She felt a moment of distant concern at the failure.

Another face leaned over. A man. Wild black hair, swollen eye bruised blue. She groped for a name. Ah, Lester.

"What's wrong wiv 'er?" he said. "Why don't she move? Why is she starin' like that?"

"Don't know." A warm hand touched her cheek. "My lady, say somethin'." Sprat's face leaned closer. "You fixed Lester." She tapped her finger against her temple. "Got all his marbles. Just like that!"

Too much effort to listen. Easier to sink into the soft silence.

⌒

THREE FACES. BLURRED.

"What's that she's holding? A book?"

A woman, face too close. Thick black hair. Cleft chin. The name arrived, dragged from a distant place. Kate Holt.

"You don't wanna go anywhere near that." Sprat's voice again, heavy with warning. "She said it's made of blood. Murdered coves."

Yes, she could still feel it, the scritch-scratch in her mind. The metal taste upon her tongue.

"Is that what she killed my brother for?"

"She saved Lester with it. I calls that square, don't you?"

"Watch yourself, girl." A sniff. Shrewd green eyes looking into her own. "I'm not complaining about the bargain. Still, she looks mighty morbid. If she's going to die, I don't want her doing it here."

"She ain't gunna die." Sprat leaning over her again, all frown and ferocity. "We gotta get her back to her people."

"Ma, she's right." Lester coming into focus, thin hand gripping Kate Holt's shoulder. "Gotta do somethin' for 'er. You don't know what it was like. I was in the dark with this chatterin' in my head and no hope."

"I saw what it did, love." Kate's hand over his, patting away the memory. "Sprat, you know where she comes from?"

"Surely do."

"Get Big Tom to put her into a hackney. Make sure she gets there."

Get where? She tried to hold on to the question. It was important. But the balm of dark silence was calling her back.

THE SMELL OF horse and old sweat. Hands, big and efficient, rolling her onto a hard seat. Cold, cracked leather beneath her cheek. Her hat, upside down on the scuffed wooden floor, amongst the straw and dirt.

"We're goin' to Twenty German Place," Sprat's voice said. "Hop to it."

"How you gunna pay?" a man's voice demanded, rough and suspicious. "How you gunna get the cove out t'other end now Big Tom's gone?"

"I got the ready—look. An' you make no mind of t'other end. This 'ere cove's quality. He's got servants."

German Place? There was something about that address that she should remember.

The world rocked, a slam of a door and a clip-clopping lurch that rolled her back against the seat. Lamps flashed past a rattling window, the yellow light sliding across a pair of small dirty hands holding her arm.

Sprat's face loomed over hers again, crooked teeth showing in a reassuring smile. "Won't be long, my lady."

She had something important to say. What was it? But the

rocking motion beneath her body soothed the sense of urgency, drawing her once again into the gentle, healing darkness.

——

A THICK FINGERTIP pulled back her eyelid, the white ceiling and chandelier above her blurring into a smear of light. Worried brown eyes edged with a swirling tattoo peered intently into her fixed gaze. Quinn. Where had he come from?

"She's in a Reclaimer fugue. It doesn't look deep. I would say she'll come out of it in an hour or two."

Fugue? But she had something to say. Something important. Something about . . . She could not grip on to the words that drifted through her mind.

"There don't seem to be any physical injuries." Darby. Voice thin and tight. "She's holding something, but I can't shift her fingers."

"It's a book," Sprat's voice announced. "She called it a jer-nell."

"Journal?" Carlston's voice, urgent.

Now she remembered. *Must not go back to German Place.*

Too late. Carlston's face hovered over her, a half-healed split across his cheekbone, mouth still bruised. She'd done that. *Amore mio.* She saw his hand reach toward the book.

Do not touch it! She screamed the words, but they were caught in her mind. No sound.

A blur, then Quinn's fingers locked around his master's wrist. "You must not get too close to Lady Helen, my lord. Let me get it."

Carlston's hand balled into a fist. "Of course." He jerked his wrist out of Quinn's grip. Eyes pained, space between his brows furrowing. "Sprat, that's your name, is it? Tell me exactly what happened."

She saw Quinn's head bend to his task. Felt her forefinger

prised from the book. She tried to fix her scream into her eyes. *No! Quinn, do not let him touch it!*

"Like I said afore, my lord. She killed Mrs. Holt's bruvver and saved Lester. He was touched in the head, real bad, but now he's not. Just like that. It's all 'cause of that book. She says it's writ in blood. Made her real sick."

"Blood?" Carlston leaned over again and she saw the realization dawn in his eyes, their black centers flaring with horror. "Get it off her, Quinn. Now! Benchley made a *Ligatus!*"

She felt the journal wrenched from her hands. The terrible weight of it shifted from her mind, the sudden ease like a sigh through her soul that pulled her inexorably away from Carlston and into the quiet grip of oblivion.

Twenty-Eight

Wednesday, 22 July 1812

HELEN SURFACED THROUGH layers of heavy languor that dragged at her consciousness. The white ceiling blurred into focus again as she fought to form one sentence through her parched, aching throat.

"Do not touch it!"

The words grated across her throat in a raw sting. She struggled upward, elbows sinking back against the give of damask cushions. She was on the sofa in the German Place drawing room: How did she get there? In the candlelight, the clock on the mantel showed that it was just past midnight, but the shutters on the windows had been left open. They framed Delia, clad in her blue pelisse, as she peered pensively down into the dark street.

"My lady!"

Beside her, Darby straightened from a tired hunch on the ottoman pulled untidily next to the sofa. She touched Helen's arm as if checking the sudden animation.

Delia turned from the window. "Helen! Thank goodness you are awake."

A small face bobbed up beside the ottoman. Sprat smiled. "See, I told you she'd be spruce."

Darby cast a quelling frown at the girl, then addressed Helen, her face softening with relief. "How are you feeling, my lady? Let me help sit you up."

She rose and wrapped her arm around Helen's shoulder, pulling her up against pillows and cushions, her broad body a warm anchor in the sudden dizzy swirl of the room.

Delia crossed from the window. She was wearing gloves as well: dressed for travel. "Mr. Quinn assured us you would emerge from your fugue soon, but I was so worried. You did not move at all."

"We were all worried," the Duke said, coming into view. He was not wearing his jacket, and his linen shirt and green waistcoat were creased, his blond hair raked back and lost to all style. He was smiling his relief too, but underneath, Helen saw an ominous solemnity.

Now she remembered: stealing away from his house, Lowry, the journal, Sprat. She closed her eyes. Of course, Sprat had brought her here by mistake. Straight to Carlston.

She opened her eyes, noticing damage around the room. Broken vases, a wall mirror cracked, a hole punched into the wall, pieces of plaster hanging from it.

"Where is Lord Carlston?"

The Duke's face pinched, nostrils flaring, piqued that her first question was about Carlston. Right now she did not have time for his sensibilities. Not with the *Ligatus* anywhere near Carlston.

She caught her maid's hands. "Where is the journal?"

Darby looked up at the Duke, deferring to his rank, her soft mouth pressed into a worried line.

"Carlston is on his way to London with the book," the Duke said, crossing his arms. "That journal, or whatever it is, did something to him. As soon as he opened it"—he waved his hand at the side of his head—"he nearly destroyed the place. Screaming about the Comte d'Antraigues and a cure."

Helen shuddered, remembering the chittering, howling presence

412 — Alison Goodman

of the journal in her mind. It must have wreaked havoc upon Carlston's fragile sanity.

"He was just like Lester, my lady," Sprat said. "All snarly an' sick an' jibbery."

"Quinn, too, my lady," Darby said. "He tried to read the book, but it made him purge over and over again. Said it was like having claws in his mind. In the end, Lady Margaret managed to look through it. She wasn't so sick with it. She found what his lordship wanted, but he couldn't tear it from the book. Just made him sicker and sicker."

"Yes, it would."

Helen released her grip on Darby and dug her hands into the soft seat, pulling herself upright. The room shifted again into a nauseating spin. She took a steadying breath, waiting for the dizziness to pass. She had to get up and follow the journal and Carlston.

"Mr. Hammond fears his lordship is going to offer the Comte d'Antraigues the whole journal," Delia said. "We—Mr. Hammond, Lady Margaret, and myself—are set on following him to the Comte's house in Barnes Terrace. Mr. Hammond is readying the carriage at this minute."

Of course Hammond and Lady Margaret would follow him, but what could they hope to do?

"Why is Carlston taking it to d'Antraigues?" the Duke asked. "Isn't the man a French spy?"

"He is also a Deceiver," Helen said. "He has offered Lord Carlston a cure and information about the Grand Deceiver in return for information in the journal." She turned to Darby. "Did Quinn go with his lordship?"

"Of course, my lady."

At least he had his Terrene by his side.

"Mr. Quinn said if you were to wake in time, to bring help,"

Darby added. "He doesn't think he and you will be enough to stop his lordship this time."

Helen met her maid's solemn gaze and nodded, acknowledging the gravity of Quinn's admission. "How long ago did Lord Carlston leave?"

"At least half an hour," Delia said.

"I must leave now." Helen swung her legs off the sofa, gritting her teeth as the world swung, then settled.

"You can't go after him; you are not well enough," the Duke protested. "Besides, you won't have a chance of catching him in a carriage. Carlston is driving a curricle, and he has his own horses at the posting houses."

He was right: she needed a light equipage and good, fast horses. A plan was beginning to form—not ideal, but she could see no alternative.

"Am I right in thinking you also have your own horses stabled along one of the London roads, Your Grace?"

She knew he did: prime horseflesh, famously bred and matched for speed.

"On the Hickstead–Croydon Road," he said. His jaw shifted. "You will go after him come what may, won't you?"

"I must."

The Duke ran his fingers through his hair. "What is it about this journal that makes it so dangerous?"

"It is part of a heinous creation called a *Trinitas* that can open the gates to Hell," Helen said curtly, pressing her booted feet against the ground. Her legs seemed sound enough.

"Glory be," Sprat whispered. She shifted closer to Darby.

Helen looked up from the test of her legs. She should have sent Sprat from the room at the first mention of the Deceivers. Well, too late now.

"Are you serious?" the Duke demanded. "You mean *Hell*?"

Helen looked at him squarely; he needed to see the truth in her face. "If you call opening a way for more Deceivers to pour into our world a hell, then yes, Hell. A *Trinitas* can also be used to kill every Reclaimer across the world. Either way, it will bring death and chaos to humanity."

Delia crossed herself.

The Duke regarded her gravely. "My own curricle and teams are at your disposal, Lady Helen. With one proviso: I will drive them. I know my horses and how hard they can be pushed."

She stood. The room, thankfully, stayed still. "I did not want to drag you into this, but I will take the offer gladly."

She caught his arm and squeezed it in thanks. He froze for an instant, then flushed, the pleasure tucking his chin against his cravat.

The door opened and Hammond strode into the room, buttoning his greatcoat. "We are ready to go, Miss Cransdon." At the sight of Helen, the determination on his face softened into a smile. "You are recovered. Thank God!" His delight sobered. "You have heard what has happened?"

"I have." Helen crossed to him and gripped his shoulder. "How bad was he this time, Mr. Hammond?"

He lowered his voice. "The worst I have seen. I think the only thing that is holding him in any sort of sanity is the promise of d'Antraigues's cure."

"The Duke and I are going after him," Helen said.

"The Duke?" It was a protest.

"He has offered his horses and driving skill," she said under her breath. "It is my best chance to get there in time. Remember, the Comte is not the only Deceiver in that house. The valet is too. I am not sure Lord Carlston could defeat one in his current state, let alone two. And if they have the reserves to build whips . . ." She shook her head.

"Miss Cransdon says Carlston has at least a half hour start on us," the Duke said. "Is that correct?"

"More or less," Hammond said coldly.

"We shall take my teams of four. It will give us the best chance of reaching London at the same time as Carlston."

"You are going to drive four-in-hand at night?" Hammond pursed his lips in soundless appreciation. "You may even catch him before he gets to London."

The Duke looked at Helen. "I will send Jackson, my tiger, back to my stables with the order. We can be on the road in fifteen minutes."

"We cannot leave quite yet," she said. "I have to get help. Reclaimer help."

"What do you mean?" Hammond frowned, the answer clearly coming hard upon his question. "Stokes! Are you mad?" He spread his hands at the impossibility. "You cannot ask him for help. Pike has ordered him to kill Carlston."

The Duke straightened. "What?"

Hammond groaned, realizing his mistake.

"Pike considers Lord Carlston irretrievably mad and has requested a warrant for his execution," Helen said, unable to keep the challenge from her voice. She regarded the Duke through narrowed eyes. Would he make the mistake of showing accord with that decision?

The Duke merely nodded.

She addressed Hammond. "Pike's dispatch was only sent yesterday. The warrant cannot have been issued yet. Besides, Stokes told me to go to him if I ever needed help."

"It is a fine line you are treading," Hammond said. "Are you sure Stokes will tread it too?"

Helen had to concede her doubt. Even so, she had been treading a fine line ever since Pike had set them on the path of finding the journal. Perhaps ever since she had met Lord Carlston.

"I am not sure of anything except that Stokes is a man of honor and I cannot stop Lord Carlston by myself."

Hammond hissed an expletive through his teeth. "Do you even know where the man lives?"

She nodded; she at least knew that.

THE BRISK MOTION of the Duke's gig down Marine Parade cleared the last echoes of the journal from Helen's body. It was just past one thirty in the morning, the moon high and brilliant, capping the waves on the beach with silver and lighting the road and town houses in bright relief. The Duke had already sent his man Jackson to ready the racing curricle for the drive to London. Now all Helen had to do was find Stokes and persuade him to come with them.

They rounded the corner onto the Steine. The large green held only a few pedestrians upon its paths, and the windows of Donaldson's Library were dark. The evening concert had finished, its subscribers long gone. Most of the night's remaining activity clustered further up North Parade, around Raggett's Club and the front entrance of the Castle Tavern.

Helen tapped her fingers against her knee, trying to contain the urgency that clamored in her blood. Hammond, Lady Margaret, Darby, and Delia had already left for London on the Hickstead Road with the Duke's advice to turn at Streatham. Sprat—sworn to silence—was in the care of Garner and Mrs. Kent for the remainder of the night. Helen gave a slight shake of her head: something would have to be done about Sprat. She could not stay in that bawdy house. Although, Helen conceded, what could be done for her entirely depended upon the night ahead.

The plan—if indeed such a loose series of possibilities could be given such a grand name—was to secure Stokes's assistance, exchange the Duke's gig for his curricle, intercept Carlston, and retrieve the journal. It was at the intercept mark that the plan became hazy. Had the journal's blood-soaked energy pushed Carlston beyond saving? It did not seem fair that the foul thing would save Lester but only increase the madness of Lord Carlston. But then, Lester was an offspring, whereas Lord Carlston was a Reclaimer. It clearly had a disastrous effect upon Reclaimer energy. His lordship had erupted into violence again at its touch; and at Holt's she had felt its chittering evil drag her toward dark insanity. It was not the same power that had ripped Lowry apart—that had come from the Deceiver energy she had somehow stored within herself. No, the journal was something entirely different.

The thought brought another wave of urgency. One thing was certain: the journal had to be destroyed. Such a foul and danger- ous thing could not be allowed to exist. Nor could it be allowed to fall into the hands of the Deceivers. Yet destroying it would also destroy the valuable information within it, including the details about her parents that she had not had the strength to find in Lester's cell.

Ahead, a stream of fashionables were departing the weekly Assembly ball at the Castle Tavern, the streetlamps catching flashes of white muslin, high shirt points, and pale tired faces.

"Not much of a crowd tonight. We should be able to cut through Pavilion Parade to Church Street without too much trouble," the Duke commented as he steadied the gray's trot along the Parade. Even so, they were still progressing fast enough that Helen had to hold on to the brim of her beaver hat. "I believe a good wedge of our fine Brighton society has gone to a masquerade ball out of town."

Helen recalled Pug's excitement at the promenade. "Yes, you are right: the Olivers' ball." She laughed; it came out dry and hard. "I cannot conceive of dancing at a ball ever again."

The Duke flicked the whip above the gray's head, prompting a new spurt of speed. "Do not say that. If you give up on dancing, then you give up on joy."

"Dancing is not the only joy."

"True, but it combines two of the most divine favors of human-kind: music and elegant women."

She glanced at his profile, keenly aware of the absurdity of discussing the glories of dance on their way to a battle with unearthly creatures. "You do not truly understand what is coming, do you?"

He turned his head, the lamps along North Parade catching the quirk of his mouth. "Perhaps not. Pike only gave me a brief history of the Deceivers and the Dark Days Club. Tell me, what are we really following to London? Is Pike right: Is Carlston irretrievable?"

Helen could not quite hold his eye. "I do not believe so."

"Is that based on knowledge or hope?" It was said gently, but with the implacability that she had heard before in his voice.

"It does not matter," she said, hands pressed upon her thighs as if the braced position could somehow protect her from the question. "They have the same outcome. I will do everything I can to save him."

"What if you cannot save him?"

The answer to that was not made of words, but of pain, lodged in her heart and ready to open into spikes if she let her mind dwell upon the possibility. Best to focus upon what she could do: find him, contain him, and, after all that, leave him before she hurt him further.

The gray climbed the Church Street hill at a quick trot, the mill of carriages around the Marlborough Row corner quickly left behind. The majority of the houses and buildings were dark, with only a few still with shutters rimmed by light. Most of the locals had found their beds by now.

"His lodging house is at number Twelve, just past Brooks Chapel," Helen said, peering into the gloom. She saw a cross silhouetted against the sky and pointed. "There."

The Duke drew the gray to a stop. "Do you wish me to come with you?"

"It is not necessary, thank you."

Helen fitted the toe of her boot onto the round brass foothold and swung down to the ground. She did not quite know what she was going to say to Stokes, but whatever it was, she did not want the Duke privy to it.

Number 12 was a plain-faced redbrick dwelling with two shuttered windows on the ground floor, two above, and a door that led directly onto the road. She looked for a knocker of some kind, but the door was as plain as the building. She balled her fist and hammered on the wood. The door rattled against its hinges and lock, the thuds booming in the slumbering silence.

There was no answer to her summons. She listened, finally finding a wheezing breath and a murmured, "What the devil?"

She hammered again.

Footsteps on the first floor, crossing a creaking wooden floor. The sound of a metal shaft sliding back. Helen pushed back her hat brim and looked up. One of the first-floor shutters opened, the window pushed out with a grating judder.

"What?" a congested voice demanded. A woman in a white cap, mid-aged, with the squinting frown of someone woken from a deep sleep, looked down, her nightgown covered by a red shawl bunched at her throat in a suspicious grip.

"I am looking for Mr. Stokes," Helen called.

"You got a nerve at this hour, young man," the woman said. "Thumping on decent folks' doors in the middle of the night."

"I do apologize. Is he there by chance?"

"He paid up his reckoning and left a few hours ago. Got me out of bed to do it too."

Stokes had left his lodging?

"Did he say where he was going?"

"If it'll make you go away, I'm to send his box to a place on Edward Street." She gave a wet, phlegmy laugh. "Moving up in the world, ain't he?"

"Edward Street?" Helen repeated. Pike had a house on Edward Street.

"Didn't I just say that? Saints preserve me from foxed fools." She withdrew her head and closed the window, the glass shivering from the force.

Helen stood at the door, marooned for a moment in the unexpectedness of Stokes's departure. Why would he go to Pike's house after midnight? Had the warrant come already? It did not seem likely—the timing was physically impossible.

Another thought lifted her head. Had Pike decided to take matters into his own hands without a warrant? Now, that was far too likely. But surely he would not know that Carlston had gone to London?

She ran to the gig, found the brass foothold, and climbed into the seat. "Edward Street," she said. "Pike's house, quick." She gripped the handhold, realizing the flaw in her plan. "Lud, I do not know the number."

"I do," the Duke said. He clicked his tongue, urging the gray into a wide turn. "If you recall, I paid him a visit after Union Street. After I saw you fight that creature so valiantly."

Helen sent him a sidelong glance. He smiled, although he did not take his eyes from the road. He knew he was being very useful. And very charming.

Apart from a dog-leg curve around Parade Green and the

Pavilion, it was almost a straight line from Stokes's former lodgings to Pike's house. The Duke barely slowed the gray from its canter across the town, drawing up to the small, neat house near the end of Edward Street in less than ten minutes. The dark windows were shuttered, only a night lamp lit above the stout front door.

Helen swung herself to the ground and regarded the ordinary scene with a growing sense of bafflement. But what had she expected? Candles ablaze as Pike and Stokes plotted Carlston's demise?

"Allow me to accompany you," the Duke said. "Pike is a difficult man, but he has already discovered he cannot disregard my rank."

Helen inclined her head, although she was not sure she was in charge of the choice.

This time there was a knocker on the front door: a well-buffed brass piece in the shape of a fish. Helen rapped its tail against the back-plate, the sharp rat-a-tat-tat loud enough to wake those on the Steine.

She focused her hearing. Movement down in the basement and up on the first floor. Footsteps climbing steps and a sigh—young and very tired.

"Someone is coming," she told the Duke. "A maid."

"You can hear her?" Half of his face was lit by the lamp, the quizzical furrow of his brow giving him a rather saturnine expression.

She nodded, resisting the urge to list what the girl was wearing—flannel nightgown and felt slippers. That would be coming very close to vulgar display.

The door opened. A little face, slightly sleep-swollen, with thick plaits of brown hair, peered out, candle in hand. Blue flannel nightgown, Helen noted, with an ugly peach shawl hastily crossed over a thin bosom and tied at the waist.

"Yes, sir?" she whispered, bobbing into a curtsy.

"Is Mr. Stokes here?" Helen asked.

"No, sir." The girl's eyes flicked up to the Duke, recognition coming with a blush. "Oh, Your Grace." She curtsied again.

"Is your master at home?" the Duke asked.

"No, Your Grace. Only my mistress. She's abed. She's not well."

"Wake her," Helen said.

Both the Duke and the maid stared at her, taken aback by the abrupt and unseemly demand.

The Duke recovered first. "Well, girl, do as you are told."

The maid curtsied. An order seconded by a Duke was an order to be obeyed. She ushered them inside a small foyer, her candle stub lighting a thin staircase leading up into darkness and a long hall, the walls of which held no adornment except a narrow table with a white porcelain tray upon it for visiting cards. Helen drew in a lingering scent of decay: Mrs. Pike's disease, ingrained upon wood and stone.

Closing the door, the maid led the way into a small parlor room, the air still warm from the banked fire in the iron grate. Two heavy armchairs were positioned before the glowing embers, and a small worktable held a folded bedsheet that was in the process of being hemmed. The maid deftly lit three half-used candles on a sideboard with her own stub, their light bringing the rest of the room into gloomy definition: a small glass-fronted bookshelf, a larger table with four chairs, and a handsome workbox set upon turned wooden legs.

"May I take your hat, Your Grace," she asked, bobbing again. "And yours, sir?"

They handed over their headwear. The girl curtsied once more and, with hats and candle in hand, left to inform her mistress of her visitors.

The Duke walked across to the bookshelf and squinted at the spines. "The Pikes have a penchant for Scott."

Does not everyone, Helen thought. She studied the workbox, wrinkling her nose at the stronger smell of putrefaction. A folded piece of embroidery showed Mrs. Pike to be a fine needlewoman. A familiar color of cardboard caught her eye. She leaned closer and smiled. Mrs. Pike was also fond of Gunter's jellies. Did Pike buy them for her? It was strange to think of him buying gifts for his wife and living in this sparse, homely space. Somehow it made him seem less vile.

She glanced across at the Duke. He had his hand over his mouth.

"Can you smell it too?" she asked.

He looked up from his scrutiny of the books. "Smell what?"

The creak of a stair turned both of them toward the door. Mrs. Pike had rallied well under the circumstances. She wore a sweeping white house gown tied loosely over her yellow nightgown, both covered by a large green Norwich silk shawl. Her hair had been hastily bundled beneath a white pleated cap, and she held up a night candle in a tin holder, the soft light dragging at the corners of her mouth and deepening the lines upon her brow. She was clearly bemused by the lateness of their call, but still had the air of quiet dignity that Helen had seen in the Dunwicks' supper room.

"Your Grace," she said, walking sedately into the room and curtsying. She turned a polite face toward Helen.

"Allow me to introduce Mr. Amberley," the Duke said.

Helen bowed, her breath held. Would Mrs. Pike recognize her as the lady she had met at the rout?

Apparently not. She curtsied and turned back to the Duke. "How may I help you, Your Grace?"

Helen cleared her throat, forcing herself not to show revulsion at the smell of rancid meat. "I apologize for the intrusion, Mrs. Pike. It is a matter of utmost urgency." She coughed again, trying to draw breath past the dank, overwhelming smell. The poor woman's disease was clearly progressing if the stink was anything to go by. It was almost as strong as the foul odor in Lester's cell. "We wish to know whether Mr. Stokes has been—"

Helen stopped, the unexpected connection between Lester and Mrs. Pike exploding into a sudden violent understanding that rocked her upon her feet. The rancid smell was not disease. It was the smell of an Unreclaimable. Sweet heaven above, Mrs. Pike was an Unreclaimable Deceiver offspring.

"Is something wrong, Mr. Amberley?" she asked.

Helen turned away, another realization buffeting her like a physical blow. All she could see in her mind was that pale rusty name in Benchley's journal: *I. Pike*. Not Ignatious Pike, as she had assumed, but Isabella Pike. The woman standing before her had killed Sir Dennis Calloway, the Reclaimer that her husband had served. It all made terrible sense: why Pike hated Carlston and was so desperate to find the journal. Sir Dennis had asked Carlston for help to reclaim a madwoman, and he had refused. In fact, Carlston had told Sir Dennis to put the woman out of her misery.

Helen pressed her hand against her forehead, as if she could slow the rush of cause and effect. In Pike's eyes, Carlston had refused to save his beloved wife and by doing so had caused the death of Sir Dennis and the loss of his Terrene power. He had been forced to seek Benchley's help and been placed in a madman's debt. A madman who had recorded the affair in his journal.

Did Mrs. Pike know?

She whirled around to the woman again. "Tell me, do you remember a gentleman by the name of Sir Dennis Calloway?"

Isabella Pike frowned in bewilderment. "Of course. He was an acquaintance of my husband. A government man as well. He died tragically, I believe."

"Yes, he did," Helen said. There was no sign of dissembling in the woman's exhausted face. "Mrs. Pike, forgive the personal nature of this next question, but do you suffer from times when you have no recollection of events?"

Mrs. Pike ran her tongue over her cracked lips. "I do. In fact, I have for many years. They cause my dear husband much anxiety. He is always searching for a cure. But how would you know that, sir? Are you a physician?"

Poor woman. She did not know that in those missing hours she was a violent, murderous creature. Helen could almost pity Pike, too: caught between his love for his offspring wife and his duty to the Dark Days Club. For years, living in a perpetual state of agony, knowing that discovery would mean the destruction of Isabella and his own ruin.

Even so, his actions had brought them all to this sorry state.

"I am also with the government, Mrs. Pike. Can you tell me the whereabouts of your husband?"

"He is gone to London, Mr. Amberley."

"When did he leave? Is he with Mr. Stokes? What prompted his departure?"

She drew back a little at the barrage of questions. "I am not sure I wish to be interrogated in such a manner."

The Duke smiled. "Be easy, madam. We are friends of your husband. I can assure you the information is of the utmost importance."

She pressed her lips together, the quandary decided with a small sigh. "He received a note just after midnight and was gone almost immediately. I am not certain, but I think he intended to collect Mr. Stokes on his way."

Perhaps it was a coincidence that Pike had left hurriedly for London, but Helen doubted it. She would wager that someone had informed him of Carlston's departure, and he and Stokes were following with violent intent. But who could have sent the information?

"Do you have the note?" Helen asked as the Duke crossed the room to stand by her side.

"No, I am afraid not. My husband burned it, as he does all such correspondence."

"Unfortunate," the Duke said. He glanced at Helen: *Time to go?* She nodded.

"Thank you, Mrs. Pike," he said. "We will show ourselves out."

"My husband is not in any danger, is he, Your Grace?" she asked.

The Duke smiled. "Of course not. You have my word upon it."

Mrs. Pike nodded; the word of a Duke must be the truth. Even Helen had to admit that, for a second, she almost believed it too.

Twenty-Nine

HELEN BRACED HER booted foot against the front dash of the Duke's racing curricle and leaned into its shift as they rounded a curve in the moonlit road to London. She tightened her left hand on the edge of the curricle's folded-back hood, her right hand clamping down harder upon the top of her hat. It was in constant danger of being snatched off her head by the wind created by the speed the Duke was coaxing from his team. He'd had the foresight to remove his own hat and jam it in the footwell between them. He had obviously driven in such a breakneck manner before.

She had to admire his skill. He had both feet braced and the reins wrapped around his gloved hands, the jut of his long jaw showing the immense control it took to handle the four chestnuts in their headlong gallop. The heavy drum of hooves, grind of wheels, jangle of the harness, and the constant jolt and jar of the curricle on the poorly dressed road made conversation almost impossible. Not that Helen sought conversation; she did not want to disturb the Duke's fierce concentration. Besides, she had more than enough to think about over the remaining miles to London.

They had already passed Lady Margaret's coach near Albourne Green. Mr. Hammond had been on the box with the driver, leaning forward as if the angle of his body could somehow quicken their pace. He had raised his hand as they passed, urging the driver to whip up the horses, but the Duke's team had quickly left them behind.

Two small flickering wide-set glows appeared in the gloom ahead, the cold moonlight sliding across polished silver fittings. Another carriage. They had already passed three other vehicles since the turnpike at Hickstead. The last had been an elegant town coach on a blind corner, their two equipages almost scraping sides. The Duke had barely acknowledged the close call, merely uttering a low curse, then returning to their thundering progress. Helen, however, had peered back through the billowing rise of dust behind them. The heavier coach had pulled over and the driver was standing up on the box, his outraged shouts lost in the road noise.

"Warninglid turnpike coming up!" the Duke yelled, although he did not take his eyes from the road. "This team will last till Crawley. We'll change there."

The oncoming carriage must have seen their carriage lamps, for it was slowly veering to the right. By the silver fittings and large silhouette it was another town coach—there were quite an unusual number on the road. Helen pressed herself back into the seat as they careered toward it. This part of the road, at least, was straight and wide.

A milestone flashed by: thirty-six miles to London. Still so far to go.

The toll keeper at Hickstead had reported that, yes, Lord Carlston had passed and in a mighty hurry, but he had not seen anyone who resembled her description of Pike or Stokes. Presumably they had taken the Cuckfield road.

The driver of the oncoming coach had slowed his team to a walk, taking no chances. A feathered head poked out of the window to see what had happened. Helen saw an instant of a woman's astonished face, and then they were past.

The keeper of the Warninglid turnpike told the same story as his counterpart at Hickstead. "Aye, Lord Carlston's been through, sir," he said, squinting up at Helen's question. "Bit less than an hour back. Couldna missed 'im. His man—huge blackamoor with some kind of heathen drawings on his face—kept sayin' his name."

Quinn, making sure anyone coming after would know they had been through.

"How much less than an hour?" Helen demanded.

He sniffed, considering the march of time. "Not much less."

"What about two other men?" Helen asked as she handed down the toll fee. "Both tall and thin. One with blond curly hair."

"Nah, I ain't seen anyone like that." He flicked through the coins, then handed up the ticket. "This'll take you through Crawley, too, sir. Are you on some kind of race?"

"Yes," the Duke said. "Open the gate, man!"

By the time they reached Crawley, the sky had brightened into shades of dawn pink, and the horses were showing the strain of the sustained speed, their chestnut coats dulled to brown by sweat and road dirt. The Duke slowed them into a tired trot as they approached the Rising Sun Inn, its long, many-windowed frontage sporting a huge black-and-white sign across the top that proclaimed POSTING HOUSE AND LIVERY STABLES. A neat fence made of white posts linked by chains demarcated the front of the inn from the road. A town coach, empty of its passengers, stood waiting opposite the entrance of the inn, the driver and an old ostler inspecting the hoof of one of its team. They looked up at the clatter of the curricle's arrival, watching as the Duke maneuvered his team in behind the larger vehicle.

"Robbie," the ostler called over his shoulder, "His Grace, the Duke of Selburn. Four-in-hand!"

A younger ostler appeared from the archway that led to the stables. He jogged over to them, touching his hat. "Your Grace."

"The grays ready for a stretch, Robbie?" the Duke asked.

The boy grinned. "Champing, Your Grace."

The Duke glanced at Helen. "Order some refreshment for us if you will. We shall be here but a few minutes."

Helen placed her hat upon the seat and climbed down to the cobbles, arching her back and sighing with the stretch of cramped muscles. She watched as the Duke drove the curricle through the narrow archway, the older ostler also looking up from his work to watch the show of skill.

"I'll check the tack," the coach driver said. He gestured to the hoof. "You'll take care of this?"

"Aye," the ostler said, taking a file from his leather apron. "Won't take long."

The driver walked to the coach's two lead horses and inspected the harness.

The inn door opened, and a waiter approached. "Refreshment for the Duke and yourself, sir?" he asked. "Claret? Rum? Ale?"

Helen's mouth and throat were parched, and she was sure she had swallowed at least three insects. What she really craved was the tart slake of lemonade, but Mr. Amberley and the Duke of Selburn would hardly order such a mild beverage.

"Ale," she said.

The waiter bowed and hurried back across the cobbled yard to the inn.

Helen walked over to the older ostler. The man looked up from the hoof and dipped his gray head. "Sir."

"Cracked hoof, is it?"

"Aye, but not bad."

"A lot of coaches on the road," Helen commented. "Do you know Lord Carlston by sight?"

"Aye. Came through a while back driving his bays, all but blown. Looked like he had the devil on his back."

"What do you mean?"

"He usually has a kind word for me an' the boys, but not this time. He was wild, pacing up an' down. In a right state."

A worrying description.

At the corner of her eye she saw the Duke emerge through the archway. A loud chatter of voices, female, turned her head to the inn door. A waiter held it open as three women and a gentleman, all in evening dress, departed the inn and headed across the short distance to the coach. The familiar squarish figures of two of the women registered first, sending a sweep of foreboding across Helen's skin. Then she heard the loud voice of Pug Brompton declare, "The last team were absolute bone shakers. I hope this lot are better matched."

Helen felt her heart punch against her chest. Pug and her mother, on their way back from the Olivers' ball. Lord, if they recognized her . . . If she were found alone in the company of the Duke . . .

She searched wildly for an escape. The four coach horses prevented any retreat over the white post fence; the ostler, bent over the wheeler's hoof, blocked the path to the archway. Pug and her party were only a few steps away. She did not even have her hat to pull down low over her eyes. Her best chance was the archway.

She turned her face away from Pug and launched herself past the old ostler. The wheeler caught her sudden movement at the edge of its blinker and shied, wrenching its hoof from the man's grip. The ostler jumped back, straight into Helen's path as the horse heaved upward in the traces. Its back legs kicked out. One hoof slammed into the driver's box with a booming thud, the other clipped Helen's hip. She staggered, the horrified faces of Pug and her companions blurring as her hands and knees hit the cobbles, the impact jarring through her bones. More painful than the glancing kick. In reflex, she rolled away from the sound of squealing horses and the scraping shift of hooves.

"Helen!" the Duke yelled. She heard his running footsteps, felt him grab her under her arms, her body hauled backward away from the distressed team. "Are you hurt, Helen?"

The aching pain had already peaked and settled. She heard a loud, familiar female gasp of recognition. Oh no, Pug had heard her name. Her untitled name.

"Get me out of here!"

She wrapped her hand around the Duke's strong forearm, her urgency cutting through the shock in his face. He pulled her upright.

"For goodness' sakes, get another ostler to their heads," Lady Dunwick commanded as the driver and the old ostler ran to the lead horses to calm them.

All attention was upon the coach and team. A chance to slip away. She took a limping step, the Duke supporting her arm.

"Lady Helen?" Pug's voice.

Helen hunched her shoulders, but Pug was not one to give up. She circled in front of them, peering into Helen's face.

"That *is* you, isn't it? Why I didn't recognize you until—" She stared at the Duke, still with his hand supporting Helen's arm. "Your Grace." She bobbed into a curtsy, her gaze darting from Helen to the Duke and back again, the story complete in her face. "Holy heavens above, you are eloping, aren't you? How wonderful!"

Lady Dunwick whirled around from inspecting her vehicle, her protuberant eyes even wider than ever. "What did you say, Elizabeth?" She stared fiercely at Helen, the moment of identification arriving with a small gargle of horror. "Lady Helen!" Her gaze came to rest upon the Duke and his hold upon Helen's arm. She inclined her head, her voice thick with disapproval. "Your Grace."

"Are you hurt, Lady Helen?" Pug asked.

"No, not at all. It was my own fault."

"Oh, now I see—it is Lady Helen *Wrexhall*!" the other woman exclaimed, a thin, hawk-nosed woman wearing girlish curls and an expression of scandalized delight. She leaned closer to the rotund man at her side, presumably her husband, and said in a loud whisper, "Viscount Pennworth's niece." Her eyes raked over Helen. "Look, Albridge, you can see the whole length of her leg!"

The man, his thick lip curled in disdain, raised his quizzing glass. "Quite," he said.

"A jade, just like her mother," the woman added.

Helen closed her eyes. Now she recognized her. Mrs. Albridge, Lady Dunwick's best friend and one of the nastiest gossips in England. Everything that transpired in the next few minutes would be broadcast to the whole of Brighton by tomorrow and London by the next post.

She opened her eyes in time to see Lady Dunwick wave the woman back. "Be quiet, Amelia." She turned her stout indignation back to the Duke. "What is happening here, Your Grace? You are obviously traveling with Lady Helen. Are you indeed eloping with my daughter's friend?"

The Duke glanced at Helen, the moment between them stripped back to the awful realization that her future lay within his next words.

She curled her fingernails into her palms. Only she was in peril—a man's reputation did not turn upon the axle of purity. Yet only his answer had any bearing upon the course of her life. If he said no, she was utterly ruined—a wanton lost to all decent society. And if he said yes—and he was going to, for it was in the sweet, possessive smile dawning upon his face—they would be, for all intents and purposes, man and wife.

"Lady Helen and I are betrothed."

She released a shaking breath, finding her hands suddenly caught within Pug's excited hold.

"I knew it!" Pug squealed. "Oh my goodness!" She squeezed Helen's hands, then stepped back and swept a curtsy. "Your Grace! How well that sounds."

"No," Helen breathed.

Pug frowned. "What do you mean? Oh, I see!" She giggled. "Well, it will be Your Grace soon enough."

"But why are you traveling at night in such a hurried and illicit—" Lady Dunwick stopped, her jaw tensing. Apparently a reason had presented itself. She regarded the Duke with narrowed eyes. "I shall be writing to Lord and Lady Pennworth at the earliest opportunity tomorrow to congratulate them upon the betrothal of their niece," she said, steel in her voice.

"I am sure your congratulations will be received with pleasure," the Duke said. "Lady Helen, the horses have been changed. We are ready to go."

Yes, she had to get away—she could not bear Lady Dunwick's horrified stare, or Mrs. Albridge's malicious glee, or even worse, Pug's beaming smile of congratulations.

She thrust the tankard into the hand of the old ostler, then walked stiffly across the cobbled yard. She must concentrate upon the task at hand. With every minute passing, Lord Carlston and the journal were drawing further and further away from them. They must continue. She could feel a pain building in her chest and knew that it was made of two words. *Amore mio.*

"It is so romantic," she heard Pug say.

"Be quiet, Elizabeth," Lady Dunwick snapped.

HELEN STARED STRAIGHT ahead as they left the posting inn and turned right to take the road out of Crawley, the last pink remnants of dawn disappearing into the clear blue of the new day. She had not spoken since she had hobbled away from Pug and her companions and swung herself up into the curricle again. It was, perhaps, not fair upon the Duke to have stayed so silent—a thank-you, at the very least, should have been offered—but she could not even voice that simple courtesy. All words were gone, lost in overwhelming humiliation and the awful impossibility of the situation.

The Duke glanced across at her now and again, but made no comment as the shops and houses gave way to high-edged banks covered in dense tangles of hazel. He was keeping the fresh team to a smart trot, partly because the winding route out of Crawley hid the oncoming road, but mostly, Helen knew, to hear her response. She twisted her fingers together. She had too many responses, none of them coherent.

"I could not see any other way forward," he finally said.

She summoned her voice. "No."

"It was presumptuous, but that Albridge woman will have the whole affair across society by tomorrow evening."

"Yes."

"Will it be so bad?" he asked.

She heard the note of injury in his voice and could not ignore it.

"Your Grace—"

"Selburn now, I think," he said with a brief smile. "Or perhaps even Gerard."

She stared down at her hands, twisting her fingers tighter. The offer of his first name was too much. Too intimate. "Selburn, what you did was most gallant, but you know I am not a normal woman.

436 — Alison Goodman

I cannot live a normal woman's life. Besides, marriage is forbidden by the Dark Days Club's oath."

He dismissed the oath with a wave of his whip. "That will not apply to us."

"You do not understand. I cannot be a wife, especially not the kind of wife that your rank requires. In truth, I can barely be a woman. I must dress as a man, go into places that no lady would even know existed let alone visit, and fight unearthly creatures. I have killed a man with power that I do not understand." She stopped for a moment, the enormity of that statement squeezing all of the air from her lungs. She gulped for a breath, pushing past the sob in it. "Yes, I have killed a man. He was a horrible man, but I killed him, and—merciful heaven—I think I was glad."

He regarded her, face drawn tight with shock. "Then all the more reason for me to be at your side. You cannot do this alone. You should not do it alone—it is too much to ask of a young woman." He checked the off-side leader, bringing the horse's gait back into line with its partner, then glanced across at her again. "We have friendship and respect, Helen, and now a mutual purpose. Many successful marriages are built upon much less. Besides, you will be at the pinnacle of society. What could be better for a Reclaimer?"

He was right: most marriages of their rank were financial transactions with not even a basis of friendship. He made it sound so reasonable. So useful. So inevitable. Yet she could feel herself resisting, as if something deep within her was curling away from him.

Apparently he could feel it too, for he said curtly, "You are thinking of *him*, aren't you?"

She rubbed at her forehead. "I do not know what I am thinking. Right now it is all too much."

"I will tell you what you should be thinking. He is mad, he killed his wife, and he is still considered married."

She gripped the edge of the seat. "He did not kill Lady Elise."

"Even if that were the case—and I assure you it is not—he is definitely the other two."

They stared ahead again. Helen rubbed her chest. It was as if her heart hurt.

"Beyond Carlston and your own obvious hesitation, a hard truth remains," he added. "Our betrothal has been witnessed by Lady Dunwick and her companions, and will be advertised to the world in short order. If you want to have any currency within decent society, if you want to save yourself and your family from further ignominy, then we must be married."

He sent the whip over the team, springing them into a gallop.

Thirty

THEY REACHED STREATHAM at around seven o'clock—five miles from London—the road already clogged by carts, herds of cattle for Smithfield, and carriages heading into the city across Westminster Bridge. It was a relief to finally take the turn for Mitcham, a shorter route, the Duke assured her, to Barnes and the Comte d'Antraigues's country residence.

"I have only been there once, for a rout, so my memory of it is sketchy," the Duke warned as he whipped up the pace from the new team that had been changed at Croydon. "As far as I recall, the house is upon the riverbank."

She heard the croak of fatigue in his voice. He had managed almost six and a half hours of driving with only brief respites at the tollgates and posting houses. She felt it in her bones too, alongside the ever-building dread of what they were hurtling toward. The keeper of the Croydon tollgate had reported that just twenty minutes earlier Lord Carlston had passed through—looking like death himself, the man had said cheerfully, and still driving at relentless speed. She squinted along the road, eyes scratchy with grit, hoping to see a plume of dust that would indicate his lordship's curricle. But twenty minutes translated into at least three miles between them, and the view was obscured by bends in the road and dense copses of trees.

She had no clear idea of what lay ahead, and it did not make for a solid plan. Even so, whatever eventuated in that house, retrieving the journal must be her priority. It could not fall into the hands of the Comte, a Deceiver.

Even as she thought it, as she pressed her hands against her thighs to lock the duty into her bone and muscle, her mind conjured an overwhelming sense of lips upon her own, the smell of soap and leather and warm skin. She drew a shaking breath and glanced at the Duke as if he might have seen and felt the overwhelming image too, but his attention was fixed upon the road. It seemed a deeper part of her had another priority: Carlston. Save him, but from what? The Deceivers? Pike and Stokes? Himself?

She shook her head, coming to an unsettling conclusion. Any plan she made would be little more than useless. Every decision must be made in the moment; a daunting prospect.

A milestone flashed by: Barnes, two miles.

Ten minutes later they rounded a corner that brought them alongside the morning-gray expanse of the Thames. The riverbank was thick with clumps of long reeds, and a majestic willow bent over the slow-moving water. A curricle stood abandoned beneath the tree's trailing branches, the horses still harnessed and their dark coats lathered.

"That is Carlston's gig!" the Duke yelled above the grind of their velocity. "I recognize those bays."

Helen felt her heart lift. He was not so lost within his madness to push his prized horses beyond their endurance.

"He and Quinn must be on foot," she said, searching the grassy riverside. "We are close, surely."

The Duke pointed with his whip at a two-story white building with a thatched roof. "There, that public house: the Sun. I am sure it is where we must turn for the Comte's residence." His whip point shifted toward the riverbank. "It is that redbrick house."

They slowed as they drew up to the Sun Inn, then made the

left turn and doubled back a little to enter Barnes Terrace. Helen leaned forward in her seat, searching for Carlston and Quinn as they drove alongside the river, which was already busy with long low boats piled high with goods. They clattered past a large malt house, and an even larger estate with the name ELM BANK emblazoned upon the iron gates. The Thames curved ahead, its wide expanse a greenish gray in the weak morning sun.

She could see no sign of two men on foot, but a coach and four stood outside number 27—the Comte's residence—with one door open, a woman half-bent inside arranging something within the cabin. The Duke slowed their pace to a trot, the drum and grind of their arrival pulling the woman up from her task—a maid by her drab gown and neat white cap. She watched them pass, then ducked back into the coach.

"Do not come inside, Selburn," Helen said, gripping his arm for a moment as he drew the curricle up outside the White Hart Inn that marked the end of the Terrace. Through the windows, she saw customers already inside its public room. Early drinkers. "This will be a fight between Deceivers and Reclaimers. You will not be able to help."

"You expect me to sit here while you go in there alone?"

"That is what the future would hold." Now he would understand what his proposal meant. "You must promise not to come in. I cannot be distracted from what is ahead."

He gave a terse nod, but she was not convinced.

"Give me your word."

"You have it," he said roughly.

Helen swung herself down to the cobbles, smoothed down the buttoned front of her buckskins, and started back the short distance to number 27.

The Comte's residence was a handsome double-fronted dwelling built in dark red brick on five levels. The household appeared to be in the midst of an imminent departure: the coachman up on his box, and the front door of the house standing open. Another maid stood in the doorway, her attention on a figure behind in the hallway. Helen saw a flash of royal blue silk trimmed with broad thread lace and an extravagantly plumed red bonnet: the Comtesse, no doubt.

Helen crossed the road, a little at a loss. She was not sure what she had expected, but it was not this orderly house. Had she some-how arrived before Carlston? She skirted the coach, receiving a dull stare from the plump coachman, and regarded the wide-open door.

"Can I help you, sir?" the maid in drab asked, looking curiously at the disheveled, hatless young man so intent upon the house.

Helen focused her hearing inside the dwelling. Beyond the two women at the door, she heard the creak of steps, the hard rhythm of labored breathing. Then the Comte's voice: "Guillaume, what are you doing here? You look awful, my friend."

"I have your pages, Louis. What is the cure?" Carlston's voice, strained into a rasp.

He must have entered from the back. Three strides and Helen was upon the doorstep, pushing past the maid and dodging the Comtesse's ample figure.

"Sir!" the maid protested.

Helen swiftly gathered in her surroundings: a small hallway, papered in green-striped silk. The only furnishing was a long hall table set against the stair casement with a large vase of pink roses upon it, their delicate perfume carrying across the air. The Comte stood on the stairs, halfway up, clad in a blue kerseymere jacket with his hat upon his head, as if he had been caught ready to descend to the coach. Lord Carlston had positioned himself a few steps below, the journal in one hand and a pistol in the other, only the barrel of the weapon in view. Road grime and sweat smeared his face, his profile set into the savagery that Helen knew only too well. Even so, he swayed upon his feet. No wonder: he held the journal tight in his bare hand. Behind him, Quinn stood with legs braced over two steps, body tensed, as if ready to catch him. Or leap upon him.

"Louis!" Helen turned at the Comtesse's irritated call to her husband. The woman still stood in the doorway, her hands spread in outraged inquiry. "Where did all these men come from?" she demanded in French. "What do they want?"

She had clearly not seen the pistol.

"It is all right, my love. Lord Carlston is an old acquaintance," the Comte answered in English, his voice measured. He dragged his eyes from the gun to glance at Helen on the floor below. "Do I know you, monsieur?"

"It is I, Lady Helen."

She saw Quinn take a quick breath—relief—although he kept his eyes on his master. Carlston did not seem to register her arrival. The elderly Frenchman above him held all his attention.

The Comte gave a forced smile. "Ah, Lady Helen. A most excellent disguise." He addressed the maid at his wife's side. "Elizabeth, take your mistress outside."

The Comtesse hitched her hands upon her hips, rouged lips pursing. "But, Louis," she said in French, "we must go now if we are to make this appointment."

He held up his hand. "Antoinette. Please! Elizabeth, take your mistress out now!"

The Comtesse murmured a frustrated "sa-sa" beneath her breath, but allowed herself to be ushered from the house.

The Comte waited until his wife and her maid had disappeared through the door, then said, "So, you have discovered Benchley's journal, Guillaume, and come to make our deal?"

"What is the cure?" Carlston rasped.

"No," Helen said. She crossed to the balustrade and looked up through its rail. "Carlston, you must give me the journal."

He squeezed his eyes shut for a moment as if trying to focus sight and mind.

"What is happening?" the Comte asked, perplexed. "Lady Helen, do you not wish Guillaume to be cured?"

A clatter from the back of the house swung Helen to face the dark passage that led beyond the hall. She heard footsteps, so fast that she had only a second to register one thought—*uncanny speed*—and then crouch into readiness as a figure burst into the vestibule. Her vision adjusted, the speed of the man sliding from a blur into the recognizable tall, thin form of Stokes. Behind him, another figure approached, caught in the treacle-slow progress of normal momentum. Pike.

Stokes came to a stop in front of Helen. The jarring shift of speed snapped her senses back into normality, bringing an instant of dizziness that resolved into Pike coming down the corridor at a run.

"Throw the journal to me, Carlston," Stokes ordered. "You must surrender it."

Carlston stared at him as if he did not recognize the other Reclaimer.

"Come on, man," Stokes urged. "You cannot give a *Ligatus* to a Deceiver!"

"What?" the Comte said, his gaze fixing upon the journal. "Benchley made a *Ligatus*?"

Pike entered the hallway, panting. "Lord Carlston!" Drawing in deep breaths, he strode past Helen and Stokes and took the first two steps, coming to an abrupt halt as Quinn turned and blocked the way.

"Do not make this worse, Quinn," Pike snapped. He looked past the big man and jabbed the air with his forefinger. "Carlston,

I order you to hand over that journal now. If you attempt to give it to the Comte, it is treason."

Carlston lifted the pistol, aiming at Pike. Did he not care that Quinn was too close?

"Look out!" Helen yelled.

The Terrene slammed his back against the wall as Carlston pulled the trigger. The blast cracked through the air, pushing Helen into a reflexive duck. The ball whirred and hit the string-board of the staircase with a dull thud. A plume of acrid smoke rolled across the hallway.

"Did you see that?" Pike demanded, lurching back down the steps. "He tried to kill me!"

Carlston dropped the spent pistol. It bounced down the steps past Quinn. The Terrene stared at its trajectory, his face pale.

Above them, the Comte declared, "Guillaume, get out! I want no part of this."

"You promised me a cure," Carlston said.

He advanced upon the Comte, forcing him back up the stairs. With a desperate glance at Helen, Quinn followed.

"Stokes, get the journal," Pike ordered. "Whatever way you can!"

Stokes started toward the staircase, but Helen grabbed his arm, stopping him. "I will get it." She rounded on Pike. "Let me try. He will give it to me."

"Too late. He nearly killed me!"

"He does not know what he is doing! The journal brings on madness. It is making him worse."

"Exactly." Pike jerked his chin at Stokes. "Get going."

Stokes pulled his arm from Helen's grasp. "I'm sorry. It has to be destroyed, Lady Helen."

"Lawrence! Lawrence!" The yell came from outside. A woman's voice: the maid. "Murder, murder!"

Helen whirled around to face the open doorway. The maid was on her knees beside her mistress. The Comtesse had collapsed to the ground in a crumpled heap of royal blue silk, her vivid face drained of color, a red stain blossoming through the lace above her left breast.

Helen's view of the two women was suddenly blocked as Lawrence, the Comte's valet, ran into the hall, dark face intent, body angled, a coppery tang of blood on his body.

Stokes clearly smelled it too, for he charged at the smaller man at Reclaimer speed. Helen followed, a step behind, catching sight of a dagger in Lawrence's hand as it flashed upward in a lethal arc.

"Watch out!" she yelled.

Stokes recoiled, his reflexes saving him from the slash at his throat. Instead, the knife connected with his chin, slicing along his jaw in a hot spray of blood. He staggered back into Helen, his desperate grab at her shoulders for support slamming both of them into the wall. The brutal impact punched the air from Helen's lungs. Gulping, she clutched Stokes's jacket, struggling to keep upright, her hands wet with his blood.

She reached out wildly with her other senses—searching for the taste, shape, sound of an energy whip around Lawrence—but found nothing. He'd not had a chance to glut. He only had the knife, yet that was deadly enough.

Opposite them, she saw Pike turning slowly to look out of the doorway at the Comtesse, locked into human momentum.

"Antoinette!" the Comte screamed. He started to descend the stairs at Deceiver speed, blocked by Carlston. "Get out of my way!"

Lawrence accelerated across the vestibule and leaped onto the hall table. The vase of roses smashed to the floor as he vaulted over the banister and landed on the step above the Comte, using the momentum to plunge his knife into the old man's shoulder. Helen heard the hilt thud against the Comte's body.

The old man gasped and buckled to the steps as Lawrence wrenched out the knife and met Carlston's attack. He held the high-ground advantage, and as Carlston lunged—journal still clasped in one hand, glass knife in the other—Lawrence aimed a vicious side-kick at his lordship's chest. As his foot connected, Carlston stabbed down with the glass knife, the blade finding purchase in the Deceiver's leg. The momentum of the kick rammed Carlston backward, the glass blade ripping through flesh and muscle.

Lawrence screamed, falling back against the wall. Carlston staggered down two steps, the journal dropping from his hand and landing against the balustrade.

Quinn charged past him and launched himself at Lawrence. The Deceiver slashed upward with his knife, ripping across Quinn's gut. Blood surged through white shirt and green waistcoat into a bright scarlet crescent. The Terrene gasped and doubled over, teetering for a moment before stumbling backward and landing on Carlston.

"Quinn!" Helen yelled. She started toward the stairs, her impetus abruptly stopped by a bloodied hand on her shoulder.

"No, you're not ready for this," Stokes panted, his other hand clamped over the gash along his jaw. "You'll get in the way. Stay here."

In the way? Before she could protest, he shoved her back and ran for the stairs.

Lawrence, seeing him coming, grabbed the journal and hobbled up the last few steps, his injured leg dragging. The Comte made a feeble grab at his ankle as he passed, but Lawrence shook off the old man's grip and pulled himself by the banister around to the next set of steps, disappearing from view.

With a roar of frustration, Carlston pushed Quinn off him. Helen gasped as the big Islander rolled down a few steps, landing

in a sprawled heap. Sweet heaven: even Quinn's peril did not penetrate the savage madness in Carlston's face. He levered himself up
and climbed the stairs after Lawrence, Stokes close behind him.

"Stay with the Comtesse, Lady Helen," Pike said, his voice slow
and slurred. Helen blinked, her senses shifting back to normal
speed. "Stokes will get the journal."

Above them came the crash of furniture, the sound of yells and
grunts. On the staircase, Quinn pulled himself upright and, bent
over his wound, followed the sounds of the battle.

"Lady Helen," the Comte rasped from the steps. Blood trickled
from his sleeve, pooling on the carpet runner. "The cure for
Carlston . . . the Grand Deceiver. Do you still want to know?"

Helen ran up the stairs and stopped on the step below the old
Comte. "Of course I do."

"Help me kill Lawrence . . . before this body expires. I will tell
you all when he is dead."

"Tell me now!"

The Comte hauled himself up a step toward the landing. "He
has killed my Antoinette. Help me avenge her, then I will tell you."

Helen grabbed the Comte's arm and pulled him to his feet.

Pike looked up through the balustrades. "Do not help him!" he
ordered. "He is a Deceiver. You cannot trust him."

"I trust him more than I trust you." More to the point, she
trusted the Comte's desire for revenge. She ducked under the old
Deceiver's arm, taking his sagging weight. "Is Lawrence the Grand
Deceiver?"

The Comte gave a ghastly wet laugh. "No. He is a Cruor. I hired
him to protect us . . . should have known he is a creature of the
Grand Deceiver."

"Do you hear that?" she said, addressing Pike over her shoulder.
"The Grand Deceiver is real!"

"Hurry," the Comte panted. "This body does not have long."

Helen gathered her Reclaimer strength and steered the Comte rapidly up the stairs, half dragging, half carrying him. She grabbed the balustrade and pulled them both around onto the first floor. From the sounds above, the fight was on the next level. Hauling the Comte with her, she took the steps, pausing for a moment at the top. The sound of bodies hitting walls and smashing wood came from the second room along the corridor.

"They are in my dressing room," the Comte gasped in her ear. "Take me."

"No! You cannot fight Lawrence." She could not risk the Comte dying before she got the cure. "I will get him for you."

She had a small hope that if she touched Lawrence, she would drain him, like last time.

She dragged the Comte to the next room, the connecting bedchamber, and wrenched open the door. Wood-paneled walls and bright patterned yellow paper barely registered; all her focus was upon the large bed set against the wall. She crossed to it and twisted her body to swing the old Deceiver down upon its yellow cover, the action prompting a hiss of pain from him.

He reached for the wound in his shoulder, the blue wool of his jacket sodden with blood. "Be quick, or we shall both lose our chance."

The door to the dressing room was still closed. Helen ran to it and flung it open. The room was shifting between blurs of velocity and moments of distinct bodies in the space: Carlston, Stokes, Quinn, and Lawrence. She blinked, her Reclaimer sight coalescing the whole into a heaving battle scene.

Carlston clearly did not know, or perhaps care, who he was fighting. He had jammed the journal in his waistcoat and was defending it with brutal kicks and punches that were, for the moment, driving back Stokes. Helen's skin tightened with fear.

There was no sign of sanity in Carlston's eyes. Only pitiless savagery. Had the *Ligatus* already consumed him?

"Lord Carlston!" she yelled.

He did not even look up. Stokes, however, checked for a moment. A costly moment: Carlston slammed his head against the wall. Stokes managed to block the next hit, driving Carlston back with a kick to the stomach.

Quinn was caught in a low grapple with Lawrence—both injured and bleeding profusely—but the Terrene was barely able to land a blow against the vicious Cruor. Even so, he did not let go, grittily taking the Deceiver's vicious punches. His shirt and waistcoat were sodden with bright blood, the black tattoos stark against the pallor of his skin.

Helen lunged for Lawrence and grabbed a handful of the man's hair, hauling him off Quinn. She held her breath, but no, there was no draw of glorious energy like last time. It must only happen when they had whips.

The valet twisted, breaking her hold, landing on his knees. She half pivoted, gaining momentum, and rammed the edge of her boot into the soft connection between his neck and shoulder. She felt the crunch of bone and ligament. He collapsed onto his side, gasping, then rolled and scrabbled onto his feet.

"*Non vi combatto,*" he said, backing away. *I do not fight you.*

The declaration checked her for an instant—why would none of them fight her?—but right then it was an advantage she would take. She gathered her strength again and spun, driving her foot into his gut, the impact doubling him over. Regaining balance, she shifted her weight forward, hooking her arm around his throat into a headlock. He grabbed at the choking hold, fingers ripping at her arm. She dragged him toward the dressing room door, the fight between Carlston and Stokes still raging in a punishing trade of blows.

Quinn hauled himself upright, his body bent over the ominous gut wound. "Do you need help, my lady?" he panted.

"No. Help Stokes contain Lord Carlston."

"Stokes is not trying to contain him, my lady," Quinn said.

Helen sent a wild glance over her shoulder, keeping her arm locked tightly around Lawrence's neck. Quinn was right: Stokes was not holding back.

"Stokes!" she yelled. "Do not kill him."

"I have my orders, Lady Helen," Stokes yelled back, ducking a vicious punch aimed at his throat. "And he is trying to kill me!"

There was no time to argue. "Quinn, protect your master," she ordered, and heaved Lawrence another few steps toward the door.

The Deceiver grabbed for the doorframe, abruptly stopping their progress, straining against her momentum, but he could not hold against her grim determination. She rammed his injured leg against the frame, his flinching pain giving her the moment to rip his hands free and drag him into the bedchamber.

Quinn slammed the door behind them. She knew she was delivering Lawrence to his death, but it was the only path to Carlston's cure.

"Here," the Comte gasped. He held a pistol—retrieved from a brace on the table—the weight of it making his hands shake. "Bring him here!"

Yells and footsteps ascended the stairs to the third floor; the fight had shifted upstairs. She had to get the cure and get it up there as soon as possible.

"*Traditore!*" Lawrence yelled at the Comte. *Traitor.*

He lunged, his body weight rocking Helen forward. She tried to tighten her hold upon his neck, but pain exploded through her foot as he rammed his heel onto her bones, then jabbed his elbow into the soft apex of her diaphragm. She doubled over, breath locked into a choking gasp, her hold loosening enough for him to leap for the gun. He was trying to finish his task.

He clamped his hands over the Comte's bony grip and slowly turned the barrel toward the old Deceiver's face.

Gulping for air, Helen lunged for the wildly weaving gun, finding a handhold around the top. She yanked, but could not pull the gun free; Lawrence's strength matched her own. All three of them grappled for control, straining to point the barrel. To find the trigger.

The Comte was all but spent, the hollows of his face grayed by the shadows of death, but perhaps he would have enough to tip the balance in her favor.

"Comte, together," she gasped.

The old Deceiver's eyes hardened with intent as she focused all of her Reclaimer strength.

Inch by inch she felt the barrel turn, its aim slowly shifting to Lawrence's face. His hot, panting breath smelled of sharp alcohol and juniper, and his dark eyes bulged from the strain of fighting against their combined effort.

Helen slid her finger down, feeling for the rounded shape of the trigger guard. There! She jabbed her finger through, finding the smooth curve of the trigger. A little more to the right and . . . The blast boomed in her ears, juddering through her bones. The brutal recoil threw her back against the bed table, and flung the Comte against the bedhead, his skull connecting with a sickening crack.

The lead ball smashed through Lawrence, the force sending out a spray of blood and bone, twisting him upon his feet so that for a moment he faced Helen. She caught a nightmare vision of blood and bone and teeth where his mouth should have been, and then he crumpled face-first to the floor.

Silence. Even the struggle upstairs had stopped. Helen grabbed the edge of the table for support.

Gun smoke hung in the air, its acrid stink mixing with the meaty smell of burned flesh. Helen wiped sticky blood and bone grit from her face, trying to fight back the burning rise of vomit. Good God, she had shot the man's face off.

Lawrence's body suddenly heaved with light, his skin glowing with an orange-hued incandescence as if lit from within by an infernal fire. A sound rose, horrifyingly akin to the howling she had heard from the *Ligatus*.

"*Mors Ultima*," the Comte whispered, a grim smile on his bloodless lips. "He is no more."

Helen had never seen the final end before. Lawrence had no offspring to shift into; she had truly destroyed him. Two deaths on her soul now: one human, one Deceiver. Lowry had been right. She was killing like all the other Reclaimers.

The light swarmed from the body and hung for a moment above the tumbled flesh form. A dark speck in the center expanded, the size of a pinhead, a button, a penny, growing and growing, pulling all the swarming light in until it seemed to collapse upon itself with an awful screaming keen, leaving just a corpse with a ruined face and blood creeping through the carpet.

"Murder! Murder!"

The cries from the street broke Helen's horror, and the startled hiatus above them. She heard the sound of wood smashing and a low gasp of pain. Carlston. She looked up at the ceiling: Was Stokes getting the upper hand? Every part of her wanted to run upstairs, but she had to learn the cure from the Comte before he died. Everything hinged upon the cure.

Voices were already calling below. She and the Comte would not be alone much longer. She stepped around the gruesome remains of Lawrence and leaned over the old Deceiver.

"Lawrence is dead, Comte. What is the cure?"

Above his coiffed white hair, blood smeared the bedhead. His breath came in short gasps.

"Tell me, what is the cure?"

He frowned, struggling to fix upon her face. "You are the cure," he said, the words almost lost in the wet wheezing. "Cause and cure. You should be bonded, but you are not." He lifted his hand and tapped her chest with a trembling forefinger. "The Grand Deceiver is not one of us, but two. A dyad. Same for the Grand Reclaimer. A dyad: you and Carlston, bonded in blood. That is the cure."

She stared at him. At the rout he had said it would take both of them—herself and Lord Carlston—to defeat the Grand Deceiver. Even then he had been telling them that they were meant to be bonded. That they would be facing two Deceivers working together.

Why did no one else know that the Grand Deceiver was a dyad? Perhaps he was lying. Carlston had said he did not trust the Comte. But where would that take her? Nowhere. God help her, she had no choice but to believe him—it was the only hope she had.

"Comte, how do we bond? How do we become a dyad? Is it a ritual?" She caught his shaking hand, trying to focus his dying mind. "How do we do it?"

He drew in a rattling breath. "Blood alchemy," he whispered. "Benchley built it."

"The *Ligatus*?" She shook her head. How could their bond be forged by such a hideous, godless creation? "No, it pulls us into madness! It will kill us."

"Head or heart?" he whispered.

She remembered his same question at the rout: Did she follow her head or her heart?

"These two are not like any other," he rasped. "*Lusus naturae*."

His clawed fingers caught at the blood-stained fob ribbon that hung from his breeches pocket. "Find—" He stopped, panting for a moment, then wrenched the ribbon free and held it up. The attached fob—a gold disc with etching on it—swung between them. He pressed it into her hand. "Find . . . Bath Deceiver. Show this." Red spittle flecked his lips. "Keep your word. Keep my son safe."

His labored breath barely lifted his chest.

What did he mean, *not like any other*? And who was the Bath Deceiver?

"Comte!"

But his eyes had fixed beyond her, sight no longer anchored in the room, and although his mouth moved with words, he no longer had enough breath for sound.

Behind her, the bedroom door opened. She spun around. Pike stood in the doorway staring down at Lawrence's body, his thin lips pursed in distaste.

"One problem gone." He looked at the Comte on the bed. "Is he dead too?"

"No, but I do not think he has long. He can no longer speak."

She pushed the gold fob and ribbon into her breeches pocket and rounded the bed, avoiding the staring eyes of Lawrence's corpse.

"Stokes and Quinn are both injured," Pike said, looking up at the ceiling. The thud and crash of combat still filtered down, but it was less frantic. Was that a good sign or not? "I don't think you are ready, but you are all I have. Get up there and get the journal. We must destroy it."

"I *am* ready," Helen said, heading toward the door. She looked back at the Comte: *dear God, let him be telling the truth.* "But we can't destroy the journal. The Grand Deceiver is two creatures working together, not one. The Comte told me Carlston and I are their opposite: a Grand Reclaimer. We need the journal to bond. That is what is wrong with him—it is the need to bond that is making him mad!"

Even as she said it, a vile question rose in her mind. If they were meant to be the Grand Reclaimer, were their feelings for one another based on nothing more than a compulsion created by this power?

"You are a fool to take the word of a Deceiver," Pike said. "If the journal is making Carlston mad, then surely it will do the same to you. I will not have two of my Reclaimers descend into madness in one night. Destroy the book."

"No. Even if there is only a slight hope that it will restore Lord Carlston, we must take it."

"He is too far gone. I order you to stop him, by the authority of the King—even if that means killing him." He stepped in front of her, blocking her path. "It is my order. Acknowledge it!"

"I no longer take orders from you, Mr. Pike," she said, unmoved by the narrowed threat in his eyes. She pushed past him, savoring the astonishment on his bony face. She knew what she must do, and he was not going to stand in her way. "I know the real reason why you want the journal destroyed. I know about your wife."

"You read the journal, didn't you?" He followed her out into the corridor. She could almost see the rapid recalculation in his face. "Then you understand Isabella had no idea what she was doing."

"But you did," Helen said, rounding on him. "You hid the fact that she is an Unreclaimable offspring and killed Sir Dennis. You made a bargain with Benchley, even though you knew he was mad."

"Of course I did—she is my wife." His face tightened into loathing. "And, by God, he made me pay for it. Even so, the *Ligatus* is part of a gateway to Hell. I order you to destroy it. Honor your oath, Lady Helen."

"My oath is to the Dark Days Club and England, not to you." The truth of the statement straightened her spine. "I am a Reclaimer and I believe the Grand Deceiver is real, Mr. Pike. Lord Carlston and I must fight them, whoever, or whatever, they are. I will not destroy the journal, not until I try to make this bond with him." She ran up the steps, then said over her shoulder, "Besides, saving Lord Carlston and the journal is in your wife's best interest too."

Pike glared up at her through the balustrade. "What does that mean?"

"I saved an Unreclaimable through that journal. If it is destroyed, your wife's only chance at sanity is destroyed as well."

His whole body stilled. "You saved an Unreclaimable?" The hope in his face hardened into bitterness. "And so you hold this over me now? I must do as you say if I want my wife saved?"

"That is your way of doing things. I will try to save your wife whatever happens."

She stopped on the landing, her voice stolen for a moment by the magnitude of the bond she was about to attempt. The danger to herself and to Lord Carlston.

She took a deep breath. "If I survive, I will save your wife." She looked down at him, standing on the level below. "I know you do not recognize it, Mr. Pike, but that is what honor looks like."

Thirty-One

THE SHOUTS AND wails in the entrance hall below had taken on a new volume. Helen peered down through the stairwell as she rounded the intermediate landing and caught sight of hats and hands and boots: men on the stairs, making their cautious way up. One of them was a doctor by the glimpse of a black physician's bag. She ran up the next rise, noting smudges of blood on the wall and banister, a sick sense of dread building with each step.

Mr. Hammond's voice cut across the sobbing and cries below, demanding to know where Lord Carlston had gone. Thank God he and the others had finally arrived. They could not help her retrieve Carlston from his madness—he was too strong, too fast, and far too lost in the journal's violence—but just their presence sent new energy through her body.

She directed her hearing upward. It was quiet, no longer any sounds of battle. Was that good, or bad?

She took the final steps at speed and rounded the balustrade, ducking back at the sight of two men on the landing: one heavy-set and slumped against the white wall; the other crouched beside him, blond and lanky. Her mind caught up with her reflexes: Quinn and Selburn. What was the Duke doing up here?

As she straightened, he spun around, a long-barreled pistol aimed at her chest.

"Helen!" He lowered the gun. "You are safe!"

"You gave me your word you would stay outside!"

She had not seen him pass the bedroom. If he had been caught in the fight between Stokes and Carlston . . . No, she could not even think it.

Unrepentant, he said, "I heard the gunshot and fighting and came looking for you." He gestured to Quinn with a bloodied hand. "Carlston's man is in a bad way."

It seemed Quinn had been heading for the narrow attic staircase at the end of the corridor; a smeared trail of blood down the wall mapped his collapse to the floor. A bloodied knife lay next to him. Both of his eyes were closed, his hands clasped over his stomach wound, blood still seeping through his fingers. His skin had turned a waxy gray, and his body had a frightening stillness about it.

Helen crouched beside him, praying she would find life. "Mr. Quinn?" She pressed her palm against his tattooed cheek. Still warm, and she felt his soft breath on her skin. "Quinn?"

No response, not even a shift in his shallow breathing.

"He was conscious when I found him," the Duke said. He pointed at the attic steps, the door at the top ajar. "As far as I know, Carlston is in the attic, but I haven't heard anyone move since I arrived. Quinn told me Carlston has killed Stokes. He kept on saying it."

Helen clutched at the wall for support: his words felt as if a hammer had hit her chest. Stokes could not be dead. *Must not* be dead. She had liked the Reclaimer, even trusted him. She squeezed her eyes shut, trying to hold back her grief and the flood of ramifications. If it were true, Carlston would never forgive himself. Nor would the Dark Days Club.

Quinn had to be wrong, or the Duke had heard amiss.

Opening her eyes, she concentrated fiercely, listening for any kind of sound in the attic. Beside her, she heard Quinn's shallow gasps, then four sets of approaching footsteps on the stairs, Pike's voice—"You can't go up there!"—and then Mr. Hammond's curt rejoinder, "The devil take you, man!" Gritting her teeth, she forced herself to ignore their arrival and focused her hearing upward. Finally she found breathing, but only one person, every inhalation pained and sick. Even so, she recognized the rhythm: Carlston. And like a counterpoint within it, that incessant pulse that reached between them. Now she knew what it was: the call of the Grand Reclaimer bond.

"My lady!" Darby ran headlong up the stairs, her broad face drawn into exhausted shadows. She checked on the last step at the sight of Quinn. "Nathaniel!"

"He is alive," Helen said quickly. "Stabbed in the stomach." She rose to her feet, making way for her maid.

Only Carlston in the attic: Had he truly killed Stokes? If so, he must not have recognized the other Reclaimer. Maybe he would not recognize her. He had called her his love, but would that hold firm against the journal and its madness? Dear Lord, she had to find a way to get through to him.

Darby dropped to her knees beside Quinn, ripping her tucker from her bodice. "Nathaniel?" She pressed the white linen against his wound. "Nathaniel, can you hear me?" She looked up at Helen. "Why is he not healing? Shouldn't he be healing by now?"

"Lady Helen!" Mr. Hammond appeared at the top of the stairs, his strained face streaked with grime, blue jacket almost gray with road dust. "Where is Lord Carlston? Do we have the journal?"

Behind him came Lady Margaret, her usual poise lost in a tumble of black curls, crumpled gown, and a dusty pelisse. Delia, her pallor and angles even more pronounced, brought up the rear. All three of them gathered on the landing.

"Lord Carlston has the journal up there," Helen said, indicating the attic. "It is possible . . ." She stopped for a moment. "It seems he has killed Stokes."

"No!" Lady Margaret stepped forward, all indignation. "He would never do that."

Hammond gripped her arm as if to hold her back.

"The Comte gave me the cure," Helen continued. "It is the journal itself." She swiftly reported the old Deceiver's dying instructions.

"But do you trust the information?" Delia asked. She glanced at the Duke, clearly seeking the support of her fellow aide. "It could be a trap for you and Lord Carlston."

"Miss Cransdon is right," the Duke said. "You cannot trust a Deceiver, and you cannot hope to go up against Carlston. The state he is in, he will kill you." He held out the pistol. "Shoot him. No, wait." He drew it back. "I will shoot him, then you will not have to deal with the sin of murder."

Too late for that, Helen thought.

"Shoot Lord Carlston?" Lady Margaret exclaimed, just as her brother said forcefully, "He would break your neck before you even raised the gun."

"He cannot beat a bullet," the Duke said.

Helen heard a sound from the attic, a heaving cough that she immediately recognized. Carlston was searching the journal again. If he had any sanity left, that would surely rip it from him.

"We will not shoot Lord Carlston," she said, cutting off the argument. "Your Grace, Hammond, take Quinn downstairs." In one sweeping glance, she gathered Lady Margaret, Delia, and Darby into her next order. "Go downstairs. Do not let anyone up here."

Darby touched Quinn's cheek, then sat back on her heels. "With respect, my lady, I am staying with you. I have trained to be your Terrene and I will not let you stand alone."

"You do not have Terrene strength or speed," Helen said.

Darby lifted her chin. "We have made our oaths, my lady. Do not doubt me now."

Helen met her maid's steady gaze and nodded. There had already been too much doubt.

"I'll be damned if I let two women try to subdue a madman by themselves," the Duke said. "It is impossible."

"We may be women, Your Grace, but we are also Reclaimer and Terrene," Helen said. "You saw what I did in the laneway. I do not need your protection."

He crossed his arms, patently unmoved by her statement. She had no time for debate. Nor did Carlston. Garnering her Reclaimer energy, she stepped across to the Duke at uncanny speed and pulled the pistol from his grip. She stepped back and held out the weapon as his sluggish perception caught up.

The Duke stared at his empty hand and then at the gun lying across her palm. "I see what you mean," he said. "But keep the pistol."

"Finally he understands," Hammond murmured. He crouched beside Quinn and hooked his hands under the big man's armpits. "You heard what your Reclaimer said, Duke: help me move Quinn." He looked up at Helen, his face grim. "You are the only one who can save Carlston, but if he is beyond help and tries to kill you, do not hesitate. We cannot lose you, too."

Helen gave one stiff nod. Pray God, it did not come to that.

⌒

As SOON AS Selburn and the others had retreated downstairs with Quinn, Helen led the way to the attic staircase, Darby following close behind.

Helen flexed her hand around the ivory handle of her glass

knife and focused her senses on the room above. Carlston's breathing held a rasping rawness—he had moved to the far right of the room—and she could smell blood, bile, and the dank reek of final evacuations.

"How does the journal bond work?" Darby asked softly. She had armed herself with the knife lying beside Quinn and was gripping it in a very skilled manner. He had trained her well.

"I do not know," Helen admitted, pausing for a moment on the bottom step. "It is built out of the blood of slain people. I would think we must offer it blood too."

"You should have kept the Duke's pistol."

Helen shook her head. She had seen what a pistol shot had done to Lawrence, and there was no coming back from an ill-timed or misjudged shot. "I cannot bond with a corpse."

They crept up the remaining four steps. Not that stealth would make any difference, Helen thought. Carlston was sure to be listening for them. He would be prepared for their arrival whatever they did, and it only remained to be seen whether he held on to enough sanity to recognize them. The best chance, she decided, was to make sure he knew who was coming and try to reach what was left of his mind.

She concentrated her senses, squinting with the effort, but could not find his position. A disturbing development. Had he vacated the room through a window, or was she merely failing to locate him?

Through the gap of the door, she glimpsed the booted feet and buckskin-clad legs of a long, lean man sprawled on the floor. The wooden boards beneath the body were dark and wet, the tiny channels between them red and glistening with pooled blood. Stokes.

Behind her, Darby drew in a sharp breath of horror. Helen felt it too—a sickened grief that wrung at her innards, and with it a deep sense of foreboding.

"Carlston," she called. "It is Helen."

She pushed open the door and stepped into the attic. Dust, stirred up into tiny currents of glittering air, tumbled and streamed through a shaft of sunlight. She registered stacked chairs, traveling trunks, an old freestanding tambour frame, and then all her attention fixed upon Stokes at her feet. His once warm hazel eyes stared up at her, glazed by death, the cause of his demise immediately apparent. A glass knife protruded from the side of his throat, the smooth, viscous creep of blood below it already flecked with dust. Helen could not move her gaze from the etched design upon the blade; the same as her own. Carlston's knife.

She caught a flash of movement just in time to block the side-kick aimed at her face. Her forearm took the blow, the weight of it jarring through her bones. She ducked as Carlston spun into another kick, missing her temple by a hairbreadth. Her blood surged, full Reclaimer speed riding in upon it. She leaped over Stokes's corpse and whirled around to face Carlston, knife raised.

His dark eyes showed no recognition. They were narrowed and cunning and fixed upon her with vicious intent, his lips drawn back over his teeth like a snarling animal. A long wound at his hairline seeped with blood, streaking one side of his face like war paint. A knife had ripped through his shoulder, slicing open jacket, shirt, and muscle into a sodden mess of red cloth and raw flesh. In one hand he held the journal, and in the other, a long paling of wood with three iron nails protruding from it.

"William!" She put every ounce of urgency and need into the call. His name had brought him back from strangling the Duke; perhaps it would draw him back again. "William! It is I, Helen."

He ran at her, stepping on Stokes's body, the corpse convulsing under his foot as if it still had life. The man she knew would never have desecrated another Reclaimer in such a way. Lord Carlston was truly gone.

He lunged, the paling aimed in a low sweep at her ankles. She jumped back, slashing at his hand, but he was too fast, pulling back into an overhead hammer swing at her head. She had no time to deflect, just managing to turn so that her shoulder took the blow. Pain burst through her back and arm, her hand spasming open. Her knife clattered to the wooden floor.

Clenching her teeth, she tried to grab the paling, but he pulled it too fast. She retreated, trying to stay on her toes, flexing movement back into her hand. He was standing over the knife.

Behind him, Darby launched herself from the doorway at human speed.

"Darby, stay back!" she yelled as Carlston attacked again.

The warning cost Helen a precious second. She dodged, but not fast enough. The paling slammed into her ribs, the iron nails biting through her woolen jacket into her flesh. She gasped as he followed it with a snap-kick to her chest. She staggered back from the momentum, the nails ripping out of her flesh. Clutching the raw, wet agony, she tried to stay on her toes, Quinn's mantra loud in her mind: *A still body is an easy target.*

She retreated another step, stumbling over the foot of the tambour frame. Its mahogany stand was at least as long as her leg: a weapon with reach. She grabbed the bottom of it, her hands wet with her own blood, and swung it up at Carlston's head. The blow connected so hard with his jaw, it smashed the embroidery frame off the end, the circle of wood flying through the air.

He dropped to one knee, momentarily dazed. Seeing the chance, she kicked at the journal in his hand. It spun from his loosened grip, landing with a slap on the floor near Stokes. She swung the tambour stand again, but he rolled clear, coming within hand's reach of her glass knife. He scooped it up, surging to his feet.

Behind him, Helen saw Darby slowly reaching for the journal, caught in human momentum. If Carlston saw her, she would be dead in a second.

Helen retreated, tambour stand held like a bat, trying to draw him away from Darby's excruciatingly slow progress. He followed, the glass knife raised. Helen felt a choking rise of anguish. Carlston would have known the knife had her protection alchemy forged into it. This man in front of her was just a savage animal, and she was barely holding her own against him.

Darby ponderously scooped up the book and clutched it to her chest, rising sluggishly to run to the safety of the opposite wall. Helen readied herself for Carlston's next attack just as a figure stepped into the doorway. The Duke, his arm outstretched, pistol in hand.

"No!" Helen screamed. She could see its course—a flash of the future in her mind—but he had already pulled the trigger.

The iron ball exploded out of the smoky ignition, its aim set for Carlston, but its course was blocked by Darby as she ran—so slowly—for the wall. Helen tried to launch herself past Carlston, but he was in her pathway, charging toward the Duke.

The bullet hit Darby under her collarbone—an awful wet thudding crack of metal chewing through flesh and smashing bone.

Helen arrived at her side in time to catch her as she staggered another step still clutching the journal, blood welling up through the blue pleats of her bodice. Her startled eyes found Helen's, her breathing shortening into panting shock. Helen took her weight against her chest and lowered her to the floor, pressing her hand against the wound. So much blood.

A low guttural snarl wrenched her attention back to the doorway. Carlston picked up the Duke by his throat and slammed him against the wall.

Helen half rose, caught between Darby and the Duke. Both in dire peril.

She ducked back to Darby, grabbed the journal from her maid's weak grip, and jammed the soft leather cover against the gaping wound. Darby screamed.

Helen gritted her teeth and pulled Darby's hands over the book. "Press hard," she ordered.

She hurled herself at the grim battle by the door. Selburn smashed the butt of the spent pistol against Carlston's head, opening up another gash across his temple in a spray of blood, but Carlston did not let go. He pounded Selburn back against the wall, the Duke's head slamming against the plaster, and raised the glass knife.

With a yell, Helen launched herself onto Carlston's back, wrapping her legs around his waist and her arms around his head. He released the Duke and staggered into the wall under her momentum. The Duke slid to the floor, dazed.

Hammond peered through the doorway.

Helen tightened her headlock, desperately trying to steer Carlston away from the other two men.

"Hammond, get him out!" she yelled.

Damn the Duke and his gun. The blaze of anger galvanized her as Carlston whirled around, trying to dislodge her from his back, the knife still in his hand. He stabbed at her blindly but the blade sheered past her thighs, his strikes sliding wild. They whirled in a lurching circle. Helen caught a dizzy glimpse of Hammond dragging Selburn out of the attic, and then Darby with the journal still stoically pressed into her wound, the binding covered in her blood.

Carlston rammed Helen against the wall, the impact crushing the air from her lungs. Gasping, she punched him in the head, managing to get a foot on the wall to lever herself some space to breathe. Somehow she had to get the journal and subdue him long enough for them both to touch it. There would be no problem with the supply of blood, she thought grimly. For either of them.

He still had her knife. And he still wanted the journal. A desperate plan formed.

"Darby, can you move?"

It came out more as a gasp than a yell, but she saw Darby nod and gather herself. So brave.

Carlston shifted, giving himself space for another brutal ram into the wall. With a formless prayer, Helen swung both feet back and planted them against the wall, her arms still wrapped in the headlock. With all her strength, she propelled herself forward, pushing all her weight up against his shoulders, praying that the leverage would be enough to topple him.

He staggered a step, then dropped to his knees, her forward momentum too much for his balance. As he crashed to the floor, Helen launched herself into a tumble over his head, the room spinning, her breath gone in a moment of panic. She slammed onto her back, her spine jarring against the floor.

"Darby!" she yelled.

She spun on her back to face Carlston. He hauled himself onto his knees. At the corner of her eye, she saw Darby crawling toward her, the journal in her hand, smearing a trail of blood on the wooden boards. *Faster*, she urged her maid. *Go faster.*

She clenched her teeth as Carlston gathered himself, knife in hand. She had to trust the alchemy forged into the blade and her Reclaimer speed.

He scrabbled forward and lifted the knife above his head, face savage and intent. Helen watched him drive the blade down toward her heart, the reflex to roll away rising like a scream through her body. The point plunged closer and closer, a foot, an inch, from her chest. Suddenly the blade veered to the right and slammed into the wooden floor.

For one precious second, Carlston kneeled beside her, locked in uncomprehending stillness. Darby flung herself forward, hand outstretched with the journal. Helen snatched it from her grasp and curled herself upright, slamming the blood-soaked binding against Carlston's torn shoulder, praying that her own bloodied hands were enough to forge the bond.

The journal heaved under her grip, searing power boiling up from its foul blood-ink and streaming into their bodies like a torrent of scorching oil. Carlston screamed with pain, and Helen's own terror scoured her throat. The shrieking howls of the slain rose through the pages, their death throes caught within their blood, their fear written into the journal's alchemy. Helen felt their anguished loss pulling her toward the darkness.

She braced against their burning force, turning her body against the attack, raising her arm as if to block a savage blow. But there was no outside enemy to deflect; all the searing power was within.

Another scream drained her of air as a golden light—her soul—erupted above her body. Gasping, she saw Carlston arch in agony under a swollen black mass of vestige energy and alchemy. Was that his soul? She could see no light at all within the snarl of power that twisted and writhed above him.

Her own soul-light swirled around the black pulsing mass, battering against its squirming walls like waves against a rock face. There was no way into the dense darkness. She fought to focus through the agony building in her head, her body shaking with fiery pain and a terrible realization: they had not bonded. He was locked too deep within his madness.

She had to free him to bond, but how?

The answer came in a horrifying rush. She must stop resisting the voices and their fear-filled madness. She had to open herself to the journal's blood power and Carlston's vestige darkness, and pull him out. The same force that had all but destroyed her mother.

No! She was not strong enough! What if she did not find her way back? What if she went mad too?

Yet if she failed now, there would be no Grand Reclaimer. No hope. Carlston would be lost forever, caught in eternal torment.

The darkness had destroyed her family. It would not destroy Carlston, too.

She slammed herself against the journal's blood-soaked binding and Carlston's arched body, and with a formless prayer opened herself to the howls of the slaughtered inscribed upon its pages. Deceivers, Reclaimers, innocents—their anguish and fear searing through her veins, their lives embedding themselves within her mind and heart like thousands of burning brands stamping their mark forever. So many lives. So much knowledge. She felt the pain of every word written in their blood—Benchley's words about her parents; Carlston; his wife, Lady Elise—then they were swept past in the agonizing deluge of blood-ink and murdered voices that fused with her flesh and bone. She absorbed them all.

The power from the journal rose louder and louder, roaring through her into a bright, molten force. It boiled through Carlston, raging toward his black, squirming prison. It swept up Darby, forging a bond through the blood-soaked binding, her screams joining the song of pain. No! Darby was not a Reclaimer. She would not survive this power. But there was no stopping the roaring voices.

The black mass of vestige above Carlston flared with light, heaving with the journal's bright fury. The blood power boiled across it like fire across a forest, consuming the foul darkness in a blistering inferno, obliterating the screeching, oily madness. Piercing light sprang around Carlston: his soul, scorched clean of all vestige. He slumped onto his hands and knees, gasping for air like a man who had not breathed for days.

She felt his heartbeat and her own meld into one frantic pulse beneath the molten force—the bond, finally forged, locking them together in an agony of union, the chaotic voices of the journal screaming through them. She had to stop them or they would drag her and Carlston—and Darby, too—into the storm of their gibbering pain forever. But how?

She forced herself past her own terror, and focused on the voices. So much fear. So much loneliness. She caught an image of a tavern girl, eyes bulging, clawing at hands around her throat. A boy shielding his head from a hammering fist. A baby alone in a crib, screaming. Dear God, a baby. All those voices bound together into one howling wounded creature, striking out with teeth and claws made of burning power. She could not save them from their brutal ends, but she could soothe them. Comfort them. She could sing their lament alongside them with a heart that had felt fear and loss too.

"I understand," she cried. "You are not alone. You are remembered."

There was no change in the roaring, chittering pain. Perhaps an open heart was not enough. Yet did not all hurt things seek easement?

She kept on calling, her voice lilting into a chant. "I understand. You are not alone. You are remembered."

The silence came so suddenly that it pitched her backward, the room spinning into a gray haze from the sudden absence of shrieking pain. She felt hands catch her and gather her against the warmth of another body. For now, the journal voices were blessedly at rest, the pain they had brought gone, but she could feel their presence in her mind like a distant hive of bees, ever shifting and softly buzzing.

Above her, the gray slowly resolved into Carlston's face, blood-streaked, the pain still etched on his face.

"Helen!"

She gave a sobbing laugh of relief, touching his jaw, his cheek, the curve of his lips, no longer set into savagery. He was truly back. She could feel the pulse between them; no longer a clawing, desperate need, but a strong steady beat of union.

"What have you done?" he said in wonderment. "We are connected. I feel it in every part of my body."

"The Comte's cure was a blood bond."

"So Louis kept his promise." He pressed his lips hard into her hair, the fierce tenderness drawing her closer against his chest. "I have never felt anything like it. So much power."

Part of her knew she should pull away—she could hear a persistent whisper rising from the distant buzz of the journal, its devastating information demanding attention—but she did not move from the circle of his arms. Surely they could have this victory, this sublime moment of completeness, for just a while.

Darby pushed herself onto her knees, dazed, brushing her fingers across her torn and bloodied bodice. "My lady, I am healed!"

Helen peered down and touched her side where the nails had ripped through her flesh. Smooth again, just as the cut in her palm had healed when she had struck down Lowry.

"Are you healed?" she asked Carlston.

"Was I injured?"

She hesitated, then with light fingers, smoothed back his hair. "You had a gash here, on your head, but it is healed now." She felt the power that linked them tingling in her fingertips and leaving a trail upon his skin. "Your shoulder, too; it was laid open."

She dropped her hand, the break of their touch bringing a tiny loss. He regarded her for a moment, clearly feeling it too, then drew a breath and turned his attention to the ripped and bloody mess of his jacket and shirt. He pulled back the ripped cloth to expose smooth skin and muscle.

"Everything seems to be healed." He gave a tight smile. "Not least my mind, thank God."

"My lady, do you know what happened?" Darby's voice held an edge of panic. "After I was shot, all I can remember are voices screaming in my head, and pain, like I was on fire!"

"The power forged our Terrene bond, too," Helen said. "You did so well, Darby. You were so brave."

She took her maid's hand. It was trembling.

"We are bonded?" Darby tightened her grip. "I am glad, my lady. But will it be a normal Terrene bond? Does it matter that we did not say the right words?"

A good question.

"I do not know." She squeezed Darby's hand. "Normal or not, I am glad we have it."

"Helen." Carlston's arms around her tensed. "Is that Stokes over there. Is he dead?"

She could not help but look at the prone body in the doorway. Merciful heaven, Carlston did not know what he had done. Darby met her eyes—should they tell him?—but Helen gave a slight shake of her head. Not yet. There was more anguish to come, but not yet.

"He died as a true Reclaimer," she said.

She felt the sorrow bow Carlston's body. "He was a good man. He will be sorely missed." He pressed his hand to his forehead. "I cannot remember much, but I do remember Benchley's journal was a *Ligatus*. Is it destroyed now?"

Helen lifted the blood-soaked book. "It is how we bonded."

He flinched. "We bonded through that thing?"

Helen opened it and fanned the pages. Every one of them was blank.

Carlston tentatively touched the smooth paper. "But it was full of writing. Full of alchemy."

"Not anymore," Helen said.

It was all locked within her mind and heart. She had absorbed all the voices, all the words, all the power. And very soon—when she could bear to retreat from Carlston's arms—she would have to tell them the terrifying truth. She was not only one half of the Grand Reclaimer. She was also the *Ligatus*.

Thirty-Two

A<small>LMOST A FULL</small> hour later, the bodies of the Comte and
Comtesse d'Antraigues and their assassin, Lawrence, were
carried to the cool rooms of the White Hart to await the coroner.
Mr. Pike orchestrated the removal, ordering into service a number
of local men who had gathered outside the house to watch the
spectacle. As ever he was promptly obeyed, his air of authority creating
some order within the murmuring shock of the day.

He and Helen stood watching from the doorway of the Comte's
house as the three bodies made their journey across the road, an
interested group of shabbily clad children circling the procession.

"What about Stokes?" Helen asked.

"I am dealing with that situation," Pike said.

Carlston was right: the man was a bureaucrat to the core and
a shrewd survivor. They needed him as much as he needed them.
Although it went against the grain, she had to put aside her dislike
and distrust.

"I watched the Comte die," he said. "It was *Mors Ultima*.
Strange, since I was sure he had living offspring."

"He does, the Comte Julien, but he did not want to destroy him,"
Helen said. "He told the truth about that, and about Carlston's
cure." She drew out the Comte's fob from her pocket and inspected
it again. The etching on it was of Bacchus, the Roman god of wine
and pleasure. Did that mean something? She held it up. "It would

follow, then, that the Comte also told the truth about an informer in Bath."

Pike glanced at the gold disc. "Looking at it over and over will not make it any more useful. There are more than forty thousand people in Bath and you only have a title, the Bath Deceiver."

"Even so, it is a start." She pushed the fob back into her pocket. "Would it not also follow that the Comte told the truth about the Grand Deceiver? Surely you must now admit it exists?"

The question brought a worrying thought. Where was Philip in all of this? He may have disappeared from view, but Helen had no doubt he was still working against them. Somewhere.

"It would seem I must allow the possibility of the Grand Deceiver, now that we know what you and Lord Carlston are." Pike squinted at her, his bony face even more haggard than usual. "You are sure Lord Carlston is restored?"

"I am certain. All the vestige darkness in him is gone." She paused. "He does not remember killing Stokes."

"That does not make him any less guilty."

Helen heard a promise of retribution in his voice. She leaned closer, meeting his eyes with her own guarantee. "He and I are the Grand Reclaimer, Mr. Pike. There has been nothing like us before in living memory. You would be a fool to do anything that would harm your greatest asset."

He gave a dry smile. "Not to mention my wife's sanity."

Helen drew back. "I gave you my word on that. It will be done."

He crossed his arms. "You should be more circumspect about giving your word, Lady Helen. You have no idea how this new power manifests or even what it involves." He shook his head. "It is hard to understand how you could absorb a written book."

"Do you need more proof?"

She had already told him three facts about himself—facts only Benchley could have known—that the whispers in her head had supplied. Along with the devastating news she had yet to tell Carlston.

"No," he said curtly. "This development, however, must stay contained. No one else beyond Lord Carlston and Miss Darby must know. Do you agree?"

She glanced at him. Here was a turnup: Pike asking for agreement, not ordering obedience. "When Mr. Quinn recovers, I suspect he will know through his Terrene bond."

Pike nodded. "Yes, you are right. Mr. Quinn, too. But that is all. We must somehow work a way for you and Carlston to explore this new level of power between you."

"Yes."

She glanced across at Lady Margaret's carriage. Selburn stood beside it in conversation with Mr. Hammond and Delia. She felt a fleeting moment of regret—more secrets—but she had vowed to keep the Duke and Delia safe, and this new situation was perhaps the most dangerous yet.

Pike followed her gaze. "His Grace apprised me of your unfortunate meeting with Lady Dunwick and her friends on the road. He tells me you are betrothed."

"He should not have done that. I have told him Reclaimers are not allowed to marry."

"As you noted, Lady Helen, there has been nothing like you before. And a man of his rank generally gets what he wants."

Was Pike saying the Dark Days Club would not stand in the way? She looked back at the Duke: to have the regard of such a man was no small matter.

Across the road, the last of the corpse bearers entered the inn.

Pike turned to regard the huddle of servants waiting in the yard. "Now I must make sure the Comte's household recollect the same series of events." He allowed his wintry smile to touch his lips. "Memory can be so unreliable." He took out his fob watch.

"One of the tavern men went to fetch the local magistrate. He will arrive soon. It is time for all of you to leave. Will you be so kind as to pass the word?"

He waited for her nod, then gestured to Elizabeth, the maid. "Miss Ashton, is it not? Will you please come this way."

Leaving him to his machinations, Helen crossed the road to the carriage. She could no longer ignore the whisper in her mind. Besides, Carlston would want to know the truth. He deserved the truth. She must put aside her own wretchedness and deliver it.

Selburn smiled cautiously as she approached. A large blue bruise had formed on his forehead, and more bruises marked out Carlston's handspan around his throat. They had not yet spoken about the events in the attic. Helen was not sure she was quite ready to discuss with any kind of equilibrium his attempt to shoot Carlston. Particularly since he had twice promised to stand back from the battle.

"Mr. Pike wants us to leave," she said. "Do you know where his lordship has gone?"

"By the river," Hammond said. "We are all set to go on to London and give Quinn some time to heal properly at Caroline Street. Will you travel with us?"

"Yes, do so, Helen, please," Delia said, touching her arm in concern. "You look burned to the socket. You could sleep in the carriage."

Selburn shifted, as if to refuse on her behalf, then caught her eye. She was tempted to say yes to Delia, but saw the impulse for what it was: childish punishment. In truth, Selburn had only acted according to his nature; he had made it clear all along that his aim was to protect her from harm. She had to remember that he had only joined the Dark Days Club little more than a day ago. She could not expect him to change a lifetime of command in a matter of hours.

"I will drive with the Duke," she said, but she did not return

Selburn's smile. They would need to come to an understanding.

She stepped up onto the carriage steps and, hooking her hands around the open window frames, peered into the cabin's interior. Mr. Quinn had regained his senses and sat propped against Darby's shoulder. Lady Margaret sat opposite, her forefinger tapping an anxious beat upon the worn leather seat.

"I am glad to see you are recovering, Mr. Quinn," Helen said.

"Thank you, my lady." He sat close enough to the window for her to see the pallor of his skin and deep lines of pain carved from nose to mouth.

Beside him, Darby clasped and unclasped her hands in her lap. She offered a smile, but her mouth had a new tightness around it, and she had an air of bracing herself, as if the world had tipped and she was struggling to keep balance. It would take some time, Helen thought, before her maid—no, her Terrene—fully came to terms with what had happened in the attic. Indeed, it would take her quite some time too.

"You are going to find his lordship?" Lady Margaret asked.

Helen nodded. "He is by the river. I am going there now."

"He would not allow me to accompany him," Lady Margaret said. She crossed her arms, her finger taking up its beat against her ribs. "Are you sure he is recovered?"

"Quite sure," Helen said.

She looked down at the ground, ready to withdraw, but was stopped by a hand around her wrist. Quinn, the urgency in his face excusing the liberty.

He leaned forward, wincing from the effort. "I haven't seen him this rattled since Lady Elise."

Helen gave a nod, and he released his grip, settling back with a soft huff of pain.

She stepped back to the ground. The story of Lady Elise was not yet over. She closed her eyes for a moment, letting the sun's warmth chase away a little of the chill that came from the news she carried.

"Are you ready to leave?" the Duke asked at her side.

She opened her eyes. "Not quite." She drew a breath. "Would you be so kind as to bring your curricle around to where we saw Lord Carlston's gig? I will join you there."

"He has made it clear he does not want company."

She let the comment pass. "Will you bring your horses around and wait for me?"

"Of course." He bowed.

"Thank you."

She watched his retreat, then said, "Mr. Hammond, will you walk with me?"

He looked at her quizzically. "It will be my pleasure."

"Allow me to come too," Delia said. "I would be glad of the exercise before the drive to London."

"No, Delia. Stay here."

She turned from her friend's disappointment. Lord Carlston did not need an audience for his pain.

The walk along the riverbank would have been pleasant if her thoughts had not been so dark. The morning had already taken up some warmth from the sun, and a number of barges and boats were navigating the wide expanse of water. Hammond clearly sensed her mood, for he did not try to make conversation. She took some comfort in his silent company and the rhythm of her long stride; no gown hem to be caught up and no thin-soled slippers that felt all stones and ruts.

Her stout Hessian boots and buckskin breeches took her across the rough road and through the knee-length grass. Ahead, Carlston stood on the bank, arms wrapped around his body, watching the water slide past. His horses, still hitched to his curricle, cropped the grass nearby.

She stopped fifty feet or so from him, halting Mr. Hammond with a hand on his arm. "I have something to tell Lord Carlston. Something that will distress him. He will need a friend after it is done, and I cannot be that friend. Not for this. When I leave, will you go to him?"

Hammond nodded. "Of course." He touched her shoulder. "But what about you? It is clear you are distressed too. Who will be your friend?"

She shook her head, feeling an absurd sting of tears at his never-failing kindness, and started across the grass.

She knew the moment when Carlston felt that she was near. The pulse between them quickened, and then his shoulders straightened. Even so, he did not turn, his attention seemingly fixed upon the gray-green water.

She walked up beside him. He glanced at her, dark eyes hooded, mouth lifting for a moment in a strained smile of welcome. The breeze ruffled his hair, showing the old scar on his temple and the remnants of the blood dried upon his forehead.

"I liked George Stokes very much," he said, breaking the silence. "A man of firm ideas and an extraordinary capacity for claret. I feel I should at least do him the courtesy of recalling the moment I killed him." His hands, tucked under the cross of his arms, clenched into fists. "I recollect nothing."

"It was the journal," Helen said. She wanted to reach across and take his hands. Uncurl his pain.

"Apparently I tried to kill you, too. Selburn told me."

"He is one to talk," Helen said. "He tried to kill you and shot Darby instead."

It brought a small smile, as she had hoped it would. "Poor Darby. A baptism of fire. But she is coping, is she not?"

"She will."

"And you? Are you feeling any effects from the *Ligatus*?"

He finally turned to face her, the soft concern in his voice echoed in his dark eyes. She had not anticipated the effect it would have on her, the rise of that pulse between them, the strength that seemed to build behind it. She saw his jaw shift. He felt it too.

She cleared her throat. "I do not know how I can hold such a heinous thing within me and not go mad, and yet I can." She tapped her fingertip on her forehead. "The *Ligatus* has receded from my conscious mind, but I know it is in there, every word that Benchley wrote, every soul he murdered, waiting for me to find a way to retrieve them. Just as I know—" She stopped.

"That I am in there," he finished. He touched his temple. "Just as you are in here, our energies combined into a Grand Reclaimer bond. So much strength waiting to be unlocked."

"Yes," she whispered. The promise of it was breathtaking.

"I cannot remember much of the last few days, Helen. When I try, there is only a dull sense of some immeasurable pain." He lifted his shoulders: an involuntary hunch. "I do, however, remember three precious moments: when you freed me from that shrieking black hell; when we bonded with all that power; and the salon, before you left. I remember what I said in the salon." He took her hand, his skin warm against her own, and pressed the curve of her fingers to his lips. "*Amore mio.* Do you remember? I meant it then, and I mean it—"

"You must stop!" She snatched her hand back. "Please. I know something about your wife. Something I have retained from the *Ligatus.* Benchley wrote about her in his journal."

Carlston straightened, the tenderness wiped from his face. "About Elise?"

Helen swallowed. She had thought herself resigned, but she suddenly could not speak past the choking tears in her throat. She curled her hands, digging her fingernails into her palms, and focused upon the small pain. Best to say it fast.

"According to Benchley, your wife was a spy working for Bonaparte. She realized she had been discovered, was facing imminent arrest, and so staged her own death and fled. She is, by all accounts, still alive and in France."

"Alive?" He stepped back as if the word had been a slap.

"Yes."

He shook his head. "A spy for France?"

He stared across the river, dark brows angled into fierce concentration. Helen could almost see the devastating recalibration of every moment he had spent with Elise de Vraine.

Finally, he tilted his head back, eyes squeezed shut. "Fool! How could I have been such a fool? So intent on Deceivers, I did not see the common spy in my own house. I wonder, did she want me suspected of her murder?" He paced a few steps along the bank. "Still alive and in bloody France." He dragged his hands through his cropped hair. "No, it changes nothing." He whirled around to face her again. "Helen, it changes nothing."

"You are right," she said. He stepped forward, but she shook her head, stopping his eager advance. "Nothing has changed. You have always been married. It is just that now she is no longer a ghost."

How it cost her to say it in such a measured way.

She looked over her shoulder at Hammond. He immediately started across the grass toward them. At the side of the road, she saw the Duke draw his curricle and four to a standstill.

Carlston lifted his head. "I truly thought Elise had been taken from this life, Helen."

She nodded.

"We cannot ignore this bond we have," he said.

Hammond was almost upon them.

"No, we cannot ignore it," Helen said. "But it does not change the fact that you are married." She hesitated, knowing her next words were another solemn bond. "Or the fact that I am betrothed."

She turned and walked across the grass toward the Duke, feeling Lord Carlston's presence like a heartbeat within her own.

Morning Post

FRIDAY, 24 JULY 1812

Marriage in the High Life

O ur Windsor correspondent informs us that a matrimonial alliance is to take place between His Grace the Duke of Selburn and the Lady Helen Wrexhall, daughter of the notorious Countess Hayden and niece of Viscount Pennworth. The ceremony will take place early in the New Year, and Lady Helen is to prepare for her nuptials in Bath with her chaperone, the interesting Lady Ridgewell. If our information be correct, Her Majesty has been formally notified of this intended union, and will condescend to grace the ceremony with her presence. The date of the nuptials has thus been determined by the Royal schedule.

Author's Note

I researched *The Dark Days Pact* with as much fervor and delight as I did the first book in the series, *The Dark Days Club*, and I possibly had even more fun.

In *The Dark Days Pact* I have once again mixed real 1812 world events with my own fiction, and a number of the characters are historical figures.

Martha Gunn was a real dipper in Brighton and, by all accounts, in 1812 she was still dipping at the grand old age of eighty-six. She is a fascinating figure; a celebrity within her own lifetime, and a favorite of the Prince Regent, who was so fond of her that he gave her lifetime access to the largesse of his Brighton Pavilion kitchens. She was called the Queen of the Dippers and many of her descendants still live in the Brighton area. I hope they enjoy and approve of my depiction of their marvelous ancestor.

The Comte and Comtesse d'Antraigues are also historical figures, as is Lawrence (Lorenzo), the Comte's Italian valet. The Comte and Comtesse were really murdered by Lawrence on 22 July 1812, and Lawrence then committed suicide (or so it is reported). The Comte was a known spy who seems to have worked for nearly everybody, including the French royalists, the Spanish, the Russians, and the English, in some cases at the same time. His wife was a former Paris Opera star and, it would seem, a rather formidable woman. Together they fled France, survived arrest and interrogation by Napoleon, lived in Vienna, and ended up in Barnes Terrace in England. Their murder is as mysterious today as it was in 1812. At the time, Lawrence's actions and his subsequent suicide were put down to the "passionate nature" of Italians, but the reason why he brutally murdered his employers and then shot himself was never really discovered. It is now supposed that the murders were in fact assassinations prompted by the Comte's spying activities, but even that is not certain. Whatever the case, the sequence of events in the d'Antraigues house on that morning was very odd and made more confusing by the conflicting eyewitness accounts reported in the newspapers of the time. I must confess that I have slightly altered the sequence of events to fit my fictional action, but for the most part the actions of Lawrence, the Comte and Comtesse, and their servants are as reported in the newspapers and the inquest report. Also, in the interest of accuracy, it is quite possible that the Comte and Lawrence were not, in fact, Deceivers.

As a side note, I visited the house where the murders occurred. It is still standing alongside the Thames in Barnes Terrace and is now called D'Antraigues. The White Hart pub where the bodies were taken is also still there. In the absence of any centralized city mortuary, pubs were used for coroner's inquests because they had cool rooms in which to store the bodies of the dead. (I'll have a beer with that corpse, please!)

Other real-life figures who are mentioned include: the Prince Regent; Queen Charlotte; Lord Sidmouth, the Home Secretary; Mr. Ryder, the Home Secretary prior to Lord Sidmouth; Mr. Wedgewood; and Comte Julien, the d'Antraigues's son (also known as Jules). The wonderfully named Committee for Secrecy was also real, and included Mr. Canning and Mr. Wilberforce, the famous abolitionist.

For me, the town of Brighton in 1812 is like another historical figure. Most of the places that are mentioned or that Helen visits were real, such as Donaldson's Circulating Library, Raggetts Club, the Castle Tavern, the Steine, Awsiter's Baths, the Lanes, including Union Street, and of course the Marine Pavilion, the Prince Regent's favorite palace. In 1812 it was not yet the Royal Pavilion, the magnificent Chinese/Indian—inspired frivolity that still stands today in Brighton. Those extensive renovations did not begin until 1815, and so the palace that Helen sees is still the classically designed Marine Pavilion. For my descriptions of Brighton, I used *A Guide to All the Watering and Sea-Bathing Places for 1813* by John Feltham, and Sickelmore's *An Epitome of Brighton* (which includes a map of Brighton from the time), and I made a number of visits to modern Brighton. For those who may be interested, German Place where Helen and her comrades live is now Madeira Place, renamed for patriotic reasons during the First World War.

I have taken a little liberty with the addition of the molly rooms to Kate Holt's bawdy house. From my research, it is not outside the realms of possibility that molly rooms were also incorporated within a more traditional bawdy house. However, in most cases separate molly houses existed, and because of the deadly laws against homosexuality, these houses were kept secret and could be disbanded very quickly if the house was under surveillance or a Watch spy tried to enter. Brighton's proximity to the army barracks and its status as a resort resulted in numerous bawdy houses, and my research reinforced the troubling fact that it would not have been unusual for a girl of Sprat's age to be found working in them.

On a less serious note, the cant language used by Mr. Hammond, Sprat, Binny, Kate Holt, Lowry, and, on occasion, Helen comes mostly from *Grose's Classical Dictionary of the Vulgar Tongue* written by Francis Grose and updated by Pierce Egan. It was published in 1785, revised in 1811 and 1823, and is now available free online. The dictionary is a fascinating journey back to the Regency era, and I wish I could have used more of the hilarious words and phrases, although a good number of them are quite obscene. Here are a few of the more respectable examples that didn't suit the book but that I just have to share with you:

Chatter broth: tea
Squeeze crab: a sour-looking shriveled fellow
Snilch: to look at something attentively
Out of print: slang used by booksellers to describe
someone who is dead

This last one cracks me up every time!

As with Book 1 in the series, if you would like to learn a bit more about my research, you can do so on my website, darkdaysclub.com, and on my Pinterest page at pinterest.com/alisongoodman.

—Alison Goodman, October 2016

Acknowledgments

I would like to thank the big cornerstone four: Ron, my wonderful husband; my best friend, Karen McKenzie; and my parents, Douglas and Charmaine Goodman.

Huge thanks, always, to Jill Grinberg, my fabulous agent, and her exceptional team: Cheryl, Katelyn, Denise, and Kirsten. The best in the business!

I am privileged to work with a fantastic team at Penguin Random House headed by my delightful editor Regina Hayes, who loves the Regency and the novels of Georgette Heyer as much as I do. Thanks also to the eagle-eyed Janet Pascal, and the wonderful publicity team including Lindsay Boggs and Elyse Marshall. Finally, kudos to the cover team of Jonathan Barkat (photography) and Maggie Edkins and Kristin Smith (design), who have created such stunning covers for the Lady Helen series.

I am a big believer in the value of writing groups and the support they provide. My two gangs—the Y. & J. Writers and Clan Destine—are a great (and madcap) source of inspiration and laughter.

A number of people have helped along the way. Thank you to Duncan Nash, John Garden-Gardiner, Alan Baxter, Amanda Mustafic, and the staff at the Royal Pavilion and the Brighton Museum and Art Gallery.

My sincere thanks also to the two back specialists who are

keeping me upright while I write Lady Helen's adventures: my chiropractor, Dr Warren Sipser, and my physiotherapist, Natalie Szmerling.

Finally, I must acknowledge the sweet hound from Hell, Xander, my dear old-man dog, whose main contributions are loud snoring, louder barking, and an insistent paw that taps my leg at four o'clock every afternoon to remind me that a daily walk is most beneficial for the constitution.

Turn the page to read an excerpt
from the final Lady Helen novel

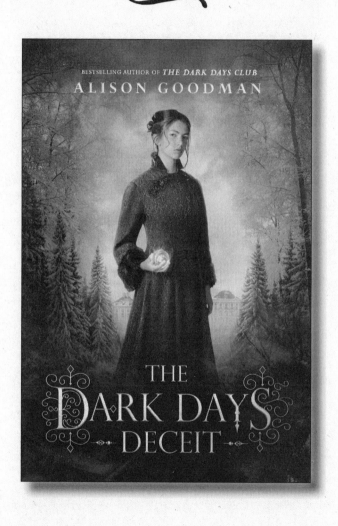

BESTSELLING AUTHOR OF *THE DARK DAYS CLUB*

ALISON GOODMAN

THE
DARK DAYS
DECEIT

Half Moon Street, 9 December 1812

My dear Helen,

Regarding your letter of 7 December, I understand that you would wish to continue your stay at Bath with Lady Ridgewell and Miss Cransdon. The company of such lively young friends would naturally eclipse that of your old aunt, not to mention the fact that your betrothed's country seat is so happily situated near that fair city. Nevertheless, I do remind you that I have not seen you since July when the Duke obtained Her Majesty's permission for you to marry. Now that your nuptials are less than a month away, I insist that I join you to help prepare for your wedding and finalize your gowns for the ceremony and ball.

I had hoped you would return to London for such important purchases, but Lady Jersey has assured me that the warehouses and drapers at Bath are equal to the task.

I am aware that Lady Ridgewell has no spare room for me, but I have had an invitation from Lady Dunwick to stay with her and her daughter at their house in the Crescent. Ever since they happened upon you and the Duke on the Brighton road before your official betrothal, Lady Dunwick has become somewhat adhesive. I will stay with her until other arrangements can be made.

I expect to travel in the next week and will write again soon with a firm date of arrival. I look forward to our reunion.

I remain always, your loving,

Aunt Leonore

One

Tuesday, 10 December 1812

—

L ADY HELEN WREXHALL refolded the letter and pressed its wax seal back together, as if she could lock away the news it contained. Aunt Leonore soon to arrive at Bath. Lud.

Of course, she loved Aunt and wanted her to be part of the wedding, but it was a complication none of them needed. She tapped the edge of the letter against the hallway table. Her aunt and uncle, along with the rest of society, were under the impression that she had spent the last six months enjoying the delights of Brighton and Bath; not, in fact, training to be a warrior, masquerading as a man, fighting Deceivers, killing murderers, and becoming one half of the Grand Reclaimer with Lord Carlston. Helen shook her head. How was she to keep all that from Aunt? It was going to be impossible.

The sound of footsteps descending the stairs drew her from her thoughts. Lady Margaret appeared on the landing above, one red gloved hand sliding along the banister, the other encased in a golden sable muff that matched the luxurious collar of her pelisse. Her brother followed behind, adjusting the capes of his greatcoat, his hat already upon his head.

"We are off to the Pump Rooms for our daily dose of foul water and gossip," Lady Margaret said, pausing at the bottom of the steps. "Will you join us after you have trained? We are all invited to breakfast with the Grays."

Helen shook her head. It was the fashion to breakfast with friends after taking the waters, but it was not one of Helen's favorite diversions; her appetite was now that of a Reclaimer, and even when she restrained herself she ate double what a lady should eat in public. "Please pass on my regrets, and Delia's too. We will breakfast here and then the Duke is calling to take us to the porcelain showrooms. I am to choose a new coffee service."

"Another one?" Hammond asked, ushering his sister past Helen. "Is he restocking the whole of Chenwith Hall?"

"It is for the Queen, Michael," Lady Margaret chided. She addressed Helen. "Has his lordship arrived yet? He and Quinn finally returned late last night, did they not?"

"They are in the cellar," Helen replied.

She had not seen the men arrive, but had sensed Lord Carlston enter the house ten minutes ago. The pulse they shared—a steady beat beneath her own heart's rhythm that confirmed their union as the Grand Reclaimer—had sharpened into a call. She felt the incessant draw of it, like a pin to a magnet. The two men had been gone a week; a dangerous foray into Napoleon's Paris to search for Carlston's traitorous wife, Lady Elise. Had they found her? Helen lifted her shoulders and let them drop, trying to shrug away the hollow unease that always came with the thought of that woman.

"We should go down and greet him," Lady Margaret said. "Perhaps he has orders for us."

"His lordship has made it clear the morning is for Reclaimers and Terrenes only," Hammond said, ushering her firmly toward the door. He cast a smile back at Helen. "Steer your betrothed away from French porcelain. We cannot have the Queen eating off the enemy's plate."

Garner, the butler, opened the door. A blast of freezing air swept into the hallway. Another bitter day, Helen thought, shivering despite the warm wrap of her woolen shawl. Outside, two wet footmen stepped forward to hold umbrellas over Lady Margaret and Mr. Hammond as they made their way to the carriage. Garner closed the door against the elements and, with a bow to Helen, retreated to the butler's pantry.

"May I go down, my lady?" Darby asked. She wore the blue gown she kept for training and stood waiting on the top step of the staircase that led to the basement, clearly eager to reunite with Quinn.

Helen shook her head. They must wait a few moments more; she did not want to give in, quite yet, to the draw of the Grand Reclaimer bond. Darby, at least, knew her regard for Mr. Quinn was built upon the man's worth. Helen's link to Carlston had been created by some heathen alchemical force that pulled them together regardless of the turmoil it caused.

She frowned at the empty hallway. "Where is Sprat? Did you tell her to come down?"

"I did," Darby said crisply. "She is most likely hiding from the idea of work, or she could be outside."

"Outside? Is she wearing her shoes? It is raining."

"I doubt it. She won't wear her shoes or her hose. I've told her over and over, my lady, but she won't listen to anyone but you."

Helen gave a nod of sympathy; Darby was trying so hard to help the girl. "I know, but we must keep in mind where she has come from. She needs time."

Darby's soft mouth tightened. "It has been a fair while, my lady, and she still cannot do your hair properly or sew a straight line."

"But she is an excellent pickpocket," Helen said, only half joking. Lord Carlston had used Sprat's more dubious skills on more than one occasion.

The quip did not draw a smile. "The other maids think she's been going through their belongings."

Helen's smile faded. "Has anything gone missing?"

"A few small things: pins and whatnot." Darby paused. "She swears she's not touched them, my lady, but she bends the truth something awful."

"Well, we must not assume she is to blame. Nevertheless, I will speak to her about it." *Again*, Helen added silently. Rescuing Sprat from the brothel in Brighton had been an easy decision, but it seemed the girl was not interested in morality or training to be a lady's maid.

With no Sprat to ferry the letter upstairs, Helen tucked it inside her long cambric sleeve and finally led the way down the steps. The beat within her body quickened as they descended. While his lordship had been away, it had been vastly subdued; a blessed relief.

She pulled her woolen shawl more firmly around her shoulders. The basement was brisk at the best of times, but during the current stretch of dismal weather it was unbearably cold. There could be no doubt that their proximity to the River Avon added to the damp chill; the house stood in the middle of a handsome row along Great Pulteney Street near the bridge, one of the newer fashionable addresses. It lacked the space they had enjoyed in Brighton, but even so, the house was a godsend. Nearly all of Bath had been fully let for the winter season and it had taken the Duke's influence to secure them lodgings at such short notice.

It could not be denied that her betrothal to the Duke of Selburn held many advantages, not least his constant regard for her comfort. The thought brought a smile. Not only was he refurbishing his country seat, Chenwith Hall, but he had also taken it upon himself to arrange a grand New Year's ball to celebrate their wedding. It was to be held in a new dance pavilion being built in the gardens at Chenwith, the crowning event of a huge Night Ice Fair that would mark their union. An enormous undertaking, but as the Duke said, their wedding celebration was to be attended by Royalty, so it must not be a meager affair.

Mr. Quinn was waiting at the doorway of the cellar, still clad in his thick coat. The windowless room currently served as their training area, and although not ideal—the only light came from oil lamps and the space was not large—it afforded the seclusion they needed as she and Lord Carlston tried to control their power. Only Quinn, Darby, and Mr. Pike, the bureaucratic heart of the Dark Days Club, knew that they were the Grand Reclaimer dyad—two halves of a whole meant to wield great power—just like their unknown nemesis, the Grand Deceiver. Yet, Helen thought, after five months they had very little to show for their efforts. It was true she could conjure the electrical fire, but they had no idea how to make the energy into a weapon, or, indeed, what role Lord Carlston was to play in the partnership.

"My lady." Mr. Quinn bowed as Helen entered the cellar. "And Miss Darby. It is very good to see you again."

Behind her, Helen heard Darby whisper, "Are you well, Nathaniel?"

"I am now."

Helen heard the smile within Quinn's reply. Such sweetness between them.

Carlston stood beside the wine racks. The capes of his coat still glistened with rain and the yellow light from the lamps gave a golden hue to the planes of his face, reminding Helen of a gilded statue she had once seen of Michael the warrior-saint. The beat of their union thundered in her ears, and she knew he felt it too. It was in the clench of his hand around the wine rack and the tension that coiled through his body as he fought the urge to step to her side.

He smiled, the carefully maintained space between them spanned by its warmth. "It is very good to see you."

"Indeed," she said. "We had thought to see you sooner." In her mind, however, she screamed: *Why did you take so long? Are you well? Did you find her?*

He raked his hand through his dark hair. "I was hoping to be back three days ago, but the news of Napoleon's impending return from Russia arrived and Paris was in turmoil, so we waited until things quietened down."

"Was your trip a success?"

His mouth tensed at the question. Clearly, not. Then again, she was unsure what would actually constitute success. Lady Elise had been a spy for France and had betrayed Lord Carlston in the worst possible way, leaving him suspected of her murder. Her retrieval could only end in her execution and further scandal for his lordship. Yet he was determined to keep searching. Was it because he still loved her?

"Paris held no answers."

He looked away and wet his lips, the unconscious action bringing a shameful rush of heat through Helen's body. Even now, after so many months, she could still feel the touch of his lips on her own. The light, sweet touch of the Duke's mouth had not in any way subdued the sordid burn of that illicit memory.

"I am sorry to hear it," she managed.

He nodded and lifted one shoulder, as if throwing off the last seven days. "We have lost more training time than I expected. Let us devote the rest of today to the problem of your power. I've had some ideas that may—"

"The rest of the day? But I cannot," Helen said. "I am engaged this afternoon to buy porcelain."

"Porcelain?" Carlston's hand tightened on the rail again. "With Selburn, I presume? Can you not put him off?"

"We must do it today or the order will not be filled in time."

His jaw shifted, his silence more eloquent than any comment.

"I am more than happy to forgo breakfast and work right through until the appointment," she added.

"Thank you," he said dryly. He took a few steps along the narrow space between the two wine racks, as much pacing as the room allowed. "Quinn, close the door. Make sure we are alone."

Quinn checked the corridor, then secured the door. He and Darby stood side by side, their unity and affection as clear as if they were holding hands. It all looked so natural, Helen thought. No confused questioning or divided loyalty.

"The trip to Paris did at least give me time to reflect upon our progress," Carlston said. He rubbed his eyes, his frustration palpable. "I feel like the third wheel on a racing gig. After all that we endured to bond, we do not even know how we are to share the power stored within you. Has there still been nothing from the Ligatus? I had hoped the new meditations would have had some effect by now."

His question brought a flare of guilt—she held the key to their power in her memory, but could not retrieve it. When the two of them had blood-bonded to become the Grand Reclaimer, she had simultaneously absorbed the Ligatus: a madman's journal written in the blood of slaughtered people and Deceivers. The author of that foul book, the rogue Reclaimer Samuel Benchley, had bound his victims' life knowledge and energy into its pages by alchemy. Now all their knowledge was locked in Helen's mind, frustratingly inaccessible, and their life energy an ever-present hum in her body.

"Nothing has come to me yet," she said, watching him pace across the brick floor again.

He stopped in front of her, eyes narrowed. "How hard are you trying?"

That was unfair. Helen crossed her arms. "I am meditating three times a day as you said I should. There is something at the edge of my mind. I just cannot catch hold of it yet."

She did, however, have a terrible sense of what it could be: the screams of a dying infant. There could only be one such pitiful voice in the Ligatus: little Timothy Marr, one of the poor Ratcliffe Highway souls brutally murdered for their blood by Benchley. Every time Helen meditated, she heard the infant's distant pitiful cry, buried deep within her mind but slowly surfacing. More often than not it was accompanied by such an aching anguish that her own sobs wrenched her from the meditation. She had told no one of it yet. First she had to control her emotions so the little voice could emerge; and then she had to find a way to contend with all the others who howled their pain inside her.

Carlston paced back to the other side of the room. "I think it is time to try another way. I have asked Sir Jonathan to join us. He has studied mesmerism. You are aware of the practice?"

Helen wrinkled her nose. The field of mesmerism was even more disreputable than alchemy. "If I recall correctly, Mr. Mesmer's theories have been wholly discredited in Paris."

"Mesmer has been discredited," Carlston conceded, "but Abbé Faria has developed a way to access thoughts hidden from the conscious mind, and he has had some success. Sir Jonathan assures me the practice is safe."

Sir Jonathan Beech was the Dark Days Club's senior Tracer, responsible for tracking the progeny of Deceivers so they could be returned to full humanity by the Reclaimers. Not, Helen thought wryly, a theologian or physician qualified to delve into the hidden mysteries of the mind and soul. Nevertheless, she must try. She held within her not only the answer to their power, but possibly a way to destroy the Grand Deceiver and the Trinitas—a three-part alchemical weapon that, if brought together, could rip open a doorway between their world and the otherworld of the Deceivers and create a hell on earth.

"It would be prudent to continue with your own meditations," Carlston added. "The closer you can get to drawing on the information, the better for Sir Jonathan's methods."

Helen nodded although foreboding prickled her skin. Little Timothy's anguish was just the tip of the pain buried within her mind. What would happen if Sir Jonathan brought out all the voices at once, as it had been when she had first absorbed the journal? She was not sure she was strong enough to withstand such an all-encompassing wave of despair again.

"When does Sir Jonathan arrive, my lord?" Darby asked, ever practical. "Will he be staying with us?"

"He arrives Thursday and stays only two days. I have arranged a room in my lodgings."

At least Sir Jonathan would be gone by the time Aunt arrived at Bath, Helen thought. Which brought her to her own news.

"Lady Pennworth is coming here to help me prepare for the wedding."

Carlston, Darby, and Quinn stared at her with similar expressions of dismay. It would have been comical if it were not so serious.

"You must stop her," Carlston said. "It is a complication we do not need."

"I know, but she will not be put off any longer. Besides, it would be deemed odd if she did not have a part in the preparations."

"Does she expect to stay with you?" Carlston demanded. "You will have to make some excuse. The risk of discovery is too great."

"She says she will stay with Lady Dunwick."

"Even so, she will demand your company every day. As it is,

you are too distracted. With her here, we will make no progress at all!"

"I am not distracted," Helen protested. "I am doing as much as I can."

Carlston snorted. "You are forever at warehouses and shops with Selburn; and when you are here, your mind is on weddings, not training or the Grand Deceiver."

Helen felt the humming energy within her rise. "I am no more distracted by my wedding than you are by your search for your wife."

At the corner of her eye, she saw Quinn wince.

"Surely we do not need so much urgency," she added, trying to moderate her tone. "I know the Grand Deceiver holds a Colligat, but it is only *one* part of the Trinitas; and they cannot get their hands upon the second part since it is in here." She tapped her forehead. "Only we know I have absorbed the Ligatus, and it will take the Deceivers years to create another. Moreover, you have told me again and again that the third part of the Trinitas is safe—whatever it may be—so it follows that the immediate danger is past. We have time to gather ourselves, to train and find our power."

"Time to get married, you mean?" Carlston said acidly. From his fob pocket he withdrew a heavy disk of gold attached to a bloodstained ribbon. He held it up before Helen, its ornate etching of Bacchus glinting in the lamplight. It had belonged to the late Comte d'Antraigues, Deceiver and spy, and he had passed it to Helen after he was attacked by the Grand Deceiver's assassin. "Louis gave us this for a reason. The Grand Deceiver is planning something, and we must find out what it is."

"We already know what was being planned," Helen said. "To unite the Trinitas, but that is now secure. Besides, there has been no sign of Philip here or in London. Surely if the Grand Deceiver was planning something, they would send their harbinger of destruction. They have every other time."

"Do you really think the Grand Deceiver has retired defeated?" Carlston demanded.

It was clear any answer other than *no* would be wrong. "I see that *you* do not," she said.

He eyed her for a moment, as if she had disappointed him. "You and Pike have allowed yourselves to be lulled into a false sense of victory—exactly what I think the Grand Deceiver wants. We are meant to believe we have stymied their plan when in fact it is still in operation—a brilliant deception that is already halfway to defeating us. Louis did not mention the Trinitas when he gave you this fob. He told us to find the Bath Deceiver. Those were his dying words, and that is where the truth of our salvation lies. The Bath Deceiver holds the information we need."

"You speak as if we have not been searching," Helen protested. "To find one Deceiver among the hundred or so here in Bath is a monumental task, especially when all are doing their utmost to hide from us."

"In five months we have found only fifteen, none of them Louis's comrade. It is taking too long." He shook the fob on its ribbon. "I need you focused on the search and our training, not on your wedding. Can you do that? Or are you in too much of a rush to appease society and marry Selburn?"

Helen narrowed her eyes. "You think I am marrying the Duke only to save my reputation?"

He lowered the fob, his face set. She knew that expression—he was deciding whether or not to step over a brink. A brink that they had, by mutual silence, avoided for months.

Do not do it, she thought fiercely. *Do not.*

"Knowing the man, what else could it be?" he said flatly. "You were compromised on the road to Barnes and you think the only way forward is to marry him. You are clinging to the delusion that you can be both a Reclaimer and the woman society expects you to be. The woman *he* expects you to be."

"Knowing the man?" she echoed. "You do not know the Duke. You see only your dislike of him. Selburn is offering me a chance to retain my reputation, that is true—but he is offering far more than that. The chance of a family—my *own* family—and a life that holds more than reclaiming and killing. A life that is sanctified by God and society."

He blinked; the barb had hit home. He could not offer her those things. It was the truth, but still, she should not have said it. She had wanted to punish him for things he could not change: a wife still alive and her own wretched confusion about their Grand Reclaimer bond.

"Your life is already sanctified by God and society," he said, his voice hard. "You have taken an oath as a Reclaimer. That is your life, and he is taking you away from it, away from your *duty*. What is worse, you are letting him."

Behind her, Darby made a soft sound of denial.

"That is not true!" Helen said.

Carlston leaned closer. "He is making you less than you are, Helen. He will not play second to a woman, and you are already stepping back."

"I am not!"

"Then show me I am wrong. Show me some damned focus!"

Helen drew herself up. She would show him focus. Concentrating all her outrage into her hands, she dragged the warm ever-present thrum of otherworld energy up through her bone and marrow and flesh until it sparked into a blaze of blue fire that engulfed her fingertips. Heat throbbed through her body, a furnace of power. She cupped her fingers, the blue humming flame in each hand slowly curling around itself until she held twin incandescent balls of hot energy, hovering an inch above her palms. Dear God, she was holding them *and* maintaining them! Her breath quickened, the exhilaration bursting out in a small huffing laugh.

The jutting challenge in Carlston's face shifted into anticipation. "Can you throw them?" he whispered.

In the periphery of her vision, she saw Quinn edge Darby back against the door.

She raised her hands, the crackling, humming blue orbs shivering at the movement. She felt them slipping, the heat ebbing. *No!* She tried to draw more energy from her center, but it was too late. Each ball pulsed with a flash of light, then broke apart into hundreds of harmless sparks. The tiny lights spun upward and hung in the air like a silent explosion of miniature fireworks, then showered down around them, flickering into oblivion.

Carlston released a long breath, his eyes dark with disappointment. "I thought for a moment . . ." He closed his fingers around the gleaming fob.

"I am sorry." She lowered her hands.

And yet, deep down, she felt a tiny treacherous sense of relief. It was all very well for him to seek their power with such fervor, but he was not the one who risked being consumed by the burning energy and howling despair of the Ligatus.

Read more from *New York Times* bestselling author Alison Goodman:

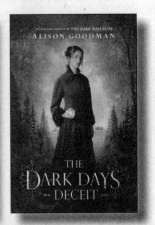